DREAM CATCHERS

Their dreams gave them strength
Their love gave them passion
And the courage they needed, they
found in each other

DREAM CATCHERS

Sometimes, despite the odds, love conquers all

Relive the romance...

Two complete novels by two of your
favorite authors

About the Authors

Kathleen Eagle—had her first book published in 1984 and has since written more than twenty romance novels, both contemporary and historical. This award-winning author has also published several mainstream novels. She set aside a seventeen-year teaching career on a North Dakota Indian reservation to become a full-time fiction writer. She is also a frequent speaker at writers' conferences and workshops. Today Kathleen lives in Minnesota with her family. Many of her stories reflect the Lakota Sioux heritage of her husband, Clyde, a Minneapolis teacher.

Bronwyn Williams—is the pen name used by two sisters, Dixie Browning and Mary Williams. *White Witch* is the first of nine books they have written together so far and is set in the area where they both make their homes and where their family has lived since the 1600s. The now-extinct Hatorask tribe is an important part of the family's heritage, so the writing of this story was a labor of love.

DREAM CATCHERS

KATHLEEN EAGLE

BRONWYN WILLIAMS

Harlequin Books

TORONTO • NEW YORK • LONDON
AMSTERDAM • PARIS • SYDNEY • HAMBURG
STOCKHOLM • ATHENS • TOKYO • MILAN
MADRID • WARSAW • BUDAPEST • AUCKLAND

HARLEQUIN BOOKS

by Request—Dream Catchers

Copyright © 1996 by Harlequin Books S.A.

ISBN 0-373-20119-2

The publisher acknowledges the copyright holders of the individual works as follows:

MEDICINE WOMAN
Copyright © 1989 by Kathleen Eagle

WHITE WITCH
Copyright © 1988 by Dixie Browning and Mary Williams

This edition published by arrangement with Harlequin Books S.A.

® and TM are trademarks of the publisher. Trademarks indicated with ® are registered in the United States Patent and Trademark Office, the Canadian Trade Marks Office and in other countries.

Printed in U.S.A.

CONTENTS

He had come to her in a dream
But she couldn't let him stay—
if she wanted him to live

MEDICINE WOMAN

Kathleen Eagle

Prologue

Paha Sapa, the Black Hills in the land of the Lakota
1819

Morning sifted through Kezawin's eyelids like a gray-clad intercessor. The dark dream fell away piece by piece, and the hideous high-pitched laughter faded. She forced her eyes open wide and covered her ears against the staccato hoofbeat of the dream's final retreat. *Too late,* came the husky warning all around her head. *Too late to cover your ears. You have heard. You have seen. You have chosen.*

Kezawin turned her head slowly, pressing her cheek into the matted curls of buffalo hair, and stole a look at the face of her sleeping husband. Iron Shell was a beautiful young man with a strong heart. For three years he had protected her and provided for her well, never complaining as he waited month after month for his wife to conceive. Now, in the gray light of morning, a terrible truth seized Kezawin's heart. She was barren. No life would quicken in the womb of a woman who dreamed as she just had. And the young husband who lay beside her, though he was as strong as any man, was endangered by her very presence in his bed.

Trembling, Kezawin eased herself from their sleeping robes. The morning chill touched her backside first. She balanced herself on the balls of her feet and her fingertips, shielding her breasts behind her knees as she backed away without making a sound. She must not wake him. She must not let him see her crouching and shivering in shame.

Slipping a robe over her shoulders, she uncoiled her body slowly as she found her moccasins with her toes. Carefully she reached for the buckskin dress that lay neatly folded on the tipi's plush buffalo carpet and clutched it to her breast beneath her robe. She could not pull the dress over her head and risk the sound of ornamental elk's teeth clicking against each other or the soft swish of fringe. Iron Shell had the keen senses of a warrior. But Kezawin was a daughter of the Lakota, and she knew how to move quietly.

Her fingers might have been greased with tallow, so awkward were they in untying the thong that secured the tipi door, which was a piece of rawhide stretched over a willow hoop. She waited a moment, settled her mind on the task, then loosened the knot with a now steady hand.

The autumn air was cold and thin. A shallow breath of it pinched her lungs. A full breath stabbed deep. It wasn't the air, she thought. It was the dream's piercing horns. She adjusted the robe closely around her shoulders as she cast a hasty glance at the pine-green and autumn-brown valley. The tipis rose from the ground-hugging mist in miniature imitation of the peaks of the *Paha Sapa*, which surrounded the village. The golden glow of the coming sun glistened in the mist and lent an illusion of luster to the tall, tan, sooty-tipped cones. Picketed near their owners' doors, the war ponies stood with necks drooping and hindquarters cocked to rest a leg. One camp dog was about his business early, scavenging the ashes of a dead camp fire for some forgotten scrap. The rest of the camp rested peacefully.

Kezawin hurried to the river. She found a cluster of sheltering pines and sought refuge while she dressed. The soft skin of the elk blocked out the light as she slipped it over her head, but the light and dark of the dream swirled within the confines of her dress and warred round and round her head. She stretched her arms, dove into the sleeves of the dress and popped her head through the neck, gasping for air. She sought the light. She *chose* the light.

She knelt in the tall slough grass that lined the low earthen wall that the river had cut for its bed. Lying on her belly, Kezawin dipped cupped hands into the icy flow and splashed handfuls over her face and neck. She shivered as the water trickled between her breasts, but she reached for more. It tingled and tightened her skin over prominent cheekbones like the deerhide stretched over a willow frame in the making of a drum.

She closed her eyes and shook droplets from her face as she struggled to shake the thought from her mind. She had not meant to compare her skin to that of the deer. The image had come into her head, unbidden. Perhaps she could still drive it away. The image flew in the face of the destiny she wanted for herself—the roles of mother, wife, woman respected by the people for her impeccable virtue, industry and skills. She had lived her seventeen years to that end, and she would not, *could* not see it all blow away on a dream wind.

Her father would tell her that the dream had deceived her young, inexperienced mind. Lone Bear was a holy man, a man of wisdom. Surely the daughter of such a man could not be touched by unnatural dreams. Kezawin pushed herself up from the ground and reached for her robe. Her father would interpret the dream. She would tell him every detail, omit nothing in her recounting of it. There were signs in the dream that she could not read, but Lone Bear would know them. He would tell her that it was not as she feared. She had not been touched by the deer woman.

Kezawin stood near the covered door of the tipi with the familiar geometric paintings in bright symbolic colors, which proclaimed Lone Bear's accomplishments. "Father," she said, knowing that her brother, Walks His Horse, would sleep through this disturbance if she spoke quietly enough. "Forgive me for troubling your sleep, Father, but I must speak with you."

"Now?" The voice she knew better than her own rattled with early-morning dampness.

"It's an important matter, Father. Something that frightens me."

A head of graying hair emerged from the tipi. Lone Bear hitched his striped trade blanket around his waist as he straightened to a height that surpassed his daughter's by a head. His eyes were assaulted by the sun's early rays, and he drew his face into a well-established pattern of protective folds. "Where is your husband, Kezawin? He is the one to be shaken from his blankets when something frightens you."

"My husband is not a holy man, Father." She felt her father's eyes upon her, although she did not lift her gaze from the toes of his quilled moccasins. "I have seen something *wakan*," she said quietly. "Something holy."

Lone Bear turned back toward the door. "This is not for my brother's ears," Kezawin said quickly. "And I need to feel the sun on my head."

They went to the river and sat upon Kezawin's robe in a grassy clearing, where crystal beads of dew twinkled in the morning sun. The long dry summer had diminished the river's power. It sloshed lazily in the confines of its banks while Lone Bear waited quietly.

"It was a dream," she said simply. "It came to me while I slept."

Lone Bear gave a nod, acknowledging the fact that his daughter had not sought this vision. She had not fasted and prayed for it. It had simply come to her.

"We were walking," she began. "We were searching for a certain plant, just you and I. I had never seen it, but you said it had red roots and I would know it when I saw it. We came to a river, but it was not like this." She indicated the water with a graceful gesture. "The water ran high, and we could not find a fording place. We walked. Then we saw a deer." She could feel her father's back stiffen at the word, even though he sat an arm's length away from her. She described the deer's motions with her hand. "It crossed the river, and the water only came up to its hocks. It—*he* had a beautiful mossy rack. Father, it was a buck. I was sure it was."

She looked at her father in the hope that this piece of information was significant, but she saw no change in his grave expression. She continued. "The deer began to scrape his antlers in a scraggly chokecherry tree, but the tree grew bigger, and soon he was entangled in its branches. I could see his eyes. He didn't panic. He entreated me to cross the river and free him."

"Did he speak?" Lone Bear asked.

"No. Not yet. I asked you to go with me, but you said that only a woman could use this ford. If I chose to cross, I would have to go alone. I asked you whether the red root plant might grow on the other side. You said it was very likely.

"I followed the trail the deer had taken across the river. He was deeply enmeshed, and my arms and face were soon bleeding from scratches." She held her arms out in front of her, turning them over to examine them. The dream burned so vividly in her mind that her unscathed arms puzzled her.

"I freed him," she said. "And then he spoke. His voice was that . . . of a woman." That part she knew to be significant, and she paused in the fear of that knowledge. "He said that he would give me the red root plant if I would stay with him. I refused, and he became angry and began chasing his tail like a dog. Round and round, round and round. My head was soon spinning. I heard the sound of a whirlwind, and I felt drawn into the vortex of the deer's wild dance. I had no thought of walking, but I was moving closer. Even as he spun, he watched me through flat black eyes. His lips curled back over his teeth, and the wind shrieked in my ears.

"Something white caught my eye. Another buck was grazing nearby, but this one was white. All white. I wanted to touch him. He raised his head, and I saw the red roots of the plants in his mouth. I walked away from the spinning deer. The white deer stood quietly until I reached him. He let me touch his face. He dropped the red root plants in my hands. He licked the blood from my arms and face with his cooling tongue.

"We walked to the riverbank and found an old woman with wild, tangled hair, sitting with her feet in the water. Across the river I could see the village, and I told the white deer that I would take the red root plants to my father. The woman laughed, and when she looked up, I saw the flat black eyes and the curling lips of the spinning deer. She pulled her legs out of the water and put her moccasins over cloven hooves, and then she sat cross-legged, unbefitting a woman. The village looked close, but it felt distant. I asked the woman how far it was, and she said, 'They are beyond your reach now. You are a fool if you stay within theirs.' And then she went to the chokecherry bush and began rubbing her head on it, tangling her hair in its branches. My scalp itched, and I wanted to imitate her actions."

"Did you?" Kezawin's father asked quietly.

"No. The white deer stepped into the water, and I knew that he was not a woman and could not ford the river there. He floundered in deep water. At my back I heard the woman's laughter, but I followed the white deer into the deep water. I followed him because he knew the secret of the red root plant and because he was beautiful, and I did not want him to drown."

"Did he drown?"

"I don't know," she said. "The gray light woke me."

"Did the white deer speak?"

"Not a word."

Lone Bear nodded as he looked across the river and into the trees. "And the spinning deer," he said. "What color was the tail?"

"It was a white-tailed deer."

Lone Bear nodded again. The whitetail came as no surprise. It was *can tarca winyela*, the female woods deer, a vision no woman sought. He would pray about this dream and consider the meaning of each detail, but there was no question in his heart about one thing. "You have dreamed of the deer woman."

Kezawin shivered and hugged herself against a cold that was not caused by the air.

"You are Double Woman Dreamer," Lone Bear proclaimed.

Chapter One

*Near the Shayen River in Unorganized Territory,
land of the Teton Lakota, west of the Missouri River
1826*

James Garrett dropped to his knees in the lush curly-leafed switchgrass and plunged a handful of plant specimens into the cold creek. The water's quick flow reduced clumps of dirt to a brown cloud on the run. He swished the leafy stalks around for good measure, then sat back on his heels to study the curious bulbous red roots. The upper Missouri River was a naturalist's paradise, and this botanical specimen was an example of the kind of find that set his brain abuzz.

He sliced the flesh of the root with his thumbnail and sniffed its juicy pulp. It had a pungent scent and a woody texture. His tongue darted out for a small taste. It burned. He scooped up a handful of water to quell the sting, spat the first mouthful into the grass and leaned down for another drink.

The sweet sound of a woman's laughter drove the bitter taste from his mind. His arm froze, and the water trickled through his fingers, flowing freely like the feminine laugh that he couldn't quite believe he was hearing. It had been well over a year since he'd heard a woman laugh like that. He raised his shaggy head slowly, half hoping to find a woman of his own kind standing on the far bank and fully expecting to see nothing at all. The Sioux people, with whom he had lived over the past year, considered him to be slightly crazy, and it was just possible that he was beginning to hear things.

The woman who watched him from the opposite side of the creek was the loveliest brown-skinned creature he had ever seen. Her braided hair was as bright and black as the wing of a raven, and merriment flashed like the quick glint of a brook trout in her dark eyes. Her white elkskin dress was unadorned except for a profusion of fringe around her elbows and below her knees, but she wore elk's-tooth earrings and a dentalium shell choker. She carried a digging stick, and a buckskin pouch hung over her shoulder. James recalled the undignified way he'd just spat in her presence, and he felt the flush of embarrassment. He reminded himself that she was not, as he'd dared to hope, a white woman, but a sheepish smile crossed his face nonetheless.

"Turn your face from my shameful behavior," he said in her language. "The taste was bitter. I had to be rid of it."

"It's good that you did," she replied, lifting her voice above the water. "The red root plant may not be eaten."

"Is it poisonous?"

Ignoring his question, she turned her attention to her digging stick, using it to loosen the roots of some plant hiding in the grass. James stood up and tucked his find into his own collection pouch. Trowel in hand, he continued on his way, following the creek bank. On the opposite side the woman kept abreast of him. The watchful eye he had trained to the ground began to stray, even though he kept up the appearance of attending to his fieldwork. She moved when he moved. She paused when he paused. She dug when he dug. He was tempted to veer away from the creek and head north just to see whether she would cross over and follow him.

The fact that she was gathering roots alone was remarkable in itself. James had followed the Missouri River northward and had spent the past eighteen months with east river groups of Sioux—the Santee, the Yankton—and now the west river people, the Teton, who called themselves Lakota people. He had mastered adequate conversational skills, observed their customs and taken a particular interest in the various uses they had for the flora of this country. He had allowed the people to observe him, too, and observe him they did. He sensed their conviction that he was a bit strange but that he posed no threat to them. One by one the much-feared Lakota bands, or Council Fires—the Brûlé, Miniconju, Sans Arc, Oglala— all had permitted him to come among them.

Now, as he explored a meandering tributary, he had made his initial contact with the Hunkpapa. Their cousins had apparently sent the Lakota version of a letter of introduction in advance of his arrival, for a hunting party had passed through his camp the previous morning and had acknowledged him by name. He had offered gifts of tobacco and had told them that he had heard of their medicine man, Lone Bear, and he wished to pay a visit to one whose wisdom was widely honored. He had known from that moment to this that he was under some watchful scrutiny, but he hardly imagined they would have sent a woman to ascertain his intentions.

Their women foraged in groups for roots and berries. They traveled in small bunches to fetch wood and water, and they worked together tanning, quilling and sewing in exclusively female circles. James had observed the courting ritual in which a young woman would stand with a man beneath his robe, but always directly in front of her parents' door. He'd watched the women form their dance lines and flex their knees to the beat of the drum in the square-shouldered, sedate form of sociable dancing that was considered proper for women. They giggled readily, but al-

ways with a demure hand shielding the mouth, always
subdued, at least in the presence of men.

This woman who followed him was an enigma. More-
over, she was persistent. Throughout his sojourn among
these people, he had taken pains not to offend them, and
he suspected that approaching a woman would be the sur-
est way to do just that. Yet, she was attractive by any standards, even James's, and she was certainly following him.

"I am of the opinion that there's nothing edible along
these banks," he said as he lifted his face to the noonday
sun. "Are you finding the same?"

"Is it food you seek?" the woman asked.

"I seek that which I have not seen before." He tucked his
trowel in his pouch and turned to her. "And I've not met
you."

"Were you seeking me, then, James Garrett?"

Her boldness prompted boldness in him. "Had I known
about you, I might have sought you, but since you have the
advantage of knowing my name, it would appear that you
seek me."

"It would appear that I have heard of you, James Garrett. Nothing more." She selected another plant and jabbed
at its base with her digging stick. "Are you in need of
food?"

He raised his hand and pointed to a grassy knoll. "My
camp is just over that hill, but I'm sure you're aware of
that." She looked up from her work and studied him for a
moment. He knew he must look strange to her with his pale
brown hair and his full beard, and he wondered if she expected him to sprout horns and a tail. But, perhaps she was
flirting with him. He firmly believed that every society had
its coy skirts, be they ruffled or fringed. "Have you food
to share?" he asked.

"If you are in need of food, I have some." She plucked
the loosened plant from the ground and cut the foliage
from the roots with the quick slice of a small glinting blade.

James strained to identify the plant at a distance. It appeared to be a specimen he didn't have. "What is that?" he asked quickly.

"Feverroot," she told him as she opened her hand to let him see the tangled brown mass. "It nourishes the fevered body."

"Is there more of that over there?" He glanced upstream for signs of a place where he might cross, his interest in the new specimen suddenly displacing his interest in the woman. "I don't believe I've seen the like of it. Feverroot, you say?"

She watched him pace the bank and realized what he was about to do. "Stay where you are," she said as she bent to untie the legging that protected her calf against the brush. "I will come."

"But I want the entire plant," he muttered. "I can find—"

"Stay there, James Garrett." She dug up another plant, moved back downstream a little way, shucked both leggings and moccasins and waded into the water. It rushed past her ankles, and soon it was up to her knees. James watched her hike her skirt up an inch or two at a time to accommodate the depth of the creek. With each step she took, he hoped for slightly higher water, but between water and elkskin fringe he saw only a teasing hint of small round knees and smooth thighs.

"I could have done that," he said as he offered his hand in assistance. "Would I be unwelcome on the other side of the creek?"

Standing knee-deep in water next to the sharply eroded bank, she stared at his hand, then offered a wary glance.

"Among my people, a man assists a woman thus," he explained. "It's the proper thing. I would not harm you."

She considered the outstretched palm for a moment before switching all that she carried into her left hand and laying her right hand in his. "You speak our language well," she noted as she stepped up to the grassy bank.

"I've had good instruction." She handed him the plant she'd dug for him, and he spoke absently as he examined the small round leaves and the matted roots. "Your cousins, I believe. Interesting people. Fine people."

"My father received word that a *wašicun*, a white man named James Garrett, wished to meet him. Our Miniconju cousins say that you walk from plant to plant with your nose to the ground, exclaiming over them in your own language as though, unlike others of your kind, you know these plants to be your relations. I have seen that this is true."

He spared her a quick smile and indicated his new specimen as he moved toward the water. "This brother of mine needs a bath. You say it's effective against fever?"

"I said that it nourishes one who has fever," she said patiently.

"And who is your father?"

"My father is Lone Bear of the Hunkpapa."

James lifted his newly washed plant up and shook the water from it, mumbling his observations about the character of its roots in his own tongue. Then her answer registered in his brain. "Lone Bear? Ah, the medicine man I've heard so much about." He levered himself up on one knee. "Your father's wisdom is widely praised."

"We have heard much about you," she told him.

"What have you heard?"

She sat upon a rock and pulled one legging over her calf. "It is believed that you are *wakan*. You have been watched but never challenged, never harmed. In fact, our cousins say that you follow a trail of plants and sometimes lose your way."

"I've never lost my way," he said, his tone indignant. But he smiled on second thought and gave a careless shrug. "Once or twice, perhaps. But it really doesn't matter. Your people have been very good to me, and sooner or later I always run into someone who's willing to set me back on course."

The woman's laughter was lilting and unrestrained. "You have not met them by accident, James Garrett. They watch after you. If you are *wakan*, then you must be protected."

He laughed as he tucked the specimen into his pouch. "My own father would find it amusing to hear you describe me as 'holy.' Were you sent to watch after me today?"

"No," she said. "I was about my own work when I saw you. You found the red root plant."

"Collecting herbs for your father?" he asked. "No doubt we all have our field assistants." She looked at him curiously, then went back to putting on her moccasins.

"May I know your name?" he asked.

It appeared to be a difficult question for her, almost as though she were unsure what to tell him, or whether to tell him anything at all. James had learned to wait for his answers without prodding with more questions. She stood slowly, avoiding his eyes. "My name is Kezawin," she said at last.

"Kezawin," he repeated, savoring the word. Soft and warm, it lingered sweetly on the tongue while it curled around the ear. "Will you take me to your father?"

"I would take the red root plant to my father," she said as she glanced at his collection pouch.

"The red root—oh," he said, touching the pouch. "It was the only one of its kind that I found. We can search for more."

"They are rare," she told him. "You may not see another one for a long time."

"What's it good for?" he asked as he peered into the pouch that hung against his lean hip. "You said it wasn't edible."

"It has healing power."

Carefully he separated the plant from the others in his pouch. "I would take it to your father, then, and offer it as a gift."

She held her hand out. "If you let me give it to him, he will know this as a sign."

"A good sign?"

She dipped her chin in assent, and he laid the red root plant in her hand.

"Will you take me to him?"

"I will come for you again, James Garrett. Don't cross the creek until I come for you." She walked away from him, and his feet were strangely heavy, rendering him unable to follow her. He watched her disappear into a stand of cottonwoods.

The air inside the sweat lodge was thick with steam. Kezawin breathed shallowly and indulged herself in physical self-awareness as a prelude to the awareness she sought. She was surrounded by darkness. The willow-framed dome admitted nothing from the world outside the layered walls of heavy hides. Kezawin sat naked, her chin hovering above her knees, inside Earth's warm, wet womb. Her hair made a cape over her rounded back, and a runnel of sweat slid between her breasts on its course to the puddle that had formed in her navel. Her belly rumbled, but she had no thought of food. She had the sound of her own breath to tell her that she was not an unborn spirit, but she had no thoughts now. She simply sat inside herself and became the breath and the heartbeat tucked under Earth's breast. She was a vessel into which awareness might sweep.

In the darkness the face of the white deer appeared with the red root plant in his mouth. It lingered, then went away again.

Brightness began as a small seed, opening in the dark and blossoming slowly into white daylight. The sun danced in the man's light hair. Like his brother, the deer, his face was covered with hair. He put the red root plant in his mouth, and Kezawin held her breath as she watched from across the creek and waited for the man to be transformed. But when he spat the bitter pulp into the grass, she welcomed the sign that he was human, and she laughed, as was her right. He spoke to her, and she studied him, as was her duty. His eyes were large and round, alert and curious. He acquainted himself with all that grew in the earth, and he used all of his senses, smelling, tasting and touching with his hands while he looked carefully with his eyes. He spoke to the plants as he removed them from the earth, making his peace with them in his own tongue. Kezawin watched him do these things, and she was filled with a strong sense of rightness.

He saw the feverroot and acted on impulse, incautious in his eagerness to cross the creek and learn something new. A wiser man would know the unknown thing to be *wakan*, holy in its mystery. She watched him pace the bank of the creek in his anxiety to reach her, and she warned him against crossing the creek until she came for him.

He heeded her warning, but she saw no fear in him. He invited her to touch him. Other men admired her, but they were afraid of her power, and they stayed away. This one offered his hand. Her name did not frighten him, nor did her laughter. He was a brave man. Or a foolish one. Or, if the signs were true, he was sent by her *śicun*, her guardian and helper, which had been represented in her dream by the white deer.

Awareness. In the dark womb of the earth, Kezawin made no thought. She saw what was. She accepted the red root plant from the white deer. Under the bright midday sun, she accepted James Garrett's hand.

James found his thoughts drifting to the Lakota woman as he went about his work. It had been two days since he'd seen her, and he was beginning to wonder whether she'd been a figment of his imagination. She had convinced him of her intention to return and take him to her father, and he kept catching himself watching, feeling himself waiting. He had to remind himself that he was not one to await any woman's pleasure. He hadn't the time or patience.

He hooked his fingers into his thick beard and scratched his chin as he watched the breakfast fire burn low. The water would heat quickly, and he had a razor in his pack within close reach. He had let his beard grow after giving his mirror as a gift to a Brûlé medicine man, but now he had an urge to be rid of the itching nuisance. Charles LaRoux, the old French trapper he'd traveled with for the better part of a year, had advised him to enjoy being liberated from unnecessary grooming, but James had not achieved LaRoux's unself-conscious state of unwash. He had, however, cultivated a dense growth of facial hair, and it occurred to him now that shaving might be in order. Indian men plucked what little facial hair they had, and a woman might well be offended by...

Stray thoughts again. Clearly the woman had not found him to be offensive. In his attempt to behave in a manner that he had thought she would consider respectful, he had refrained from approaching her. But she'd followed him. Perhaps she was simply curious about him because he was white. On the other hand, it was quite conceivable that she was interested in him as a man. He had turned this notion over in his head many times since he'd met her. Even though he had not numbered women among his objectives for this expedition, James had half a mind to exercise his considerable masculine charm and find out whether the latter prospect was true.

He tossed a pan of water on the fire as he came to his feet. The sound of hoofbeats enjoined the hissing of the coals, and James jerked his head around. She was coming. His thoughts entertained no other possibility. She crested the hill on a small buckskin mare, and James caught himself grinning broadly at the sight of her silhouette etched against the morning sky. She sat astride the horse with as much grace as any rider he had ever seen. Her only tack was a blanket and a strip of leather looped around the horse's lower jaw for a one-piece bridle and rein.

James quickly tucked his white lawn shirt beneath the leather belt that held up his buckskin britches, as well as both of the sheaths for his knife and trowel. His mouth went dry as he watched the woman draw near. Her face was burnished by early-morning gold, and her white elkskin dress appeared to be gilded. The yoke was heavily embroidered with red-and-yellow porcupine quills, and the tin-wrapped tips of fringe at the bottom of the dress jangled softly as the pony pranced.

"Hello!" he greeted her in English as she slid down from her mount. He continued in Lakota. "It's good to see you, Kezawin. You must have heard my thoughts this morning."

"You considered coming to our camp on your own, did you not?" Her mare stood ground-tied, as though the rein were invisibly bolted into the grass.

"I thought perhaps you had forgotten about me. May I offer you breakfast? I, myself, have just eaten."

Even though she had eaten, too, she accepted the offer as a friendly gesture and knelt beside the circle of ashes that had been his camp fire. The spit-roasted rabbit he served her was still warm, and she knew she'd been given what would have been his midday meal.

James sat on his heels and stole surreptitious glances at her as she ate. Impolite as it was to watch her, he couldn't help himself. He knew she'd dressed for this occasion, and his Lakota vocabulary had become a jumble in his head. The quillwork on her dress was superlatively crafted. The brightly colored geometric designs were intricately worked into tight, perfectly ordered rows. Her dentalium shell choker and delicate shell earrings glistened as prettily as pearls. She had rouged the center part in her lustrous black braids.

"You look fine this morning," James said, fumbling for the right words. The last thing he wanted to do was embarrass her and drive her away. "Your dress is beautiful. You're a very skilled craftswoman, I see."

"My work is highly prized," she acknowledged without looking up from the food she nibbled on.

"I will know your husband before we are introduced," he said in the way of a man who fished with a baitless hook. "He will be the one who wears the finest shirt."

She held the meat still and spoke quietly. "He wore the finest shirt when I saw him last, James Garrett. If you are wise, you will not speak of him."

"He is dead?"

She nodded.

"How long?" he persisted.

"Seven winters."

"So you live with your father?"

She looked up at him. "I have my own lodge."

He knew how unusual that was, but he didn't question her further on the matter. There was a strange, light-hearted feeling that had come to him with the knowledge that she had no husband, and it was that feeling he would question later, when he had more time.

"Have you spoken to your father about me?" he asked.

"He was pleased to receive the red root plant."

"I found another," he told her. "They do seem to be rare."

Her face brightened with her smile. "It's good that you've come. You are the first white man who comes seeking medicine. My father has discussed this matter with others who have observed your kind. Some said there might not be a wise or holy man among you." He laughed, and she was glad he hadn't taken offense. "The red root plant is a good sign. We've been waiting for such a one as you."

"You knew my name."

She dismissed it with a gesture. "I knew you by the red root plant. Your name meant little to me."

It was difficult to hide his sudden flush of indignation. "Perhaps it means something to your father. You said the Miniconju spoke of me."

"Yes, they did." She finished the meat and cleaned her fingers on the grass. "We were prepared for James Garrett, whom they called a strange but harmless white man. But my father, Lone Bear, wishes to see the bearer of the red root plant." She stood, then added thoughtfully, "For that we had not expected a white man, but the signs are very clear, James Garrett. And I'm happy that you're not a true deer."

"A deer?"

She was not given to explaining herself, James realized. He accepted it as the female prerogative to be totally enigmatic. Without asking more questions, he packed up his gear, distributed it between his packhorse and his saddle horse, and followed her the four or five miles to her camp. As they approached the collection of tipis erected on the high ground above the creek, James saw one sentry standing on top of a hill. He knew there were more whom he would not see unless they wanted to be seen. He was glad he had waited for Kezawin to escort him.

As they approached, the camp came alive with curious eyes. Three young boys chasing one another and leaping over tipi stakes in a game of kick-my-tail-off stopped dead in their tracks and watched the two riders pass. Four young girls paused on their way to the creek, taking a moment to gape and giggle. One whispered to the others, but the old woman who waddled along behind shooed them toward the thicket of wild plum bushes on the creek bank. The girls hurried on, but the old woman stopped to adjust her picking apron and steal a good look at the strange sight for herself before she clucked to her dog and waddled away. James grinned at the sight of the big gray dog, who dragged the triangular travois that was lashed to his back and trotted behind the girls with his tongue lolling. He looked much like the wolf who might be counting the trusting chickens who were headed for the bushes.

Three women peeked over, under and around the willow frame of a meat-drying rack as they arranged strips of raw meat and flicked their hands at persistent flies. Nearby, a child turned for a moment from the baby she was entertaining, whose cradleboard was suspended from the branches of a cottonwood sapling. Even the infant stared.

James could only guess what aspect of his appearance might seem the most peculiar. During the past eighteen months he had traveled with other white men, but he had struck out on his own in search of Lone Bear, the renowned medicine man. He was suddenly acutely aware that he was a minority of one, and he wished he had taken the time to shave.

Kezawin stopped in front of a tipi on the southeastern side of the camp, which numbered more than thirty tipis. James followed her lead and dismounted as a tall lean man with graying braids ducked out of the tipi door. Kezawin took James's reins and introduced him to her father, Lone Bear.

"My daughter will unload your horses and turn them out with the rest, James Garrett. You will be my guest. It has been decided."

James followed Lone Bear and sat next to him on the men's side, the right-hand side of the tipi, which was richly carpeted with the hides of buffalo. Lone Bear sat against a willow backrest, and James was aware of the neat arrangement of Lone Bear's belongings, but he took care not to pointedly survey the man's home. They discussed nothing until they had shared a pipe, and finally Lone Bear said, "I have heard that there are medicine men among your people, but I have not yet seen one for myself. Are you a healer, James Garrett, an interpreter of visions, or do you have other powers?"

"I am what my people call a naturalist." He used the English word because he could think of no equivalent concept in Lakota. "My special interest is in botany—plant life. I collect all species of plants, observe where they grow, how they grow, their cycles, the animals who feed upon them."

Lone Bear nodded as he listened. "A plant-taker, then. Will you take great numbers, like the beaver-takers?"

"I will take only a few," James assured him.

Lone Bear nodded again. "You must be a healer, like my daughter."

James lifted his brow. "Your daughter is a healer? I assumed she was gathering herbs for your use."

"She does sometimes, but more for herself. Kezawin has such power as a healer. Many of the women come to her, and even some men when they have exhausted all other channels."

"But no one spoke of her," James protested. "They all say that it is Lone Bear who is the great shaman of the Hunkpapa."

"I am," Lone Bear said, eschewing false modesty as a waste of time. "But Kezawin's destiny is most unusual, and her ability to find the right leaf or root to drive harm from the body is remarkable."

"I have an interest in observing your uses of plants," James said, purposely avoiding any mention of an interest in Kezawin or her destiny. "In the time I've spent here, I've gained respect for what the shaman does, what he knows."

Lone Bear considered this for a moment and then nodded again. "It is possible that a *naturalist* might understand some things. From your description, your word *naturalist* fits any Lakota, but some, of course, are more observant than others. Have you the patience to learn from us, James Garrett?"

"I've studied for many years, but I believe that you can teach me things that our wise men in the East don't know."

"I can teach you nothing, but there is much you might learn. Do you have a vision? Will these observations you make serve your people in some way?"

James gave the question some thought. He did not doubt his own destiny for a moment, but he wasn't sure the Indian would understand it or appreciate the gravity of it. "I keep a journal," he said finally. "Much like your winter counts, except that I use words instead of pictures. When people read my journal, they can hear everything I say with their eyes. My work will be published so that many people will learn what I have discovered on this journey." He realized that Lone Bear would understand *published* only in the context of the oral tradition of the Lakota *eyapaha*, the one who broadcasts news to the village, but it was the closest word he could use.

"Then your people will all want to come here."

James smiled and shook his head. "I don't think so. Their homes are planted in the ground, like those of the Mandan, the Earth Lodge People, and they have their farms and their families. Their lives are different. They wouldn't like this place."

"Many white men of the French tongue have come to stay. They have married our women and planted their houses in the ground. We trade with them. Most of them cause no trouble."

James made no comment about the French. He owed his facility with the Lakota language to just such a Frenchman, but James was a man of science, and Charles LaRoux was not. *Joie de vivre*, had been the Frenchman's simple goal. No matter what tongue they conversed in, James and LaRoux did not speak the same language.

"I won't cause any trouble, either, Lone Bear. I shall take but a few plants with me when I leave. I've come here just to learn."

"Do you hunt for meat?"

"Only to feed myself. When my aim is bad, as it often is, I go without." James watched the old man weigh his answer, wondering whether he'd just diminished himself in Lone Bear's eyes. He knew the younger men would provide meat in return for the shaman's services, but Lone Bear appeared to be particularly fit for his age. "Do you?"

"I claim choice portions following a hunt, as is my right." Lone Bear tapped the ashes from his pipe into the fire pit, signaling the end of their discussion. "While you are here, you will improve your aim, James Garrett."

"I'll do my best," James promised as he uncrossed his legs and stood to take his leave. "But I tell you quite honestly, hunting is not my sport."

"That is as it should be. We take the life of the four-legged so that we two-legged might have life. This must be marked in your journal, James Garrett. You must teach your people that killing is not a sport." He put his pipe away in its quilled leather case. "Even the French who have lived among us for a long time are misguided in that way. Perhaps there are not enough *naturalists* among you."

James smiled. "We are a rare breed. Many people think men such as I are just a bit crazy."

"You are here because you are crazy. You are *wakan*. That which is mysterious and holy dwells within you." Lone Bear stood to hang his pipe bag on its willow stand. "Build your shelter next to my lodge, James Garrett. My daughter will cook for us both."

"I promise to contribute to her cooking pot whenever I can."

James spent much of the day selecting and trimming the poles to build his lean-to next to Lone Bear's tipi. He covered the frame with oilcloth and willow branches and built a stone fire pit in front of the structure so that he could burn sage to chase away the mosquitoes at night. While he worked, he offered a greeting or a nod at the least to each passerby who stopped to give him a curious once-over. The first man who stopped insisted that James pivot the structure a few degrees so that the entrance faced due east. Because erecting the lodge was woman's work, the man did not offer to lend a hand, but he gave a nod of approval when the change was made, then went about his business.

When the shelter was built and his gear was stashed inside, James gathered soap and shaving equipment and headed for the creek. He trimmed his hair and removed what he could from his face with a pair of scissors, stropped his razor and set about the task of shaving without benefit of a mirror. The first nick in his skin had him grumbling, but by the third he loosed an oath condemning the beard, the razor and the soul of Charles LaRoux. Down on one knee, he rinsed blood-tinged lather from his blade and took an angry swipe at the last of his beard. A sudden peal of laughter nearly caused more bloodletting from James's tender neck. He turned and found Kezawin's eyes bright with amusement.

"Ye gods, woman!" Since the expletive was lost on her in English, he sought more composure in Lakota. "You should know better than to startle a man who has a blade at his throat."

"I have never seen a man hold a knife to his own throat. It's a strange ritual." She took a step closer as she surveyed his face.

"My beard is too thick to pluck hair by hair as the men of the Lakota do." He splashed a handful of water on his face.

Kezawin extended her hand and offered him a small pouch. "When I saw that you were slashing your face a moment ago, I went back to my lodge to bring you this. It will stop the bleeding."

James stood up slowly, pointedly glancing down at his bare chest. In eighteen months he'd gone from pale-skinned scholar to the deeply tanned outdoorsman, and he was not ashamed of his physique, but his parlor etiquette was deeply ingrained, and her laughter made him uncomfortable. "Once again you've caught me off guard."

A man's bare chest was no novelty to Kezawin. She smiled. "A man should always be aware of everything around him, James Garrett. Even when he is busy mutilating his face. Take this."

He used both hands to fold his razor as he looked first a the pouch, then into Kezawin's eyes. "I might have come down here to bathe," he said.

"Not unless you wanted to bathe publicly."

He glanced down at the pouch again. "I cannot see where to apply it."

She stepped close to him and opened the pouch. "Your face must be numb after the scraping if you don't know where you've cut yourself." She took a small amount of clear salve from the pouch and dabbed it on his chin. "I will tell you when to wash your face again. The bleeding will have stopped."

A tangy scent reached his nose. He searched his brain but failed to determine the source of the salve from its smell. "What is it?"

"It is a mixture of herbs with the gum from the yellow bark tree."

"Will you show me this tree?"

"It doesn't grow here," she said. "If you stay with us long enough, I will show you. It is from the hills to the south."

She treated each cut with painstaking deliberation, and he was keenly aware of her warm breath against his neck, the closeness of her body to his bare chest, and her scent, which was a combination of wood smoke and something sweet. He dug his fingers into his palms and reminded himself that he'd asked her to do this for him. Now he didn't quite know what to do with the racy feeling she triggered in him.

"Your father has invited me to stay for a while. I've built my lodge next to his."

"I know."

He cleared his throat. "I don't wish to strain your resources, Kezawin. My hunting prowess is nothing to boast about, but I will make every effort to put fresh meat into your cooking pot."

"That is not why you're here," she told him as she daubed salve on his neck.

"Tell me what you mean," he said quietly. "You seem to have your own ideas about my purpose in being here."

"It may not yet be *your* purpose, James Garrett. I believe you have much to learn before it becomes truly yours." She lowered her hand from his neck, but she took only half a step backward. "Will you scrape the hair from your chest, as well?" she asked as she studied him boldly.

"Would that improve my appearance?"

She glanced up quickly and smiled. "Your face is much improved, James Garrett. It's a handsome face after all."

"After all the hair is scraped away?" He chuckled as he rubbed his hand over his smooth jaw. "Did you expect me to look like a plucked goose?" She laughed and shook her head. "I would have you call me James."

"I have said it wrong? James Garrett," she said carefully.

"No, just James. Garrett is my family name. James is *my* name. It's what you should call me."

"James," she repeated. "You have stopped bleeding, James. You may wash—"

With one cautious finger he touched the rows of quill work on her shoulder. "What is this purpose you have in mind for me, Kezawin? What must I learn?"

"That it is neither my purpose for you, nor yours for yourself that will—"

"You speak in riddles, when the plain truth is that you don't want to back away any more than I do." One corner of his mouth drew up in a teasing smile. "What is this purpose you speak of?"

She had not been touched by the strong hands of a man in a very long time, and this man's hands rested easily on her shoulders. He was too ignorant to have it be otherwise, and yet it felt good, and she looked into his eyes and welcomed his ignorance for the moment. To him, she was simply a woman, and he was not afraid to be close to her in the way of a man who is drawn by instinct to a woman. Kezawin banished all thoughts and let the woman in her be drawn to the man, but just for this moment.

He slid his hands over her shoulders and down her arms, touching soft elk hide, then warm woman's skin. His palms tingled with the contact. "I don't know the word, Kezawin," he said quietly, and he cupped her face in his hand as he spoke low, his voice softly persuasive. "But what I'm going to do won't hurt you. It works best if you close your eyes."

She made no move to touch him, but she did not move away. He kissed her tentatively, touching his lips to the corner of her mouth and then, lightly, the middle. She lifted her chin, and he whispered again, "Close your eyes, Kezawin." He moistened his lips and slid them over the fullness of hers, hardly moving, hardly pressing until her lips parted for him. His heart leaped in his chest, and he slanted his mouth across hers and gave in to the need to fully taste her mouth.

When he ended the kiss, he looked down at her, expecting the willingness he'd tasted on her lips to be reflected in her eyes. Her hot dark stare startled him, and although she still had not laid hands on him except to apply a healing salve, he felt as though she held him in the grip of her small hands and shook him hard. He could not have mistaken her response so completely, he told himself. He was certain she had welcomed his kiss. And then unexpectedly the heat in her eyes vanished, and she laughed.

"You find that so amusing?" he demanded. James Garrett was no inexperienced, fumbling boy, and no woman had ever sneered at his advances. "Forgive me, but I could have sworn the invitation was there."

"You are a foolish man," she said with a hint of regret in her voice. "It is I who do not wish to harm you, and yet you stand here, filling your chest like the courting grouse, daring me to strike you down."

"Strike me down?" It was his turn to laugh. "You would kill me for kissing you?"

He used the English word because he had not learned to court a woman in Lakota, but she understood him. Already they had taken a step beyond words, and the danger in that step frightened her. "I would not want to see you dead, James. You must not touch me as a man might touch a woman."

His brow drew down in his confusion. "I did not force myself on you in any way, Kezawin. Nor would I. From the first, when you came upon me by the creek, you have been—" He scowled as he mentally recounted each flirtation. "What kind of woman are you?"

"I am called Double Woman Dreamer," she told him, and she waited for him to shrink back. When he did not, she took it as another sign of his ignorance. "I have dreamed of the Double Woman, the one who is at once a woman and a deer. I have the power to heal."

"So your father told me."

"And did he tell you about the dark side of my power?" James shook his head slowly. "Two men lay dead because of me. Both my husband and my brother. The power of the Double Woman can destroy a man's medicine."

"I have no medicine, Kezawin. I'm a scientist. You'll not dream me dead." He pointed to the sheath on her belt. "Unless you plunge that knife into my heart, you'll not—"

"My dream told me that you would come, James. Our destinies are entwined. You are the bearer of the red root plant. But there are two sides, like the faces of the Double Woman, and you must take care not to touch me even . . . even if I would seem to want you to. I would need no knife to kill you."

Her dark eyes told him that she did not doubt the truth of what she said, and though he understood none of it, her conviction was unnerving to him.

Chapter Two

The crack of rifle fire shattered the peace in the piny woods. The buck's legs buckled as the sound reverberated in the hills, and a hearty "Eee-yahhh!" chased the echoing shot with ecstatic ripples. As often as not James's gunfire had signaled the flight of his prey rather than its fall, but here was a true shot and a clean kill. He wondered what kind of reception this offering would earn him from Kezawin.

Lone Bear would accept his guest's hunting success the same way he did all the failures, offering neither praise nor censure. Lone Bear's gods were credited with providing the meat whenever James made a kill, and when James returned from his occasional hunting forays empty-handed, Lone Bear found no fault with his efforts. But he was certain he had noticed a glint of pride in Kezawin's eyes whenever he'd presented her with a gutted carcass to butcher.

Gutting the carcass was far from his favorite task. He dropped to his knees beside his kill, lashed its back hooves together and prepared to hoist it over a tree limb, quietly explaining to it all the while that the job was as unpleasant for him as it was for the dead animal and that he could do just as well on a diet of dandelion greens and wood sorrel if it were not for the carnivorous appetite of his host.

Kezawin stood quietly behind a stand of pine samplings and waited for James to finish praying in his native English. Clearly he understood the need for pardon and praise when the deer's life was taken to nourish the human body. He was an unusual white man, to be sure, but then, her vision had shown her how unusual he would be. The white deer was rare, indeed. When the praying had stopped, she stepped away from her cover.

"Will you share the fresh liver from your kill with me, that we may both be made strong by it?"

Clutching his broad-bladed knife, he whirled at the sound of her voice, the surprise instantly doubling his pulse rate. "Where did you come from?" he demanded.

She lifted the strap of her collection pouch over her head. "I have some things to show you after we feast."

"Feast?" He glanced down at the carcass. Since he had always done his hunting on his own, he had made a practice of disposing of the offal, but he knew that a Lakota hunter would consume the raw liver on the spot. The idea was not an appealing one.

"Your medicine grows stronger every day, James." She took the knife from his hand and rescued the choice red organ. "As does mine. Your deer brother would share his power with us now." She sliced a portion of the liver and handed it to him before cutting some for herself.

The meat dangled from his fingers, limp and dripping with blood. He watched Kezawin eat hers, and it struck him that the process appeared no more indelicate than slipping a slithery oyster from the shell to the mouth. He thought he might manage it if he thought no more about it and did it quickly. He accomplished the haste but not the interruption of thought, and in a moment he was bolting from her sight. The sound of her laughter did nothing to quiet his rebellious stomach.

When she brought the water bag she'd taken from his saddle, she found him leaning against a tree. His face had lost its color, and she thought it a shame that he couldn't finish the succulent liver, which would restore him. She offered the bottle with a smile, and he snatched it rudely.

"I gave it a try, Kezawin. How could you laugh at me like that?"

"You ate it so quickly," she said, imitating the motion. "And it returned just as quickly. Were you offended because a woman had not waited to eat her portion until you had finished?"

"I was offended because it was raw!" He swished some water around in his mouth and spat. "You made it look better than it tastes."

"Since you never bring us the heart or the liver of your kill, naturally I assumed you were accustomed to consuming them on the hunt."

"Naturally." He tipped the water bag to his mouth again, but the taste of blood lingered. "I was actually beginning to warm up to the sport, but this leaves something of an unpleasant taste in my mouth and an unsettled feeling in my stomach." He laid a hand over his flat belly and shook his head.

"This will help."

James flinched at the sprig of wild greenery Kezawin held up to his mouth.

"But you must chew it slowly and not wolf it down," she warned as he eyed the greens uncertainly and then glanced at her.

She smiled reassuringly, and he found that the temptation to eat from her hand was irresistible. He nibbled cautiously.

Once again she was reminded of the shy animal who had foretold this man's coming, and she stood still and let him take what he would until his lips brushed against her fingers. His cool blue eyes became soft and warm when they met hers. Her heart went out to him even as she told herself it would have to a child who trusted because he was ignorant of danger.

"What am I eating?" he asked, chewing slowly as she had instructed.

"We call it bee plant. It grows in the mountains to the west, but this is something I wanted to show you. I found some nearby." She took another sprig from her pouch and handed it to him.

"Is it unusual to find this plant growing in this area?"

"It is." She produced another specimen from the bag. "I believe this one is not yet in your collection, either."

His face brightened as he examined the two botanical samples. "I must see the habitat," he said eagerly. "These hills are a veritable treasure cache, Kezawin." He flashed her a smile. "A gold mine for the likes of you and me, fellow naturalists that we are."

She questioned his use of an English phrase. "Gold mine?"

"Just an expression," he said with a shrug. "A place that yields up treasures such as these. Of course, Lewis and Clark described many new species in the journals they kept when they made their journey through here twenty years ago, but their task was more general, and they missed these wonderful mountains."

"*Paha Sapa* is a holy place. Its treasures, as you call them, are many. That's why we come here every summer."

"Show me where you found these," James insisted.

She shook her head and offered up a coy smile. "I have meat to butcher now. Tomorrow I will take you there."

James scowled at the carcass that hung by its legs from a tree. "Infernal horned beast," he grumbled. "Such a nuisance, this meat-making."

"I heard your victory cry when you hit the mark with your noisy rifle." Her dark eyes twinkled, and James saw that inkling of pride in them again. "I think there's a hunter in you, James Garrett."

Kezawin kept her promise the following afternoon and many days after that, leading James to hilltops and stream banks in a continually fruitful quest for botanical discovery. Occasionally Lone Bear joined them, but as often as not he declined his daughter's invitation, and James and Kezawin pursued their mutual interest alone. James found each new foray to be fascinating, but his guide was becoming even more so.

She had a tender regard for every plant they uprooted and an insatiable curiosity about every note he made about them in his journals. He explained the way his science called for grouping every species into classes for the purpose of study, and he showed her the characteristics by which they were deemed related. The concept that plants came in families made perfect sense to her. Her people also grouped themselves into clans, or *tiośpaye*. She needed no journal to keep track of what he told her; she repeated his explanations back to him, and he noticed that she began arranging her own collection as neatly classed botanical bunches, keeping, as she said, families together. During his days as a laboratory assistant at Harvard, he'd never had a more enthusiastic pupil.

She had wandered away from him one afternoon as they foraged on foot in the pine-covered hills the people called *Paha Sapa* because they appeared, from a distance, to be black. A sudden thunderstorm took him by surprise, and by the time he ducked under a protective rocky outcropping, he was soaked. He waited, thinking surely Kezawin would return to the vicinity where she'd left him, but the moments slid past like the falling rain, and she did not come.

James began to worry. Perhaps she had stumbled into a bear's den, or perhaps she'd simply stumbled, fallen and now lay twisted and helpless on the rocks somewhere. He left his shelter and followed the path she had taken when he'd last seen her. In the pouring rain he called her name. The echo of his own voice answered. Panic seized him, and he began to run. The soles of his moccasins slipped in the muddy carpet of fallen pine needles, but he pressed on, raising his voice again and again against the thunder. *Something's happened. Something's happened.* His heart pounded with unreasoning fear, and his shouts became hoarse as his throat tightened. "Kez-ahhh-winnn!"

"James!"

He stopped, his chest heaving as he searched the rain-drenched woods and wondered whether he was hearing things. "Kezawin, where are you?"

"I'm here!" Her face appeared amid the dense boughs of a huge sheltering pine. "You're getting wet, you crazy man! Come inside."

Her laughter heated his blood, turning cold fear to hot anger as he plowed his way through knee-high saplings and dove into her shelter, a dry cocoon in which she'd managed to build a small, nearly smokeless fire. He found her crouching under the natural lean-to where there had been an attrition of a few lower branches and the higher ones swooped down to form a small den. She watched him crawl in while she hugged her knees and unleashed that free and infuriating laugh of hers. James snatched her up by her shoulders and shook her once. Her laughter died, and she gazed up at him, startled by his blazing eyes. His face was so close to hers that water dripped from his hair and fell on her nose, her cheek, into her eye. She didn't blink.

"Woman, you will never again laugh at me," he warned, his voice hoarse from shouting. "I have suffered this indignity long enough, and I will tolerate no more of it. You are willful and brazen. You fly in the face of your own conventions. Women of your kind do not conduct themselves in this unseemly fashion, and yet you—"

"Women of my kind?" she asked calmly. "What do you know about women of my kind, James? Your running around in the rain amuses me. It makes me laugh."

"My running around in the rain!" he bellowed, giving her shoulders another quick shake. "I couldn't find you. I called out time and time again, and when you didn't answer, I feared for your safety, Kezawin."

"My safety?" She resented the strong hold he had on her shoulders, but the look in his eyes did not threaten her. To her amazement, she saw that the anger had become remembered fear. "But it's only rain, James. I thought you would find shelter for yourself." Tenderly she touched his cheek and repeated, "It's only rain."

He peered at her in the dim light, and the haze in his mind began to dissipate. The tension went out of his shoulders as he relaxed his grip on hers. She was safe, after all, and untouched by the rain other than the drops he'd brought her. He thought he must look quite foolish at the moment, while Kezawin, with her dark eyes shining up at him, was a beautiful sight. He drew back and tried to push the notion of her beauty out of his mind as he leaned his back against the trunk of the tree. He was thoroughly uncomfortable.

"Are you afraid of the rain, James?"

He tried to laugh it off as he shook his head, but she touched the shirtsleeve that was plastered to his arm, and he stopped laughing. "My mother died in the rain." The words were out before he'd even thought about them, and when he heard them, he wanted to take them back. "She was quite ill, you see, and she wandered outside in the rain. There was no one looking after her." He shrugged. "She would have died anyway, as sick as she was, but someone should have been with her."

"You have not put aside your grief, and this death haunts you." She moved away slightly, as though the haunting might somehow touch her, too. "I see that you have yet to make your peace with the one whom you blame for not being with her. Is it yourself, James?"

He turned his attention to the small fire pit and the low-burning flames, and he shook his head. "I was just a boy, and I was just as sick as she was. My father left us in the care of his—the people who worked for him. Some of them became ill, too. Others fled."

"Then I see that you must make peace with your father before you can put aside your grief. Is it this bad feeling for your father that drives you so far from your people?"

"Drives me?" James scowled as he ruffled his hair with his fingers and flicked a shower of droplets in all directions. "Nothing drives me. I'm here because the Boston Society of Naturalists has agreed to publish my work, and my sponsor, Ezra Breckenridge, agreed to pay the expenses for this expedition."

The confusion he saw in her eyes gave him a sense of satisfaction. She had overstepped her bounds with all her speculation, and, of course, what did she really know? The very word *society* was difficult to translate into something she might understand. He used *akicita*, which referred to the warrior groups to which Lakota men belonged, but the concept was hardly comparable to the Society of Naturalists, a group of highly educated men. Even the concept of a fraternity did not relate to Kezawin, who was, after all, a woman. Reassured by the notion that he had elevated the conversation well above her head, James smiled and told himself there would be no more slips of the tongue unless, in these cozy quarters, they were literal.

"Boston is part of a place called Massachusetts, which is an Indian word, and it is what we call the place where I live," he explained after he had concluded it might be the one thing she would understand of all that he'd said.

"And where your father lives?"

"No. My father lives in Virginia, which is far away from Massachusetts."

"And so these others you spoke of sent you here," Kezawin said. "Why? Are the plants in Massachusetts not as good as those that grow here?"

He laughed. "Some are the very same, but many are different. The Society simply wants to know more about the West and all that grows here."

"And you are their scout?"

"No, Kezawin, I'm a scientist. I need to know, too, because I...I just need to know, that's all." His patient smile hinted at his conviction that few people understood that need. "I also need to publish my work, but I am a poor scholar who has no money of his own to accomplish these things, and I therefore depend on the financial backing of men like Ezra Breckenridge. But I'm sure none of this makes any sense to you."

"I understand that what you're telling me has little to do with why you are here." Her smile was equally patient. "Except that you need to know. That, I believe, is important to you. And you attend to some things very well. Much better than other white men."

The compliment warmed his smile. "You say I know nothing of Lakota women. What do you know of white men?"

"I know that most of them are poor observers, but not you." She cocked her head to one side and looked at him curiously. "Why did you fear for my safety, James?"

"I told you why. I told you more than I intended to tell you. Quite obviously it was a foolish notion I had that a man is responsible for a woman's safety. But you—" With a gesture he indicated their dry, comfortable niche in a world turned stormy. The rain fell steadily all around them, but the thick pine thatch eliminated all but an occasional trickle. "You were well able to take care of yourself. Who would have thought to find such a shelter in a tree?"

"A porcupine, perhaps." A man and a woman, Kezawin heard him say. She was a woman no man dared take responsibility for, but he spoke of them as man and woman. Unthinkable. Recklessly Kezawin savored the thought, promising herself that she would put it aside in a moment. "Tell me what you feared," she said quietly.

His shoulders quivered slightly, whether from chills or his active imagination, he was unsure. "You might have slipped and fallen, or some wild animal might have—"

She reached out slowly, and for one sweet moment, he thought she might embrace him. Her eyes suggested it, but her hands went to the buttons on his shirt. "You must let the fire dry this," she said, "and warm your skin."

Had any other woman made the suggestion, he would have had a ready response. This was a woman who kept him guessing, and that idea brought a slow smile to James's lips. Guessing could be fun, too. She unbuttoned his shirt, her small hands slow but sure, and when she reached his belt, he leaned back. His smile broadened. Undaunted, she pulled the shirt free of his pants and peeled it back from his shoulders. The dusting of light hair across his chest was a curiosity, and she rested her hands in the middle of it, testing its texture.

"Now what happens, Kezawin?" She glanced up and saw a man's look in his eyes. "If I touch you, will you laugh in my face as you so often do?" He touched her cheek with the tips of his fingers. Her lips parted as she lifted her chin, but she said nothing. He ran his fingertips over the side of her neck and continued downward, over the neckline of her elkskin dress.

"Not yet amused?" he asked in a throaty tone as he sat up slowly. "Your dress is not wet. I have no excuse to touch you as you touched me." Just the tips of his fingers. Just the slightest pressure and the slowest descent. Skin against skin against skin. His touch made her nipple tighten. "There's my excuse," he whispered, and he covered her mouth with his.

Her fingers curled in his chest hair, and she opened her mouth to drink deeply of his kiss. She responded only as a woman, wanting what a woman wanted, feeling the delicate need, like the quick flutter of a brightly colored wing. His way was different, but it had been so long since a man had touched her, and that man had been as young and inexperienced as she. Now here was warmth sparked by something different, and yet not different. It was still man and woman, just as he had said. But when he groaned in the way of a man whose needs would soon transcend his reason, Kezawin knew the moment had to be over for them.

He made no move to draw apart, but he straightened and rested against the trunk of the tree, tipped his head back and gave her a heavy-lidded stare. She put his shirt over a branch and added dry tinder to her fire. There was no room for either of them to move about and no way to distance themselves mentally from each other. The awareness of breath, flesh and heat was tangible, and the attraction between them had redoubled itself with a kiss.

"Perhaps it's time I knew more about this kind of woman you say you are, Kezawin," he said quietly. "Are you the kind who makes a man crazy with her games?"

"That would not affect you, James." Her laugh was brief and guarded. "You are crazy already."

"I believe you are one of the few people, Indian or white, who knows that isn't true."

"I know you to be *wakan*," she reminded him. "That much I know."

He waved the notion of holiness away with his hand. "Why do you tease me, Kezawin? You spend a great deal of time with me, and I know you find it pleasant to…to…" He waved his hand again, as though the words he wanted might be somewhere in the air. Finally he looked at her straight and hard. "Why do you laugh at me? No, why do you laugh the *way* you do? The other women are… different. Demure. *Feminine*. I don't know," he said, dropping his hand in exasperation. "It's as though you have a secret—a grand joke that none of the rest of us knows anything about."

Sitting with her legs tucked under her, she scooted closer, her dark eyes anxious. "Did I look different when you kissed me, James? Just before or just after, did you see anything change in my face?" Even as he shook his head slowly, she waved her hand above the part in her hair. "Perhaps on my head?"

"No. Nothing but a woman's eyes, a woman's mouth."

"Good. That's good."

A woman's eyes, he thought as he sought to plumb their depths for whatever this secret might be. They were soft and wary, like the eyes of a doe, but set in the smooth-skinned, fine-boned face of a woman. "What else could I expect to see?"

"I am Double Woman Dreamer." Her voice became hollow as she said the name. "In a dream I have seen the Double Woman, who is able to change herself from woman to deer and back again. I am not like other women. Laughter comes to me, and I do not try to control it. My quillwork is unsurpassed. I have the power to heal."

"Those are wonderful gifts, Kezawin. Laughter, creativity and a healing touch, all residing in one lovely woman." He saw that none of this comforted her, and he had a disturbing thought. "Is this why you never seem to be included when the women gather in groups for quilling or picking fruit or butchering? Are they jealous of your skills?"

Kezawin laughed freely once again. "Suspicious, perhaps. Wary, I would say. Never jealous."

"I think you're wrong. I've seen how much is offered for your quillwork. I've seen the women come to your lodge and bring their children for whatever it is you do to alleviate their aches and pains. And I've seen the way they clear a path for you when you pass by." He touched her cheek. "I think you're very lonely, Kezawin. I believe I am your only friend."

"The Double Woman Dreamer has no friends," she said, avoiding his eyes. "I dreamed that you would come and that we would help one another. You follow a road that lies next to mine."

"We are special friends, then. A society of two." He smiled at the notion that she thought she had dreamed of him before she ever saw him. It was an endearing fantasy. "The naturalist and the medicine woman. It's a poetic alliance, I think."

She smiled, her eyes brightening at the thought that she might at last belong to a group, however small. "We must have a name for our society," she decided. "What did you call the ones who sent you here? The society of the Massachusetts place."

James laughed, pleased with the fact that she'd remembered the name of his home. "The Boston Society of Naturalists, which is hardly as imaginative as your *akicita* names, the Kit Foxes, the Brave Hearts and the others."

"Ours will have a secret name so that no one can steal its power. But I have not heard you sing of this alliance. Have you done so?"

He had used the Lakota word for *song* as a close approximation for *poetic*, and her response brought more meaning to the remark. He smiled warmly. "I should sing like a bird if only you would stop leading me this merry chase."

"Chase?"

"At least give me more than one kiss at a time."

She glanced away.

"I would stand with you before your father's lodge and kiss you beneath a courting robe if that would please you more," he offered.

"Your touch brings me pleasure, James. I will not deny it. I have, for so long, taken care not to desire any man because I would not take the form of the deer woman. I will never let her use me that way—not if I can help it—and if I have led a chase, as you say, then it is possible she may have—" She clutched her breast suddenly and looked at him with dread. "She may have slipped inside me, or I may have—"

"Kezawin, that's nonsense," James insisted, half-laughing. "Were I to find myself suddenly kissing the lips of a deer, I assure you I would remove myself from the embrace."

"You would be dead," she said without emotion. "It is not a risk a wise man would take."

"But if you have dreamed of me—"

"We are to share our knowledge, James, and nothing more than that. And perhaps it is true that you are to be my only friend."

"I don't think I would mind that," James said with a smile.

It was a season of plenty for Lone Bear's people. Prairie fires the preceding fall had burned off much old grass, and after plentiful spring rains, a thick new green carpet covered the hills and plains. Great herds of buffalo grazed the land contentedly, moving at their leisure, and the people were never far behind. A campsite might serve them for a week or a fortnight by James's count, and then one morning they would be on the move again, lodges struck and travois loaded within less than an hour of the singing of the announcement that it was time to move on.

When the signal came, Garrett was caught up in the excitement of being mobile again. A wave of restless energy seemed to flow through the camp as each person tackled his assigned tasks. No discussion was necessary. The plans had been made by the *wakincuzas*, the ones who decide, and an official leader had been chosen from among the warrior societies. For the rest of the people, the destination was a matter of trust, and they enjoyed the anticipation. They might be headed for a site they had used in summers past, or maybe the scouts had found a new variation of an old theme—a place where water, grazing, firewood and windbreak were all in good supply. For the Lakota, the land traveled over was as much a part of being home as the encampment was, and James Garrett found himself absorbed with the love of changing scenery.

It had taken some adjustment. Before joining Lone Bear's band, James had traveled with LaRoux, the Frenchman, and sometimes with two or three of LaRoux's trapper friends. They had moved from camp to camp as their fancy and the friendliness of the Indian people permitted. Now he followed the rules of the band, some of which he learned the hard way. The most difficult requirement was that everyone stay within the bounds of the march. Behind the scouts the *wakincuzas* marched at the front, and the police surrounded the people on the sides and at the rear. No one fell behind, and no one wandered off to hunt, not even for botanical specimens. When James threatened to break the rules, Kezawin warned him that the *akicita* would be forced to destroy all of his belongings, including his collection and his journals.

Once he accepted the rules, he found that there was much individual freedom to be enjoyed. When the band was on the move, they would make several stops during the day and camp for the night on ground that never failed to yield something worthy of the naturalist's inspection.

Even more interesting than the discoveries he was making about the land were his observations of Kezawin's work. He had begun to regard it as Kezawin's calling because, although in his opinion it had no scientific basis, what she did seemed to be effective. Her herbal medicines were used to treat wounds, animal bites, festering cankers, internal complaints and the infirmities of the aged. Occasionally a woman would even bring a horse or a dog for her to treat. Even though he was not privy to her consultations, James kept an eye out for improvement in Kezawin's patients, and, more often than not, what he saw amazed him. He had little faith in medical doctors, who, among other shortcomings, had failed his mother, and who generally had little to offer for a wounded limb other than the suggestion that it be lopped off. The notion that Kezawin's healing skill was bestowed by a dream was one he regarded as utter nonsense, but his observations of the results of her remarkable work began filling his journals.

The journey seemed circuitous at times—west, then north, then east. It took them from the hills through stretches of prairie to the foot of a range of high mountains and back to prairie again. One landmark that James found most impressive was a rocky tower that seemed to have thrust itself from the ground in some long-past volcanic upheaval. Its steep sides were deeply grooved as though some demon in the earth had clawed at the mass as it escaped the underworld and shoved its way toward the sky. The band made camp within view of this monolith, and James could barely contain his excitement at the prospect of exploring the area.

"It has many names," Kezawin explained as they approached the wooded base of the structure. "Some call it the Bear's Lodge. We call it *Tiipašotka Wakanšica*, The Tower of the Bad God."

"A fitting name," James said as he tipped his head back to watch a cloud sail past the soaring pillar. The ancient Greeks would have coveted its fluted symmetry, he thought. "Are you afraid of it?"

"It's a holy place," she said. "We regard it with respect. We shall take nothing from the ground here."

"But we might find something—"

"Nothing we can't find elsewhere. It is not a matter of fear, James. It is a matter of showing respect."

"Is there a way up to the top?"

"The falcon has a way," she said with a laugh.

"Perhaps something wonderful grows up there." Pebbles skittered under his moccasins as he sidestepped a scrub pine and scanned the summit. "There might be something magical up there—something that would give me power over the deer woman's curse."

"It's not a curse as long as you use the proper caution." A smile danced in Kezawin's eyes as she repeated, "It is a matter of showing the proper respect."

"I've known few women who commanded quite the level of respect from men that you do, dear Kezawin. Are you sure there isn't some small measure of fear involved?"

"Not on your part, certainly." She swept her hand in the air to dramatize the tower's height. "Go ahead, James

Garrett. Scale *Tiipaśotka Wakanśica* and count your coup. Bring the magic down from the top."

"There's a way," he said as he looked up. "One could find a way with the proper tools and enough ambition."

"We will go to *Mahto Sapa*, Bear Butte, which is east of here. That one you can climb, and there, perhaps, you will seek your vision. I think this ambition of yours lives in the absence of vision."

"I think they're one and the same." He put his arm around her as they walked. It was an intimacy she had come to permit and one he had come to enjoy because of the comfortable closeness it afforded them. "In my world the men would be afraid of you, too, simply because you are too smart. I'm going to miss you."

James had often spoken of continuing his life in that distant place he called Massachusetts, but for Kezawin the idea of his future there was a distant thing, as well. His mention of leaving was another matter. In her world, the people moved when it was a good day to move, and that was the day they spoke of it.

"You are leaving now?" she asked.

"No, but soon I'll have to. I don't want to get snowed in along the way."

"You'll need meat."

"I have yet to bag a buffalo. Before I leave, I'd like to do that." He pushed a low-hanging branch clear of both their faces and smiled down at her as they walked together. "I would like to bring you a buffalo."

"Then you must hunt for one." The smile she returned was full of mischief. "And if you cut out the heart and eat it before his blood has cooled, then you will gain the strength of the—"

"Arghh!" he groaned as he bent down and scooped her off the ground. Laughing, he bounced her a couple of times, hefting her slight weight. "Do I have to pass another of your bloody tests to prove my strength? What about this?" He tossed her up again. "I think I shall scale this rock with you on my back to prove that I have all the strength of the buffalo bull. How would that be?"

Kezawin laughed along with him. "If you don't want the best parts of the carcass, bring them to me. Better yet, I shall go with you."

"What? And scare the game with that impudent laugh of yours?"

"Not at all," she protested with a toss of her head. "I shall see that you don't catch sight of some new bloom and lose the trail."

"Oh, ho," he declared with mock solemnity. "The magic lady has a practical side. Food first, flowers for the potions later. Let's try it, shall we?" He nodded toward the top of the tower. "They say we're both *wakan*, touched by the gods. Let's put ourselves to the test. Perhaps we can fly."

Her eyes followed the direction of his gaze. The strange grooves seemed to pull the spirit upward with the promise of the chance to soar. "It's a beautiful thought, but that is not to be our test," she told him.

He lowered her moccasined feet to the ground slowly. Her body slid against his, and he knew what his test would be. He breathed deeply of the scented oil she used on her braids. It was one of the many things about her that had once seemed strange, even distasteful, but now gave him pause only to think, ah, yes, the sweet smell of her hair.

She had become an exotic fantasy, the more desirable because he could touch her but he could not move her. Her will was as strong as his, and her mind—could it be?—just as quick. In a richly appointed parlor or on a polished ballroom floor his tongue was as artful as any man's, but standing there beneath the wide blue sky in the shadow of *Tiipaśotka Wakanśica*, a piece of earth that stood in stark contrast to its surroundings, he had told a woman that he would miss her when he left. He had used no art—a startling slip that left him feeling unarmed, which was no way to face a test.

They stood close. Kezawin had not taken her hands from his upper arms, and James had not moved his from her back. It was in his mind to try to steal another kiss and see how much pleasure she would allow herself before her superstitions came back to haunt her, when he noticed that something at his back had caught her eye. She raised a wide-eyed signal that he was to turn cautiously.

An albino buck returned their stares. For a moment the three were rendered motionless by a delicate balance of wonder and fear that bound them hypnotically together. The late-afternoon sun filtered through the pale green leaves of a stand of cottonwoods and created a mottling of shadows on the deer's white back. As he lifted his head and twitched his nostrils high in the air, one garnet eye glinted in the sunlight. While they could no more look away from the creature than they could draw breath, James and Kezawin linked hands and let the electricity in the air flow between their bodies until the buck turned and darted back into the trees.

Kezawin glanced down at their hands and then up at James. His eyes reflected her own awe. "You saw him, too?"

"Magnificent," he replied, his voice hoarse with wonder. "Celestial. A rare sight, truly. I have never—" He frowned at her when he caught that familiar haunted look in her eye. "That was a buck, Kezawin. It could not have been your deer woman."

"But I have dreamed of him, too," she said quickly. "It was he who first brought the red root plant. And then you came."

James looked back at the spot where the albino had disappeared into the trees. "You're saying the white deer was my harbinger, then."

She knew he didn't appreciate the power of her dream, and even though he had told her on more than one occasion that the *wakan*, the realm of mystery and holiness, was no mystery to him, she knew that he really did not understand. No matter how simply she might try to explain her *šicun*, her spiritual guardian, James was not yet open to the concept. Yet the white deer had brought him to her, and now that he spoke of leaving, the white deer showed himself to James. What was the meaning?

"I knew you when I saw you," she told him. "We shared something immediately, and there's more to be shared. Not," she added quickly, "as man and woman but as—"

"Colleagues," he supplied in English, but the only Lakota word he could use was, "*Kolas*. Friends. Friends of the plants and—" he gestured in the direction of the buck's retreat "—friends of the white deer."

Kezawin brightened. "Yes. Friends of the White Deer. That will be our secret name. I've learned much from you, James."

"There's more I would learn from you before I leave. Would you permit me to watch you administer your medicine?" He saw that the suggestion was alarming to her. "To the children, perhaps. Let me see how you use the herbs we've collected. Let me make notes. It would add a new dimension to my work. My people would learn a new respect for—"

"My medicine might not work for them. It might not even work for you. You would be required to prepare yourself."

"I'll do whatever you ask. I'll take part in the ceremonies, or whatever you say. Perhaps your father will allow me to observe his medicine if he sees that you trust me."

"If my father will perform *inipi* with you, you will be purified in the sweat lodge. Then you may learn of my medicine. As for my father... as I told you, you are more observant than most white men."

Again the compliment warmed his smile.

Chapter Three

Thunder Shield often watched Double Woman Dreamer, often admired her, but always from a safe distance. It was one thing to stand aside while her father claimed a portion of meat from his kill, as was their right, or to stand beside his wife, Red Calf Woman, when she offered a pony for Double Woman Dreamer's healing for their daughter. It was quite another to loaf in the shade and watch the way her dress hitched up a little on her hip when she reached to drape a filet of venison over the highest pole of her drying rack. Noticing the curve of her ankles and the sleek shape of her calf and taking pleasure in the way his body yearned as he watched was deliciously unsafe. Such a pastime could only be indulged from a distance, for this was Double Woman Dreamer, whose looks could kill a man.

She was his younger brother's widow, and if Thunder Shield had been foolhardy enough, he could have claimed her for his second wife. Red Calf Woman was not as industrious as some, and she would be glad for the help. She had mentioned more than once in recent months that her own sister, Walks Slow, was already nineteen winters and without a husband. She was without a husband for good reason, for her hips were as broad as a man's shoulders, and she never seemed to have her wits about her. She was far from Thunder Shield's choice for a second wife.

He scratched his bare back against the bark of a cotton-wood tree and considered the woman who would have been his choice for a first wife if only he had waited a couple of years in choosing. In that time Kezawin had become such a beauty that his younger brother, Iron Shell, had competed long and hard to win her favor. Even though she bore him no children, Iron Shell was the happiest of married men for three years. And then she had become Double Woman Dreamer. Iron Shell had been advised to leave her, but he would have none of any man's warnings against his wife, and he had paid the supreme price. Her power had been too strong for the young warrior. Not long after his wife had had her vision, Iron Shell was killed on a horse raid among the Pawnee. Double Woman Dreamer's brother had fallen in the same raid. There was no mistaking the measure of her power.

Neither could a man ignore her beauty, which became a stronger lure as the years passed. More than one man had thrown caution to the wind and tried to court her. It was not uncommon for one who had dreamed of the deer woman to defy the tenets of Lakota propriety and become openly promiscuous. Although Double Woman Dreamer lived as no other woman lived, alone in her lodge, and acquired a reputation for her healing power and her unsettling laughter, there had been no gossip. No man claimed intimate knowledge of her, and no woman had seen any sign. The people were inclined to accept her friendship with the white plant-taker as part of the mystery of two who were surely *wakan*.

Thunder Shield was not. It turned his stomach sour to see her drying the meat of the white man's kill next to the darkening strips from the flank of buffalo meat that Lone Bear had claimed from Thunder Shield. The white man had brought down nothing larger than a deer, and for that he used a rifle. Thunder Shield doubted that James had the skill to hit the mark with a lance. And yet this puny offering of venison seemed to please the woman.

What was worse, Thunder Shield had, on occasion, chanced to observe the two of them foraging for all manner of plants. The white man showed no respect for himself as he groveled in the ground, even stooping to the point of gathering wild turnips and plums like a woman. When Double Woman Dreamer laughed that unsuitable laugh of hers, the white man hadn't the decency to be embarrassed for her. Often he laughed with her. Thunder Shield had never seen them touch each other, so he could not accuse them publicly, but he wasn't certain this James Garrett was truly *wakan*, and his blood grew hot when he thought of what might be between them. Thunder Shield was as brave as any man, and he dared take no more pleasure in her than he did at this moment. If James wasn't crazy, then he must have been ignorant.

Blood that was already hot began to simmer when Garrett appeared. Thunder Shield strained to hear the exchange of words as the tall white man offered Double Woman Dreamer a handful of wildflowers and some remark about finding the blooms without losing his way. Thunder Shield took her laughter as a sign that the gesture seemed as foolish to her as it looked to him, but then she praised Garrett's "tracking skills" and offered him food. Before he had given his action sufficient thought, Thunder Shield pushed away from the tree trunk and emerged from the river bottom thicket, approaching the couple.

"Ho, Garrett! One might take you for a brother to the buffalo. You do so much grazing."

James knew the stocky man as one who had an eye for Kezawin. Thunder Shield's hungry looks were hardly subtle, even when his wife was standing beside him, but given the contrast between the two women, James found the man's behavior perfectly understandable. Irritating, but understandable.

"I've learned that we are all brothers to the buffalo, and there's much to be said for our brother's fare." James gave

Kezawin a conspiratorial smile. "Especially when it earns a man an invitation to supper."

"Will you be eating your own kill or mine, Garrett?"

"Whichever happens to be in the pot, I should think." Turning to Kezawin again, James added, "I had thought to do a little fishing today. If I have any luck, perhaps you would welcome a change from red meat."

"A change from antelope and venison, you mean," Thunder Shield said. He snapped a dry stalk off a tall yucca plant as he edged closer. "Some say the size of the game is the measure of a man."

"Is that so? Some say the size of a man's ears is a measure of his intelligence, but in your case the equation doesn't seem to add up." James smiled, trusting the insult would be taken tit for tat.

"Scouts have located a large buffalo herd. It's time we permitted you to hunt with us, Garrett. You've loafed around our camp long enough." Thunder Shield's smile accompanied his return volley. "Let us see whether you're any kind of a man at all."

"Stop this nonsense," Kezawin snapped. "A medicine man is not expected to hunt buffalo. He is—" She glimpsed a scruffy brown camp dog sneaking through the grass to get a jump at her drying rack. "Ssst!" The dog skulked away, and Kezawin turned her scowl directly to the two men. "I am entitled to a portion of your kill, Thunder Shield. Your wife comes to me, and so do your children. And you, James Garrett, you are my father's guest. You are not required—"

"By what right do you call yourself a shaman, Garrett?" Thunder Shield demanded.

"I call myself a scholar, a vocation that has no meaning here. But I will not be called a coward by any man. I'll join your hunt."

"It's a good day to die, Garrett." Thunder Shield snapped the twig in two and dropped it in the grass. Turning on his heel, he called back over his shoulder, "Leave your rifle. It will do you no good, anyway, and I would not have you shoot one of us by mistake."

As he watched the man disappear in the camp circle, James wondered how he'd suddenly earned himself a rival. For weeks he'd been tolerated, watched—an object of some curiosity, but considered harmless enough. "Leave my rifle?" he mused. "How am I supposed to kill anything without it?"

Kezawin grunted with disgust and disappeared into her tipi. James followed.

"I haven't had much success with a bow," he said as he let the flap fall to cover the doorway. "I've tried it once or twice, but not seriously." Kezawin turned a hard look on him, and realized he'd committed a breach of etiquette. She glanced left and right in the way of a woman checking for personal things she may have forgotten to put away. "Excuse me," James offered with half a smile. "May I come in?"

"Have you a death song, James? This may be the day you will sing it."

"I'm sorry." Palms raised in mock self-defense, he stepped back. "I know this is rude, just walking in like this, but I didn't know it was a capital offense."

"And I thought your good sense outweighed your pride, but it must not be so with any man, not even you."

"You said I should hunt for a buffalo," he reminded her.

"I did not say you should participate in a surround."

"A surround? What's that? He said they were going hunting."

With a sigh, Kezawin reached for a buckskin pouch that hung from of the ribs of her lodge. "You have no medicine, no weapons, no skill in these matters and no sense about—"

"I have a rifle," he insisted as he watched her untie the pouch. "Some of the other men have rifles. Is there some rule against using one to hunt buffalo? The beasts are so big

I can hardly miss. One shot and I'll have my kill and my self-respect, and you'll have—"

"It won't be like stalking a deer, James. You must follow the orders given by the *akicita*. If you make a move before the signal is given and scare the herd, the *akicita* may destroy your property when you return. If you break ranks, they may flog you." From the pouch she pulled a rawhide thong, to which a disk-shaped amulet was attached. "Your rifle would do you no good. There would be no time for reloading it."

He ducked to allow her to put the necklace over his head. It hung in the deep V of his shirt, and he took the disk in his hand, running his thumb over the smooth surface. He lifted his gaze to Kezawin's warm brown eyes and smiled. "Does this mean I'm wearing your colors?"

"I will pray that the *šicun* of the white deer will protect you. This is made from an antler. Not from the *white* deer, of course, but he is the one who brought you here."

James dismissed her concerns with a wave of his hand. "Kezawin, I'm not going to put myself in any danger. If I don't kill anything, it won't be—"

"Men who are trained for this from boyhood anticipate danger when they ride in the surround. You are not trained for it. For you—"

"For me?" He hooked his hands low on his hips. "You think it's too dangerous for me? Too difficult, too tricky? What else? I came here alone, Kezawin—on my own—to a land I knew nothing about, inhabited by people who were strange to me. I'm not a hunter or a soldier, but I take risks to do what I do, and that . . . that . . ." He jabbed his finger in the air and thought better of using the word that came to mind. "That posturing braggart who is *so well trained* suggests that I haven't got the nerve to go out there and hunt those dumb, woolly beasts with his little sporting brotherhood. Well, I've got a piece of news for both of you. I'm—"

"You are a good horseman, James," she said evenly. "Control your mount. Guard yourself against *tatanka*'s horns. Do not ride into the center of the herd, and remember, do not disobey the *akicita*. Thunder Shield is a member, and he seems to have taken a disliking to you."

James shifted his weight from one leg to the other as he reclaimed his composure. "He's jealous," he said with a shrug.

"Jealous?"

"He wants you, and he thinks I'm in the way."

Kezawin shook her head. "Thunder Shield is my brother-in-law. He knows better than anyone what the Double Woman Dreamer does to a man's medicine."

"That doesn't stop him from wanting you. I've seen it in his eyes. He looks at you the same way I do." But he saw the fear in her eyes, and he tried to allay it with a chuckle as he laid his hand on his chest. "Since I have no medicine, there's nothing here for your power to destroy."

Kezawin took no joy in the knowledge that his cocky attitude would soon be eradicated by a test for which none of his experience had prepared him. "Come. We will go to my father. Perhaps he will give you a lance that has some power."

There was little talk among the hunters as they rode through the tall grass, following the scouts who had located the buffalo earlier in the day. Their approach was downwind, and they carried nothing, wore nothing that might jingle or clatter. James had been told to leave his saddle behind because the leather squeaked. Like the others, his upper body glistened with grease, which overpowered human scent and served as protection against the sun and biting insects.

Had it not been for his light brown hair, blue eyes and skin that had tanned to a golden hue rather than bronze, James would have looked very much like the thirty other men, who moved with the gaits of their horses as if they were all of a piece. James wore buckskin breeches, much like their leggings, and his hair, which nearly reached his shoulders, was kept in place with a deerskin headband. He carried a three-foot lance, given to him by Lone Bear, and he had a spare that he'd secured with a loop over his horse's withers. The others carried bows and quivers of arrows, but Garrett knew that for him such equipment would have been useless baggage. The hunt promised to be an adventure, and if by chance he should make a kill, that would be a bonus.

At the top of a hill, they could see the herd—not a large one by Great Plains standards, but numbering in the hundreds and grazing contentedly in the broad valley's thick grass. Instructions were given in sign, and James paid close attention. The hunters were divided into two groups, and he understood that his group would circle wide and approach the herd from the opposite side. He was watching the exchange of hand signals when his horse suddenly bolted under him, as though the animal had been stung. Within a few prancing steps the big sorrel was brought under James's firm control, and he looked around to find the entire party scowling at him—all but Thunder Shield. With a pointed glance at the amulet that hung around James's neck, the stocky warrior gave an ominous smile, and James noticed that the end of his quirt handle was carved in a sharp point.

So this was the way of it. James made up his mind to stay clear of his newfound rival as they formed a column and headed out to take up a position on the other side of the herd. Once in place, the two columns closed in slowly, and now it was the experienced hunting ponies that were hard to control, anxious to get on with it. But like James himself, who was prepared to take a few stabs at a buffalo just to make a good showing, his horse was merely along for the ride.

Then the herd began to stir. Shaggy heads were raised one or two at a time, and an undercurrent rose with them among men, mounts and prey. Complacency became awareness. Restraint became daring. For one breathless instant the inevitable was apparent, and every nerve was exposed to the tension in the air. Then one huge bull leaped into motion, and the cry came from the leader, *"Hoka hey!"*

Suddenly there was a whirlwind of galloping horses, stampeding bison and a melee of shrieking, yelping men. The lead bull was turned back into the herd by a quick rider, and the bunching buffalo began running in circles. The mounted hunters fired a volley of arrows and charged the confused beasts with their lances. James found himself surrounded by whoops and shouts, bawling and bellowing, the smells of dust and blood, horse sweat and greased men. His heart pounded as he dug his heels into his mount's flanks, raised his lance and charged into the brown thickness with his own rousing, "Eee-yahhh!"

It was hard to find an animal without an arrow or a lance sticking out of it somewhere. Everything was part of the blur of motion. James guided his horse with his legs and took several wild stabs at fleeing prey, succeeding only in hanging on to his lance. The energy of the initial attack had surprised him as much as it had the buffalo, and he was caught up in the frenzy. But soon he realized he would do better to take aim, and he saw that the others sought to puncture a lung by driving the lance between the ribs. The task looked easier than it was.

After several near misses, James rode up beside a young bull, raised his lance aloft with both hands and drove it home. The bull bellowed, spun and charged its killer. James watched with horror as a deadly horn gouged his thigh. His horse wheeled, and the horn slipped away again, leaving only the searing pain behind. The bull went down on its knees, then flopped over on its side.

James jerked off his headband and tied it above the wound, twisting the ends around his knife to make a tourniquet. He wanted out, had to get out, but the hunters and the hunted swirled around him. He tried to make his way around one young brave's mount, but the horse suddenly reared, and James saw the cause. A bull the size of a locomotive had lowered its head for the charge. The horse came down, impaling itself on the big bison's horns, and the rider fell to the ground.

The young man scrambled to his feet and looked around him. There was only a sea of buffalo and the white man, James, who saw the cloud of uncertainty and the spark of fear in the hunter's eyes. He reached out. "Come on! Get up behind me!" With an agile leap, the young man took the seat James offered.

· When they had ridden clear of the knotted carnage, the young man asked for the use of James's horse. "I haven't made my kill yet."

"Hell, I saw what happened to your horse," James shouted. "I got one. You're welcome to a share of it."

The young man's heated look told James what he thought of the offer as he slid over the sorrel's rump. He jerked his chin toward the spare lance. "Give me that, then."

"You're going back at it on foot?"

The brave snorted in disgust and turned on his heel to return unarmed to the fray.

"Come back here!" The young man turned, and James tossed him the lance and slid off his horse, favoring his wounded leg as he landed heavily. With an expletive for which there was no Lakota translation, he handed over the reins. "I don't want your death on my head. Go get your supper, but bring me back my horse. I'm not up to walking back to camp."

Within a short time it was over. Though some of the animals had escaped to graze other prairie flats, the grass of this one was strewn with buffalo carcasses. Sees The Enemy, the young man who had borrowed James's horse, had made his kill, and the women were coming to butcher, load up their packhorses and carry the meat and hides back to camp. The thrill of James's success had lost its edge as he sat in the grass and let Sees The Enemy help him bind his wound.

It pleased him to see Kezawin arrive leading a pack-horse. He knew it was not a measure of her faith in him, for all who would eat were expected to have someone there to butcher. The elders and the shamans were entitled to claim choice portions, but the good hunters had more meat on the ground than their women could handle, and no one would deny a share for the "tail-tiers," those who were without hunters. Food-getting was a communal effort with communal benefits.

The women searched for arrows and lances marked with their hunters' signs and set to work. James knew he ought to be returning to camp to tend to his leg, but he sat in the grass on a gently sloping hillside and watched. He could see no sign of surprise when Kezawin identified her father's lance and unsheathed her knife. She hadn't looked for James at all, but he believed she knew where he was. He believed she felt him watching her. He wondered self-indulgently whether she knew he was hurt. He'd stemmed the flow of blood, but whatever damage lay beneath his buckskins ached like a son of a bitch. It pleased him, though, to watch her belly-slit the beast he'd brought down himself.

When she'd finished packing the meat and the hide, Kezawin headed for the spot where her hunter waited. His pride suddenly pricked him, and he managed to mount his horse before she reached him. They rode to camp together, but the words he wanted to hear from her never came. The story of his hunt babbled in his head, but since she said nothing, he kept it to himself.

"You must go to my father's lodge," she told him when they reached camp. "He will make medicine for your wound."

James scowled. He had given a chunk of his flesh to feed this woman, and now he was being dismissed. With his teeth clamped together over the demands he wanted to make, he wheeled his mount and trotted him in the direction of Lone Bear's tipi, punishing his injury with the jarring gait.

"Lone Bear!" The leathery face appeared in the doorway. James slid to the ground, exerting tremendous effort to keep his knees from buckling. The blood stain was spreading on his breeches again. "Can you do something about this?"

"I'm ready for you," the old man said. "Picket your horse and come inside."

Picket his horse? He was seeing black spots before his eyes, but his stubbornness kept him going until the horse was secure. Lone Bear's gesture indicated a buffalo robe pallet, which James gratefully dropped upon, grumbling all the while in his native tongue. "It isn't something a woman could appreciate, anyway, the speed, the thrill, the...the... Damn her, she could show some concern. She could pay some attention. It isn't every day that a man—"

"Kezawin tells me that you often speak to the plants in your language as you take them from the ground," Lone Bear said as he tossed a sprig of sage on the small fire that burned in the center of the tipi. "Is this part of your medicine?"

"Kezawin says I have no medicine." Through the haze of smoke and black spots, he saw the creased face. "I made a kill, didn't I? I came back alive, didn't I? I've got good medicine. I've studied. I've been no man's field assistant. I've identified . . . I've named . . ."

James was talking to the wind, talking nonsense, and he knew it. Lone Bear helped him replace his pants with a breechclout, and he lay there, his head swirling with his pain while he rubbed his burning eyes and listened to Lone Bear's chants. Lone Bear bound his leg, and the chanting continued as the smoke rolled on. Damn the smoke, he thought. Damn the beast with its stabbing horns, and damn the fickleness of women. He'd shown her he could do it, and he wanted to hear her admit it. He wasn't without courage.

He was tired of hearing about this medicine thing. She had the power. *She* had the medicine. He knew he had to get back to a civilized world where a man was respected for his work—important work—work that would go down in the annals of science, and damn her! He'd risked life and limb for a bundle of meat, and she hadn't even acknowledged his efforts.

Sometime during the course of Lone Bear's ritual, James had fallen asleep, but he awoke in the dead of night, and his leg was throbbing. The old man was asleep. The air in the lodge was heavy with smoke and ashes. The embers in the fire pit smoldered. Moonlight streaming through the smoke hole at the apex of the lodge made a sooty haze. Gingerly James touched his thigh and felt the heat and swelling. He heaved himself from the bed and stumbled out into the night. Her door was several yards away—several long, painful yards.

"Kezawin!" he whispered. "Let me in. I need your help."

The rawhide door slid away, and he ducked through the opening, grabbing at the hide as he passed through and landed on one knee. He pitched forward into her arms. "No chants," he groaned. "No smoke. It's festering. Lance it...drain it. Give me...whatever you..."

She lost her robe in her struggle to hold him up, and his cheek slid against her bare breast. His back was slick with sweat and grease. The second thing she would do, she decided, was bathe him. She tried to get a grip on him, and he nuzzled her and groaned. The bath might be third or fourth, she amended as she deposited him on her own bed. First, she reached for her dress. Then she added wood to the dying embers in her fire pit and filled a buffalo's stomach, or paunch, with water. When the cooking stones were hot enough, she dropped them into the water to make it boil.

The swelling in James's leg had tightened the bandaging. Now the wound was hot and angry. Kezawin would fight it with more heat. She applied a hot wet chamois compress, but James sucked his breath through his teeth and threw the first one off. Kezawin calmly reheated it, reapplied it and held it in place.

"Good God, woman!"

"Do you want my help or not?"

"Your father nearly suffocated me, and now you scald me."

"You will keep your voice down."

He dropped his head back on the pallet and sighed. "I'm sorry. It's just that it's . . . gotten worse."

"You should have taken care of it right away."

"*You* should have taken care of it right away." He wanted to bite off his tongue. He had no intention of letting her think he felt slighted by her lack of concern. "You're the medicine woman," he added.

"I don't treat men."

"You're treating this one."

She looked at him, and her eyes softened. "So I am." Taking the soft piece of deerskin up, she turned quickly to dip it into the hot water again. "Why did you wait for me to finish the butchering? The other hunters had gone. There was no need—"

"Were you surprised that I made a kill?"

Gently she laid the chamois over his ragged flesh, but she avoided his eyes. "It was a good kill. You put only one hole in the hide."

"But were you surprised?"

"You're a strong man and a good rider."

"Did you think I couldn't kill a buffalo without using a rifle?" he persisted.

"You were untested." She soaked threads of sinew and one of her precious steel needles in hot water. She wanted everything hot, hotter than the fever in his leg. Blood and pus flowed from it now, carrying the illness out of his body.

"I've been tested now," he said stubbornly. "I passed, didn't I?" He heard the adolescent swagger in his voice, and he managed a thin chuckle. "I surprised myself, and that's the truth of it. I've never liked to hunt, but I felt compelled to prove that I could do it, and once I found myself in the thick of it all—" he lifted his head to be sure he had her attention "—it was exhilarating, in a way. The surprise, the fear, and then the throwing off of fear—it was exciting until that damnable beast gored me." He saw that she listened with only one ear as she busied herself with boiling something. "What's that?"

Kezawin handed him a dry sprig, and he launched into an automatic examination by sniffing, turning it over and over to see it in the best light, sniffing again. "The tea from this will calm you," she said.

"I'm calm. Where can we find this? Can we—"

She laughed. He was talking like the plant-taker again. "It grows in dry country far to the west. I traded for it. After I stitch the wound I shall give you another tea to nourish you and help your spirit drive away the sickness in your leg."

"I'll need my journal," he said, and he lifted his hand in the direction of his lean-to. "I must take notes on everything—" She handed him the book, and he looked up at her, astonished. "You took my journal?"

"I have your plant boxes here, too."

He braced himself up on one elbow. "Why? What would you want with my—" Understanding dawned in his eyes. "You thought I would get into trouble on the hunt today, didn't you? You thought the *akicita* would come back here and destroy my belongings."

"There was that chance." She brought him the tea in a rawhide bowl. "If the man is sufficiently penitent, often the *akicita* will collect items from the people to replace what was destroyed. This work of yours could not be replaced. It was my job to protect it."

"Thank you." Steam from the bowl carried a pungent odor to his nose, but when he sipped, he found the taste surprisingly pleasant. "You're right. There was that chance. Thunder Shield nearly had my horse on the run just before the surround."

"I have no desire to explain anything to Thunder Shield, but if it will keep him from scheming against you, I will swear an oath that I am no man's woman and that I am to be no man's—"

He gripped her arm. "You'll do no such thing. What is or is not between us is not his business. I don't know what you take me for, but I'm not a coward. I'm not afraid of Thunder Shield."

"I know you are not a coward, James. I never thought you were." She cupped her hand beneath his and helped him raise the bowl toward his mouth. "Drink this now. The stitching will be painful."

Kezawin washed him while the tea did its work, making him groggy and relaxed. Not unlike a bit of fine old brandy, he thought as he gave himself over to the pleasure of her ministrations. The throbbing in his thigh had become a dull ache as the heat she applied drew out the infection. He smiled at the way she rubbed his chest in smooth circles and told himself that soon he would be throbbing elsewhere.

"You are leading me a merry chase again, Kezawin."

"Do you prefer to smell like the buffalo?" she asked. "I am chasing the smell from your body."

"Mmm. Keep chasing." He gave her a sleepy-eyed smile and drained the bowl, then added, "I was referring to the feeling I got earlier that you hated to see me go off on this hunt for fear that I might be injured. But when I was injured you—" He set the bowl aside and tried to make light of his complaint with a halfhearted shrug. "You chose to tend to the buffalo instead of me."

"And you chose to watch me while you sat there bleeding."

"I wasn't bleeding. I'd stopped the bleeding, and I didn't think it was too bad. But you didn't know that." He angled his head to get a look at her eyes. "I thought we were friends. A society of two, we said."

"You should have gone to my father immediately," she insisted, avoiding the eyes that would demand more of her than she could permit herself to give. "I have treated men on few occasions. Only when a man is desperate does he come to me, and then it seems that often . . . he loses his battle."

"That's why I came to you before I got desperate. Kezawin—" He caught her chin in his hand and turned her head toward him. "You thought enough of my work to take it under your wing for a while. What about me?"

"I would not want to embarrass you, James. A woman grieves over a man only after he is dead."

James's shoulders shook with silent laughter as his hand slid away from her face. "So you refuse to flutter over me, do you?"

"If you die, I shall cut my arms and my hair and keen most pitifully since there will be no one else to mourn you properly."

"If I die!" He nearly choked trying to contain his laughter. "You mean I have to *die* for your concern? Is there not one bit of sympathy for the wounded friend? Not one, 'Oh, poor James'?"

She laughed with him. "Shall I call you *onśila*? Poor thing! It is what a woman says to a child."

"Ah, I see. That's why you avoided me. A woman may not show her sympathy for a man whose leg has nearly been torn off by a raging fire-eyed beast, is that it?"

"*Onśila,*" she crooned, letting him see the mischief in her eyes as she petted the soft springy hair on his chest. "Would sucking at a woman's breast help you to heal your wound?"

"It might," he said with a slow smile. "It couldn't hurt."

"And would—" The suggestion stuck in her throat. His eyes were soft, warm and inviting. Deep in her womb, there was a slow stirring, a persistent yearning to lean closer, to touch, to entreat. The tea had produced the soft glaze in his eyes, but Kezawin reminded herself that she had had no tea. There was something else at work in her, something insidious, something she must not allow even the smallest berth within herself.

She took up her needle with a vengeance against that thing that would not let her be. She believed it to be the same thing that made pus in James's wound, and she would fight it, drive it out. She spoke coldly. "Today you have hunted the buffalo and made a kill. You are not a man to be pitied."

James was too warm to feel the chill. "I like your medicine," he said, smiling. "I shall forget my bid for sympathy if I may have more tea."

"Try not to move," she said as she poised the needle for the first stitch. "And I shall try to work quickly."

He closed his hand tightly around the edge of the curly hide upon which he lay, and, still smiling, he turned his face toward the fire. "The breast is another matter, however. I shall not forget your soft breast."

When at last he slept, Kezawin covered him with a red trade blanket and sat beside him, admiring his face. She didn't mind the shadow of his beard anymore, nor the pale color of his hair and his skin. Many times she forgot to think of him as a white man. She had tried to forget that he was a man at all, but that was impossible. Too often she saw the man's look in his eyes, and she felt an answering stir within her belly.

When the runner had brought the news of the successful hunt and recounted the hunters' injuries, her heart had thudded in her throat. Then she saw that James had bound his own wound, and she went about her business, all the while knowing he must have pain. If he had been killed, he would have been the victim of his own male pride, and his destiny would have gone unfulfilled. She did not pretend to understand the nature of that destiny, but she knew that somehow it was bound with hers. The white deer would not let her forget that.

But the deer woman would not let her forget the other side of her fate. Kezawin feared the same part of herself that was feared by others, the part that seemed to fly in the face of all decency. It was the part that mocked her femininity, the part that made her long for a man while it denied her a permanent place in his life. The gifts bestowed by her dream made her unique among women, and that uniqueness was its own curse, for she could never again truly be one of them. Stories were told, stories that rang with the authority of tradition. It was said that this one's grandmother or that one's uncle had actually seen the metamorphosis take place—deer to woman, woman to deer. A man must never lie with the Double Woman Dreamer, for who could trust such a woman? After the dream, one never knew.

Kezawin knew. She had experienced the urgings of the deer woman in visions of herself and this man that made her dewy, as though she had been touched, and left her craving in the knowledge that she had not, could not, would not be touched. Her laughter was a signal to all others to beware of her power. Beside it, a man's medicine might crumble. It was said that she might use it to charm him, seduce him, lure him to his death.

Not this man, she told herself. When she had heard the news of his injury, her heart had cried out, *not this man*. She would fight those awful, wondering stirrings even as the care she felt for him continued to deepen.

And it had deepened. With tentative fingers she touched his warm face and saw that the contrast between her skin and his was pleasing to the eye, like a soft piece of buckskin dyed with a berry stain and decorated with white quillwork. She brushed his hair back from his face and saw its contrasts, too, in the thick hair the color of a pronghorn's back, tumbling in soft disarray over a high forehead, and the strong stubborn chin, stubbled and square.

No longer the face of the strange white man, it was a face that brought her sunshine in the morning, a promise of a day filled with good things to be shared. It was the face of her friend.

Yes, she thought enough of him to take him under her wing for a while. And he would buoy her up with the warm smile of a man who saw her as Kezawin, not Double Woman Dreamer. But because she knew who she was, they could never be lovers.

Through the open side of James's lean-to, the morning sun touched his aching leg. When he found that the leg would not support his weight, he fashioned a crutch from the limb of an ash tree and tried to carry on with his business. By midday he was back in Kezawin's tipi, his leg swollen and infected again. She repeated her treatment, offering him more herbs to fight the infection from the inside. Lone Bear stuck his head in a couple of times to inquire about his guest, but he offered no advice. Some men did not respond to a shaman's medicine, but few chose the alternative the medicine woman might offer them. Because this man was both white and *wakan*, no one could predict his actions.

By nightfall James's body was plagued by high fever. Kezawin worked over him, draining his leg, bathing him, forcing him to take what concoctions she could offer and praying all the while that her medicine would not overwhelm his own.

"Don't take my leg," he croaked with a dry tongue. Kezawin slipped her hand beneath his head, and he lifted heavy eyelids. She smiled at him as she brought a bowl to his lips, but he blocked it with his hand. "I want to come out of this with two legs, Kezawin. Do you understand? *Two* legs."

"I understand."

"That's not part of the treatment, huh? Hacking off limbs?"

She shook her head. "Not for a friend. If you were one of the Crow people, or one of the Pawnee, I might consider it."

"Doctors back home do it to friend and foe alike."

"I would never offend you that way," she promised. He let his hand drop away from the bowl and accepted the drink. "The healing happens inside you, James. I can nourish you and try to draw the illness out, but you must call on the powers that give you life. You must pray."

He heard her earnest plea, and it shook him to the core. It reminded him of a small frail woman whose prayers had been uttered between desperate gasps for breath, and of a man who spoke of prayer, then closed the door, leaving the room dark, his footsteps echoing in the hallway. James swallowed the bitter potion and pushed the bowl away.

"I have no faith, Kezawin. I have only will. My own stubborn will. That's my power. That's my *sicun*."

"Your will does not give you life, James."

"I *have* life. Where it came from, what power made it, what it is I am not certain. I only know I have life now, and I shall not give it up." He took the bowl back and drained the contents. "Neither am I willing to relinquish my leg. Your medicine works. I know it. I've seen it." He gestured toward the foot of the pallet. "Hand me my journal so I may make notes on this treatment of yours."

But as soon as she put the book in his hands, he fell asleep again.

James recovered gradually from his leg wound, and as he did, he kept his journal close at hand. Kezawin showed him the medicine she made, not only for him, but for others, and he filled page after page with notes. This much they shared, but whenever he tried to touch her, she drew back. Whenever their laughter settled into smiles, then into soft hungry looks, she turned from him and went her own way. Their days were filled with each other, but she refused to speak of nights. When he spoke of a man's loneliness, she asked him to speak of something else. Her medicine had cured him, but her mythology was driving him crazy.

Lone Bear performed the *inipi* for James, but it proved to be an empty experience. Kezawin tended the fire outside and rolled hot stones under the buffalo-hide walls as they were needed inside the dome-shaped lodge. The small lodge filled with steam, and James sweated until he was light-headed and impatient with the smoke that made his eyes burn in the dark and the old man's monotonous singing. The two men went from the steam-filled lodge to the cold river, after which James dressed and went looking for Kezawin to tell her that he felt clean but uninspired.

As the days passed, they spoke less and less. It was the time for grass to turn from green to lifeless dun and for the hot wind to fill up the ears and isolate the mind, but the changes were more than seasonal for the society of two. One morning Kezawin emerged from her tipi to find that James's shelter had been dismantled and that he was gone.

Chapter Four

Boston
Winter of 1827

Ezra Breckenridge was a man of wealth and power. His grandfather had secured the Breckenridge fortune as a merchant in colonial Boston. His father had established political influence as a member of the Provincial Congress, and his mother had, by virtue of the fact that she was one of the Boston Dexters, contributed social standing to the family's list of credits. Ezra had successfully continued those traditions. Money crowded its way into his pockets along with politicians and highly-placed friends. Those aspects of his life were well in hand when he sought to add his own chevron to the Breckenridge family crest by pursuing loftier interests. He became a "man of science."

At the age of fifty he was not about to take up the study himself, and his son, Orson, failed in the vicarious achievement of Ezra's personal goal by getting himself booted out of Harvard in his freshman year. The alternative, then, was to become a patron of science. Financing a promising young naturalist's expedition into the continent's interior promised to affix the name of Ezra Breckenridge to a piece of work that would survive him in a way that no brick monument could. It would bring him the respect of learned men.

At last the wandering protégé had returned, which meant that a celebration was in order. The Breckenridge home in Cambridge was ablaze with light, and carriages lined the driveway as the rich, the influential and, indeed, the scholarly alighted upon the cobblestones and mounted the steps to the white-columned porch of the huge square frame house. Immediately upon his return to Boston, James Garrett had delivered a vast collection of neatly pressed and mounted botanical specimens, which were displayed on every table, sideboard, shelf and mantel in the several rooms in which guests would be entertained. They would, as well, meet the man of the hour, the man who had followed Breckenridge's instructions so admirably.

Breckenridge listened with one ear to the polite conversation being traded at his elbow while his other ear attended to the voices that filled the foyer after each knock at the front door. James was late, and Ezra Breckenridge did not appreciate being kept waiting. One could not be expected to discuss the collection with the more erudite of the guests assembled in the drawing room without some commentary from one's field assistant.

"We're anxious to have Garrett back in the lecture hall," one of the men was saying. "He's a fine teacher."

"It must have been a splendid adventure," the other man said. "If I were twenty years younger, even ten, I think I'd have a look at those great Western mountains and deserts myself. Have you seen the journals, Breckenridge?"

"What? Oh, no, not yet. I believe he means to turn them over tonight. I do hope he doesn't make too much of a production of it, considering the work we have left to do before anything is committed to the printed page."

"Yes, I daresay you'll spend much time consulting."

"Any piece of work bearing my name—"

"Any piece of work that boasts the auspices of Harvard University—"

"Certainly must be—"

"Above the pale."

"Yes, yes, above the pale."

"Indeed, fine young man."

"Extraordinary scholar."

"Excellent mind. Courageous mind."

"Indeed."

Breckenridge's smile was thin and lifeless. It would not have served his ego to reveal his anxiety over the tardy appearance of a field assistant. He cocked his ear toward the foyer. "Ah. I believe our adventuring colleague has found his way to our door."

James Garrett squared his shoulders and stepped across the Breckenridge threshold, telling himself that one hour of parlor chitchat would be his limit. After one hour, he would select from the long list of places he'd rather be and excuse himself to attend to a pressing matter of some sort. He handed his top hat and his velvet-collared black cloak to Breckenridge's butler and ran his hands quickly through his hair. He still hadn't adjusted to the shorter style.

He had provided Breckenridge with a duplicate of his Western collection, which should have been sufficient entertainment for the evening. James resented the summons to appear as part of the display, but it was one of the unwritten rules that one humored the wealthy man who exhibited a hobbyist's interest in science. Let the man dabble as he would. Give him the vehicle he had chosen to impress his equally wealthy friends, and he would do his part to further the cause by investing in another project. The academic community depended upon the endowments of the rich. Pure science, which was but a source of passing curiosity for most people, was widely financed by the dabbler. James knew his duty, and he had come to perform it with as much charm as he could muster, after which he would welcome a tankard of ale at the Green Dragon.

"Welcome! Welcome, my boy." Ezra Breckenridge's hand fell heavily on James's shoulder as he turned to his guests and gestured with a flourish. "Ladies and gentle-men, welcome the man who spent two long years in that unsettled territory west of the Mississippi River, gathered the specimens you see and brought them back for our edification and enlightenment. Mr. James Garrett."

James dipped his head in response to polite applause. "Ezra Breckenridge is a great friend of science," he told the gathering. "His sponsorship made the venture possible, and I thank him for that."

In the midst of the obligatory applause, Breckenridge leaned closer to ask, "Where are the journals? Did Hector stash them aside with your hat?"

"The journals?" James glanced around the crowded drawing room. "I saw no reason to bring them to this event."

Breckenridge's scowl came too quickly. It took him a moment to recover his bland smile and give James's padded shoulder a patronizing pat. "We'll talk later. Everyone is anxious to meet you. Of course—" his signet ring flashed in his solicitous gesture to include a third party in their conversation "—you know Professor Harding better than I do."

James offered a handshake to the plump white-haired man who stood near Breckenridge's elbow. "Good evening, sir."

"Quite a good evening for you, Garrett."

"For all of us," Breckenridge added.

"Would that we could all have made the journey with you," the professor said. "But you've brought us the far horizon, Garrett, and we're anxious to hear the stories that must accompany this remarkable collection."

James had carefully selected the stories with which to regale Breckenridge's guests. They wanted to hear about the bear and the bison, the splendor of the mountains and the strange ways of the Indians. He spoke of the Lakota, even offered a taste of the language, but he said nothing of Lone

Bear or Thunder Shield or Sees The Enemy. He jealously guarded Kezawin's name.

After he had given James time to mingle with the guests, Breckenridge ushered him into his study and shut the door. The party became a distant buzz while the host took his seat in a commanding high-backed upholstered chair behind a polished inlaid desk and produced a neatly penned document from one of its drawers.

"This is our agreement, my boy. In return for my financial backing, I am to receive a complete collection of labeled specimens *with* commentary."

By nature the scene was one to tie James's stomach into a knot. The words "my boy" were unpleasantly reminiscent of "young man," and the man behind the desk gave him a familiarly accusing stare. Reminders of his father brought out James's icy reserve. He reached inside his coat and drew out a cheroot.

"Care to join me?" The invitation was merely perfunctory. When Breckenridge waved the offer away, James stepped over to the fireplace and took his time lighting the cigar with a bit of kindling. He puffed, then drew the cigar from his mouth and studied the burning tip for a moment as though he were observing something of greater import than Breckenridge's statement. Finally he took a chair.

"I expected you to turn the journals over to me tonight," Breckenridge said.

"You seemed anxious to display the specimens. I had those prepared first. My commentary on the collections, which includes a representative of everything I collected, will be delivered shortly."

"I want your journals just as they are. There's no need for refinement of any kind at this point, Garrett. Knowing your reputation, I'm sure you were quite thorough. I am anxious to publish the findings of the Breckenridge expedition as soon as possible, and I have already arranged for—"

"My journals are my property," James reported flatly. "I assumed that you would donate the specimens and the commentary I shall provide to one of the institutions you endow, but you may do with them as you please. The journals are personal, and they are mine."

"I beg to differ, Mr. Garrett. We both know that the journals contain the meat of the work."

"That's true." James drew slowly on his cigar and created a blue veil around his face. "I set out to assemble a botanical collection, to classify it and to describe it, and that I have done. Beyond that, I met with a world we know nothing about, and my journals contain observations from that world. That, sir, is a piece of work that is not mentioned in our agreement and to which you have no claim."

"I have a claim to anything resulting from the Breckenridge expedition. I paid for it, and I own it."

James eyed the man through a lazy haze of smoke. His journals were filled with wonders that were beyond Breckenridge's poor power to imagine. He could never own them. Some of what James had written would not be published, not by himself or anyone else. His memories were not for sale. What would be published by James Garrett and no other person was a work that had taken a direction he had not foreseen. While the earlier part of the work was thorough, enlightening and definitive in its field, it was the journalizing of the past few months that made the work unique.

"I assure you that I will fulfill my contract with you, Breckenridge. You won't be disappointed with my commentary, which will be carefully written in layman's terms. It will be pleasant reading. You can have it printed, claiming your sponsorship on the title page. I'm sure your friends will find it amusing." James stood up and took one last puff on his cigar before tossing it into the flames that licked the firebox inside the classically constructed fireplace. He had lost the taste for strong cigars. An open camp fire and a long-stemmed pipe filled with the soothing taste of *kiniknik* would have appealed to him more. Shared in the ritual of the Lakota, the pipe might have tempered the growing anger of both men.

"You'll regret resisting me on this, Garrett. The journals are mine. You would be hard-pressed to find an attorney in this town who would be willing to represent you should this matter land in court."

"Then I shall represent myself."

There was a soft rapping at the door. "Are you in there, Father?"

"Yes, yes, come in," was the impatient reply. Flat brown eyes set in a round rubicund face peered around the door. "What is it, Orson?" Ezra asked.

"I thought you might be having some sort of trouble, sir. Our friend isn't holding out on us, is he?"

"Come in and close the door, Orson." Ezra pushed his chair back abruptly and circled the desk. "I believe Mr. Garrett realizes how foolish it would be for him to offend me. Isn't that right, Mr. Garrett?"

James glanced at the blotchy-skinned son, who stood in front of the door with his arms folded over his chest, then returned his attention to the ample-bellied sire. In another few years he thought they would make a fine pair of bookends. "It was not my intention to offend you," he said. "But neither do I intend to give you my journals. If you take offense, then so be it."

"I'll see that no one else finances your work," Ezra blustered as the color began to rise in his face. "I'll see that no one else gives you a penny. I can do that, you know. Do you realize that with a few well-placed words I can make certain no one will ever hear of the brilliant young naturalist, James Garrett? Peddle your journals where you will, young man, you will be outmaneuvered in this."

James's humorless smile gave his blue eyes a cold glint. "Do you intend to outlive me, too? Your present apoplectic state bodes ill for you, Breckenridge."

Orson stepped away from the door. "Are you threatening my father, Garrett?"

"I've had enough of this," James said matter-of-factly as he headed for the door. "This little soiree has ceased to entertain me. You will get the commentary we agreed upon, but the journals are mine." Orson stood his ground two feet in front of the door as James paused to drill him with his eyes. "Excuse me." James gave Orson a moment to size him up. The shifting of the eyes assured James of Orson's self-doubt, and he swept the junior Breckenridge aside with a brush of an arm.

"Your work will never see print," Ezra warned, his voice quavering with anger. "Your expeditions are finished, your career, your reputation—"

"I bid you good night, sir."

James headed directly for the Green Dragon, where the Medford rum and the friendly company soon improved his mood. Having reacquainted himself with friends and fellows from the university, he traded tales and raised his glass for toast after toast. The yellow light from the tavern's oil lamps threw tall shadows on the wall—winsome serving girls in silhouette and the shapes of brawny dock workers rubbed shadowy shoulders with scholars, merchants and politicians. No story was too farfetched nor overly ribald, and the only weight thrown around was that which bellied up to the bar.

"Say on about the woolly-headed buffalo, Garrett. How much spearing did you have to do to bring him down?"

"Puts me in mind of the time I sailed to Africa. Saw the most amazing creatures. Rhinoceroses. Elephants."

"Did you bag an elephant, Cap'n?"

"Almost. Had him in my sights."

"But this buffalo. How big did you say he was?"

"Big enough," James told the crowd. "Big enough to feed your family for an entire winter."

"Not ol' Charlie's pack o' brats. Fourteen last count, right, Charlie?"

"How 'bout the women, Garrett? How much spearin' did you do with them wild redskin wenches?"

James set his glass down carefully and studied the grain of wood in the table.

"Puts me in mind of the native women I saw in Africa. They wore very little, of course, and when you're trading, you learn to pick and choose. The young ones—"

"Lakota women do not have red skin, nor do they—" James glanced up. He was surrounded by expectant leers.

"What color skin do they have?"

"What color is it under their—"

"Enough!" His chair clattered to the floor as he came to his feet. He saw their surprise and realized he'd surprised himself. Truly he knew only one Lakota woman, and he'd risen to her defense. He sought to regain his customary self-control. "The, uh . . . the Lakota women are quite modest. Quite reserved, actually."

"You mean they wouldn't give you a tumble, Garrett?" There was a round of chuckles. "Handsome specimen like yourself?"

"Or maybe they was all hags."

"Maybe he didn't know the right words."

"Or the right price. Did you offer them a bit of—"

"No!" Anger flared in his eyes, even though its source was elusive. James had always been a sporting sort when it came to a little harmless ribbing among friends. He took up his glass and tossed down the last swallow of the potent rum. It gave him a warm feeling and put a smile back on his face as he sat down again. "I had nothing to offer but clumps of weeds, my friends. The ladies were not impressed."

"The next time you go on one o' these trips of yours, take along a few trinkets," someone suggested. "A man can use a little diversion no matter where he wanders."

"Beads and weeds, beads and weeds. I've got a length of somethin'll give 'em what for."

James joined in the laughter. Everyone knew Charlie had all he could handle at home. The faster the rum flowed, the fewer boasts any of them could hope to make good. But when a peal of light female laughter rose above the bass tones, the image of a woman half a continent away appeared to James. Her hair was black and glossy, and her face was covered with rain. Mink eyes flashed as she laughed, and his heart quickened. He jerked his head around.

The woman had red hair and berry-colored lips set in a pallid face. She laughed good-naturedly as she served tankards of ale to the men at a nearby table.

"Betty's as wild as any red savage," a voice at James's elbow confided. James turned, and his old friend, John Glover, gave him a knowing smile. "She's given you the eye several times tonight."

"Has she, now."

"Quite blatant about it, she's been. I think your hunting story caught her fancy."

A slow smile spread across James's face. His hunting prowess had finally garnered its due respect. He raised his voice across the room. "Mistress...Betty, is it? Would you be good enough to refill my glass?"

Betty hovered over James's table, leaning over to top off tankards, and treated James to an unobstructed view of her ample bosom. He pushed his chair back from the table and offered his lap when she said she was anxious to get off her feet. She smelled of ale and kitchen grease, and he wished for wood smoke and sweet grass. He pushed that wish aside, admonishing himself to wish realistically. Betty was real.

She ran her hands over his shoulders, assessing his physique beneath the padding of his coat. "Lusty one, ain't you? Strong enough to bring an elephant down with a spear."

"Buffalo," he corrected, and squeezed her waist. She laughed lustily and wiggled her bottom against his lap. He closed his eyes, nestled his chin in the ruffle of her scoop-necked blouse and nuzzled the valley between her breasts. He pushed the din of the tavern to the edge of his brain. There in the corner of his mind he found a soothing memory of brushing his hot face against cool firm breasts.

"I can get us a room upstairs," Betty whispered.

James lifted his head and looked at the woman. He was half-surprised to find curly red hair instead of sleek, black, beautiful ... God in heaven, reality could be such a disappointment.

She misread his dark expression. "You'd have to pay for the room, but I wouldn't charge you nothin'."

"You're very generous."

"I like you." She smiled, and he saw that she had green eyes.

"Why?" he asked. "Have you had a vision of me? A bolt from the blue promising that I would come?" She looked puzzled. He gave her the kind of pat on her hip he knew she could understand. "I like you, too, Betty. There's nothing complicated about you or your offer." The look he gave her was blatantly sexual. "And I shall come. That much I can promise."

"No hurry," she said, then whispered in his ear, "Just take your time and enjoy your friends. I'll make the arrangements." She sat up and made every effort to dazzle him with a smile.

The smile did nothing for him. There was no mystery in her eyes, nothing to engage his imagination. But she engaged his sex, and that was all he needed. "I have a room," he whispered back. "It isn't far."

Ingersoll's was one of the more reputable lodging houses in Cambridge, and it was for that reason that James chose to usher Betty through the back entrance and up the dark narrow twist of a stairway to his room. He warned her to avoid the fifth step, and each of them bypassed the creaky tread. The hour was late, and James knew he risked eviction if the other boarders were disturbed. In the cold night air he had lost his initial enthusiasm for the plan he had conceived in response to Betty's squirming on his lap. The sooner he could tend to the needs he'd long neglected and send the woman off with a heavier purse, the better he'd like it. Her glassy-eyed smile and her hiccupy giggle were beginning to irritate him.

He intended to whisk Betty in ahead of him as he opened the door, but the shadowy figure standing in the middle of his room stopped him cold.

"What are you—"

The hulking figure tossed his cloak back over his shoulder, briefly blotting out the moonlight coming through the small window behind him. James stepped over the threshold as he pushed Betty behind him.

"What do you want?" James demanded as he loosened the fastenings on his own voluminous cloak, shoved it to the floor and tossed his hat aside. The intruder edged away from the writing table. A bit of steel glinted in his hand.

"He's got a knife!" Betty whispered at James's back.

"I've got nothing worth stealing, man. Be gone and we shall forget we ever—"

The dark shadow lunged across the room, but James was ready with a shoulder block. They crashed to the floor together as James grabbed for the arm that brandished the weapon. The intruder's cloak became a third party in the grappling. They rolled together and became entangled, struggling for control over the deadly blade.

James realized the man's superior strength and inferior agility as he sought to gain the cloak as an ally. If the heavier man managed to reverse their positions and land on top, James would be lost. Betty's cry for help filled his ears, and the intruder's hot, sour-milk breath assailed his nostrils. In one quick move he tossed the cloak over the man's head, rolled him over on his stomach and pushed his face against the floor. The man grunted and convulsed as though he dangled from a noose. Then he was still.

A single taper bathed the room in shadowy unreality. With his chest still heaving from his efforts, James pulled himself off the cloaked hulk on the floor and rose on one knee. A second taper joined forces with the first, and there was a gathering of voices. James looked up. Mrs. Ingersoll held her candleholder aloft and stared with wide eyes. Her flannel nightgown flowed to the floor like cream. Mr. Lorry from down the hall crept closer with his taper, and Betty hovered behind them. There was a buzzing of curious voices in the darkness beyond the door.

"Who is this?" Mrs. Ingersoll demanded. Her face fell into a scowl, and her eyes darted to indicate the cowering woman behind her. "You know we do not permit this, Mr. Garrett."

James glanced down at the cocooned intruder, up at Betty's huge glassy eyes and finally at Mrs. Ingersoll's outraged face. His shoulders shook as he gained control of his breathing. Relief combined with a feeling that he was surrounded by absurdity, and laughter bubbled in his throat.

"What is the meaning of this, Mr. Garrett? What have you done here? This is a respectable house. I won't permit such goings-on in my—"

"Look! There's blood!"

Mr. Lorry pointed to a dark pool seeping, gathering, growing beside the bundled attacker. James rolled the man over and peeled the cloak back while Betty's tongue suddenly sprang to life. "He was waitin' in here, just waitin'. He had a knife. When Mr. Garrett told him to just go on out peaceable, the bloody thief went for him, just like—"

The knife was buried to the hilt in the man's belly. James felt for a pulse in his neck and found none, but he detected something tucked beneath the man's coat. He pushed one lifeless arm aside and found two leather-bound books. He motioned for more light, and Mr. Lorry stepped closer, curiosity and candle both ablaze. James turned the dead man's face toward the light.

"Damn you, Orson. If you weren't so fat you could have stuck the journals in the front of your trousers. They might have saved your worthless life."

At the inquest, Betty and the witnesses from Ingersoll's Lodging House helped James clear his name, but he was not allowed to reclaim his journals. Upon his return to Ingersoll's, he received notice of his eviction and a summons to a meeting with Barkleigh Harding, who was the chairman of the Botany Department at Harvard. Harding met him in a tiny cubicle at the back of a dusty storage room near the laboratory. James interpreted the arrangement as a sign that the level of his acceptability had slipped a notch.

"I'm sure you realize that this Breckenridge affair has become a sticky business for us here," Harding said as he took a seat on one of the tall wooden stools that stood near a bank of oak cabinets.

James planted his foot on a lower stool and braced one hand on his knee. "The man broke into my room," he said evenly. "I was forced to defend myself."

"We know that, James. Breckenridge is a pompous man, and his son was a fool."

"There were no charges."

"Good," Harding said, nodding. "That's good, James. I would hate to see you rotting in prison over a thing like this."

"The authorities are holding my journals."

"No." Harding glanced away. "No, they're not. Breckenridge demanded them with his son's personal effects."

"He has them, then?"

"I have them." Harding leaned forward, bracing himself on his thighs. "He wanted me to sort through them. He plans to publish the findings of the Breckenridge expedition, but, of course, the findings are over his head."

James offered a humorless smile. "The mourning for his son seems to have gotten short shrift."

"I suspect that vengeance will take precedence over mourning, James, and I suggest you look to your own safety."

"What's to be done with my journals?"

Harding pondered the question for a moment. "I'm not quite sure what to make of your journals. Whether they be fact or fiction, they are certainly fascinating. I was unable to set them aside until I had read every word."

"Fact or fiction?" James fairly exploded at the suggestion. "Sir, you know my work. I have studied your own work, Nuttall's, Say's. I know my predecessors by heart, but I daresay the depth of my work, *my* journals surpassed anything accomplished thus far in the territory west of—"

"You daresay so, do you? Just what was all the hocus-pocus with the Indian woman, James? You seem to have gone beyond the bounds of simply observing primitive culture. In fact, I would say you gave some credence to her heathen practices, coming dangerously close to crediting her with medical knowledge, or, worse yet, some God-given power to heal."

James's pulse pounded in his ears. The man spoke of Kezawin, and James felt like a traitor. He had never intended to expose her to this kind of unsympathetic scrutiny. He wanted to write about the things he'd learned from her, but he had planned to edit the journals so that she would not be labeled sorceress or witch by those who knew nothing of her life and her traditions. Not that their labels would ever touch her in her world, but they would touch him, and how would he respond?

"I said nothing of God or supernatural power," James pointed out. "I took note of her herbal prescriptions, and I observed their effect insofar as I was allowed. She treated an injury of mine with amazing success."

"Yes," Harding acknowledged with a thoughtful nod. "That was interesting. I should tell you that your...shall we say, sentiments toward the woman are apparent in your writing."

"I came to respect her. I learned a great deal from her."

"As much as you learned from me or from Thomas Nuttall or Thomas Say?"

There was an undeniable challenge in Harding's hard look. His white hair and the soft folds of aging skin only served to add weight to his authority. "Of course not," James acquiesced quietly. "She is uneducated and...and untutored in scientific or philosophical thought." In his mind he saw a clear picture of her face, and it was as though she had heard him denounce her. His heart ached, and he groped for some way to redeem himself. "You must understand that she is—"

"A savage, James. Their brains are smaller than ours, you know. They are simply incapable of participating in a higher level of—" He waved his hand in a gesture of dismissal. "Of course, you know all that. You were out there for two years, and you have a man's needs. I trust the woman was attractive in her own way, and you—"

"Sir, I beg you to return my journals."

Harding stood slowly, his joints protesting the weight they were required to carry in their advanced years. "I sympathize with your dilemma, James. It is a piece of work that contains moments of genius. On the other hand, there are certain aspects, certain elements, certain implications—" He waved a hand in a dramatic lecture-hall gesture. "It could ruin you, and you know it. Fascinating as they may be, pagan superstitions must be termed 'nonsense' by the scientific mind. One must not seem to portray such rites as anything but—"

"Their rites had no part in my study. I described the use of herbs in treating injury and disease."

"By a woman who thinks she can turn herself into a deer. Good God, man, you'll be the laughingstock of the scientific community!"

"I had no intention of mentioning that aspect of her life. It has no bearing—"

"No bearing! It's hocus-pocus, I tell you. It's one thing to observe the primitive and describe them from the viewpoint of a civilized, intelligent, English-speaking, God-fearing white man, but it's another thing—" Harding was displeased with the emotionalism he'd begun to display, and he reined in and tempered it with scholarly reason. "Much of your work is, as I said, valuable, enlightening, deserving of attention. I intend to placate Breckenridge by publishing it as his work, with you as his field assistant."

"His field assistant!"

"And James," Harding cautioned, "I suggest you disappear for a time. Visit your family in Virginia. Perhaps in two or three years, when Breckenridge's furor over his son dies down a bit, you can come back and be reinstated with the university."

"I am relieved of my teaching post, then?"

"I'm afraid so. We cannot risk losing Breckenridge's generous endowment."

The stagecoach left Scollay Square at three o'clock in the morning. At that hour the huge conveyance lumbered over the cobblestone streets of the sleeping city without interference from other traffic. It rumbled over the ruts of the Boston Post Road and headed south. Covering about six miles to the hour, it would take at least two days to reach New York—two days for the traveler to mull over his plans.

James had no plans. He had given considerable thought to putting the elder Breckenridge in a grave beside the younger one, but some measure of reason had intervened. Professor Barkleigh Harding, a man James had once admired, had sacrificed one man's career for the good of the university. Perhaps he'd been prudent, but James wondered how many others might be cast adrift in deference to the same cause.

Harding's parting warning that James must now look to his own safety was a concern that James had all but set aside, until he had tried to engage an attorney's services to help him recover the journals. No one had been willing to take his case. He heard several conflict-of-interest excuses, and one particularly cool-mannered lawyer told him that he might want to be as far from Boston as possible should new evidence surrounding the circumstances of Orson Breckenridge's death come to light.

Once he'd exhausted the legal channels, James considered what was left. The journals had been stolen from him through legal channels. In order to get them back, he had to play the game. He had gone to Harding's office late in the day to return his keys, say his farewells, play the role of the gentleman who understood the old professor's position and would be grateful to see his name listed as an assistant on the Breckenridge project. The recognition would help him establish himself elsewhere, perhaps in New Haven. They had laughed, agreeing that Harvard's loss might be Yale's gain. James returned his keys. Harding tossed them in a drawer, locked his office and went on chatting as they strolled together for the last time down the deserted corridor.

When they reached the foyer, they shook hands and went separate ways. Harding was off to a dinner engagement. James circled the building, readmitted himself with a duplicate key and returned to Harding's office, where his master key made burglary an effortless operation. He knew that in Harding's mind the journals belonged to the university, and logic dictated that Harding would have kept them there. James found them in the drawer with his keys.

The coach bumped along in the early-morning darkness, and James thought about Harding's suggestion that he return to home ground to lick his wounds. Home ground. He had left his boyhood home near Falmouth on the Rappahannock River with his father's threats ringing in his ears. Eternal damnation awaited the son who refused to honor the wishes of his father. His father wanted James to be a tobacco farmer, but James had no interest in farming, and he took pleasure in defying the wish of the father who had left a gravely sick child and a fragile wife to die in the rain. With an inheritance from his maternal grandfather, James had paid for his "Yankee" education. He had not been home in more than ten years, and he had no wish to return now.

Word of James's hand in Orson Breckenridge's death had undoubtedly reached Falmouth and Ridge View, the Garrett farm. His father would insist that James had killed a man in defense of some intellectual nonsense and that his place in hell was assured. Then he would offer James a chance to redeem himself. He'd need only tuck his tail between his legs and do his father's bidding. And how that old man would relish playing the role of magnanimous father to his prodigal son!

James had no taste for farce. He had no apologies to make to anyone. His life was still his own, and he had his journals. There were also the pages of new journals to fill. James Garrett's life's work would carry *his* name, not his father's and not Ezra Breckenridge's. What had seemed like a dead end was clearly a fork in the road. He would ride the coach to the end of the line, then head west again.

Chapter Five

Paha Sapa, The Black Hills
Summer, 1827

The Moon of Ripening Chokecherries was a time when the sun made the days long and warm and invited the men of the Lakota to fulfill their vows by offering the Gaze at the Sun sacrifice. The bands of Teton Sioux gathered on the banks of Spearfish Creek in the bosom of *Paha Sapa* for the twelve-day Sun Dance ceremony. They came to hallowed ground where, since the beginning of the old ones' collective memory, the men had pierced their flesh and sacrificed their own blood for the good of the people. It was a sacred time, when mothers brought their babies forward for ear piercing, when young men sought their first visions and mature men reached for higher levels of visionary experience, and when women sought signs portentous of love, a fertile womb, a successful birthing.

In her search along the creek bank for the thick-stalked bulrush, Kezawin had found such a sign—a spear of gama grass with four heads—a promise of love. Her discovery had brought forth a burst of laughter. Surely *Tunkaśila*, the Grandfather Above, intended this for her amusement, that she should find it and not the others who searched together in their groups. She had thought of leaving it for a more likely candidate, but, no, this was her find, and she tucked it carefully into her leather pouch. In the privacy of her lodge, she took it out again and rubbed the stem between her thumb and forefinger, making the heads dance.

"Daughter, I have news to tell you."

Kezawin put the stalk of grass under her sleeping robe and added a sprig of sage and a piece of dry cottonwood to her fire. "You are welcome here, Father," she announced.

Lone Bear ducked inside and took a man's place at the back of the tipi, where a willow backrest provided him with comfortable seating. He accepted Kezawin's offer of fruit and jerked meat, but he took only small portions. He was anxious to tell her what he knew.

At last, when he had eaten, Lone Bear launched his news. "Our friend Garrett is a captive of the Skidi." He watched Kezawin's eyes widen.

"James?" she whispered, then summoned a stronger voice. "Was he taken after he left us last summer?"

Lone Bear shook his head. "Two white men were riding with a Yankton scout. The Skidi took only the whites and left our cousin for dead. His relatives found him and brought him here for healing."

"How long ago?"

"Two days."

Kezawin knew what that meant. Three more days. The summer solstice was a time for ceremony there in the hills, but in the flat country not far to the south, the hated Pawnee, to which the Skidi band belonged, honored their gods in this season, as well. The Lakota Sun Dance lasted twelve days, but the Pawnee ritual took only five. Kezawin's brain buzzed with an invasion of images—a party of three, a whirlwind of dust and horses, yelping riders with hair roaches bristling like quills over the crests of their shaven red-painted heads. And in the midst of it all was the face she had not forgotten. She heard the pounding of the horses' hooves and the racing heartbeats, first his, then hers.

"Our cousin is safe," Lone Bear went on.

The sound of her father's voice drifted in the periphery. Wise words meant nothing now. Only one truth was clear to her. "He cannot be left to the Skidi."

"They may have killed him," Lone Bear said quietly.

"No. If he were dead, I would know it."

"How?"

Kezawin looked at her father, and he saw that she had an understanding beyond explanation. In that moment, James Garrett lived. His heart beat as surely as hers did. "The Skidi might know of me," she said. "Many people have heard of the Double Woman Dreamer from Lone Bear's band."

"If word has reached them of your beauty, they will be ready to take you, and Garrett will still die."

"I must prepare a sweat," she decided. "I must be clean, and my head must be clear enough to receive a good plan."

Kezawin traveled alone. She knew that no weapons would protect her once she reached the land of the Pawnee, and she carried only her skinning knife. She recognized, too, that it was her own will that led her on her southward journey, but she had conceived her plan in the steam of the sweat lodge, and when she had worked it all out in her mind, the air in the lodge had seemed to lighten.

The Pawnee were earth-lodge people, and they had long been enemies of the Lakota. The horse Kezawin rode and the one she led would be tempting prizes, as would the bundles she had lashed to the packhorse. She, herself, would be of value, as well. A woman was a potential child bearer first and a laborer second. Either way, she would be valuable property. By now they had spotted her, and they knew she was theirs for the taking. They were simply watching to see what this lone Lakota woman was about.

Flat sunbaked plains stretched endlessly before her, but she had seen the signs of a village nearby. There had been horse dung, and the grass had been grazed. The Pawnee were not rich in horses like the Lakota, but they had a few. Kezawin knew that the sentries would show themselves before she would ride close enough to see corn patches or the earthen mounds that she had heard about but had never seen.

They appeared all at once at the top of a rise. Four of them approached on horseback at an easy gait. Kezawin's buckskin mare pricked her ears, but Kezawin held her gait steady, matching the riders'. Her heart pounded, but she stared straight ahead and gave no sign of fear. Her only advantage was the sheer audacity of her action, and she counted on impressing them with nothing but that. Only when they put themselves in her path did she slow her pace. She came to a halt and gave the sign that she had come to talk.

The four men scowled beneath heavy brows. Their smooth scalps glistened in the sun, and their war clubs were handy. A fleeting picture of her skull being bashed open like a ripe squash ran through Kezawin's mind, but she squared her shoulders and suffered their perusal of her. They would know the meaning of the deer hooves that dangled from her belt, and even if they had no respect for Lakota medicine, they would see that only a woman with strong power would ride alone into the land of her enemy. She was obviously not lost, and by this time they had assured themselves that she was, indeed, unescorted.

The four men exchanged a few words and then wheeled their horses as if on signal. One brave took the lead while the others dropped back to surround Kezawin. They rode together in tight formation until they crested a ridge. On the sprawling flat below, Kezawin saw the bright green leaves of young cornstalks flickering in the midst of tawny grass, and beyond that were the Pawnee lodges, popping from the ground and sprigged with grass like the round bald heads of the men who dwelled in them.

Kezawin hid her thoughts behind an expressionless face as the four men led her into the village. Some of the people climbed onto their earthen roofs to get a good look at the Lakota woman who came to their village unbound and leading a packhorse. One child lost ground in his effort to scramble up the side of the house behind his older brother, and as his feet skidded in the clods of dirt he'd set rolling, he let the backward motion take him while he craned his neck for a sliding peek at the strange woman. On the roof-top above him, a little girl tugged at her mother's skirt, and Kezawin could hear the foreign words spoken in a familiar tone, putting off the child's demands for just a moment.

Her Skidi escorts led her to the bread-loaf-shaped entrance to one of the larger lodges. One of the men spoke to another and sent him on his way. Then the remaining three dismounted and signaled to Kezawin to do the same. An older man emerged from the lodge, and the three spoke to him in deferential tones. The full curve of each of his ears was pierced and adorned with looped strings of beads and fine bits of bone, which rattled softly as he nodded, listening. He spared Kezawin a glance, and she made the sign that she wanted to trade. He looked surprised.

The man who had been sent away appeared again, followed by a young woman. He barked a command, and she stepped closer to Kezawin. "I am Sweet Grass Woman, once Yankton, now second wife to Sky Runner of the Skidi."

The young woman spoke haltingly in the Nakota dialect, which bore enough similarity to Lakota that Kezawin had little trouble understanding. "I am Kezawin, daughter of Lone Bear of the Hunkpapa. I am also called Double Woman Dreamer."

Sweet Grass Woman took a single step backward. Kezawin lifted her chin and waited calmly. When the older man questioned her, Sweet Grass Woman had much to say, but Kezawin was more interested in the men's reaction than in the gist of Sweet Grass Woman's introductions. The wariness in their eyes was a good sign.

Sweet Grass Woman realized her own value when all attention turned to her as she translated. She threw her shoulders back and relayed the message of the men who had taken little notice of her until this moment. "Mark Of The Badger, chief of the Skidi, says that Double Woman Dreamer does not appear to be a fool. He wishes to know why a daughter of the Hunkpapa would come here to trade with the Pawnee."

"I am told that the Skidi took a white captive several days ago. I believe I know this man. If he is the one, then I wish to buy him from you."

This news prompted some discussion between Mark Of The Badger and the leader of the scouting party. Sweet Grass Woman waited patiently to relay his reply. "The Skidi have two white captives. The strongest of the two is being prepared for Tirawa. Mark Of The Badger has not yet decided about the other one."

James was as strong and healthy as any man. Kezawin shuddered inwardly, thinking no other white man would please the Pawnee god more than he would. "The man I seek is *wakan*," she said through her interpreter. "I, who have dreamed of the deer woman, have also dreamed of this man. He is a holy man and must be protected. He has medicine that will make mine stronger. That is why I have come to you without fear. My *šicun*, the white deer, has brought me to buy this man."

After more discussion among the men, Mark Of The Badger gave the matter some thought and finally relayed his offer. "Let us see what you have to trade."

Kezawin unloaded her packhorse and displayed four buffalo robes decorated with quilled borders. The vivid colors and superb work were, Sweet Grass Woman noted, signs of the work of one who had dreamed of the deer woman and could therefore call herself Double Woman Dreamer. Kezawin offered a pipe bag, a pair of saddlebags and a saddle blanket, all decorated with the same uniquely designed quillwork. Although Mark Of The Badger was not visibly impressed, the offer was clearly more than any white captive was worth.

"Mark Of The Badger accepts these gifts and the two horses," Sweet Grass Woman translated. "You may take your captive and return to your people unharmed."

"It must be the man I seek," Kezawin said.

"Mark Of The Badger says that one has already been chosen for Tirawa. You have traded for the other one."

James's arms ached like the devil, and his right foot had gone to sleep again. Since his capture he'd spent much of his time trussed up and braided like a knot of fancy bread. He wondered how soon these people planned to bake him. He found his situation particularly frustrating because he wanted nothing more than a chance to move about freely and observe Pawnee customs and habits, even partake insofar as he might be permitted. Instead, he was permitted almost no movement at all.

For a time they had kept him in the same lodge with Red Girard, the hulking young trapper who had broken several Pawnee bones before they'd taken him down. James had spent an entire day bound back-to-back with Girard, long enough for each to become thoroughly sick of the smell of the other. From the first, the Pawnee had taken an interest in Red's strapping physique and his flaming hair, and Red had worried aloud that he'd probably broken some chief's son's nose and would pay dearly for the transgression. He assumed that they were trying to decide where to hang his hair when it was all over.

Neither of them knew much about the Pawnee beyond the fact that they were enemies of the Sioux, which meant that James's proficiency in Lakota would not earn him any friends among his captors. After a time Red had been taken away, and James had been left in the corner of the huge earth-walled lodge with the chief's horse. Each morning he and the horse were taken outside. The animal was permitted to graze, while James was allowed only a few moments to tend to his needs before he was herded back inside and tied up again. At night he was taken to water, and then he and the horse were returned to the corner and secured there with leather thongs.

James fastened his mind on the shaft of light that shot through the center smoke hole. Everything else bore down on him and threatened to bury him alive. The air smelled dank and earthy, and he struggled with the oppressive darkness. The inside of his nostrils were coated with dust, and a gash he'd received on his neck in the initial scuffle with his captors was festering. Without his hands he could do nothing to help himself.

He anticipated the origin of every sound outside the lodge. The dwelling housed a dozen people, the members of what appeared to be three related families. James didn't blame them for spending most of the daylight hours outside, but he was glad when a woman or a pair of children would spend a few moments within the lodge. Even though they ignored him, he welcomed their company and some relief from the boredom.

There was something going on outside the lodge even now. With his cheek pressed against the packed-dirt floor, James strained to listen. The deep rumble of men's voices was too distant to allow him to discern anything other than the fact that a conversation was in progress, but it was a form of distraction. It was something living, something human, and James felt dangerously out of touch with both elements.

The old man, his "host," entered the lodge with a buffalo robe over each arm. James peered across the room, and when the shaft of light struck one of the robes, he noticed the quillwork. The intricate designs were Sioux. The sight touched his heart the way a piece of his mother's needlework might have. He thought of the airy tipi with its opaque walls, the floor carpeted with buffalo robes and the smell of meat boiling in the cooking pouch. A woman entered, carrying more decorated goods. A second woman followed. The entryway was like a tunnel, which echoed the sounds made by those who approached and made for a moment of wild anticipation. James knew before she came through the door that it was another woman, because he could hear the soft click of elk's teeth and the music the tin-wrapped ends of the fringe on her dress made. She entered as a shadow and moved toward the light.

He knew the days and nights in this hole had broken him at last. He had lost touch with reality, and his mind saw only what it wanted to see. Kezawin.

And Kezawin saw that James was the man she had purchased. Relief poured through her like the first hot soup after a long fast. She moved quickly to kneel beside him and slip her hand between his face and the dirt floor. He uttered her name, and she felt the warmth of his breath on the inside of her wrist. He closed his eyes and turned dry, cracked lips against the same spot. Her stomach tightened, and she longed to examine him thoroughly as would the mother of a newborn, but she turned instead and said over her shoulder, "Ask Mark Of The Badger if I may cut the slave's bonds. I have paid dearly for him, and I want him whole and healthy."

"Slave?" James croaked while the translation was made on the far side of the room.

"I have purchased you, James Garrett. You belong to me now."

"Better you than him."

Permission was granted through Sweet Grass Woman, and Kezawin unsheathed her skinning knife and sliced through the rawhide that bound James's hands behind him and fastened his wrists to his ankles. He groaned as his blood rushed to his extremities while Kezawin helped him to sit up. He looked at her, blinking several times as if to clear his vision. He reached out to touch her braided hair, then her cheek. His fingers trembled against her skin.

"You must not touch me, James," she whispered. Her voice was as unsteady as his hand. "You are my slave."

"How did you find me?" he asked. "How did you know I was here?"

She peeled back the collar of the shirt that had become a filthy rag and examined his neck. It was too dark to see, so she leaned close and sniffed for signs of flesh rot. "What else have they done to you, James? Is there anything—"

He grabbed her shoulders. "Are you here alone? You didn't come here alone, did you?"

"You must not touch me," she repeated as she shrugged his hands off. "You *are* my slave. I would see to your wounds if you would tell me what damage has been done."

"Just what you see," he said impatiently. "Kezawin, who's with you? Who brought you? Who's looking out for your safety here?"

"No one came with me. The Pawnee is our—"

"I know," he said, cutting off the word as though it might be a curse. "I know that. Woman, you've lost your mind. You are as crazy as your people think I am. These people have had me tied up here for days—God knows what they have in mind. What made you think one woman, one crazy little woman—"

Laughter threatened to ruin her staid demeanor as she sealed his lips with two fingers. She couldn't hold back the soft smile that had blossomed in her heart when she heard his words of concern for her.

When she took her fingers away, he added, "One very beautiful, very brave woman."

"We will not be permitted to leave until tomorrow, and we will have to walk."

"Walk?"

"The two horses were part of the price."

He digested the news with a quiet sigh. "There was another man taken prisoner with me, a trapper named Girard. Somehow we have to secure his—"

"We will talk of that later," she said as she stood up and offered him a hand. "Are you able to stand?"

He got to his feet on his own, but his legs wobbled, and he finally steadied himself with an arm around Kezawin's shoulders. "I'm not touching you. I'm leaning on you."

"You are like a newborn calf."

"I felt as though I'd been crammed back into the womb these past days." He glanced up at Mark Of The Badger and Sweet Grass Woman, who had become a half-interested audience. "Is he going to let us walk out of here?"

Kezawin nodded to Sweet Grass Woman, who relayed the question. "Mark Of The Badger will permit you to go as far as the river. Your slave should be washed. One might mistake him for a horse."

Mark Of The Badger pinched his nose as he told his joke and laughed all the harder when he heard the Lakota translation.

"One did, in fact, mistake me for a horse—one near-sighted old—" James grumbled. "I would not be apt to commend Pawnee hospitality to my friends, but I can think of a few enemies I might like to see—"

"Hold your tongue, James," Kezawin warned as she helped him to the door. "We are still guests here."

They bathed separately, and when Kezawin returned to the spot James had chosen for his bath, she found him dressed only in a pair of wet knee-length drawers. His buckskin trousers and ragged shirt and socks were flapping in the breeze on a nearby bush while he sat on a fallen cottonwood and struggled to pull his boots over bare feet. Kezawin laughed merrily, and she wondered what kind of white man could have been chosen over James, who looked as healthy and appealing as any man she had known. He looked up and delighted her with a boyish grin.

"One of these times you will catch me without a stitch, and then we'll see who has the last laugh."

"*Tuki*, white man," she teased in a way of a woman challenging a man's boast. She set a pouch and several other items down beside the fallen tree where James sat.

"Remember that the Double Woman Dreamer laughs at anything that amuses her."

"And if you find that you have paid dearly for a joke, Double Woman Dreamer, who should laugh then?"

"The deer woman," she said as she tugged at a dead branch and pulled it free of a thatch of silver-leafed buffalo berry bushes. "I am never more than one step ahead of that wily trickster. I cannot forget that she has two faces."

"None more beautiful than the one that came for me today. When you came into that dark pit and stepped into the light, you looked so like—"

He wanted to say *an angel*, but it occurred to him that in his world he'd seen no dark-skinned likenesses of angels and that he could think of no Lakota word for the concept. Yet if ever an angel had interceded in his life, it had happened today. His mother had spoken of angels when they had both been gravely ill, and he had imagined brightfaced, golden-haired creatures in filmy white frocks. But the one who had stepped into that hellhole's single shaft of light wore the skin of the elk decorated in earth's warm hues. She had hair as black as the raven's wing and eyes that mirrored his pain the moment she saw him. She was at once the essence of heaven and earth, and when she had knelt beside him and lifted his face out of the dirt, she'd lifted his heart, as well.

Even now he was a little stunned and slow to act. She paused in her efforts and looked at him, waiting for him to complete the comparison. What had she looked like?

"Something *wakan*," he said as he realized his tardiness in lending a hand. He jumped up from his seat and pulled the dead branch clear of the living ones. He tossed it to the ground and turned to her. "You were a ray of hope that shattered my despair."

"You were a pitiful wretch," she said, avoiding his eyes. She broke a dry limb off the branch, remembering how relieved she had felt the instant her eyes had adjusted to the lodge's murky interior and she could see that the man on the floor was truly James. "I must tend to those wounds lest you become wolf bait."

"*You* wound me, Kezawin, even as I sing your praises." He broke off two stout sticks, measured one against the other and searched for a third.

"I hear no singing. I doubt that your people can make a good song, for I have never heard you—"

The third stick snapped between his hands as he raised his voice in close approximation of a traditional Lakota song. He composed the lyric on the spot and fashioned a tripod as he sang softly to her.

"She comes to me
Happily am I delivered
She takes me from darkness to light
Woman whose eyes soften with mercy
She comes, she comes."

He looked up at her only after he had finished his song, and he saw his own surprise reflected in her eyes. He wasn't sure where the song had come from, and now that the notes had taken flight and there was only the sound of the lazy river and the look of surprise in Kezawin's eyes, he felt like an awkward youth. "You were . . . quite a sight."

"Because you needed someone."

"Because it was you who came."

They built a fire pit together in silence. Kezawin soaked James's tripod and set it in place, and when she had water boiling in the paunch she had borrowed from Sweet Grass Woman, she took bits of bark and dried buds and prepared an infusion to treat James's wounds. He watched her without asking questions. The fire crackled and hissed, while at his back his shirt and pants flapped in the breeze. The warm afternoon air smelled like freedom.

She bathed his neck in the hot liquid. He jumped reflexively at the first application, but his skin made its adjustment, and the heat became a source of comfort. For the time being he gave little thought to what ingredients might have gone into the concoction as he leaned back against the fallen cottonwood and gave himself over to Kezawin's care.

It was good just to look at her, to admire the details that had lodged themselves unstintingly in his memory and to take fond note of those that he must have overlooked months ago. Her eyelashes were long, dark and absolutely straight. He had not remembered that spiky straightness. But he had not forgotten the way her eyes crinkled at the corners when she laughed, nor the way light and shadow accented her angular bone structure. There was nothing cool or hazy about her. She had a summer face. Her skin enjoyed a love affair with the sun.

"The woman who translated for you must have been with the Pawnee for some time," James said finally.

"She is Yankton, but she has a Pawnee husband. She was probably taken captive long ago."

"Why didn't they take you?" he asked. She glanced up at him, then continued to bathe a scrape she had located on his side. "Are they afraid of you, too?"

"The Yankton woman told them of my medicine. They saw that I dared to come among them and that I came alone."

"Why did you do it, Kezawin?" When she didn't answer, he caught her hand. "Why?"

"Why did you come back?"

"My work was not finished." He couldn't tell her he had no place else to go.

As a courtesy she accepted his answer, but she pulled her hand from his and continued to bathe him.

"You could not have known they wouldn't kill you," he persisted.

"Death is always a possibility. They may kill me yet, James. They may kill you." She gave him an enigmatic look, one that could almost have been a challenge if it had not hinted at fear.

"I'll give you my word, I'll say nothing to offend them. I'll not do anything foolish. You've risked enough."

"I have traded valuable goods for you," she reminded him as she swabbed his neck with a viscous potion that smelled of mint. "You are mine until I say otherwise."

He nodded once and lifted his gaze to the river's far bank. He smiled. "I understand."

When they returned to the village, a voice hailed them in French, and they turned to find Red Girard enjoying a meal in the shade of one of the smaller lodges. One woman hovered nearby while a second offered him more food.

"This is the life, *n'est-ce pas, mon ami*? I see they've given you a woman, too." Red laughed. "There's been quite a procession of them bringing me food and whatnot. I think I'm supposed to take my pick, but each one seems prettier than the last."

James opened his mouth to reply, but Kezawin grasped his elbow and murmured, "You must say nothing."

James turned his answer into a hesitant smile and waved to the man.

"Ask them for some clothes, Garrett," Red suggestion jovially. "You look like the very devil. Look at me!"

James took note of Red's new white trade-cloth shirt and the strings of hair pipe and beads that hung around his neck. He nodded, still smiling broadly as he muttered aside to Kezawin, "They've certainly taken a liking to him. It must be that French charm."

"Come away, James," Kezawin insisted with an urgency that puzzled him.

While they were sharing the evening meal with Mark Of The Badger's family, they heard men chanting at either end of the village. James thought it a pleasant custom, this lifting of voices at the end of the day, though this was the first time he had heard it during the week he'd spent in captivity. Associating the word *pleasant* with any part of the Skidi had not occurred to him, but now that he was free—almost free—he noticed that the men were ready to perform their version of retiring to the drawing room for a smoke while the women gathered up their wood and clay bowls and the kettles they had acquired in trade.

Not unlike children of any race, the boys were intent on plying some craft with their fathers, for they had brought forth bundles of sturdy cherry wood shoots and laid them at the elders' feet. There was much discussion as Mark Of The Badger and his older sons or sons-in-law broke open the bundles and apparently instructed the youngsters in making their selections. James concluded that it was time for arrow making.

"We must sleep," Kezawin announced abruptly. "We have a long journey ahead of us."

"I don't know whether there's room in my stall for the three of us," James grumbled as he uncrossed his legs.

"Mark Of The Badger's daughter provided a robe and showed me where we are to sleep." She caught his smile. "Remember your place, James. Remember our situation."

He tried to remember. He tried to keep their precarious relations with the Skidi in the forefront of his mind as he lay inches from Kezawin's warm body beneath their borrowed sleeping robe. He wondered what she had on her mind as she lay there next to him, stiff and still as a corpse and trying to make herself breathe evenly. She wasn't fooling him. Two of the women had come to bed. One snored, and the other wheezed. But Kezawin was wide awake.

"Kezawin?" he whispered.

No answer.

"I hate this pile of dirt. I don't want to sleep in a lean-to, either. When we get back, I want to sleep in a tipi."

Silence.

"We must speak to Red before we leave tomorrow. If he chooses to come with us, I don't think they would stop him. Do you?"

One long, deep breath. No answer.

"On the other hand, he seems to be having a pretty good time of it. They must prefer the beefy sort."

Silence.

"They took my journals. I'm having the devil's own time keeping people from—"

"They gave me your books," Kezawin whispered harshly. "They kept what they could use, but they have no use for your precious books."

"Ah, good, then I—"

"Stop this, James. I have no wish to face tomorrow's sunrise after a sleepless night."

"Good night, then," he clipped, and turned his back on her. He closed his eyes and counted backward from a thousand, and his critical awareness of her finally melted like paraffin. He drifted on the muffled rhythm of a distant drum.

But Kezawin's thoughts were full of the smiling white man with hair the color of blood, and she could not sleep.

Mark Of The Badger roused them before daylight. Kezawin clutched the sleeping robe to her breast while the Pawnee elder bound James's hands and feet once again. She could see that others stood in the shadows of firelight, waiting. James offered groggy protests, but he did not fight.

"You cannot take him," Kezawin demanded, hoping the desperation that spun in her head did not sound in her voice. "I have paid for him. We have an agreement, Mark Of The Badger. No man of your stature would break his—"

"Mark Of The Badger does not claim your slave." Sweet Grass Woman stepped closer. "The white man must not leave the lodge now. You must see to it, Double Woman Dreamer. Later, when Tirawa has been satisfied with our petition for good crops and good health, you will both be permitted to stay or go, as you wish."

Mark Of The Badger gave Kezawin a hard searching look. He carried more lengths of rawhide. He glanced at James, then back at Kezawin. She nodded dumbly, and he turned and strode out the opening. In the far corner she heard the clatter of wood. It was the gathering of weapons, a sound all women dreaded.

"What the hell is going on here?" James demanded in English. His hands were tied behind him, and his feet were bound together, but he managed to roll over and sit up. He turned to Kezawin, who huddled behind the buffalo robe, and he continued in Lakota. "What are they doing? Why did they tie me up like this? Did they think I would interfere with their morning prayers?"

"I have never witnessed this practice of the Skidi, but I have heard stories."

"Stories of what? What are they doing?"

"It is not the way of the Lakota. These people have strange ways, just as your people do." She reached for her dress and slipped it over her head. He thought her eyes seemed markedly wilder when her head popped through the neck opening. "When it's over, we can return to the Lakota. We will sleep in a tipi, and there will be no—"

"What are they doing, Kezawin?"

She said nothing. He resumed his practice of listening for whatever muffled sounds might be heard through the thick earthen walls and trying to guess what they meant. The village seemed to be mobilizing.

"Are they being attacked?" he asked. "Is that it? Cut me loose, Kezawin. Trust me. Let me—"

He heard an anguished shout. Someone called his name. Red Girard? James concentrated on the sound. He heard it again. "What are they doing to Red?" He peered at her through the dim light, searching for answers. "Kezawin?" His heart pounded as the shout came again. "Kezawin! What are they doing to Red!"

"You cannot help him, James. You must not try."

"My God, they're going to kill him. Kezawin, they're going to kill the man!"

Kezawin hugged her knees. She closed her eyes and gripped her own forearms, digging her nails into her skin. Morning light eased its way through the smoke hole and into the lodge.

"You must . . . you *must* cut me loose."

"I must take you back to the Lakota," she said quietly.

The voice had moved to the west end of the village, and Red's cries were desperate and angry. "Garrett, you son of a bitch, help me! They're going to burn me alive. Do you hear me? Where the hell are you, you coward? Damn you, you've got to help me!"

"Kezawin, please," James whispered. "We can't just sit here."

"They would kill you, too, James."

"Garrett!"

"Kezawin, we have to do something." His struggle against his bonds was useless.

"I must take you back to the Lakota," she repeated. "That's all I know."

"Kezawin, I know that man. I traveled with that man. Cut these off. Cut them now!"

His shout was enjoined by a distant agonized cry.

"He will feel no more pain," Kezawin whispered. "They have made a quick, clean kill, and the rest will not matter."

"Oh, God."

"You could not have stopped it, James. Had they chosen you, I could not have stopped it."

Outside, the morning was pierced with thunderous cries. James's shoulders slumped as he lowered his forehead to his knees. Kezawin touched his hair, and he shuddered. "You knew," he groaned.

"I knew."

"You could have told me." He lifted his head and stared at her as he realized the import of what he'd said. "If you had told me last night, I could have done something."

"You are not a warrior," she said. "You are a medicine man. You are *wakan* and must be protected."

"Protected! What kind of woman are you? How could you save one and let another—"

"I paid the price for the captive who had not been chosen. Until I saw you, I did not know which man I had bought."

They stared at each other as they listened to the frenzied cries outside the walls. "You should have told me," he said, controlling his voice. "A man decides for himself, and you think me less than a man."

"I think you are meant to be more than just a man. The Pawnee did not choose you, because the white deer chose you first."

"So *you* say."

"You cannot know your destiny when you are puffed up with pride, James Garrett. Your friend is dead."

The crazed shouts were dying in the distance now as a different voice claimed James's ear. A single male voice, a mournful cry, plaintive and hollow with sorrow.

"He's dead, you say? Then what can that be?"

"I believe that is the grief of the man who took him captive," she told him. "He was required to make the kill. Now he grieves, for he has taken a life."

James shook his head in disbelief.

"Your friend is dead, James. You had no power to prevent his death. Put aside your male pride and mourn for him."

Chapter Six

Mark Of The Badger's parting gift to Double Woman Dreamer was a horse. It was not as fine an animal as the two she had traded, but it would serve her well on her journey. He hastened to add that she was welcome to remain among the Pawnee, for it was clear that her medicine was strong, and her courage was unique among the Lakota. If she stayed, he said, she could keep her slave and no man would interfere with her. Kezawin graciously declined his offer, explaining that she had a strong vision of where she must be and what she must do, and she dared not ignore those requirements.

James said nothing. By the time Sweet Grass Woman had ducked into the lodge to tell Kezawin that Mark Of The Badger wished to see them, he had ceased to struggle. He wasn't even sure he wanted his bonds cut, for they had become the only reality in the midst of a nightmare. His hands and feet were tied. He was incapacitated. Everything else was too absurd to be real. He said nothing when Kezawin cut him loose, but he rubbed the soreness out of his wrists, gathered his journals and emerged from the lodge like a man who walked in his sleep. Someone handed him a bundle, which he dutifully lashed to the gift horse's back. He might have suggested that Kezawin ride, but he said nothing to her. When the time came, he led the horse, and Kezawin walked behind.

As they passed through the village, James peered at the solemn faces of the people. He didn't care that his actions might be considered rude. He didn't think about it. He thought about the young boys bringing bundles of sticks to their fathers for arrow making. They had worked side by side, old instructing young. How had they used the arrows that morning? Who had used them? Each face he passed was suspect. Was it you? he thought. What part did you play? Dark eyes, all of them, dark and inscrutable, full of terrible secrets. There were traces of soot on their faces and bits of white ash in their hair.

James had seen nothing. He was there, but he was not there. He was not to blame. He had heard the cries, but he was bound, tightly bound, hand and foot. Is there blood on your hands, young fellow? Don't show me. I don't want to see. I was not there. There stood the woman who had brought food to a man she knew she would kill. How could you do it? his eyes accused. How could you call it anything but murder? How can I call you anything but savage?

They were headed west and then north. At the west end of the village on a barren knoll stood two charred poles and the smoldering ashes of a fire. Nothing stirred. The midmorning sun made the moist summer air heavy with heat, and the smell of burnt blood hung in the air. James stared in hot judgment at the place as he passed. Kezawin attended to the earth, as was her custom. She stopped to dig a few plants, then caught up with James, who set a steadfast pace and did not vary it. They walked without exchanging a word until late afternoon, when the need for water drew the packhorse to a spring-fed pond and a shady resting place.

"Sweet Grass Woman gave us dried meat," Kezawin said as she pulled the bundle off the horse's back and took a rawhide pouch, a parfleche, from the rolled trade blanket. "I found roots to boil with it if you wish to make camp here."

"I want none of their meat."

She let the dictum stand in silence for a moment. "I hope the roots will be to your liking," she said finally. "It is a bit early in the season, but they don't look bad. I will cook them first and add meat to my portion after you have eaten."

He watered the horse and brooded while she cooked. He ate in silence, then brooded while he watched her eat. He told himself the smell of the Pawnee meat turned his stomach, but in truth it did not. The wild roots had not satisfied him, and he brooded over that, too. It irritated him that Kezawin had cooked just what she knew she would eat, and when she was finished, there was not a morsel left in case he had changed his mind. He brooded while she cleaned up from the meal.

"Do you realize what they did to him?" he asked, breaking the silence.

The cottonwood leaves rustled overhead. "I have heard many stories," she said quietly.

"They didn't burn him alive, did they?"

"No. They shot him with an arrow first, from side to side, under the arms. Death came quickly."

"Why did they keep yelping and screaming, then, and why—"

"It is the Skidi way. It is not the Lakota way. I cannot explain it."

"But you prevented me from doing anything about it."

"I was not the one who tied your hands."

"No, but you wouldn't *untie* them."

"Is this the way the white man grieves? It seems a strange way to ease your loss, this counting the things you might have done. Death hears none of this."

James sighed and tipped his head back. He watched a cloud roll by. "They were all in on it, weren't they. I could see it in their eyes. Even the children."

"What did you see?"

It took him a moment to put the words together. "Blood lust."

Kezawin puzzled for a moment, and then she realized that he had used Lakota words for an idea that was not Lakota. Blood and sexual desire did not belong together. A woman's menstrual blood was taboo for a man. She could only guess what he might have meant by the paradoxical term he had contrived, but she decided not to question him about it. Instead she said, "You have taken life yourself, James."

He stared at her. It unnerved him to hear the words. How had she known? His fingertips felt cold, and his palms became clammy as the blood rushed to his face and pounded in his temples. Her eyes were dark and inscrutable, like the eyes of the Pawnee villagers. He had filled his ears with his own protests and consigned the blood to them, but now the eyes were Kezawin's. And she knew him.

"That wasn't murder," he said more desperately than he'd intended.

"No. Not when you need the animal's flesh to nourish your own. Not when your family is hungry. But life is never taken without regret." She looked at him anxiously. "When you take a plant, do you not express that regret in your own language? Usually you say something for each one."

James's mind reeled with confusion. What was she thinking? Then relief settled over him. She didn't know about the man he'd killed. That was good. It didn't matter what she was talking about, because she didn't know, and he had just realized that he didn't want her to know. One moment she was intuitive beyond what was humanly possible, and the next she was utterly naive. If she imagined him saying some kind of prayer when he dug up a plant, she was mistaken, of course. As often as not he muttered his observations to himself, but there was never any regret. He was a scientist, for God's sake. And he hadn't committed murder, either. He had defended himself. There was no point in trying to explain that to her and no earthly reason for him to be so ill at ease.

"As you say, hunting and plant collecting do not constitute murder," he said in a calmer voice.

Since he had chosen not to hear what she said, she set her thoughts aside and asked, "Have you had much success with stealing?"

James was shocked. "What kind of a question is—"

"We need another horse."

"Oh, yes. A horse." He had stolen nothing but what was rightfully his, which couldn't be considered stealing, could it? Perhaps the Lakota would consider it stealing, in which case they would honor him for his single success. "Who could I steal a horse from?"

Kezawin smiled. "Anyone who turns his back for a moment."

He had already tried it once. They had come across a small band of people camped in a draw. Kezawin had identified them as Ponca, and she'd said that they would be an easy mark. When he asked why, she said proudly that the Lakota people with their cousins the Yankton and the Yanktonais had "moved those Ponca people aside long ago." James had sized up the little family band and decided he might be able to move the four women and the several youngsters aside—one or two at a time—but there were three men with them who might not be so easily budged. Besides, they only had four horses. He told himself that the Ponca must be close to their village, so they didn't need the horse he wanted as badly as he and Kezawin did.

Gauging the distance between the grazing horses and the breakfast camp fire, James had decided that he had the advantage of surprise. But stealth was not his strong suit. He had rushed his move and stampeded the horses in four directions, making his escape only because he was mounted.

After four more days of doing more walking than riding, he had decided to try it again. They had seen signs of a small party of horsemen in the area, and after they had made camp, James told Kezawin that he was taking a short ride. She had said nothing, and now as he crouched in grass that stood as tall as a horse's back and downwind of a five-man hunting party, he wondered at the trust she had shown him. He was loathe to have her witness another failure, but if he was killed, she would be left alone and horseless there on the prairie. He wondered whether it had occurred to her that he could decide simply to ride away.

But, then, she didn't know that he had run once before. She couldn't know the taste that running left in a man's mouth, the bitter taste of his own bile.

He had located the hunters' camp at dusk, then doubled back to the river and returned, having covered himself almost completely with mud. Night had fallen, and he smelled the fat dripping from the meat on their spit into their camp fire. The aroma brought out the claws within James's belly. He decided that when he got back to his own camp, he would break his fast. He'd eaten enough roots. He wouldn't make any explanations; he would simply take jerky from the parfleche and tear into it with his teeth. It had been an arduous march with only one horse and no time for hunting forays. Principles were fine, but a man had to eat.

But first he had to get the job done, and this time he wouldn't rush it. His own horse was staked just beyond the rise, out of sight of the camp. He was going in on foot this time. He felt a mosquito pierce the skin on the back of his neck. Mud offered some protection—although an occasional pest managed to penetrate—and also interfered with his scent. He covered the insect with his palm and silently pressed the life out of it. This time he would wait until the men slept. *This time* he would come away with a horse.

He closed in inch by agonizing inch, pulling himself on his belly across the last several yards. He used Kezawin's skinning knife to cut the first horse's tether. The animal went on grazing. The second horse took a few unhurried steps and found better grass. As James sliced the third tether, he thought of Kezawin again. When he'd asked for the knife, she had given it to him. She had not questioned him. She'd extracted no promises, nor had she offered words of caution or advice. Had she forgotten that he'd failed once? One more tether, he told himself. The fifth horse, the stout buckskin—that one had his name on it.

His heart leaped in his chest as he sprang onto the buckskin's back and let loose with a brash, irrepressible "Eee-yahhh!" The other four horses scattered as James bent close to the buckskin's neck and dug his moccasined heels into its flanks. The horse leaped and shot after them as though his hindquarters were tightly coiled springs. James heard the hiss of an arrow as it whizzed past his ear, but he fastened his mind on the rise. The buckskin's powerful hindquarters catapulted them over the top. On the downhill slope he stretched his gait, and James leaned off the left side and concentrated on the staked horse. He reached out, caught the rawhide tether and gave it a jerk as the buckskin careened past the docile old mare.

The tether became a firebrand as it slid through James's fist. "Eee-yahhh!" he yelled again, pouring the pain into his fury. The small wooden stake tied to the end of the rope smacked the curled edge of his hand, jerking the docile mare to life. Four horses galloped into the night, and two streaked after them.

Kezawin had their meager provisions packed and ready. They rode to put some distance between themselves and the victims of James's coup. Beneath a star-sprayed predawn sky they made camp, sheltered within a valley of stark, eroded clay mounds. A silty creek provided water for the horses. Kezawin examined the stolen buckskin as she picketed both animals where they might reach what tufts of grass were available. The stout gelding was painted with black streaks of lightning and signs of hail. His tail was bound with red deerskin, and a swatch of the same dyed leather was attached to his bit. It was evident that James had counted coup on a Lakota war party, perhaps a group of her Brûlé cousins.

Kezawin smiled secretly. His success was not to be underrated simply because he had raided an ally. They would have killed him if he had been less cunning, careful or quick. She would not make him feel foolish by telling him that he had counted coup on a party that would have helped them. James had earned his victory. She thought it would be fun to see those five warriors return to their village on foot and hear what stories they would tell their women.

"Boil enough meat for both of us," James hailed as Kezawin brought what scrub wood she had found. He clutched a strip of his shirt in his rope-burned hand. With his good hand he had dug a fire pit and surrounded it with stones, and his voice was full of exuberance. "I feel as though I haven't eaten in days."

"You know, James—" The firewood clattered to the ground, and Kezawin straightened with hands on hips. "I traded a great deal for you. I think I may generously permit you to boil the meat to suit us both."

James laughed and reached for the parfleche. "The world's best chefs are men, dear Kezawin, as you shall soon learn."

"I said *I may.*" She gave him a bright smile, and he saw her pride in him couched in her teasing manner. "It is more likely that I will decide to cook for us myself."

"I'm well on the way to purchasing myself back from you," he told her. He squatted beside the pile of wood and began breaking it into shorter lengths. "The buckskin is yours, and he is twice the horse your mare was."

"Yes, he is. Geldings are best for endurance, and the buckskin is as swift as the wind. That's why I can never ride him."

"But he's even tempered," James protested as she knelt beside him. He braced his hands on his thighs and looked at her with earnest concern. "You can't be afraid to ride him, Kezawin. Not you. I hid in the grass, waiting for the right moment, moving so carefully, all the while considering my choice. Of the five, I picked the buckskin, and I chose him for you because he was the best. You traded a buckskin away for me, and I brought you a buckskin."

"I traded a mare. She was dependable and pretty, but she was not a fast horse. A woman may not ride a fast horse."

"Why not?"

"A woman will make a fast horse slow."

He drew one eyebrow down and hiked the other. "How?"

"By riding it. If a woman is allowed to ruin a good horse, it is well-known that her family will suffer."

Her expression left no room for doubt. She did not question the validity of this time-honored discretionary measure. James considered the idea for a moment. It seemed a convenient way for a man to keep his wife's hands off his best horse, but for a man who had anticipated the light he might bring to a woman's eyes with the best gift he had to offer, this bit of folklore was annoying.

"I stole the horse for you," he insisted. "I thought you would be pleased."

"It was a bold, brave move. I will honor you with a robe painted with your story."

"*I* wanted to honor *you*." He gestured dramatically with his wounded hand. "You saved my life."

"Is this horse a gift, or is it payment for your freedom?"

"It's a gift!" he bellowed. He clamped his jaw shut and took a deep breath, searching for his rational self. "It's a gift, even if I do owe you my life. Right now the horse is all I have, and I want you to—" He extended his hand in supplication, and he saw the blood-soaked bandage. "I *stole* that horse," he reminded himself. He glanced up at Kezawin. "I'm offering you a stolen horse as though it were my own to give."

"It was a fine coup," Kezawin said enthusiastically. "One against five, and you had no weapon."

"In truth, I have nothing of my own to give you. Nothing that would express my—"

"You have your books."

He gaped at her. "My journals?"

She nodded.

"What would you want with my journals?"

The look on James's face reminded her of the proud man who had once offered the Double Woman Dreamer anything he owned if she would cure his wife's fever. She had named his Appaloosa brood mare, and his eyes and his mouth had become pinched. "What do you want with my spotted mare?" he'd asked. Kezawin had glanced at the man's wife, whose eyes were downcast, and she had agreed to accept one mare of any color.

She leveled her gaze at James. "What would I want with your swift gelding?"

"What would you want with a man?" he challenged. "Why would you buy a man, Kezawin?"

The question hung in the air between them.

"I can accept the gift," Kezawin said quietly, then added with a shrug, "but you will have to be the one to ride him."

"Fine." He snapped another dry stick and tossed it into the pile they'd made together, then struck the flint angrily and made sparks fly. "It's probably true," he grumbled. "You probably would make him slow."

James belonged to Kezawin now. The story of how Double Woman Dreamer had come away from the Skidi camp unharmed, bringing the plant-taker with her, gave strong testimony to the power of her medicine. The white man was hers to do with as she pleased, and the old ones noted that she seemed to put him to good use. Her medicine was clearly stronger than his, but he had something he called *science*, and along with that he used the white man's books. The wise ones speculated that if the white man was cautious enough, the deer woman might not kill him and Double Woman Dreamer's medicine might be stronger than ever. To that end, James the plant-taker spent long days with the medicine woman, but he spent his nights in Lone Bear's lodge.

He chafed under the invisible yoke. At first he made light of his indentured condition, but it was clear that he was expected to do Kezawin's bidding as long as he stayed with the Hunkpapa. He was free to move about the camp without any physical restraints, but he was not his own man. He owed Kezawin his time and his labor, and he was constantly aware that it was *her* work that he was doing. No matter that her work was exactly the object of his interest, it bothered him that she chose the time, the place and the means for it to be done. On more than one occasion it occurred to him that he might just walk away, and then he remembered the ways of the Skidi and decided he could serve a little longer as field assistant to Double Woman Dreamer.

James did his share of hunting and fishing, even tanning, but every task became more arduous as summer pressed on. The days grew hot, and no rain fell. Game ranged far in search of better grass. For those who gathered roots and berries, the harvest was meager, and those who gathered medicine needed a sharp eye and great patience. Stream beds shriveled and cracked like old skin as the river's network of arteries hardened for lack of rain. Men of vision sought high places, stretched their arms and cried to the sky. The grassy hillsides turned tan, and only the dust grew more plentiful.

The band had moved westward into the rugged Missouri breaks, encroaching upon Crow territory. Doggedly they followed the foraging game. Hunters went out in small parties—brothers, friends, fathers and sons—and James formed a new bond with Lone Bear, who showed him that squirrels and magpies made good meat on a day when there was nothing larger available. James came to enjoy fishing.

Impatient with pole fishing, Lone Bear recalled younger days when he could wield a pronged spear with as much agility as a bear using its own paw.

"The river is slow this summer, and the fish are sleepy," Lone Bear observed one afternoon as he studied the activity in the shallows. "They're not interested in your grasshopper, Garrett. There are too many grasshoppers around this summer."

James flexed his shoulders and scratched his back against the furrowed bark of his oak backrest. Lone Bear had set out enough snares to trap anything that dared to scamper among the trees that shaded the meandering riverbank. One way or another they'd have something to eat before the day was over, and James was content to have it the lazy way. He watched Lone Bear poke around a deadfall, and he assumed the old man was searching for better bait. "Grasshoppers are as good as grubs," James said, but he really had no preference.

Lone Bear found the long forked pole he'd been looking for, and he set about sharpening the prongs and carving barbed notches in the crotch. James ignored the project until Lone Bear handed him the finished fishing spear. "The best time to learn to fish is when the fish are lazier than you."

James sat up slowly. "Lazier than—"

"You can learn, Garrett. You're quicker than you used to be." The folds in his face rearranged themselves as he smiled. "And I've slowed down some."

James knew his scowl was wasted on the old man. He set his pole down and accepted the spear. "What am I supposed to do with it?"

"Take off your pants. It's too hot for them anyway."

James had not worn a shirt since Kezawin had brought him back from the Pawnee, but he clung to his buckskin breeches simply because he dreaded the final indignity of baring his legs. He'd taken to wearing a breechclout under his britches, and he was relieved when the sight of his pale legs elicited no audible snickers. Lone Bear motioned for James to wade into the water.

"Like so, Garrett," Lone Bear instructed, going through the motions. James saw the enthusiasm of youth hampered by an old man's body, and he was drawn into the sport by an urge to imitate, to do what the mentor had once done. He crouched the way Lone Bear crouched, and they waited together. When a fish approached, James lunged, splashed, speared, and the fish swam away.

"Is that how you made your coup on five hunters, Garrett? The fish are no less wary than they were. Try again."

Each try was a closer approximation of success. "Patience," Lone Bear repeated quietly. "Let him come to you. Welcome him. Welcome him. He will come."

James waited. When the water from the last splash stopped dripping, it was replaced by the sweat from his brow. He took a quick swipe at it and assumed his frozen stance once again. Out of the corner of his eye, James could see his trainer holding the same position, waiting. The sun pulsated on James's back, and a bead of sweat gathered at the tip of his nose. Between the pillars of his legs, into the shadow of the colossus shimmied a silver-finned fish. Silence, stillness, waiting, waiting...thunk! Lone Bear became the imitator as James wielded the spear to its mark, and both men whooped victoriously.

They shared a meal on the riverbank, neither complaining of the meat's silty taste. Lone Bear spoke of other summers without rain and the lean winters that followed. The notion troubled James as he imagined snow on the ground and hunger in Kezawin's eyes. It seemed incumbent upon him to provide for the three of them. His skills were sharpening, he told himself. He had proved that again today.

"Why did you let Kezawin ride into Pawnee country alone?" James asked without preliminaries.

"You were her friend. I told her of your capture because I knew she would mourn your death."

"But she came after me alone."

"Who else would go?"

It was a candid question, all the more chilling because the answer was, truly, no one. No one from this world, no one from the world he'd left behind. It took James a moment to find the will to press on quietly. "You should not have allowed her to go there at all. There was every chance they would have ignored the valor of her act and murdered her in some terrible way."

"How could I have prevented her from going? It was within her to do what she did."

"She's a woman, Lone Bear. She should be protected."

Lone Bear shrugged. "She is Double Woman Dreamer." He paused, considering the white man's challenge before turning it back on him. "Who dares threaten her?"

"She risks her own safety thinking this medicine will protect her. It's all she has." He chuckled humorlessly. "She has an aging father and a so-called slave, but everyone else is either fearful or disdainful of this deer woman thing, and she has no friends. Surely her father—"

"Who dares protect her, Garrett? You?"

"Certainly." Lone Bear's hard stare made James shift uncomfortably. "While I'm...as long as I'm..." He floundered, then added hastily, "I have no fear of Kezawin's dream. I respect her. I respect her as a healer, as effective as any I've seen, but I don't believe her dream can kill me. And I have learned that she is not a woman who permits—" No matter what James had learned, he could see that Lone Bear knew more, both about Kezawin and about himself. "She's a good woman," James said. "A daughter to take pride in. A woman to be respected."

"So you have offered more than protection, and she has left you alone in your blankets." Lone Bear nodded solemnly. "I have wondered how much there was between you."

"No more than she has allowed." James's very scalp was growing hot. He had never spoken thus with a woman's father, and he felt the man's eyes boring into him in search of his private thoughts. He tried to erase his favorite imaginings by clearing his throat. "We have a friendship, Kezawin and I."

"I rode against four Crow warriors to save a friend once," Lone Bear recalled. "But I don't know any man who would walk into a Skidi village alone to free a friend." He pondered for a moment. "Kezawin seeks to protect you from the deer woman, but perhaps the deer woman has no power over a white man." He smiled. "Or perhaps she has no taste for white meat."

James might have suggested that perhaps Kezawin herself had no desire for him, but even in his worst moments of frustration, he knew better.

Whether he rejected the concept of the deer woman, James could not deny that he saw two distinctly different Kezawins. Within the perimeter of the village, she stood apart from him even as they worked together. He had learned his part in each regular task and needed little instruction. They consulted over the medicine she made, took food in the traditional way with the men served first and stood together at the edge of the community's activities like marginal members. But when they were away from the village, foraging for medicine or food, Kezawin showed James a different face. Her private smile was spontaneous and unrestrained. A flash of that smile could make James feel like a different man.

One day they came upon a huge prairie dog town. As Kezawin and James reached the top of a grassy rise, the town below leaped into action. A rodent lookout yipped his warning, and all of his relations dove for the nearest burrow. Kezawin laughed and flopped on her belly in the grass, motioning for James to follow suit. Grateful for the protection of the buckskin shirt she had given him, he knelt beside her, then extended himself with all the indulgence of a weary elder. They had been walking all morning, and he could use the rest.

Stretched out side by side, they parted the grass and spied on the sprawling village of small earth mounds. Within a few moments, furry little heads began to appear. By twos and threes the creatures tested the air and nosed their way above ground. James glanced askance and saw the first inklings of Kezawin's smile in her dark wistful eyes.

"Your father would have his snares out if he were here," he suggested quietly.

"Not until the prairie dogs have put on a good layer of winter fat." The smile bloomed as she cast him a glance before scooting ahead for a better view. "Look, James. See how they tear their food with their hands and put it into their mouths like little people? They are one with us, and we would not take them without asking."

"And do they grant you permission to boil them up for supper?"

"The spirit of all living things grants us permission. *Sometimes*. Sometimes they get away, and we go hungry. But when we take them for our food, we ask them to nourish us, and they do. And we grieve for having taken their lives."

He rolled over on his back and folded his hands on his stomach. "If I'm going to eat them, I'd prefer not to become friends with them first."

"They are one with us," she repeated as though she were instructing a child. "Like the buffalo and the deer. Only a friend would give his life to nourish you."

"They don't ask to die."

"No, and neither do we. Some days are theirs, and some days are ours. We nourish them, too."

He thought of the proverbial fattened corpse fattening the worm, and he chuckled. "Do they thank you for it?"

"Yes. By feeding us. We are part of the circle."

He lifted his head and stared at her. He saw the rouged part in her hair, the white elk's-tooth earring lying against her brown skin and the light of universal insight in her eyes. *Only a friend would give his life to nourish you.* He rolled over again and propped himself on one elbow while he laid the grass aside with a careful hand.

The busy little animals had forgotten the intruders and returned to their activities. Some of the older ones had jobs to do—earth-moving, grass-cutting, nest-shredding—but others, especially the smaller ones, wrestled, chased one another, petted and played. Everyone found time to socialize.

"Do you see how they are?" Kezawin said excitedly. "They kiss, just the way you do. See that one? He reaches up with his hand and caresses the other's cheek, and they kiss and kiss." She giggled. "Such a funny thing to do."

"Look how they enjoy it," James said, grinning now. "Look, that one combs the other one's hair. She's smiling. She likes having her hair combed. See? She kisses him back."

"Ah, but he turns to that other one now and kisses her."

"And the first one will have none of it," James exclaimed softly. "She pulls him around by his shoulder, and there he goes, down on his rump. And the tussle is on!"

"The second one is no longer interested."

"She's too fat anyway. It's the first one he wants. Spirited little wench. She'll give him a run for his—" James looked at Kezawin and laughed silently. He had no Lakota word to finish the phrase.

"She'll lead him a merry chase?"

He rolled on his back again, grinning up at her, and lifted her thick jet braid from her shoulder. "As you do me. Let me comb your hair," he said as he untied the bit of leather that held it at the end. "Like the prairie dog, with my paw." She stifled a giggle. "Just between friends," he added as he loosened the plaiting from the bottom. "You have beautiful hair. I see that now."

"What did you see before?"

"I saw...black hair, thicker and blacker than any I'd ever seen." He undid the second braid and separated the three hanks before lifting his hands and plunging his fingers into her hair, lifting it away from her head. She smiled as he stretched his arms slowly, letting the rippled hair slide through his fingers. "You see how good that feels? Your friend unbinds you and sets you free."

"My hair."

"Your hair." He smiled. "It's longer than my arm."

She touched the wisps of sun-bleached hair that fell across his forehead. "Yours grows longer, too."

"Shall I let it grow?" he asked as he returned his fingers to their starting point to run them through her hair again. "Shall I braid it and wear a band around my head to keep it out of my eyes?"

"If it gets in your way."

"Comb it for me," he urged. "With your fingers."

Her fingers were shy at first, but they took more and more until she had a handful of thick fine hair. "It's softer than mine—like the back of a horse's ear. Or like beaver, close to the skin."

"And yours shines like the blackbird's wing. I thought of it so many times after I left."

She trailed a finger along his cheek. "You have a handsome face. I see that now."

"What did you see before?"

"I saw light-colored skin such as I had never seen, and I thought this would be fine for winter skin, to blend in with the snow, but in summer—" She shook her head. "Then I decided it was not so unattractive."

"Not so unattractive, hmm?"

Her eyes brightened. "And now I see the face of my friend, James, and it is a good face—a face that makes my own skin feel warm when I see it."

He smoothed her hair behind her shoulder and basked in the light of her eyes. "Does your skin feel warm now?" he asked.

She nodded.

"Mine does, too. See how we are?" He curved his hand around the back of her neck and drew her closer. "'He reaches up and touches the other's cheek, and they kiss—'" her lips touched his hesitantly "'—and kiss.'" Her hair fell to one side and made a curtain as his lips touched her hungrily. He took her in his arms and rolled over her, the look in his eyes no longer teasing. She saw the entreaty in them, and she lifted her chin and met his open kiss eagerly. He prodded her lips apart with his tongue, then flickered and flirted, coaxing her tongue to play with his.

"Such a funny thing to do," she whispered when he gave her the chance.

"If you laugh, I won't be able to do it." He brushed his lips against her cheek and inhaled the scent of dry grass and dewy skin.

"I won't laugh."

This time she parted her lips of her own accord, and he slid his body against hers as he rose on his elbows to approach her from another angle. It was as though his flint had struck steel. The spark that flashed between them set them both aflame in that nest of grass under the hot sun. They exchanged deep, probing kisses and writhed against each other, stoking the fire. They were melting together, blending breaths, tasting the salt from each other and harmonizing in urgent, elemental tones.

He wanted her. He'd never wanted anyone this much, so much that the deep physical ache made it impossible to remember how her clothes worked. He pressed his face against her breast and rubbed his forehead over the ridges of quillwork that edged her dress. He needed her. He slid his hands over her hips, letting the soft chamois skirt caress his palms and allowing the need to build. He lifted his thigh against the hardness of her mound and made her moan. He needed to feel her skin next to his. He needed to bury himself inside her, and she needed him to touch the deepest part of her.

"Help me, Kezawin."

His voice cut through the thick mist of desire. *Help me.* She heard his pain, and an image of blood gushed forth inside her head. She had pierced him somehow. She closed her eyes tightly and fought to control her erratic breathing. She would not let it be. She would *not* let it happen.

She gripped his shoulder. "She will not have you, James. I swear to you, she will not . . . I will not . . . *we* will not . . ."

He raised his head. His pulse pounded throughout his body, and his chest heaved against her. "Kezawin, I want to make love to you."

"Don't look at me, James," she begged. "Please don't."

It took a moment to get his bearings and steady himself. The woman in his arms was steeled for an assault, and he could have sworn moments ago that they were storming a castle together. He took her chin in his hand. "Open your eyes," he ordered quietly. "Look at me." When she complied, and he saw her fear, he smoothed the hair back from her face and whispered. "I would never hurt you, Kezawin."

"I know that," she said quickly. He pushed himself away from her, and she sat up, brushing the grass from her hair. "Are you in any pain?" she asked.

"Pain?" He felt damnably uncomfortable as he got to his feet and watched the prairie dogs scurry into their holes.

While his back was turned, she looked at her hands—yes, they were still hands—and quickly touched the top of her head. She straightened her dress as she stood up. "You were not . . . there was no injury, then."

He turned to her and let her see how it was with him. "You were once a married woman. I assume you've known the extent of a man's passion." She parted her lips to answer, but he spoke again. "No, there is no injury. No apparition maimed me in any way for daring to kiss the dreaded Double Woman Dreamer."

"You must not take her lightly, James."

"And you must not take me lightly! I am made of flesh and blood, Kezawin, not drowsy illusion. I walk on two legs, not four, and I have no twigs growing out of my head. I don't apologize for being a man rather than a rodent, and I *am* a man! Those poor dumb creatures are no brothers of mine. I am a man!"

He gestured as he spoke, but the creatures had been smart enough to take to their tunnels when he'd started shouting, so he had no one to point at but himself. He swung around, coming face-to-face with Kezawin once more. Her eyes were wide, and a sudden breeze riffled her hair, just as he had done with his hands. He reached out to touch it, and he lowered his voice.

"I am a man, and you are a woman, Kezawin. That's the way it is. For all your wisdom, you cannot find a way to change that basic fact."

Chapter Seven

As a toddler, Mouse Face Boy had been coaxed into a tree by his brother, Blue Heels. He had fallen and broken his hip, and the small bones had not mended properly. Blue Heels, who at the age of thirteen winters should have been spending all of his energies preparing himself for manhood, now devoted himself to his younger brother. It was Blue Heels who made certain that Mouse Face Boy seldom wanted for amusement or ample portions of his favorite foods, and who often carried the lame child about the camp on his strong young back. With so much attention from his older brother, Mouse Face Boy hardly complained, but the pain was ever-present in his hip.

Their mother, Many Plums, had tried to find ways to relieve the boy's pain. Her efforts to protect him had kept him closer to her than the Lakota believed was healthy for a boy of eight winters. Finally she took the risk of requesting the medicine of the Double Woman Dreamer. Mouse Face Boy happily reported that his hip didn't hurt as much after he saw the medicine woman, and he demanded her treatments regularly.

At first Many Plums forbade Blue Heels to take Mouse Face Boy to Double Woman Dreamer's lodge, but both boys objected to the separation. Like all Lakota mothers, Many Plums indulged her boys. And since the medicine woman had gone to the Skidi village and brought back the white man, her medicine had been widely praised. A boy might be safely treated by the white man under the powerful auspices of the Double Woman Dreamer. Many Plums instructed Blue Heels not to look the beautiful medicine woman in the face, always to stand near the door of her lodge and to see that when she came near Mouse Face Boy she did not touch his male parts.

Blue Heels watched from his post beside the door. The white man applied a warm poultice to his brother's hip, followed with a cooling compress, then repeated the process. The older boy saw nothing improper in the way the Double Woman Dreamer stood to the side and prepared the medicines to be administered to Mouse Face Boy, who remarked many times about how good the treatment felt. The white man gently wrapped and unwrapped the boy's hip while Mouse Face Boy told stories about the crow he kept for a pet.

Satisfied that his brother was not in any danger, Blue Heels began playing a game with himself. He dared himself to get a look at the Double Woman Dreamer without actually looking her in the face. He would stare at the floor for a long time, then let his gaze sneak up to her quilled moccasins, the fringed bottom of her dress, up the tail of her belt to her waist, to the yoke of her dress, and then he would try to decide which way her face was turned. She was beautiful from the neck down, but the beauty he saw each time he risked a glance at her face made him swallow and swallow, and still his mouth was dry. He had to give himself a moment before he started the game again.

James knew exactly what Blue Heels was doing, and on the one hand he sympathized with the boy. He remembered being thirteen and having sumptuous thoughts about his friend Raleigh Brown's older sister. Then, in the next moment, it galled him to watch the young man making snake eyes at Kezawin and thinking about her that way. He said as much after the boys left, although he tried to slide his remark off his tongue without looking up from his journal.

"Young Blue Heels has a case of what my mother used to call puppy love."

"What did your mother mean by that?" Kezawin asked as she hung her medicine bag on its peg. "You've told me that your people have some foolish taboo about eating puppies."

"Not like that," James said with a laugh. "Puppy love has nothing to do with puppies. It has to do with young boys. Blue Heels has lost his heart, and to an older woman, as most of us do the first time. The boy has excellent taste."

"He loves a woman?"

"He has the distressed look of a boy whose skin has gotten too tight on him. If he had gathered the nerve to lift his chin, he would have devoured you with his eyes."

Kezawin turned away from the bag slowly and scowled at James, who sat against her willow backrest scribbling in his journal. "I didn't look at him, James. You saw that. I said nothing to him."

"You didn't have to. He was completely smitten by your presence." He heard the tightness in his voice, and this time his chuckle came more naturally. "I had the urge to throttle him for his insolent thoughts, because I knew them so well. I would not relive those days for all the—" He saw the worry in her eyes. "Yes, I confess to having experienced the male urge to mark territory a moment ago. One male urge recognizes another. The young pup had thoughts of sniffing around, but fortunately for him he lacked the nerve."

"I did nothing unseemly," Kezawin said as if reassuring herself that she actually knew what had taken place. "Not once did I laugh or tease either of the—"

"Kezawin, when a thirteen-year-old boy sees a beautiful woman, he wants to gawk, and he wants to run and hide, both at the same moment. His impulses embarrass him. You did nothing unseemly, I promise you."

"It's good that you were here to see that it was so. I want no harm to come to those children." She sat down beside him on the curly buffalo carpet, tucking her legs to one side in the manner that was proper for a woman. As though she might be swearing an oath on the contents of his journal, she spread her hand on the page that lay open between his knees. "We can help Mouse Face Boy, you and I, but we must be cautious. He's young, and the medicine is strong. When he broke his hip, some bad spirit settled into the joint, and it gives him pain when he moves."

"We call it arthritis," he told her.

"A bad spirit with a name is still a bad spirit," she said with a shrug. "How do the white shamans treat this arthritis?"

"With no more success than you're having—in most cases, maybe even less. But I was thinking. In one of your pouches you have a root that you must have gathered east of here, one that I think we might try. We call it poke-root."

"You must show me the one," she said, her interest piqued. "I have stored some of my medicine in families, the way you explained last summer."

He smiled. "I noticed that you had. And I've been noting your names for plants in my journal." He thumbed through several pages and read, "*Pannunpala.* 'Two-little-workbags-of-women.' I like that better than *Asclepias speciosa*, or even 'snowy milkweed.'"

"It is good food," she said, returning his smile. "It is used when a woman's milk is slow in coming, but you also had it in your soup last night."

A voice outside the door interrupted them. "My daughter, I have news to tell you."

Quickly Kezawin made more space between herself and James. "I have tea ready."

Lone Bear sat on the man's side of the lodge and accepted the steaming bowl of herbal tea. Kezawin served James tea also, then took her place on the left side.

Lone Bear drank deeply and grunted his satisfaction. "*Ohan.* It warms an old man's throat."

"It has a touch of the food-of-the-elk," James reported, referring to the plant he had once thought of as bee balm. He knew that the tea's principle ingredient was lavender hyssop, which the Lakota called "leaf-that-is-chewed," but, according to Kezawin, it was the food-of-the-elk that soothed the throat.

"You are learning, my friend." Lone Bear sipped his tea several times more before he gave his news in the same tone he might have used to speak of the flavor of the drink. "Your brother-in-law waits for you in my lodge. He has spoken to me of marriage."

James's grip on his bowl faltered, and he scalded his tongue.

"Thunder Shield seeks marriage with me?" Kezawin asked, surprised.

"His medicine is strong, he says. He sees that your glances do not wither the white man, and he doubts that you would endanger such a one as himself." Lone Bear sipped again, then added, "He is obligated to bring his brother's widow to his lodge, he says. In a vision he was told that he must set this matter aright or things will not go well for him."

"*Tuki!*" James blurted out, and when he looked from Lone Bear's eyes to Kezawin's, he realized he had used a woman's expression instead of a man's. "Is that so?" he said, correcting the slip with an expression reserved for a man's use. He sought a tone as unruffled as Lone Bear's. "Did his vision forget to mention the deer woman?"

"No man dreams of the deer woman," Lone Bear said, dismissing the remark. "Thunder Shield's offer must be given careful consideration. You must speak with him." Kezawin nodded. She waited until her father had finished his tea, and then they left the tipi together, leaving James behind.

He plucked at a coarse curl on the buffalo rug and stared at the door. She had agreed to speak with the man, James thought. Nothing more. He took up his journal and his pen and reached for ink, jamming the point toward the target. He missed and tipped the bottle.

"Miserable damnation!" he muttered as he mopped at the spreading black stain. "Fortunately, the lady of the house has a slave to take care of such mishaps." Furiously he blotted and rubbed, blotted and rubbed. "She wouldn't marry that insufferable peacock;" he told the mess he'd made. "That's what she went over there to tell him. One wife is more than enough for that popinjay. Obligation, my ass."

He took up the pen again and tried to remember the process they had used to treat Mouse Face Boy. There was the desert chaparral Kezawin had gotten in trade, the chickweed and the bee balm. No, the bee balm was in the tea. There was birch bark. Yes, and milkweed. Two-little-workbags-of-women. Milkweed was in the soup she had made, not the poultice. A fine soup. He had brought home nothing but rabbit, but she had looked at him in that glowing way she had, and she had turned his catch into something quite delicious. In his thoughts he heard the word "home," home to Kezawin, and he found it a curious concept. He slept in Lone Bear's lodge, took his meals at a camp fire and helped pull up stakes and move at intervals he had not begun to be able to predict, and yet the thought had come to him naturally—home to Kezawin.

"Things won't go well for him," he muttered. "Miserable bigamist. I'll say, things won't go well for him."

What was that puffed-up prairie chicken saying to her now? Was he spreading his feathers and doing his courtship dance? Was he telling her that the size of the game was the measure of a man? What kind of medicine did Thunder Shield have, anyway? When was the last time he eased a crippled boy's pain? But here was Lone Bear with the news that Thunder Shield had proposed marriage, and off the woman went.

It's not important, James told himself, and he read the last word he'd written in his journal. "Weed." What weed? A weed is a weed. He barked a mean laugh and printed boldly. "'Frailty, thy name is *Woman.*'"

James had worn a path in the buffalo robe carpet by the time Kezawin returned. "Red Calf Woman told me about a place where I might find buffalo berries," she said as she reached for her picking apron. "It's a place near the river, and she says that it offers the shade from a western bluff in the late afternoon."

"Who is Red Calf Woman?" He'd aimed for an easy tone and missed the mark.

"Thunder Shield's first wife."

"His *first* wife," he acknowledged with a raised eyebrow. "How generous of her to share her personal berry patch with you."

Kezawin kept her head down as she tied the doeskin apron at her waist. If she looked up, she knew she would laugh. "We were friends when we were girls. I had no sisters, and she and I were like sisters then."

"I should think if you were wives to the same man, you would again become as close as sisters."

"Thunder Shield said that I would keep my own lodge because I have dreamed of the deer woman, and he would not wish to have me touch his weapons, his food or the place where he sleeps."

James slammed his journal shut and tossed it aside. "Interesting notion of marriage, this man has. Would he consummate it without having you touch his precious person?"

Kezawin took a deep breath and kept a tight rein on the threat of an outburst of laughter. "We did not discuss his precious person," she managed to say, still without looking up. "I suggested that he see to the needs of his wife's sister, Walks Slow."

"Walks Slow, too? Does that make you number three?"

"Thunder Shield spoke unkindly of Walks Slow. I'm sorry I made the suggestion, for I think he would treat her badly if he took her to his lodge. I pity Red Calf Woman for having such a one as Thunder Shield for a husband." She held a buckskin pouch out to him. "Will you pick buffalo berries with me, now?"

His heart felt lighter, but she had yet to tell him what he wanted to hear. "Will I? Does the slave have a choice?"

"The friend has a choice." With a woman's knowing smile she stepped closer to him. "Thunder Shield came to my father's lodge to get a second wife. He left with no more than he had when he came."

"You refused him?"

"If I could have another husband, it would not be Thunder Shield. He is without honor. He has a greater duty to marry Walks Slow than he does to marry me. Walks Slow does not learn quickly or in the same way other people do. She is *wakan* and must be protected, but Thunder Shield has no sense of his duty."

"And so you refused him," he prompted stubbornly.

She took his hand and pressed the pouch against his palm. "I refused him. A man without honor would be an easy mark for the deer woman."

"It is an outrage." James took the pouch, then caught her hand. He waited until she looked up at him. His quiet voice trembled now with indignation. "How dare he suggest such a demeaning arrangement to you? It is he who is unfit to share your bed, and I am personally insulted by his insolent proposition."

"It is Thunder Shield's right to propose marriage to his brother's widow, even though it is a foolish—"

"It is *not* his right to degrade you this way. If there were such a thing as a deer woman, she would curse him—"

Kezawin covered his mouth with a quick hand. The boldness of her action surprised her, but his words had to be stopped. "I refused him, James," she whispered as she slid her hand away. "Let that be an end to it."

"He should be horsewhipped, Kezawin. He should be challenged. I should—"

"Why? Marriage is easily offered, easily refused." She felt his desperation in the way he gripped her hand.

"The man has a wife!"

Kezawin lifted one shoulder. "He wants another one."

"That greedy, prideful—"

"I think Thunder Shield behaved exactly as he always does. I don't believe he was possessed when he made his offer." She frowned as she tried to recall every nuance of the proposal. "Still, it may have been so. Why else would a man propose marriage to the Double Woman Dreamer?"

James glanced through the cone above his head and took a deep, cleansing breath. "Men have been bewitched by beautiful women since the beginning of time. Thunder Shield is just like the rest of us, but he hasn't the decency to acknowledge the true source of your magic."

James's hand felt sure and strong on Kezawin's shoulder. She saw the fervor in his eyes, and she wanted to tell him that it didn't matter what Thunder Shield was like. James was a man whose strength matched her own. No other man made her see herself as a woman before she could remind herself that she was the Double Woman Dreamer. He refused to allow her to deny her womanhood, and there were times when she hated him for that. There were times when her femininity was an aching thorn in her flesh. But she knew that even as she hated him for keeping her birthright alive in her, she loved him more.

"There's magic in your eyes, Kezawin," James said. She looked up at him as if to verify the words, and he let the magic calm him. "And sorcery in your smile. If a man makes a fool of himself over that, it's his own fault, not yours."

"The deer woman does not visit your people?" she asked.

He shook his head slowly.

"No white woman has ever destroyed a man's medicine, taken his power and made him do her bidding?"

In his mind he saw an apple and a serpent instead of a deer, and some primal part of his male self instinctively avowed the guilt of women. But the deer woman was different, he told himself. Kezawin had to bear the burden of the deer woman alone because it was her dream. Yet she refused to be the noxious or even the capricious woman her dream gave her license to be.

"I don't think you can take my power," he told her. "I have given it much thought. It seems to me that the deer woman has no influence over a man who has no fear of her, and I have none. Why should I? The woman others know as Double Woman Dreamer saved my life."

"It was my destiny to bring you safely here, just as I led the white deer safely across the river," she told him.

"Why?"

"Why is a question that burns inside you like a hot brand, James. You know so many things, and still the question burns. Just know that it had to be."

He wanted no philosophy now. He caressed her shoulders, expressing his desire for physical answers. "I know you had your own reasons for snatching me from the jaws of your enemy."

I wanted to see the way the sky lives in your eyes, she thought. "It is true that I could not let you die at the hands of the Pawnee."

"Then you could not harm me yourself, could you?"

"I don't know." It was warm, and the skin of the lodge seemed to envelop her with him. "I have two faces, and I cannot tell—"

"You have one face," he insisted as he cupped his hand under her chin. "One lovely face, and, yes, it haunts me. You haunt me as no other woman ever has, but it's you, Kezawin. Not some evil spirit."

"You would tell me if you saw her in me?" she asked in a small voice.

"I would tell you." He stroked the cap her braided hair made. "Remember when I unbraided your hair?" A wistful smile was her answer. "I could free you the same way. I could teach you not to fear the woman who laughs without hiding behind her hand."

"It is not proper for a woman to laugh that way," she whispered as she watched his lips come closer.

"It seems proper to me." He kissed her softly, then brushed her lips with a plea. "Put your arms around me, Kezawin." When she did as he asked, he kissed her again. He touched her tongue with his, and she lifted her heels off the floor as she tightened her arms around his waist. Their kiss was hot and moist, like the air in the tipi, and he loved the heat. He wanted more of it. He peppered her face with the spice of his kisses and nudged her heavy braid aside to taste her neck.

"I feel this way whenever you kiss me," she confessed.

"What way?"

"The way a woman feels when her man is close." She slid her hands along the ridges of his muscled back and pressed herself against him, giving the molten feeling inside her leave to intensify. "If you were surely safe from her, I would be what you ask—proper or not."

He put his arms around her and held her close. "Not for him," he muttered fiercely. "For me."

"Only for you," she whispered into the pocket of his neck.

"Ah, Kezawin, I'm no better than he to tempt you thus." He rubbed his hands over the soft elkskin that covered her back and pressed his lips against her hair. "I have no bed to offer, and I live from day to day. Tomorrow is a dark and murky place. I cannot face it until sun chases the shadows away and it becomes today."

It was an emptiness within him that troubled her, but one from which she could not deliver him as she had from the

Pawnee. A man without a vision lived exactly as he had described. He was as vulnerable as a man who stood naked in the buffeting wind. All day long he sought knowledge, and he knew much about the world around him. But he did not know his place in it.

"It will come to you," she said. "You will wait, and you will listen. It will come to you."

What *it* was he could not imagine. Likely an ignoble end to a life that had once shown promise, which was nothing he would offer to share with a woman. He leaned back and offered an apologetic smile instead. "But the berry bushes won't come to us. It's cooler there, you say?"

"So I'm told."

As they emerged from Kezawin's tipi, the hot breeze felt good against sweat-damp skin. They walked among the gray-peaked tipis, headed for the opposite side of the camp and the river beyond. The village was quiet and lazy in the afternoon heat. They saw that Mouse Face Boy and Blue Heels had found a spot on the shady side of their mother's lodge, where they were turning dirt and water into a herd of miniature clay horses. James stopped to admire their work and to inquire about Mouse Face Boy's hip, which he learned was "not so bad today." Mouse Face Boy showed James his crow, whom he was trying to teach to say "Sapa," the name he had given the bird. Kezawin stood several paces back and enjoyed watching James with the boys.

Farther on, a breeze funneled itself between two tipis and made a little dust whorl dance across their path. James thought he might wash the dust off his body after they had gathered berries. Maybe before, he amended as he glanced back at Kezawin and smiled. Cool water would tamp a lot of things down.

"Where are you going in such a hurry with this slave of yours?"

Kezawin's step only hesitated, but she kept walking even as James stopped. Thunder Shield was best ignored, and such an impertinent question was not deserving of an answer. But James whirled to face him, and she knew that a woman's forbearance would not keep the peace this afternoon. She turned slowly and saw the telling stiffness in James's neck.

Thunder Shield was not alone. The stocky warrior stood near an empty meat-drying rack with two of his friends. The sun glistened on three levels of bronze shoulders, and their bare calves were coated with dun-colored dust.

"He waited for you in your lodge," Thunder Shield accused, jerking his chin at James. "I offered to make you a wife, but you prefer to take this white man to the riverbank and wallow with him in the mud. You are—"

"*You* are out of line," James growled. "And you *will* apologize."

"Stay out of my way, root-digger." Thunder Shield edged closer, while his friends stayed where they were. "This woman disgraces my brother's memory. Let us have an end to this pretense of virtue, Double Woman Dreamer."

James made certain that Kezawin stood behind him, where this foulmouthed lout could not touch her. He flexed his knees, ready to spring if the man should try. Thunder Shield squared his shoulders and puffed up his chest, approaching at a cocky angle. James watched and waited. The creature would slither. The creature would slide. *Welcome him. Welcome him.*

"I accuse you of many men," Thunder Shield shouted. Suddenly there was more life in the village than had been evident all afternoon. Heads appeared. Necks craned. Thunder Shield glanced this way and that, assuring himself that he had been heard.

"You have no proof, Thunder Shield," Kezawin said quietly. "I will bite the snake."

"Then you will be struck down for a liar, and I will be the one to—" Thunder Shield slid his hot gaze in James's direction. "You would dispute me, root-digger?"

"I would cut out your lying tongue."

Thunder Shield drew his knife from its scabbard and sidled like a preening cock. "You might try," he taunted, smiling, "if only your clout were not empty, like a woman's."

The two lunged, clashed and detonated the hot afternoon. They struggled within a circle of paralyzed fascination, no eye missing a trick, but only the combatants moved. They grunted with the strain of total exertion, muscle pushing against muscle for control of the blade, which glinted high against the neutral blue sky. A bare leg kicked up, and James tumbled, then rolled in time to avoid certain death. Instantly he was on his feet, and they circled each other, both sucking deep gulps of air and fine dust. Thunder Shield brandished the knife.

Kezawin watched in silent horror. She would permit no distracting cries of protest. In the heat of the sun, she felt the chill of death pass through her, and she dared not speculate. She dared not look away or even draw breath. She knew that James carried no weapon.

Thunder Shield darted, and James dodged the deadly blade. Another swipe left the brave open for an instant. James plunged headlong for his opponent's midsection. They grappled again, rolling and writhing in a tangle of limbs. The dust nearly blinded them both. Each reversal was met by an exertion of more will than wit. The knife was knocked loose and snatched up again. There was a thrust, a grunt and a sickening gurgle. Thunder Shield stared unseeing at the neutral sky while blood poured from the side of his neck and puddled in the dust.

Wretched, high-pitched keening split the sultry air. James stumbled backward, and Red Calf Woman took his place, flinging herself on her husband's body. With each heaving gasp, James welcomed piercing air into his lungs. Thunder Shield's chest was still.

James raised his arm and turned the bloodied knife over in his hand, staring at it as though it were something for which his brain had no name. Hoarse words came from his throat in English, and the name he uttered was one he had not called upon in years.

"My God." He looked around him, searching for something real, and he found Kezawin. Her eyes met his for just a moment, and then she lowered them and stared at her feet. He dropped the knife and stumbled toward the river.

A cloud of blood surrounded his right hand as he plunged it into the sluggish water. He ripped a handful of grass from the bank and used it to scrub both hands. He rubbed the wad of roots, dirt, spiky blades and bristly seed heads over his skin until it turned red and burned. His mind was as cloudy as the water, and all he could think about was cleaning death off his hands.

He knew she was there beside him, not because he heard her unhurried approach, but because he felt her beside him. He wiped his hands on his buckskin-clad thighs and turned slowly to face her. She knelt there, Madonna-like, her eyes glazed with shock and sorrow. Sick with shame, he turned his face away again.

"It happened so quickly," he said.

"Like lightning, a flash of anger unleashes its fury, and a life is over."

"I did not intend his death." Devoid of emotion, his voice was only a thin slice of its former self. "It was his knife."

"Your threat was empty," she said. "You carried no knife."

"It wasn't completely empty." He lifted his gaze to hers. A spark of heat returned to his eyes. "I wanted to rip out his tongue with my bare hands to stop him from lying about you."

"Then you *did* intend his death."

"No!" He dropped his forehead into his hand and tried to rub the throbbing away. "No, I didn't. I intended to beat him until he stopped taunting you."

"He was taunting you, James."

"He insulted us both." He sat back on his heels and studied her face. He burned inside with shame, and the look on her face somehow made it worse. He had done it for her. Didn't she realize that? Where was her gratitude? Where was her relief? Perhaps she'd not had time to realize either. "He insulted *you*. You are the finest woman I know, and I could not stand by and listen to that and count myself a man."

"Yes," Kezawin said quietly. "That is what he told you."

"What would you have me do? I was fighting for my life, woman. The man had a knife, and he was trying to kill me with it."

"I know. It was his pride against your pride, and yours was the stronger."

"The hell, you say! Since his pride got him killed, I dare say it was *his*—" He smashed his fists against his thighs, and his eyes flashed with his rage. "His stupidity! You said marriage was easily proposed and easily refused. How easy is it to kill a man! A man stands his ground, refuses to let another take what he values most, and before he can utter 'peace' and be on his way—"

"'Peace' was never uttered," she said. "But there was time for other words."

"I did not intend his death," James insisted. "It was he who sought mine. It was he who called you a whore."

"Which I am not. It is for me to defend my virtue, and I will do that in the proper way." She covered his fists with her hands and stroked them until they relaxed. "If he had killed you, I would have died, too."

"Then why do you judge me?"

"I don't judge you. A man is dead by your hand. Even though he would have killed you, now your own spirit grieves."

"I grieve for his widow," James insisted. "Not for him."

"Then I grieve for all of us."

* * *

Thunder Shield's family built his scaffold and mourned his death for four days. The men pushed small pegs into their arms and legs, the women slashed their limbs, and all of the relatives cut their hair. At the end of four days, the body was raised to the scaffold, and Thunder Shield's favorite horse was told to follow his owner happily. Amid terrible wailing, the horse was shot at close range so that it would die instantly, and its tail was attached to the scaffold. The wailing continued until friends led family members away from the bier.

James watched and waited for his punishment to be meted out by Thunder Shield's friends. No one spoke to him. No one seemed to realize he was there. Kezawin mourned, but as always she participated on the fringe of the community. She kept herself apart from him, and he thought it fitting that even the ostracized should have someone to ostracize. Surely they would punish him when all of this was over.

Perhaps they would both be punished. He began to imagine that he and Kezawin must be equally despised and that they would share some dreadful castigation once the funeral ritual was completed. He brooded as he watched the final proceedings from a lonely vantage point on a hill. The wailing had filled his head for four days, and he would welcome an end to the torment. He anticipated the moment when the community would turn to him and give him whatever they felt was due him.

Nothing was due him. No one came to demand an eye for an eye. No one spoke of the fight; no one called him a murderer. Finally, in the privacy of her lodge he admitted to Kezawin that he had fully expected punishment.

"You punish yourself," she said. "There were witnesses, and no one denies that you defended yourself."

Relief eluded him. He turned the news over in his mind, and he could not make sense of it. It wasn't finished. There was a knot in his gut that told him it wasn't finished. Perhaps the knot would be there until he was punished somehow.

"The trouble will pass," Kezawin promised.

James glanced up in surprise.

"At the river you said that you stood your ground when he tried to take what you valued most. What did he try to take from you?"

The dead man's name was not to be spoken. James's face became cloudy as he recalled that hot afternoon. "You," he said at last. He raised his brow and admitted, "But then, you don't belong to me."

She touched his shoulder. "The trouble will pass when you know what you value most."

Chapter Eight

The man who had questioned Kezawin's virtue was dead, and James contended that the question was settled. Kezawin's honor had been defended because Thunder Shield's lying tongue had been stopped. But Kezawin knew that the death of her accusor proved nothing. Her people honored virtuous women, and Kezawin wanted it known that she was virtuous. Most people pointedly avoided her because they feared her power, but no one had cause to accuse her of the kind of sexual promiscuity that tradition ascribed to the deer woman. She had waged a continual war with that part of herself, and she had never seduced a man. No one could claim that she had. Ten days after Thunder Shield's funeral she had announced that she would give a feast and make the ritual known as Biting the Snake.

"But this is madness," James insisted as he dropped wild turnips, one by one, into a pouch. "You are inviting them to humiliate you publicly and then dine at your expense."

Kezawin knelt beside a large rawhide bowl. The elk's teeth that were stitched to the yoke of her dress clicked softly as she worked her granite pestle over the dried meat in the bowl. "I have been accused of lying with many men," she reminded him without looking up from her work. "There will be much gossip and speculation until I hold the ceremony and put an end to it."

"Let them talk among themselves." He tossed another turnip with the reluctance of a boy who had to put his marbles away. "No ceremony in the world will put an end to gossip. People thrive on it." Plop went another turnip. "To stand up in front of these people and let them tell their fanciful tales as you propose to do is ludicrous. Who knows what—"

Kezawin lifted her chin and eyed him in challenge. "Do you believe that I have lain with men other than my husband?"

"Of course not." He loaded up the rest of the roots in one handful, then tossed the pouch aside with a sigh. "You have not lain with me. That much I know."

"And that is what each man knows." Snapping her attention back to her work, she mashed harder, twisted the stone and pulverized the meat and the words with studied intensity. *That much you know. That much you know.*

"But there will be lies told, Kezawin."

"Who would lie?" she asked tonelessly.

"Thunder Shield."

"The one you speak of is dead," she told the deepest part of her bowl.

"He lied about you, and two of his cohorts were standing by. They're still standing by to take up his cause, and each one will have a tale to tell, mark my words."

Kezawin sat back on her heels and balanced the rock against her knee. "If a man claims to have lain with me, he will pay the price for his lie when he bites the knife. The one you speak of did not bite the knife, and if he were here, he would not repeat his claim this day."

"Who holds the knife while the liar bites it?" James asked. He sat cross-legged, and he leaned in her direction with his forearms braced against his knees. "Perhaps I should have waited. All I ever wanted to do was cut out his tongue."

"A man who feels the knife blade against his tongue knows how close is calamity to the tongue of one who lies. One who speaks the truth has nothing to fear."

"And what about this biting the snake?"

She turned the mottled gray rock over in her hand as if she were inspecting it. The grinding end had been worn smooth. Her mother had used it, and her mother's mother before her. Honest women. Good-natured and industrious women, all, and their honor was never questioned. But the deer woman had not disturbed their dreams. Kezawin squared her shoulders and looked up at James. "I will swear that I am virtuous, and I will bite the snake."

"Good Lord, woman, I will not stand by while you put a snake in your mouth. There must be another—"

"It is important that you be present. You were mentioned. You must tell them that I have not come to your blanket." She reached for a stick and held it up for him to see. "This is the snake I will bite."

"Kezawin..." He shook his head, bracing his hands against his knees. His chest was bare, and he felt a rivulet of sweat trickle down his breastbone. "People lie. People who have something to gain will make all manner of claims. I have seen the way some of them go to great lengths to avoid you. You cannot believe that a piece of wood or the blade of a knife will mean anything to the people who treat you this way."

"Will you take the oath?"

"Yes. I count myself as honest as any man, and more so than most. But if I had taken you under my blanket and made love to you, as I've wanted to so many times, I cannot say that I wouldn't deny it if a small lie would spare you humiliation."

She watched a drop of sweat slip into the smattering of light curly hair on his chest. Last summer she had thought the hair on his body was unattractive. Now she had to pull her eyes away from his golden tanned skin and her thoughts from his reference to lovemaking. They must talk about lies and truth now, for his uncles had apparently neglected his education.

"What is a *small* lie?" she asked.

"One that harms no one. In a case like this, the lie would protect, and the truth would bring harm. What is between us is a private matter. It concerns no one else."

"But if you lied about it, *I* would know. I would see that your oath could not be trusted. And *you* would know," she emphasized, extending the hand that held the rock. "You would say to yourself, 'This small lie is not important,' and the next lie would come more easily. Soon neither of us would value your word, and truth would hold no meaning for you. You would be easy prey for those spirits that do mischief. And, of course, if we had joined—" she added with a shrug, "if we *had* made love as you say it, there would be no ceremony today."

"All right," he said, holding his hands up in defeat. "I see your point. But I'm not the one we have to worry about, am I? I'll gladly bite the knife and say the truth. But what about Thunder Shield's friends? What about his family? Some of them may have their stories already prepared, Kezawin. How can you be sure that everyone who attends this gathering will tell the truth?"

"Almost everyone I know will attend the ceremony."

"Exactly. And how do you know that every one of these neighbors and relatives of yours has the same high regard for truth that you have?"

"Because it is what they taught me."

He watched her add dried chokecherries to her bowl and grind them into the meat. After a few quiet moments, she lifted her soft woman's voice in a wordless tune that struck him as too cheerful for the occasion. He didn't really have a clear picture of what was to take place later that day, but he had been helping her gather food since yesterday, and he knew she planned to feed a crowd. He had seen her donate food to many a feast, but never had she hosted one herself. She was always included, yet never truly a participant in the festivities. Even though most of the people were cordial to her, there was always a mutually honored distance.

Now it was her chance to give a party, and she hummed a tune as she prepared for it. James thought his heart would burst as he watched her. In a few hours she would put herself on trial. Whatever the trappings, whatever the tradition, Kezawin's honor was at stake. She would tell the people what she had done and what she had not done, and she would ask them to believe her. If they shunned her, he swore to himself that he would rage at them for their blindness. He imagined her spreading the table before them. He imagined them eating her food, then walking away without a word of kindness for her. His lips parted on the thought of another plea, but instead he watched her spoon thick tallow into the mixture. She stirred it, and the scraping of the rock against the bottom of the bowl added an element of percussion to her song.

His thoughts drifted on as she sang, and he saw her, dressed in her beautifully quilled elkskin dress, submitting to the humiliation of a pillory in a New England town square. Next he imagined her sitting in a dunking stool of old, protesting her innocence while the townspeople jeered. And then he saw himself lurking nearby. He wasn't raging. He was mute. A proper Bostonian gentleman collared him. "Do you know this savage?" the man demanded. "She is a heathen, is she not? Has she been your whore?"

This woman a whore? This woman whose healing infusions make small miracles every day? This woman whose bright-eyed laughter is as musical as the song she hums while she works? I would sell my soul to spend one night in her arms, but she refuses me. Not one night. Not one sweet tryst by the river, not one gentle coupling.

Not one night, the top-hatted Bostonian said with a laugh. But what about a thousand, or a thousand times a thousand? What do you want from her, and what are you willing to give? And for how long, and at what price?

Think, Garrett. Would you make her your whore or your wife?

"I have not slept with her," was easily said. It would cost him nothing. For a man of little faith, "I would sell my soul" was easily said, as well. In his own way he denied her, and perhaps his way was the most dishonest of all. Would he take his empty oath and walk away?

Kezawin took up a handful of the ground mixture she'd made, and she studied James's face as she pressed the ball into a patty. "The ceremony troubles you," she reflected, "but it will show that I may still be honored as a virtuous woman. No one dares to lie and bite the knife or the snake, lest something hideous befall him." She looked at him curiously. "Your people have no such ritual?"

He slid closer and reached into the bowl. She thought he wanted a taste of the *wasna*, but she smiled when he made a patty and laid it in the parfleche next to hers. Many times she had told him there were things that, as a man, he need not trouble himself to do, but he seemed to enjoy busying his hands in her matters while they talked. Perhaps he had had no uncles to teach him the things that a man might do.

The slick texture of the mixture reminded him of his mother. He remembered thrusting his hands into her bowl when she made sweet cookies, and he remembered the stories she told that often ended with a trust-in-God moral. She, too, had been an honest woman. He concentrated on forming the perfect ball as he explained, "When a white person goes on trial, he must lay his hand on a Bible and swear that he will tell the truth. The Bible is a book made of stories about the white man's God."

"*Tos*," she said with a nod. "Yes, that makes sense. That person would not dare to lie after making a vow on such a book."

"If he does, he is charged with perjury, which is another crime."

"*Haho*, you see? A lie is not overlooked."

"Maybe not in court, but in other matters..." He squashed the ball flat between his hands. "People lie to get what they want. That has been my experience. That's why I came back." Her puzzled expression prompted him to continue. "I had intended to publish my work of last summer, but the man who put up the—who provided the supplies and the equipment, the horses, the..." He had words for everything but *capital*. "That man wanted to say that the work was his, which was a lie. It was my work, and it must be published as mine."

"Then you must offer a gift to the *eyapaha* and send him around to tell about this work. You will tell him to announce your name and not the other man's."

He smiled. "It must be published in books," he explained. "Many books, so that people will know what I have learned about the plants that grow here and how they are used."

"But this is your medicine."

"I would tell others about it, but I would have them know that these are *my* findings. Mine and ... and yours."

She watched his face color, the way it always did when he learned something the hard way, and it was her turn to smile. "You will announce my name, too?"

"Your name appears on every page," he confessed. "But lately I've wondered just how much I should tell."

"I've shared secrets with you because I believe these are things you were meant to know. And you have shared your secrets with me."

"They weren't secrets, Kezawin. Any naturalist could tell you—"

"Our medicine will not work for other shamans. I have my vision, and yours is yet to come, but who else can know these things? Surely not this other man. He cannot have our medicine. He lives in that faraway place you call Massachusetts."

"Yes, but he has a piece of my work, and he tried to steal more."

"If he makes this claim for himself, he will suffer some terrible loss. These things happen to those who make a public lie." She rubbed a greasy forefinger over the back of his hand as a gesture of reassurance. "You need not worry about this man. If he has no honor, there is no medicine strong enough to protect him."

Indeed, James thought, Breckenridge had suffered the loss of his son, and the memory brought with it another stab of guilt. Another life that he had taken. Another secret kept.

"You *do* worry," Kezawin said. "It's only because you do not understand. After the ceremony, you will."

It was the craggy voice of old Whirling Water that called the women to the center of the camp first. After they had gathered, she circled the camp once again, calling the men. Chosen for the herald's duty because she had lived a long life, ever faithful to her husband, Whirling Water walked among the tipis slowly and with great dignity as she invited every man to come forth and let it be known whether he had had sexual relations with any woman at the gathering who was not his wife.

James dragged his feet as though he were headed for a wake. The old woman's ominous intonations gave him a sick feeling in the pit of his stomach. Witch hunts were no longer a threat in the civilized world, he told himself, yet this ceremony suggested the makings of one. If the Pawnee sacrificed captives to their gods, what might the Lakota do to a woman accused of adultery?

The feast they had spent two days preparing together was spread on blankets in the center of the women's circle. James scanned the circle and found Kezawin sitting solemnly with the others. Her beauty struck him as a curse, for he could not doubt that every other woman in the circle must be jealous of her and every man covetous.

The men gathered outside the circle of women and waited until Whirling Water charged them with the duty to point out from among those women who were gathered any with whom they had been familiar. No one rushed forward. Agonizing moments passed, and James wondered how long it was necessary to wait. Surely they could all see that she was innocent. Lay it to rest now, his mind shouted, but he kept his peace and waited with his hands clenched together behind his back.

Then a man stepped forward. James drew a deep breath. Runs His Horses, a young man, tall, handsome—why this man? James had not noticed that he was a friend of Thunder Shield's. What was he trying to do? James scowled, and the pulse in his neck throbbed as he watched Runs His Horses slowly make his way around the inside of the women's circle. He walked past Kezawin, then reluctantly stopped, shuffling his moccasins in the fine dust.

"I met this woman, White Otter's Tail, at a wooded place in the hills. I have known her intimately."

James exhaled slowly.

Whirling Water handed Runs His Horses a knife, which he placed between his teeth. He repeated his accusations. All eyes turned to White Otter's Tail, the second wife of Four Strikes. The young woman sat with her hands folded in her lap and her eyes downcast. Whirling Water offered her a stick, but White Otter's Tail shook her head.

"Aiieee!"

James jumped at the sudden outraged cry. He turned just as Four Strikes shoved his way past the men who were standing behind James. The older man, who had counted coup many times and was well respected, stalked around the perimeter of the circle. White Otter's Tail's eyes grew big and bright with terror as she leaped to her feet and stumbled several steps backward. The crowd leaned in her direction as though she were suddenly possessed of a magnetic attraction.

Four Strikes snatched up handfuls of dried buffalo dung from a pile at the edge of the human circles, and others followed suit. Stunned, White Otter's Tail stood like the doe who was cornered by the hunting party and paralyzed with fright. They pelted her with filth until she came to her senses, turned and ran. A few men and women chased her briefly, hurling their odorous parting insults. That settled, they returned, and the circle formed again. Runs His Horses, who had simply stood aside while the crowd dealt with his former lover, returned to his place unchastised.

Whirling Water repeated her charge to the men, and once again silence followed. Have they had enough? James wondered. Or would one spectacle whet the crowd's appetite for more? If someone accused Kezawin, he would be unable to hold his tongue. He would take her from this place. They needed her; they came to her for healing, and what did she get in return? He would take her from here, and they would go... somewhere else.

Kezawin waited. She sat with her back straight and her head held high. The serenity on her face bespoke a woman who understood her values and had not compromised them. She would wait until they were satisfied. If no one spoke in her behalf until the moon rose, she would wait.

At last Many Plums came forward and bit the knife. She said that Double Woman Dreamer had made good medicine for her son, and she had neither seen nor heard that the medicine woman behaved improperly. Parched Mouth, sister to Many Plums, testified similarly. One by one the women at the gathering bit the knife and upheld Kezawin's respectability. The fact that none of them had been accused served as a commendation for them, too, and each woman came forward proudly to bite the knife, for it was because of her unchallenged reputation that her own opinion was held in high esteem.

When Kezawin's gaze finally fell on him, James knew that it was his turn to speak. He stepped into the center of the circle and took the knife.

"It was suggested that I have known Double Woman Dreamer in a sexual way." He surveyed the crowd, paying special attention to the faces of the two men who had been with Thunder Shield when he made the accusation. The dead man's name could not be mentioned, but he wanted them to know that he remembered. "I bite the knife and tell you that the suggestion is a lie. Although we have spent much time together, Double Woman Dreamer has never lain with me."

He looked back at Kezawin and saw that she held his journal on her lap and a hopeful look in her eyes. He understood. He took the journal from her, held it out and spread his hand over the cover.

"Among my people, such an oath is sworn on a sacred book, and Double Woman Dreamer knows that this book is sacred to me. Before all of you I swear that I have not been intimate with this woman." He looked at Kezawin now, and saw that her eyes were downcast. "I *have* known her, however." She looked up quickly. "I have known her to be a woman of amazing courage, for she faced her enemy alone to set me free. I have known her kindness, for she has fed me and tended my wounds, and I have known her wisdom, for she has instructed me." He scanned the crowd again as he lowered the book to his side. "I have lived among you for only a short time, and my words may not be worth much to you, but know this: Double Woman Dreamer is a good woman. In my experience, I have never met her equal."

When James had returned to his place outside the women's circle, Whirling Water handed Kezawin a stick to represent the snake, which she bit and made her vow. The people heeded her oath carefully, for if she swore that she would be faithful to her husband, she could not marry again. Instead, she swore that she had been faithful to her husband, and the people nodded and said *waśte*. They were satisfied. The men went on their way, and the gathering of virtuous women was left to share their feast.

The lavish feast had depleted Kezawin's stores and made it necessary for James to step up his hunting efforts. He decided to conserve his supply of powder and shot for winter and improve his skill with the bow and arrow. Lone Bear, his hunting mentor, was willing to accompany him on occasion, but more often he hunted alone. In the quiet hours of early morning or the time of purple twilight, he stalked the pronghorn and the whitetail deer, all the while sorting through his thoughts.

In the days since she had held her feast, Kezawin had not spoken of the ritual. James had wanted to broach the subject many times, but each time he held back, thinking that he would let her bring it up, and then he would question the sense of the whole procedure. No, he would question nothing, for he was prepared to lay down his civilized judgment regarding the behavior he had observed. Again, no, he would not judge, but he would present her with a scholar's objective views. As he repeatedly turned the event over in his mind, he began to realize that nothing was as clear to him as the fact of his own confusion. Kezawin had been exonerated. White Otter's Tail had been humiliated. Had he witnessed something sacred, or profane?

He had not seen White Otter's Tail around the camp, and he dreaded hearing any news of her fate. She was a *second* wife. If her life was similar to the one Thunder Shield offered Kezawin, was White Otter's Tail so wrong to do what she did? The memory of the onslaught of buffalo dung haunted him, and he knew it was not simply a result of his concern for White Otter's Tail, but the knowledge that it might have been Kezawin.

What if she had been accused, and the man had bitten the knife? She would have bitten the snake, most certainly, but whom would they have believed? The one who had counted coup in battle, or the one who had dreamed of the deer woman? When the scene flashed through James's mind, often he saw bits of filth strike Kezawin's white dress, lodge itself in her hair or break open on the side of her face. At the thought, he might clench his fists or his jaw and let an arrow fly, generally missing the target.

In the time they spent together, James and Kezawin spoke of the properties of various plants or the scarcity of ripe fruit. He suggested new ways she might use the flour she would grind from the root she called the Cheyenne turnip, and he talked of experimenting with seeding edible wild plants and returning the following season to see whether they had multiplied. Kezawin knew he had other things on his mind. He would speak of them when he was ready.

Then he saw White Otter's Tail, and what he saw sickened him. She was scraping a hide that was staked to the ground, and her hair hung about her face, unbound and swaying with the motion of her work. He *thought* it was she. He wasn't certain, because her hair hid her face, but he was curious enough to pause in his tracks and wait. Later he realized that she didn't know she was being watched, and then he felt like an intruder of the worst kind. But that feeling came when it was too late to withdraw, too late to spare her yet another moment of shame.

She sat back on her heels and wiped her brow with the back of her wrist. With a flick of her hand she tossed her hair behind her shoulder, paused, and then, as if she dreaded it but could not resist, White Otter's Tail turned her head slowly and looked at James.

Her eyes were bleak and cavernous, and the place where her nose had been not long ago was now a third empty black hole in her once-pretty face. For one long, awestruck moment, James could not look away. She gave him that moment. It was the public price that tradition demanded she pay, and she lifted her chin as if to invite James to gape his fill. The corner of her mouth twitched. For an instant she terrified him with the threat of a smile. He blanched, and when he gained control of his legs, he turned and fled, his stomach churning.

James sought Lone Bear out to tell him what he had seen.

"What would you do with an unfaithful woman?" the old man asked. It was another hot, dry afternoon, and

Lone Bear had rolled up the walls of his tipi on two sides and was lounging in the cross-breeze.

"I wouldn't have betrayed her in front of the whole community if I had been the one to dally with her in the woods," James insisted. "Runs His Horses should have kept his mouth shut."

"I see that you are of one mind with the lover, not the husband."

"No, I don't say that I would... Runs His Horses's behavior was hardly exemplary when he... But he compounded it by divulging his indiscretion in public."

"The deed was done. The woman had been unfaithful to her husband. It was Runs His Horses's duty to say that White Otter's Tail did not belong in the circle of virtuous women. It was Four Strike's right to cut off the nose of his unfaithful woman, for in that way he can be certain that no other man will want her."

"Why didn't he simply leave her or send her away?"

"He could have divorced her," Lone Bear agreed. "He chose not to. She is free to leave him if she wishes."

"He could as well have shot her," James muttered. "It might have been kinder."

"Such things have been known to happen. I have also known men to kill one another over women." He shook his head. "These things are not good. They cause hearts to harden and cousins to take sides against one another. Better to cut off the woman's nose and have done with it. The women will think about this for a long time to come." He offered James a strip of jerky to chew on and keep the mouth moist. "How does the white man punish the woman who is unfaithful?"

It was an embarrassing question. "We don't cut off her nose," was the best James could think of to say for his kind. He ripped off a bite of the chewy meat and held it in his mouth, savoring the gamy flavor.

"There is no punishment, then?"

"I wouldn't say that. Adultery is certainly not..." He would have to confess that most men would assert the right to mete out some punishment before they left the faithless baggage and shot the lover, but somehow none of that seemed as bad as cutting off the woman's nose. "But, you see, we are permitted only one wife—one at a time, that is—and we try very hard to keep that wife quite satisfied."

"And are the white men satisfied with one woman?"

"Well, yes, they are." He rolled the jerky to the other side of his mouth. "Most of them. Some of them."

Lone Bear laughed. "A warrior is always questing, is he not? It is for the woman to guard her virtue. That is what the women tell the young girls. A virtuous woman is honored by her people. She attends the feasts for virgins before she is married, and later, if she has been faithful to her husband, she sits in the circle with the most honorable women. One who defiles the circle will be denounced, as you have seen."

"It could have been Kezawin," he said aloud for the first time. "Anyone could have made a false claim against her, and who could have proven him wrong?"

"Make a false claim and bite the knife?" Lone Bear's expression indicated that the idea was too outlandish to consider further. "I had only one wife," he reported. "One wife was enough for me. She sat in the circle of the most honorable women all her life. One wife, if she is a good worker and produces children, is enough for most Lakota men. More than that—" He dismissed the notion with a wave of his hand. "Too much squabbling. As you say, keep one wife satisfied. Women are demanding. You can't please two. Four Strikes was asking for trouble if you ask me."

One woman was all the trouble James could handle. She filled his mind and left room for little else. The summer celebrations wound down, and the Lakota began separating into smaller bands. James hoped that fewer people might mean more time alone with Kezawin as the Hunkpapa divided itself into smaller groups. But fall meant more foraging, more hunting, and in a lean year the tasks consumed all efforts. James had to content himself with working near Kezawin, watching her and thinking how good it would be to hold her again.

He made a fair showing in the fall hunt, bringing down two cows and a young bull from a herd that the dry weather and sparse grass had thinned. He stayed to help Kezawin and Lone Bear with the butchering and traded commentary with his neighbors over the work. The success of the hunt lent a festive atmosphere as the people labored over the carcasses that were strewn about the dull brown flat. Part of James's kill was claimed by tail-tiers, and he saw that it pleased Kezawin when he stepped back and invited her relatives to share.

Lone Bear boasted that his white protégé had finally acquired some useful skills, and that he also showed promise of becoming a medicine man, perhaps not a *wicaśa wakan* like himself, but a *pejuta wicasa*—a man of herbs. James might have taken exception to the idea that he was only "promising," since he was highly educated in that area, but he said nothing disrespectful. Coming from Lone Bear, "promising" was complimentary, and James was given the opportunity to bask publicly in the old man's approval. Again he saw the satisfaction in Kezawin's eyes.

The hunters feasted with their families, and everyone danced in celebration that evening. Buffalo dancers reenacted the day's events to the compelling heartbeat rhythm of the drums. For the first time, James felt that he, too, must dance to celebrate the people's good fortune. The power of the drum made his blood surge, and the life force within him was immediate in a way he'd never known before. Time and space were nonentities. James was not an individual. He danced as one of the hunters.

With thoughts of cold water on his mind, James stepped out of the circle of bright firelight and into the darkness. Someone wrapped in a blanket came toward him. Even

before his eyes adjusted to the dark, he knew it was Kezawin.

"The women's dance circle is one short," he told her.

"I have been dancing." She nodded toward a spot just
outside the circle. "You were too caught up to notice.
That's good."

"I'm thirsty."

She led him to her lodge, ducked inside and returned with
the buffalo's bladder that she'd filled earlier from a spring.
He tipped it up and let the cool water run down his neck as
he drank. In a moment he knew he would feel the night
air's chill, but now he was hot from the dancing. When he'd
had enough, he handed her the bag, but he wasn't ready to
go back to the dance.

"There's been so little time for us lately," he said.
"Couldn't we just talk?" He glanced around. White
moonlight brightened the camp, and the conical lodges became dark shadows against the night sky. There were embers in several fire pits, and they were within view of a circle
of four of the older men who were sharing a leisurely pipe.
Down the way a pair of men's moccasins stood toe-to-toe
with a pair of women's moccasins beneath a sheltering
blanket. James's eyes glittered with childlike excitement as
he looked down at her. "Let's try that."

With a smile she handed him her trade blanket, and he
held it over their heads, surrounding them with a dark curtain. The drumbeat faded into the background as the duet
of their breathing filled the improvised tent.

"It's a small blanket," he whispered. "Come closer and
put your arms around me."

"It's not a small blanket." Still, she did as he asked.

"What are we permitted to do in here?"

"Talk."

"That's all?"

"Nuzzle."

"Nuzzle?"

."You know—" She stood on her toes, stretched her neck and rubbed her cheek lightly against his. Her eyelids passed across his lips, and her lashes tickled the corner of his mouth. He got the idea. They made circles and lazy eights over each other's faces with their noses, touched foreheads, inhaled the warmth of each other's breath.

"Nuzzling is nice." Her eyebrow was a small soft pelt for his lips to stroke. She pressed her lips, warm and moist, against his neck. Sweet torture, he thought. These people loved to test the limits of their endurance.

"Let us be prairie dogs," she whispered.

He glanced up. There was an opening above his head, and he could see stars. They could have been prairie dogs, bedding down in their tight, cozy burrow for the night. "You mean we are permitted to kiss?"

"Our feet are firmly planted on the ground, and no one sees our faces."

With his arms held high, he made love to her mouth, tilting his head first to one side, then the other. His kisses were alternately tentative and bold, and she responded with a shy nip or a flirtatious tongue. For James it was at once delicious and infuriating.

With a pathetic groan he broke off kissing her. "A man must have arms made of steel to court a woman thus."

"A Lakota man has mighty shoulders and strong arms," Kezawin said with a sigh. She slid her hands up to his shoulders and kneaded them. "When he can no longer hold up the blanket, the next suitor gets his turn."

James took a quick peek outside. "No competition tonight. It's a good thing, too." Lowering his arms was almost as painful as holding them aloft, and he groaned with the effort. "I think this is a sport for younger men."

"Is it so for white men, too?" He gave her a puzzled look as he draped the blanket around her shoulders. Pulling it snugly about her body, she explained. "Sometimes I think it is a sport for men, like a horse race, or... or even like a horse raid. Many parents tie a belt around their daughter's waist and pass it between her legs to discourage the young men. A maiden must be chaste before marriage, or she will be found out and bring shame upon herself and her family."

"And I have witnessed what happens to a married woman."

On a silent agreement they strolled at the pace of two who had no desire to be anywhere else. "I cannot help feeling sad for White Otter's Tail," Kezawin said.

"Why didn't she stay away from the ceremony?" It was one of the questions he'd pondered the most since the incident had happened.

"If she had, then Four Strikes would have challenged her. We all know who sits among the honorable women and who does not."

"She was trapped, then," James surmised. "I should think it would have been preferable to face her husband in private."

"Perhaps she hoped Runs His Horses would not be there. Perhaps the other women said, 'Come, White Otter's Tail. Let's go to the feast,' and there she was. Unable to hide. Unable to say that she did not hear the call. Trapped, just as you say." Kezawin shook her head sadly. "It must have been a bad time for her."

"Not as bad as what followed."

"Four Strikes has not divorced White Otter's Tail," Kezawin pointed out. "Her family would have little pity for her if she were sent back to them after such a disgrace."

"And there are no consequences for Runs His Horses?"

"He will not be considered for *akicita* membership. When men fight over women, it is not good for the people. A man who causes bickering and bad feelings loses face. A woman, too."

"Cutting off someone's nose seems a harsh punishment," James said, but the indignation he meant to express was lacking in his tone. The more he thought about it, the less willing he became to set himself up a judge.

"What would your people do?"

"Don't ask me that. I've thought about it a great deal since I talked about it with your father. My people don't compare favorably, I'm afraid. I put myself in Runs His Horses's place, and I cannot say that I would have played by the rules."

"The rules? You see, it *is* a game."

"Sometimes," he admitted. "And games are played for amusement. It's best not to let the game get out of hand—a lesson one learns as a child when things get rough and someone gets hurt."

The drum pounded out the rhythm of a grass dance, and Kezawin's heartbeat tagged along. "Are we playing a game?" she asked quietly.

"Last summer I was full of games. I thought you were beautiful and fascinating, and I wanted you. I thought that this dream of yours was the only thing keeping us apart. A year later..." So much had gotten out of hand, he thought. So many things had gone too far. For a scholar, he seemed to require many lessons, and he wasn't even certain what he had learned.

No, that wasn't true. He was sure of one thing. "I killed a man because he wanted you the same way I wanted you. I know now that I might have caused you more harm by loving you than his demands and accusations could ever cause. Your virtue protected you from the harm he would have done. I might have taken that from you."

"I might have given it up," she said. "If I had, it would have been my choice. I have no husband. No one would have cut off my nose." They had reached a stand of plum bushes, and she stopped and turned to look up at him. "I know that you spoke from the heart when you praised me before the people. I was honored when you said those things. When you called me a good woman, I knew that it was so."

"Never doubt it." He started to touch her cheek, but he sensed that the night had eyes, and he drew his hand back.

"Sometimes," she said in a soft shy voice, "the heart makes its own rules. I care for you, James. Respect is a good thing. Honor is a good thing. But I cannot close my eyes at night without recalling the way I feel when you touch me. And when I think of it, I try to feel that way again just by remembering. I try to bring you close to me in the darkness."

He stepped as close as he dared, instinctively protecting this intimacy. "I've done the same," he whispered. "In the quietest hours I've thought of going to you. I've told myself I wouldn't wake you. I would only watch you sleep."

"You would have found me awake."

"I would not have forced—"

"You would not have had to. I—" She lifted her chin and told her secret softly into the hollow of his neck. "Sometimes I think of you, and I touch myself because I—"

"Ah, Kezawin, I thought I was the only one who—"

"Would the deer woman make me do that?"

"If there is such a creature, she's going to make us both crazy by keeping us apart. I want to marry you, Kezawin." Once the words were out, he knew it was, indeed, what he wanted, even though he had dismissed it as an impossibility each time the idea had occurred to him. What could he promise her?

"You want to touch me, James. Beyond that, you have no vision."

"And you?"

"I want you to touch me, and beyond that . . ."

He drew her behind the bushes before she could say another word. Her blanket slid to the ground, and he caught her in his arms and held her close, because he wanted her to feel the extent of his need for her. If nothing else, their needs were complementary.

"I'm not playing any games with you, Kezawin. I can't go on like this. I keep thinking that we are inhabitants of two different worlds, but I can't think of living in either one of them without you anymore. I'll do whatever I have to do to prove myself to you. I'll have a vision, if that's what you want.''

She drew back from him and laid her hands against his roughened cheeks. ''There's nothing I require, James. I care for you, and that is that.''

''Enough to be my wife?''

She closed her eyes and willed the deer woman to go away so that she could tell him yes. ''I am barren,'' she warned in a hoarse voice.

''You had no children with your first husband. Perhaps I can give them to you.''

She looked at him again, and she allowed herself to wonder whether it might be possible. In the dark she saw the spark of promise in his eyes. ''You must perform *inipi* for your own sake, not for mine. Cleanse yourself, James. Be certain this is right for you.''

Chapter Nine

He had tried it once before, and nothing had happened. He had nearly choked on the smoke and produced a bucketful of sweat. A year ago the *inipi* ritual had opened James's pores, but not his mind. But he decided to try it again, and when he did, he agreed to do it, not for Kezawin, but for himself. He had long held that something was missing in the context of his life, and no matter how hard he studied or worked or strove, it was still missing. Of late he had considered the possibility that something was missing within him.

He wanted it to be something concrete, something he could simply identify, acquire and add to himself. Something like a wife. Kezawin refused to let the solution be that simple. He believed that she cared for him, but there were times when he sensed that she also pitied him, as she might pity someone who was missing a limb. Even as his respect for her increased daily, so did her sympathy for him. He didn't like it. He knew damn well what she thought he was missing, and the fact that he even wondered whether there might be a shred of truth to this exotic idea made the scientist in him uncomfortable.

He had once scoffed at the notion that this medicine, this personal power her people prized so highly, might be something he lacked. His confidence had been unshakable at a time when he was certain he knew more than they knew about almost anything of real import. He had documents to prove it. In their primitive innocence they were unimpressed with his great wealth of knowledge. They were unenlightened, he told himself.

And yet, he was lacking something, and he had begun to feel the lack inside himself. The lack *of* himself. His life had been a series of severances, a chopping of ties, one by one. He was disconnected. He was drifting. There were times when he thought he might be within reach of a mooring, but he drifted away again. Finally he explained his frustration to Lone Bear and asked the medicine man to perform *inipi* for him once more.

It had been a warm autumn day, but the night chill was sharp. James had not been allowed to help with the preparation of the beehive-shaped sweathouse, and Lone Bear seemed to take each step with excruciatingly slow deliberation. James was anxious. He wanted to get on with it. But the placement of every detail was crucial to Lone Bear, and he would not be hurried.

The willow frame had been covered with hides, and a pit had been dug in the center of the hut. Lone Bear handled the dirt carefully, using it to form a path from the small round house and a little mound at the end, which Lone Bear termed *unci*—grandmother. He covered the floor of the hut with sage.

Kezawin had gathered the cottonwood for the fire, and it would be she who would tend the fire and roll the stones into the lodge, just as she had for James's first *inipi*. This time James gave more attention to the elements of the ritual, and Lone Bear responded to James's interest by explaining each step. He had chosen the stones carefully. He called them ''bird stones,'' and showed James that they were dull, earthy, never shiny, and that they had designs on them like quillwork. They were too hard to burst in the hot fire.

The lodge's entrance faced west, and on that side Lone Bear placed a buffalo skull and built a small rack where the pipe would stand. James was told to place six small bundles of red willow bark tobacco near the skull as his personal offering. Kezawin filled a quilled deerskin bag with spring water. Outside the lodge, the coals in the fire pit burned red-hot, and the stones were ready. James savored the night breeze on his face as he waited for Lone Bear to call him into the lodge. He shivered with anticipation. When the word was given, he set his breechclout aside, crouched and entered the earth's womb like one of the four-legged ones. The flap dropped behind him, and the world became small and dark.

Lone Bear had purified the interior with an incense of sweet grass. Six rocks came in under the flap, one by one, glowing in the dark like red meteors on their way to the center pit, the very core of the earth. Lone Bear chanted as he tossed finely ground cedar, which made a shower of minute white sparks over the rocks. He lit the pipe, smoked, then passed it to James. They rubbed the smoke over their bodies. Lone Bear's chanting continued while he dipped sage into the cold water and sprinkled it over the heated rocks. The steam hissed as the rocks exhaled earth's breath, and Lone Bear sang," *Tunkašila*, grandfather, *hi-yah, hi-yah*."

James relaxed in this dark private place while the smoke crept up on him. Lone Bear talked with him of mundane things, then chanted and sprinkled more water. Kezawin pushed more rocks inside, and the process continued until James was suddenly overwhelmed by smoke and steam. His first instinct was to defend himself against it as he had a year ago—to take shallow breaths and concentrate on getting through this with a minimum of discomfort. But this time was meant to be different. He took a deep breath, and the heat seared every organ in his body. He coughed and groaned, but he refused to give in to his body's protests. Slowly he sucked in another breath. This time he felt the soothing penetration of something warm and moist, something life-giving. He exhaled and filled himself again.

Lone Bear recognized the sound of one who had just re-lived his first breath. It was at once painful and exhilarating, and the newborn one would gorge himself like the man parched for water, until he fell on his face. Before that happened, Lone Bear lifted the flap and gave James a breath of cooling air.

"When you need air from the outside," Lone Bear instructed, "say *mitakuye oyasin*. All my relatives. Say that when your lungs are ablaze, and we will help you."

Lone Bear's singing continued, and James joined in. They smoked and spoke of the good feeling it gave them to be there together. Each time Kezawin pushed a rock beneath the flap, they said *pilamaye* in recognition of her participation.

"She shares this with us," James said.

"Yes. She is with you."

"Mitakuye oyasin."

Each of the four directions was honored with smoke and beseeched in prayer. James had a sense that the earth breathed power into him. Each breath seemed to inflate him, both physically and mentally, so that there was more room inside him for meaningful things.

Hope. He wanted to offer what he had learned in some useful way. Lone Bear prayed for this.

Sorrow. He told Lone Bear that he had taken two human lives, and the faces of those men haunted him. Lone Bear prayed for this.

Joy. James spoke of Kezawin and the life he wanted to make with her. Lone Bear prayed for this, also.

Gratitude. He had looked death in the eye four times that he could name, and his life had been spared.

"Recite them," Lone Bear instructed.

"I contracted an illness as a child," James recalled. "Many died. I lived."

"Tunkašila."

"A man came to my room to take what was mine. We fought. He died, and I lived."

"Tunkaśila."

"I fell into the hands of an enemy. A man who was with me died at their hands, but a friend risked her life to save mine."

"Tunkaśila."

"A man threatened to take my woman's good name. We fought. He died, and I lived."

"Tunkaśila."

Naming his closest brushes with death gave James a heady feeling. Four times. Was it four escapes, or four times delivered? Lone Bear credited God. Was it God or luck? James had never been much of a gambler. If it was luck, then there was no order, no guide, no reason, but if there was a divine hand in all this...why? Why James Garrett?

"Will it come to me here?" James asked. "Tonight?"

"Will what come to you, my good friend?"

"Some kind of answer."

"Not if your question is 'why?' Such an impudent question will echo in the hills, and *Tunkaśila* will shake His head, and the *Taku Wakan*, the kindred spirits, will not speak."

James bit off the question and laughed. "Maybe 'why' isn't the right question this time. Maybe it's 'who' and 'what.' Who am I? And what am I supposed to do?"

"Those are two questions, my friend. You seek a vision, and for that, you must go to the hill. *Hanble ceya.*" In the dark there came another steamy hiss. "First things first. Here you cleanse yourself. You prepare. When you are open to the answers, they will come to you, but be ready. Sometimes we are unprepared for the answers we receive, and we want to throw them back."

"It would be a relief to know."

"A relief from what?" Lone Bear asked.

"Uncertainty."

"Your vision will not make you *Tunkaśila*. You will always be uncertain because you wear the fragile flesh of a man. But there are four living parts to your soul, and one of those parts will allow you to be the best man you can be if you understand it properly. You have been given great gifts. When you know those gifts, as I believe you truly do, you know who you are. Go to the hill and find out how to use them."

Both men left the lodge together and bathed in the spring-fed pool that was just down the hill from Lone Bear's tipi. James's heart was as light as his head, and the cold water made his skin sing. "I'm ready now," he said, his voice charged with enthusiasm. They wrapped themselves in wool trade blankets and returned to the tipi, where they found Kezawin waiting.

It was as though she had known James's decision before he had made it. That didn't surprise him. This night, all sounds seemed to harmonize, and all thoughts seemed to point in one direction. She had made a fire and had meat simmering. Lone Bear would eat, but James would not. They all went inside together.

"I have made this for you." The buffalo robe Kezawin held up for James's inspection was decorated with strips of quillwork done in red, yellow and black geometric designs. "It is the hide from your first kill. It will keep you from the cold."

James let the trade blanket slide to the floor. He was naked, but this was not a time when it mattered. Kezawin walked behind him and wrapped him in the robe. She came back with another gift.

"I have filled this gourd with four hundred and five small stones," she said. "One stone for each different kind of tree. Take your brothers with you." She handed him the gourd, and James's academic mind automatically raced to count species of trees. Another part of him, a part he had only recently begun to heed, told him to stop counting. Trust that there are four hundred and five trees in the land the Sioux bands walk, and believe that Kezawin knows every one of them.

She unsheathed her skinning knife. "You will take something of me with you, also."

She pushed her wide sleeve up, hooked it over her left shoulder and poised the knife on her upper arm.

"Kezawin, no!"

Lone Bear laid a steadying hand on James's arm. "Hold the gourd and let her fill it with her sacrifice. She will give forty pieces of her skin to help you."

She had already sliced one small bit from her arm. James extended the gourd and watched her take the skin from the point of her knife and add it to the collection of tiny stones. She repeated the process until her arm ran red with streams of blood. In his anguish, James felt each bite of the blade. In her self-denial, Kezawin did not.

Lone Bear led James to a hilltop not far from camp. It was not the hill that he had used so long ago, for they were far from the campsite where many Lakota medicine men had gone to the hill for their first visions. But it was a place that had been the site of other *hanble ceya*, for the small pit had been dug and dug again so that even the harshest elements never completely erased it. Lone Bear gave James a pipe before he turned and made his way back down the hill. Wrapped in his robe, James nested in the earth's curved palm. He listened to Lone Bear's footfalls until they faded in the night, and he thought he was alone.

He sat still, cradling the gourd with its precious contents against his naked belly. The night wind whispered in the grass. A small creature scurried across a barren stretch of ground just below him, and suddenly a winged silhouette swooped from distant heights, stretching clawed feet to snatch and hold. There was a squeak of terror, but the night bird, wings outstretched, hardly broke stride as it pushed off with a single unruffled stroke.

James's head was still light from the sweat bath, but he was no longer empty. The wind, the grass, the small gopher and its powerful predator had each taken a place in him. But there was room for more. He smoked the pipe, praying to the four directions and the earth and sky as Lone Bear had instructed him to do. Then he cleaned the bowl carefully. His belly was empty, and the bowl reminded him of food. He realized that he had no physical hunger. His head was lighter now, airy with the smoke. Smoke was *wakan*, Lone Bear had said. It rose from the pipe to the spirits, taking a man's prayers, but the man draws its power back through the stem of the pipe and into his body.

James wrapped his robe close about him and buried his face in the curly hair, curving his body around the gourd. He felt warm and secure, as though he had returned to a safe place, one that he had known long ago. He made himself still and quiet, and he listened. He heard the sound of rushing air and the flapping of wings. Something brushed the back of his neck. Wait, he told himself. Be still. Let him come to you. Welcome him. Welcome him.

It was not a hawk or an eagle. It was a gray owl with yellow eyes, and it perched on the bare brown bones of a winter cottonwood. While James watched, the owl presided over a parade of specters. Among them James recognized the two he had killed by the gaping holes he had made in their bodies. He braced himself for their censure, but they went their way without regard for his presence.

Then his mother appeared, and she led a procession of people who followed in a human chain with their hands firmly linked. They were Lakota people, old and young, and he was filled with an overwhelming sense of dread. He felt himself moving toward them, trembling all the while. He reached for his mother, but she slipped through his fingers and sped away like a wisp of smoke. Her diaphanous form disappeared into a hole in the ground beneath the cottonwood tree. Desperately he grabbed for the others who followed after her, but too many of them were made of air. Only a few hands of solid flesh touched his. He saw only hands. He avoided looking at faces.

"Garrett."

Lone Bear's voice was a splash of water that washed the whole tableau away, and James raised his head. He peered into the dark. "Lone Bear, have you come for me?"

But for the rustle of wind in the grass, the night was quiet. James clutched his knees and waited. His head felt heavy now, his eyelids leaden. He dropped his forehead on his knees and closed his eyes.

"Don't look for me, Garrett," came the voice in his ears again. "Listen. Have you seen the white deer?"

"No," James replied into the center of his body. "I've seen only death. I want to go back to camp."

"It is as I told you, Garrett. Wait for the white deer. Let him come. Welcome him. Welcome him. *Hi-yay-yay-yay. Hunh.*"

James waited. He had no sense of the passage of time. He was beyond time, and his only connection to anything tangible was through Lone Bear's voice and Kezawin's flesh. Within the buffaloskin sac Kezawin had made for him, he curled himself into a tight ball and made a womb of himself for the gourd. It felt warm and alive, balancing there against the sac between his thighs that held his seed. He thought of a toy wooden chicken he'd once owned in which a succession of smaller chickens nested. The smallest one held the egg. Generations. Reflections inside reflections. Begin with the egg. End with the egg. Shield the future from the night and begin again tomorrow. Begin with the egg.

He waited. When fear struck him hard, he held fast to the warm, dark, safe place. In such a place, he had prepared himself. In such a place he had cleansed himself. In such a place he could be still and listen. Then he would hear Lone Bear's song, faintly at first.

"Let him come. Welcome him. Welcome him. *Hi-yay hunh hunh. Hi-yah. Hi-yah.*"

And James was no longer afraid.

The darkness receded. The world became light. When the white deer appeared in the bright mist and came forward, he carried a bag made from the skin of a badger. He trotted around James, round and round like a creature from a carousel, and James circled with him until he got so dizzy that he sat down hard in the dewy grass, laughing. Thoroughly elated, he flopped on his back and watched the blue sky revolve overhead.

The white deer came to him, nuzzled him and dropped the bag next to his ear. Inside the bag James found a collection of plants, a trowel and a pen, and a few gray feathers that had been gathered together. At the bottom of the bag he found the deer amulet that Kezawin had given him, two black stones and a small bone whistle.

"You are White Deer's Brother," Lone Bear's voice said. "You may not eat the flesh of your own kind. You are a healer. Use your gifts well, and lives may be spared. You know many things, but there is more. Even death can be your teacher. Listen to your heart, White Deer's Brother."

When James opened his eyes, it was raining. He tilted his head back, and the first drop hit him in the eye. It was gray daylight, and the raindrops were multiplying, waking him, washing his face. He opened his mouth and let the cold rain slake his sudden thirst. He felt as though he'd been out of his body for a while, but now that he was back in it, it was making demands. His stomach rumbled roundly as he forced aching muscles to move still joints.

"Garrett!" The voice was Lone Bear's. James settled back once more like a turtle in his shell, prepared to hear more instructions, but this time the old man came walking up over the hill. "If you have seen nothing yet, you might as well come down and try again another time. You will soon be sitting in a mud pit."

James pulled his robe around his shoulders and rose from the vision pit on unsteady legs, but when Lone Bear saw his face, he knew his young friend had experienced something so beautiful and overpowering that it would be called *ša* — red.

James tried his voice. "How long have I been up here?"
"This is the fourth sunrise."

Among the Lakota, every momentous occasion required a feast no matter how lean the hunting season had
been, and a wedding, no matter how unlikely a pair the
bride and groom made, was a momentous occasion.
Thunder Shield's wife and his parents, his closest relatives, would remain in their lodge during the festivities, but
the rest of the camp had turned out to witness the marriage of Double Woman Dreamer and the strange white
shaman.

James had experienced a successful *hanble ceya*, returning from the hill with a song, and Lone Bear had interpreted his vision and proclaimed his medicine to be strong
enough to withstand the power of the deer woman. Many
people were skeptical, but Lone Bear had Bear Medicine,
which was the most powerful kind. Within days after
James's vision, Lone Bear performed the *Hunka* ceremony, the waving of the horses' tails, in James's honor. In
the ritual taught the Hunkpapa by their Oglala cousins,
Lone Bear made James kin to the Lakota and promised to
help him in all things, as was proper for a blood relative.

James had, at Kezawin's suggestion, gifted his prospec-
tive father-in-law with the buckskin horse that he had stolen on their way home from Pawnee territory, formally
announcing that he wanted her for his wife. Now he waited
for her to be brought to him. The marriage was called *Wi-
yan he cinacaqupi*—"He wanted that woman, so they gave
her to him." The guests were satisfied that this was true
when they saw the look on his face when he first glimpsed
his bride. Standing there in the white elkskins that she had
made for him with quillwork in black-and-gray symbolic
designs, he had only one horse to offer, but he wanted her.
And so they gave her to him.

Her father had put her in a fine saddle on one of his own
best horses, and he led her through the camp with great

solemnity. James's heart thudded like late-summer thunder as he watched them approach. Her black braids were wrapped in white ermine, and her forehead was painted with a strip of red, the color of great promise. She glistened like a jewel in the golden rays of the autumn sun, even though her eyes were shyly downcast. James wondered in that moment who he thought he was to claim such a regal bride. He waited for her beside Lone Bear's lodge, which was the closest thing he had to a home. He was an impoverished interloper, a small man, an unworthy man. And then she lifted her chin, and her lashes unveiled onyx eyes, which found him unerringly. The loving look she gave him made him worthy.

She, too, was dressed in white elkskin, and he had seen her in the dress before, although she doubted he would recognize it. She had added some quillwork and elk's teeth, as befit a bride, but it was the same dress she had been wearing the first time they met. He looked almost as surprised by the sight of her now as he had then, but this time she saw so much more. He was James, and she would be his wife. Her heart soared as she beheld his sun-brightened hair framing his dear, handsome face and the promise of a clear summer's day in his eyes.

Lone Bear handed James the horse's reins and stepped back, giving his daughter away. James had been instructed to picket the horse beside what served as his family's tipi, but he instead stepped up to the horse's side and reached for Kezawin in a totally indecorous gesture. She laughed and slid off the horse and into his arms. Her eyes bright with joy, she lifted her chin, inviting his own sign of approval. He dipped his head and covered her mouth with a kiss that would tell the world, "This is my wife."

Let them see, he thought, and if she turns into a deer this very moment, I will follow her to some secret bower where I can live with her and protect her from all slings and arrows.

Let them see, she thought, that this is the man who is not afraid to touch his tongue to mine, taste my love and be my husband.

They saw the strange gesture, and some even smiled and nodded their heads. Others shrugged and followed their noses to the food, mumbling that it was the kind of behavior one might expect from a white man and one who had dreamed of the deer woman.

After all the guests had been fed, gifts had been given and relatives had been honored in the traditional rites, there was still the dancing. As soon as the sun had slipped behind the hills, the air had taken on a seasonable chill. The women wrapped themselves in blankets and took to their side of the huge festive fire to do their sedate form of dancing, but the men, mimicking the prancing prairie chicken or the hunter in pursuit, easily expended enough energy to throw off the night's chill.

James stomped circles in the dry grass with the rest of the men, vigorously displaying his style for his new bride. Proper decorum demanded that a man make a pretense of being unaware of the women's dance line, but James glanced Kezawin's way, caught her attention and smiled. He would gladly have traded his new moccasins for a single waltz. He was tempted to snatch her away from the line of solemn-faced women and whirl her about the camp fire to a tune he was conjuring in his head.

Kezawin understood the eager look in her husband's eyes. She had no notion of stepping across the grass with him in three-quarter time, but she saw his need to hold her, and she wanted nothing more at that moment than to be held by him.

But the drum demanded the dancers' attention, and when the beat wound down, the men signaled with their dance whistles that the music must go on. When next James checked the women's dance line for his bride, she wasn't there. He went looking for her, but each person he asked either covered her mouth with her hand and giggled, or slapped him on the back and asked him whether the celebration was over for him so soon.

Finally he followed his instincts and headed toward the edge of camp, and there he saw that a fire burned inside her lodge. He could remember no other dwelling that had beckoned him to come home the way this one did. The dew cloth doubled the thickness of the lower fourth of the structure and formed an opaque, shoulder-height tier of dim shadow. Above that the cone glowed with the warmth of a tan lamp globe. And the sooty peak took on a darker tone again, as though it had been drizzled with an icing of ash. A wisp of white smoke escaped through the top flaps to welcome him. A mountain with a molten interior, he thought as he stretched his stride. A sweet confection. A woman's breast. Feet, move faster; it's our wedding night.

He could smell sweet grass smoke when he ducked through the door. Kezawin sat with her sleek legs and her small feet tucked demurely to one side as she fanned her hair with a quill brush in the heat of the small fire. James's mouth went dry. He straightened slowly and watched the damp silky hair cascade over her shoulder as the brush released it bit by bit. She looked up and smiled, and he swallowed hard. As an afterthought, he pegged the door shut.

"I became somewhat nervous when I couldn't find you," he managed to say as he took a tentative step on the soft carpet. "I thought maybe you had changed your mind and gone a-hiding."

"You gave me that man-look," she reminded him, and her eyes danced with the memory. "I wanted to bathe myself in sweet-scented water." She had also put her wedding dress aside and was dressed in a supple, unadorned elkskin shift.

James laid his hands on his chest and felt the dampness of his shirt. "I should have thought to do the same, but I saw the fire, and I could think of nothing but—"

His face colored, and she longed to lay her hands against his cheeks and see how warm they felt. "I shall bathe you, if you will permit me to."

He laughed as he skinned the damp shirt over his head. "I would permit you to drown me, my love, if that be your wish, but I must touch your hair first and smell this sweet-water scent."

"You would spend your wedding night touching your wife's hair, James Garrett?" she teased.

"I would wrap myself in your hair," he told her as he untied a long pouch from his waist, then undid ties and thongs and sent his moccasins and leggings the way of the shirt. He stood before her, naked now but for his breech-clout, displaying the lean length of his body made golden tan by the Lakota sun. "I can think of no more luxurious way to dress myself after a bath. But here—" He held up the pouch for her inspection. "I have a surprise for you."

From the pouch he produced a long, suggestively shaped cedar flute, which bore an adjustable pitch changer carved to resemble the headless torso of a horse. Each of the five finger holes was painted red, as was the acornlike mouth-piece. James tossed the leather sheath aside and held the flute aloft.

Kezawin's eyes lit up. "A Big Twisted Flute. Where did you get it?"

"From Buffalo Dreamer, of course. The only one who makes them. He says that when I play this for you, you will be unable to resist me." He walked around the fire and sat beside her near the sleeping robes. "He was amazed at how quickly I mastered the music." James had neglected to mention his previous experience with wind instruments. As he made himself comfortable in a cross-legged sitting position, Kezawin slipped a braided wreath over his head and arranged it around his neck. He held the leafy gift to his nose and smelled the tangy fragrance of calamus.

"Muskrat food," she called it. "Do you like the scent?"

He chuckled. "I'm sure it improves my own."

"I saw how well you danced," she offered with a smile. "You are learning so many things. Did Buffalo Dreamer teach you any songs?"

"Your husband is not such a dolt that he doesn't know the price of the flute includes the love song." She smiled while he positioned his fingers on the stops. "Prepare to be properly wooed, sweet woman."

She sucked her own lip between her teeth as she watched him place the knoblike mouthpiece in the center of his lower lip and carefully close his mouth around it. The minor key was reminiscent of an erotic whistling, like a lilting night call from a heart in hiding, a lover's hopeful entreaty. The plea was one that drew the heart from a woman's breast.

Kezawin moved behind him, took a piece of soft chamois and dipped it into the infusion of warm, scented water she had prepared for his bath. She washed his back while he played, and the woody scent of the water combined with the calamus to form a fresh masculine scent. She scrubbed in soothing circles over the long, corded muscles in his back, and then she rose on her knees and gave the same attention to his shoulders and upper arms. She dampened the sun-lightened hair that had grown to reach his shoulders, before nestling her mouth near his ear as she reached past his shoulder to tend to his chest.

"Those who might be returning from the dancing will hear your music and think that Buffalo Dreamer himself is playing," she whispered. "Maidens must cover their ears and hurry home tonight—no, please, play on." He smiled around the mouthpiece before closing his lips around it again. In the distance the dance drum added its persistent ta-tum, ta-tum, a cadence inspired by the loping buffalo, but James's love song softened the sound.

"The young men will be on the prowl," Kezawin whispered. "And husbands are saying to their wives, 'I ache for you, *mitawin*. Ease me.' Such is the power of the Big Twisted Flute. The horse, you see—" she pointed to the small carving on the flute, and even through her shift he felt her breasts press against his back "—is most eager among the four-legged creatures to mate. Don't stop playing yet. Your music has magic. I would hear more."

She replenished the warm water on her cloth, forked her thighs around his buttocks and reached beneath his elbows to wash his thighs. She started on the left side, working from the outside and moving gradually toward the inside, and down and down, achingly close, perilously, preciously close. The tune warbled, and Kezawin moved to the right side.

She touched the ridge of scar tissue, his badge of honor from his first buffalo hunt, and she thought, later I will touch my lips here, and he will know how much I respect his courage. She slid her cloth over the inside of his thigh, and when she had come as close as she could, she dropped the cloth and slipped her hand into the place where his breech-clout gapped away from his body. When she cradled the softest, most vulnerable part of him in her palm, the music stopped.

She untied the thong at his hip. The clout fell away, and she stroked him until he groaned. "Ah, Kezawin, you have all the magic."

Magic. Deer magic. She pressed her forehead into the center of his back and wrapped her arms around his chest. "I am too bold. I must not be too—"

"Kezawin, no." As quickly as he could manage on unsteady knees, he turned to her and took her in his arms, crooning, "No, none of this. I am your husband now, and I won't let you—"

"*Don't* let me, please." She took his face in her hands and felt the heat she had caused. "Swear to me, James. If I become a wild thing—"

"I shall match your wildness with wildness of my own," he vowed, and turned his face to press his lips into the center of the gentle palm that had held him a moment ago.

"No, no, you must promise me. If I should change...if you see anything, if you hear any strange sounds, you must leave this place as quickly as you can. You must not—"

"I promise," he whispered as he guided them both to their knees. Filling his hands with her hips, he slid the soft leather up and down, teasing himself with the knowledge of her nudity underneath the shift. "You'll not hurt me this night unless you turn me away. I ache for you, *mitawin*."

A mixture of fear and desire cavorted in circles inside her head, but the dizziness was not something she wanted stopped. "I want to give you ease. I could not turn you away, and that is why you must—"

"I must see you." She lifted her arms and let him peel her dress over her head. Her hair spilled over her breasts, and he thought, yes, a little at a time. He trailed his fingertips up the sides of her thighs, over her hips, across the small, soft curve of her belly. "I must put my child there, Kezawin. I believe we are meant to have children."

"You have seen this?" she asked hopefully.

"I feel it now." He moved the curtain of hair, tucking it behind her shoulder, and admired one fine, full breast. "You will suckle my child here," he promised as he lowered his head to sample her lovely nipple himself. "Like this."

Something inside her strained to give him nourishment in response to his lips' gentle tugging. She plunged her fingers into the rabbit-soft thickness of his hair and held his head close even as he exposed her other breast and treated it the same arousing way. "Our babies will have to share their mother's breasts with their father," he told her as he took her in his arms and eased her back to the bed he could now call theirs. He settled over her and stroked her forehead. "Put aside these worries and love me," he whispered between kisses. "You cannot harm me with love."

"You would make love with me face-to-face?"

"I would make love with you any way you want. Put your arms around me and whisper your wishes in my ear."

"Face-to-face is good," she said as she flattened her hands at the small of his back. "That way you can watch...to make sure—"

"To make sure I give you pleasure," he finished for her. His hands strayed from her breast to her belly. "I want to see it on your lovely face. Don't be afraid, Kezawin. I love you, and I will be gentle and make you ready for me."

"I'm not afraid of you," she whispered.

"Not afraid?" He took her hand and placed it on the would-be invader that waxed tumescent with his need. "Then you are a brave woman, and you deserve a brave husband. Have you a place for me?" He searched carefully, as a blind man might, learning each curve by texture, until he reached his destination with two sentient fingers. "Yes, you do. Small and round and warm. A man must tread lightly here. Lightly, gently, like this."

He stroked her as though he had feathers for fingers, tended her until she moaned, and he smiled against her temple and whispered, "You will cleanse me. Yes, there, you see? Your body makes this for me. For your husband. You will take me inside and make me clean."

She opened herself for him, and he knelt between her thighs and pressed himself against her, rotating his hips to tease until there could be no more teasing. He wanted her to tell him, but she held back. She must not entice. She must not seduce.

"Don't let me—"

"I won't," he ground out, and with a slight shift of his weight, he sheathed himself inside her. He pinned her hands on either side of her head and laced his fingers with hers. "I won't let you be anything less than a woman. Five fingers, Kezawin. Five on each hand. They'll stay that way. I promise you."

He stroked her inside, and she rose, rose, rose. She flowered for him, and he moved deeper. She felt something different. Something inside her was changing. Too much feeling. Too many flowers. "James!"

"Wrap your legs around me," he commanded. "Yes. Beautiful. Let me fill you...fill you..."

"Please open your eyes," she whispered. She had no control. It was up to him. "Watch me...watch me..."

He saw her through the white haze of his pleasure. Her eyes were glazed with ecstasy and wide with fear. "I see a woman," he whispered. "A woman's face, a woman's body...taking her man's seed."

They nested in curly buffalo hair and explored each other in wonder, delighting in the contrasts between two bodies—one male, one female; one light, one dark; one large, one small—that had come together, each adding to the other. Together they were so much more than they had been separately.

The shadows of a dying fire flickered over the slanted walls. Kezawin moved her fingers through the fine smattering of hair on James's chest, and she dreamed of one possibility after another, while James wondered how much of her belonged to him.

"What if I decided to go back East?" he wondered idly. "Would you go with me?"

She lifted her head and stared at him. "Back to where you lived as a white man?"

He laughed. "I live *here* as a white man. You could live there as a Lakota."

"I could *die* there as a Lakota."

"I would protect you," he promised. "What would you do if I decided to go?"

Carefully she laid her cheek against his cheek and pushed back her fear. "I am your wife," she told him. "I would go with you. If the *wakincuzas*, the ones who decide, chose to move the camp tomorrow, and you would not go, I would stay with you. And we would die together."

She had promised him complete devotion. No Lakota wished to be separated from his community. He rubbed her shoulder, telling her that he understood. "There are things

I would show you," he said quietly. "Just to amuse you, I think. I would like to see the world that spawned me through your eyes. But I don't belong there anymore. The part of my soul your father told me I would find—that part of me would die there."

"Then you will not take me away?"

He shook his head and combed his fingers through her hair. "And I will not go without you."

She turned her lips to his chest in gratitude, then snuggled against his side and watched the flickering fire again. "In the winter you must paint your achievements on the dew cloth," she said lazily. "And I shall paint them on a robe. You must paint with pictures, and I shall use designs to tell the stories."

"What makes you think I can paint pictures?" he asked as he wrapped his hand with her hair.

"Men make pictures, and women make symbols."

"Why?"

She kissed his flat nipple and lifted her head to see whether she had changed its shape. "Because it has always been so."

"Then I shall paint a picture of my greatest accomplishment directly across from the door," he decided. "A picture of the woman I have wooed and won...and undressed."

"No!" She laughed again and pinched his leg with her toes. "You must paint the buffalo hunt and the horse raid—those things."

"Ah, *those* things. If I'm to spend the winter painting, I should be permitted to paint what I want. I could make a picture of the time we saw the white deer."

"Was he part of your vision?" she asked as she braced herself up on her elbows and watched him play with her hair. "My father said that you had a powerful vision."

"Did he tell you about it?"

She nodded toward the badgerskin bag that hung on its own special rack. "He only told me how to make your medicine bag."

Lone Bear had told him that White Deer's Brother was his secret name, the name the spirits would call him. Its power would be broken if James told the name to anyone. He must heed the white deer's warning. His brothers would help him feed his family, but he, himself, must never again taste venison. James's vision was more than a personal dream, Lone Bear told him. It was a vision for the people, and even Lone Bear seemed troubled by the fact that a white man had been given such a vision. It was for that reason that he had performed the *Hunka* rite and waved the horses' tails over James's head, declaring his kinship with the Lakota.

It troubled James, as well. Why him? Lone Bear called him a healer, and with that much he could be comfortable, for he was a naturalist, and with Kezawin's teaching he had become an herbalist. It was the specter of death that left him with a terrible feeling of foreboding. Lone Bear reminded him that death would come, and no healer would ever change that final truth. But James's gift would help many people, and he must search for the wisdom to use it properly.

He knew that Kezawin did not expect to be told the particulars of his vision. He smiled at her as he spread her hair across his chest. "He also said that my medicine was strong enough to withstand the threat of the deer woman, but you were terrified the whole time we were making love.

"Not the whole time. Something happened that made me feel too wonderful to be terrified."

James's chest swelled with pride. "Your first husband was a boy. Now you are married to a man who can make that happen whenever you—" The cloudiness crept over her face again. "Forget about all that, Kezawin. Please. I'm sorry I mentioned him."

"Three men now," she reflected. "I want to believe my father's judgment, but the deer woman is powerful, too. Three men have died."

"You aren't counting Thunder Shield, are you? I'm the one who's responsible for his death, not you."

"It concerned me. You fought because—"

He touched two fingers to her lips. "There is something I would tell you about myself, Kezawin. Something I should have told you before." He took a deep breath and let it out slowly as he searched for the words he needed. "I have taken the lives of two men." He looked into her eyes and did not find the shocked expression he expected. "The first one I killed in a fight last winter. This man came to my room to steal my journals, and I caught him. We struggled. He had a knife, and I ended up killing him with it. It's a story that seems to be repeating itself with me."

"Have you made amends to his family?"

"There were witnesses who saw that I was defending myself. I was not charged with any crime."

He had not understood her question, and she reminded herself that he must learn this for himself. One day he would acknowledge the need to untie himself from these deaths, and he would know what he must do.

"This is why you came back?" she asked.

"The dead man's father has much power. I was relieved of my..." He realized that "teaching post" would mean nothing to her. "I was no longer welcome in the place where I have lived and worked."

"Were you cast out?"

He knew that banishment was the most severe form of punishment among the Lakota, and he heard the note of sympathy in her voice. "Not exactly."

"Then surely your relations would help you."

"There is no love between my father and me. My work was my life, and my life there was over."

She pillowed her head in the hollow of his shoulder and put her arm around him. "And now it begins here."

"Yes, it does." Indeed, he could think of no better place.

"I believe your medicine must be strong. Our lovemaking was wonderful and red, was it not?"

He turned her in his arms and smoothed her hair back from her face. Anything red was the finest there was. "It was the truest red I've ever known," he told her. He touched her cheek, then trailed his fingers along the side of her neck.

"And I did not change, did I?"

"I saw nothing but Kezawin," he assured her as he slipped his hand beneath one full breast and lifted it slightly, just to admire. "And Kezawin is all woman." He ducked his head to taste one puckering nipple, which reminded him of a dark ripe plum. "My woman," he whispered.

And he knew that it was he who would never again be the same.

Chapter Ten

James fancied himself something of a writer and a passable musician, but he had never had any interest in painting, and with good reason. The frustration it caused made him want to throw things. He held the bone brush up to his face and examined the sharpened tip through the fine mist of his breath. The rib was porous enough to hold the paint, but it wasn't pliable. He wondered how good a dart the thing would make.

"The horses are wonderful, James. See how the buckskin chases the others toward the door."

When he turned from his work on the dew cloth canvas, the look on Kezawin's face chased the scowl from his own. The quills, which she held in her right cheek as she softened them with her saliva, made her smile sweetly lopsided. "I'd kiss you for the compliment," he said, "but your mouth looks lethal right now."

Her laughter overrode the melancholy echo of winter wind. She selected one of the points protruding from the corner of her mouth and pulled out a root-dyed quill. "The male porcupine would know the way to avoid his mate's quills," she teased.

"The human male may soon pull the pricklers from his mate's mouth and give her something better to soften."

"Ayyy," she scolded good-naturedly as she feigned wide-eyed shock. "The male porcupine has better manners."

"The male porcupine isn't expected to paint pictures on the walls of his den." He waved his bone brush at the stylized figure he was working on. "Look at this. This doesn't look like a deer. It looks more like a jackrabbit with horns." She giggled. "If you choke on your quills, woman, your insolence will be well-served."

"But the horses are wonderful," she reminded him. "They're headed straight for the door. I can imagine them tearing outside, rearing up and plunging into the snow."

"Hmm." He studied his painting of the previous week. "They'll never be museum pieces, but you're right; the horses will pass."

"You must paint a man with yellow hair riding the buckskin."

"I'm not finished with it yet," he told her. He took up the tortoiseshell paint pot again and dipped the tip of his brush into a close approximation of white, which he'd achieved by mixing boiled hide scrapings with light clay. He studied his horse again. He'd be satisfied if he could get the deer to look more like a colt than a rabbit. One more try, he thought as he began applying the paint.

"I'm not sure I can make anything resembling a man," he continued absently. With his nose inches from the wall, he was concentrating on the deer's head. The slant of the wall didn't help matters much, but he thought it was probably easier than painting the ceiling of a church. "I've been trying to remember the painted markings of the buckskin—some sort of dots, I think, and something else. I want to get those on there."

He leaned back for an assessment. Much better. *Much* better. Garrett, you might just impress them at the Louvre after all. "You must remember those markings. You were quick to wash them off."

"I do remember them."

"Good." He added a touch to the albino deer's antlers, dropped the bone brush into the pot of white paint and shoved it aside. He took up the pot of black. "Let me get this right. How did those markings go?"

"It might not be good to show everything you saw on that horse," she suggested without looking up from the quills she was splicing into her design.

"Why not?"

"Because the owner would be identified by those markings."

"I became the owner when I stole the horse." He would never have thought he would discuss his own theft with pride, but he'd learned there was a kind of art in that, too. Here it was legal if you got away with it. In his world, it was only legal for people who had enough wealth and power to make it so.

"Besides, the original owner is not apt to come calling and see the evidence on our walls." Her silence brought him up short. "Is he?"

Kezawin went on quilling.

James backed away and surveyed his horse fresco in a new light. "Kezawin, whose horses did I steal?"

"They were not close relations. Just some Brûlé cousins. They should have been watching more closely."

James groaned as he set the pot of black paint next to the white. "Brûlés! They would have *given* us a horse to get us home."

"It was very dark that night."

"And you never told me."

"It was a fine coup, James. They would have killed you if they could have, but you were too clever and too quick. You got away." She nodded toward the painting. "Put yourself on that horse where you belong. Just leave off the markings."

It took him a moment to get over feeling foolish. Then he laughed, remembering how pleased he had been with his narrow escape. Among the Plains tribes, stealing horses was almost a game. In the white world—again, it depended on whose horses were stolen—a man could get himself hanged for his trouble.

James grabbed several pieces of firewood from the pile near the door and added them to the fire. "I don't want to be around when your cousins meet up with Lone Bear if he's riding that buckskin."

"They will be too embarrassed to admit that they were so careless."

Taking a robe from their sleeping pallet, he moved to sit beside her to enjoy the heat from her body on this dark and lazy winter's day. He draped the robe around them both. "I think I shall decorate our walls with ink drawings of plant specimens," he suggested. "That I can do well."

"What kind of story would your drawings tell?"

"The story of what brought us together."

She thought this over, trying to imagine how such a thing might take shape on their dew cloth.

"Something a bit different," he suggested. "It would look just like a piece of work that hung in my mother's bedroom. Like you, she enjoyed doing needlework." He remembered the strip of embroidered tapestry that had been his first botanical text. He had committed the herb sampler to memory many times over as he'd listened to his mother read aloud to him.

"But you wore such plain clothes when you came here." She slipped another quill from her mouth and talked around the three or four still poking forth. "The woman you speak of died long ago, and you had no wife. I thought it was sad that you were without a woman to apply designs to your clothes. You seemed . . . *unśica*."

"So you thought me pathetic, hmm? Just like a woman to pity the single man, while most of us manage to be unaware of our pitiable state." He touched the strip of quillwork on his shirt. "But you have dressed me well."

"You have brought me many hides."

He knew she was being generous. A Lakota hunter might have brought home twice as much game as he had, but

James figured he had done well enough by his small family. "When I lived among the whites, I used to pay a tailor to make my clothes. Even if I had a wife, I would have worn those plain clothes. That's the way white men dress, particularly—"

"How do the white women dress?" she asked.

He thought back and realized that his own tastes had changed. "Their dresses are long, with big skirts. They like more decoration than men do, but it's different from what *we* wear—you and I. For instance, they wear brightly polished stones."

"Stones?"

"Polished. The kind that glitter. They make necklaces and bracelets out of them."

"Shells and teeth are not as heavy as stones, and they make much prettier decorations. Perhaps the white women use pony beads like the ones the traders bring on their pony pack trains."

"I don't know. I never paid much attention to fashion. I used to see beads sometimes in shawls or maybe hair coverings, but, no, I don't think they do much of that."

"Many of our women have changed to the beads." Kezawin held out the unfinished moccasins and touched the even row in a feminine gesture, giving them both a chance to admire the orange-and-yellow design. "I prefer to use quills."

"It makes a more handsome design."

"Of course, it takes more skill." She glanced up at him, her eyes twinkling.

"Indeed, far more skill," he agreed. Her eyes met their match when his danced to her tune. "Only a lazy woman would use beads."

"And those white women can't even do that much."

"They're ugly, too, most of them."

"I suspected so, although I've never seen one. If they're so lazy, they must be fat, as well."

"Fat as cows."

She giggled. "And they must quarrel with their husbands when they want more food." He nodded. "And they must have voices like crows and skin like—"

He laughed and nodded, remembering how Raleigh Brown's older sister, whom he'd once thought to be the incarnation of Venus, had broken his adolescent heart by getting married. She had inadvertently mended it again by putting on twenty pounds almost immediately thereafter.

"Now tell me what they are really like."

"They are like any other women, I suppose." He moved to sit behind her, scooting close to her back so that he could watch over her shoulder. "Some plain and some beautiful, some lazy and some ambitious. There are those who would have been anxious to tell the whole world what a fool I'd made of myself by raiding our ally's camp. Others might have let it pass with a quiet little dig. 'Oh, incidentally, that was my cousin's horse you stole.' A few..." He adjusted his robe around his shoulders, making a warm shell of himself for her. "The pearls among them would do nothing to diminish a man's heroic moment. A man would be crazy if he found one of those pearls and didn't marry her."

She turned to look up at him. "It *was* a fine coup."

He smiled. "Especially if that pearl of a woman happens to use quills instead of beads."

"You tease me," she said, and made a pretense of going back to her work. She was down to two quills in her mouth.

"Tease you? I tell you truly that I have never seen such a quiller. If I had, I would have married her long ago. It amazes me how quickly—" one quill was now left in her mouth "—you work those things into the design."

"These are swallows," she pointed out. "The sign of the deer woman. It is thanks to her that I have this skill."

"And your healing touch. I don't think she's such a bad old girl." Kezawin tossed back a warning glance. "I'm not taking her lightly," he added quickly. The sharp end of the last quill looked mean. "Obviously she has power. Look how good this is. What kind of a dream would I have to have to improve my painting?"

"I think practice would be the best thing."

"Mmm. That's the hard way." James smiled secretly as the last quill came out of her mouth. "You may have to be satisfied with a mediocre artist. My talents lie in other directions."

Kezawin carefully folded the quill around the sinew, smiling to herself in just the way her husband did. "What directions would those be?"

"Shall I take out the Big Twisted Flute?"

"Only if you plan to accomplish nothing else the rest of the day."

"I plan to accomplish my most sacred duty." He took the moccasin out of her hands and set it aside with her awl and her bladder pouches full of quills. She turned, and both smiles were discovered. "Getting you with child."

"You have taken this duty quite seriously," she said quietly as she touched his bristly cheek.

"It is one that demands my constant attention. Now that you've removed the weapons from your mouth—"

"I have no defense against these quills on your face."

He kissed the corner of her mouth. "I'll shave again in the spring," he promised. He wondered whether it was his promise or his kiss that precipitated the sweet mewling sound she made beneath his arresting mouth.

"My brother's injury ails him today."

The announcement came through the door like a whoosh of cold air. James lifted his head and stifled a groan at the sight of Kezawin's softly parted lips. She consulted with a look. He gave an almost imperceptible nod.

"Bring Mouse Face Boy," she invited loudly enough to be heard outside. "We will try to help him."

On the end of a long, slow, helpless sigh, James went to unpeg the door.

* * *

Blue Heels kept his post beside the door as always, wrapped in his robe and keeping close watch on the proceedings while Mouse Face Boy chattered away. Blue Heels wondered at the power of the white man's medicine. After all, he had taken Double Woman Dreamer as his wife almost four moons past, and there he sat, strong and healthy as ever. Blue Heels had been certain the man was doomed. Double Woman Dreamer was simply too beautiful to be a wife to any mere mortal. Blue Heels had thought it fitting that she remain chaste, and that he might follow her example, keeping himself pure in honor of his secret love for her.

He hated the way the white man looked at her. It was wrong to look at her in the face; everyone knew that. Blue Heels had stolen many glimpses and thought for sure he would die while he was looking at her. Looking the other way also made him feel as though he might die. Her power was awful. Her beauty was awful. The way he ached inside every time he thought of her was almost unbearable.

And here was his brother, showing off Sapa, the crow, and chattering like a magpie with both of them as though they were just ordinary people.

James made every effort to preserve Mouse Face Boy's modesty, keeping his breechclout in place while he treated his hip with hot and cold wraps. The effectiveness of the treatment was evident in the child's elevated spirits, but James could have done without the flapping crow.

"Say your name," Mouse Face Boy coaxed. The thick leather wrapping that protected the boy's hand from the bird's claws was in tatters. A crippled wing prevented the crow from flying, but not from flapping each time its owner pet its breast. "Say 'Sapa.' Show my friends what a smart boy you are."

"*Rawwk! Raaawwwk!*"

James dodged an undulating wing. "Almost said it that time."

"He really can say his name," Mouse Face Boy insisted. "He doesn't like to make mistakes in front of people, so he just makes crow sounds. Come on, Sapa. You know how to say it. Sahhpahh. Come on."

"Perhaps this will help." Kezawin offered Mouse Face Boy a handful of meat tidbits.

Blue Heels broke his customary silence. "You'd better not spoil him." Three heads turned in surprise, and Blue Heels wanted to pull his robe up over his head. Instead, he stretched his neck and cleared his throat, hoping to steady his unpredictable voice. "My father says we might have to eat that bird before this winter ends."

"No, we won't," Mouse Face Boy countered. "There are plenty of dogs around, and *Ate* thinks he knows where he can find deer. He's going out tomorrow."

"And I'm going with him." Blue Heels risked a quick glance to see whether Double Woman Dreamer was impressed. *Haho!* She was smiling. He squared his shoulders, adjusted his robe and prepared for the worst.

"Look, Sapa. Meat. Now say your name, or I won't—" the beak was quicker than the hand "—or I won't give you any more. Sahhpahh."

When the treatment was done, Kezawin sent the boys on their way with a parfleche of dried meat, which they were invited to take to their mother. After they had gone, she put a ration of meat and dried turnips into her boiling pouch while James cleaned up from his painting. She could feel his displeasure, but she asked nothing. She knew that he would tell her what bothered him when he had the words ready.

Finally he took his place at the back of the tipi, seating himself against the willow backrest. "It isn't just ourselves, you know." He realized he'd begun in the middle, which indicated even to him that he was uncomfortable broaching the subject. "We have your father to provide for, as well."

It was his way to start by telling her something she already knew. She took her place at the willow backrest to his left and waited. After this curious announcement he would surely get around to saying what was on his mind.

"I don't think you ought to be giving so much food away," he said flatly. "Lately it seems that anyone who comes to you for medicine goes away with some of our food."

"Food is growing scarce."

"That's exactly my point. I don't mind your giving the children something to eat, but you gave them a good portion of what we had left."

"You remember that Many Plums spoke for me first and bit the knife when others hesitated. She has many mouths to feed."

"I know." He took up a coyote pelt and arranged it on her lap with the hair side next to her. "I remember well how she spoke. But the drifts are waist deep out there in some places. The last two times I went looking for game, there was nothing. Even the wolves have gone elsewhere."

"It's a bad winter."

"I know I'm not the best provider, Kezawin, but I am trying to keep meat in the kettle."

"It's the same for everyone." She laid a comforting hand on his thigh. "You've done well. Better than many of the other hunters. It pleases me to honor you in this way."

"What way?"

"By giving away meat. And you must know that sooner or later we shall receive what is owed us. When the weather is warm again, they will remember us for the medicine we have provided."

"When the weather is warm again, we won't have this problem." He stared into the fire, avoiding her eyes. "For right now, I just think we should hold back a little more. Things could get much worse before they get better."

"Hold back?" The concept was foreign to her. "You mean, keep it for ourselves?"

"I mean not give so much away," he clipped.

"As long as one of us has food, we all eat."

"I'm not suggesting we let anyone starve."

"We have enough for now. You'll find something soon, and we'll have fresh meat. I gave away venison, James. You have not eaten venison, so we have much to share."

"You and Lone Bear eat venison." He sighed impatiently. "I'm just saying we need to save enough so that we don't go hungry."

"Have you never gone hungry?"

He thought for a moment, then shook his head. "Not for any length of time."

"There may be hungry times before the warm winds come to take the snow away. The place where you lived as a white man must be wonderfully bountiful if the white people never go hungry."

Never covered too much ground, but he wasn't sure how he could explain the reality of haves and have-nots. "I haven't personally . . . not myself, nor my own family. You see, my family was fairly wealthy. We owned quite a large . . . Not that there aren't some—quite a few, really— poor people, people who have little. I, myself, lived a very simple—"

"Then your family would help the others, wouldn't they? You would sponsor feasts and give many gifts."

"Some, yes. There is charity, of course, but you can't help everybody."

"Why not?"

"Because then you would have nothing left."

"When you have given until you have nothing left, you will be highly honored. Then people will give you what you need, and it will be said that you are a generous man." She shifted her legs, tucking them to the other side of her seat, and adjusted the coyote robe. James had a capacity for generosity, she thought. Someone had neglected his training.

He scowled as he studied the yellow flame. The whole idea sounded almost biblical. Idealistic. People didn't live that way. Finally he shook his head. "No, I can't . . . Then you've become a charity case yourself. You can't give *everything* away."

"It is a bad sign when a man has too much. It means that he has not sponsored feasts or ceremonies, nor has he helped his relations. It means he has not given."

"But if we give until we have nothing left, and no one else has anything left—"

"We will all be hungry for a time." She saw that this frightened him more than other dangers he had faced. She moved closer and linked her arm with his. "But the Moon of the Birth of Calves will come. It always does. And imagine how green the grass will be after all this snow. *Tatanka* will eat and eat, and he will be so slow and fat that he will say, 'Take some of my flesh, Lakota brothers. I have plenty.'"

James ran his finger along the edge of her hair, smiling as he lifted it away from her face and smoothed it back. He often asked her not to braid it, and often she indulged him. "I will not have you go hungry. I shall go out again tomorrow. If I have to find enough meat for the whole camp, I *will* keep you fed."

They were brave words, she thought. Proud words. They had lived at the edge of camp, always a part of it but never completely included. They were more independent than most, but Kezawin knew that they were not self-reliant. Without each other, they would be like two hollow drums, but without the people, they would die.

"It is not for one man to feed the camp," she told him. She knew this time he would be gone for many days. It was so hard to forget the way her first husband and her brother had gone off full of youthful confidence. The deer woman had seen to their deaths. James must not go alone. "In times like these, small hunting parties may have better luck than a single hunter."

* * *

James swallowed his pride and paid a call on Catch The Bear, Many Plum's husband. The winter hunting parties were mostly family affairs for just a few men. But Kezawin was right. It was not wise to hunt alone in the deepest part of the winter, and one man alone was less effective than a small group. He told himself that Catch The Bear owed him something, but he made no such suggestion to the beefy man who was father to the slight, sickly Mouse Face Boy. He simply asked to be included with the party. Catch The Bear agreed without hesitation.

The camp had moved farther west in its quest for retreating game. In recent years, the Lakota had expanded their hunting grounds into what had once been Crow territory. As the rivalry continued, the Crow people were pushed west of the Greasy Grass River. This season, it seemed, so had the game. Catch The Bear's party followed signs for days, covering more ground when they chose to lead their horses and travel on snowshoes.

Winter hunting was an arduous, methodical task that involved none of the frenzy of the summer buffalo surround. It was a hardship to venture so far from the main camp. Even if the weather held, the days were often sullen and dim, the nights long and frigid. Long-distance tracking required stamina and determination. Trapping required unlimited patience.

Catch The Bear led a party of five, including his two brothers, Painted Shield and Two Broken Arrows, Blue Heels and James. James soon learned the value of group effort, and although much of the game was small, the hunters managed to take what they could find. One man was always left with the cache and the horses, while the rest competed with the wolves for the deer or antelope that still roamed the eastern slopes of the Bighorns, grazing near the underground seeps where they might still find forage.

James hated being left with the job of guarding the camp, especially in the waning daylight when the cool white sun threw a splash of pink and gold in the sky, then slunk behind the mountains. It was a time when the eerie lack of sound made his skin crawl. He was tempted to watch the sun, give it a parting curse for deserting him, but when he noticed a pricking of horses' ears and heard movement in the brush on the slope below him, he stretched out on his belly and cocked his rifle.

Anyone from his own party would have called out. He scanned the slope and picked out the offending brush. If it were an animal, it was soon to be meat. A man—well, he'd better be saying his prayers. Another bush moved. More than one man, and they were waiting for dusk, when they would make shadowy targets.

If they were Crow, James realized that for every one he detected, there were probably two who had not given themselves away. He figured they were just out of range, and he decided he would not wait for them to come to him. The only cover was a stand of three or four cottonwoods between him and the brush, and that was where the horses were tied. James concentrated on that destination and pushed all distractions from his mind.

He sprang to his feet and fired at the first bush as soon as he darted within range. The return fire came just as he dove for the trees. One horse backed up, loosening the half hitch at the end of his rein and breaking free of the tree. James braced his back against a tree and reloaded his rifle while the horse took off, drawing more fire. Within seconds he had mounted another of the horses and was charging the second scruffy bush. The Crow warrior tried to dive clear of James's charge, but his efforts caught him a bullet in the face.

Catch The Bear, on his way back from the hunt, heard the fracas. On snowshoes he skimmed the crusty snow, topping the rise above their camp in time to watch James ride over the heads of his would-be ambushers. Delighted, Catch The Bear shed his snowshoes, mounted up and joined James in chasing the last two Crow braves into the draw, where their own horses waited. James was more interested in the two extra Crow horses, and he rounded them up while Catch The Bear gave a rousing whoop and a half-hearted chase, letting the two outrun him in the deep snow.

"Two scalps and two Crow ponies!" Catch The Bear shouted to James as he trotted back. "That's a good day's work, my friend."

"I can use the horses," James said. "Taking Crow scalps would weaken my medicine."

"Since I backed you up, I shall take them myself."

James nodded. "Be my guest."

Catch The Bear dropped to the ground near the corpses, which lay in a macabre sort of tête-à-tête. James watched him deftly slice away the top of the scalp and wondered how Catch The Bear would reconcile his actions with regret for taking a life. Of course, Catch The Bear had not killed the men. James had.

"We travel tonight," Catch The Bear announced when the other three hunters returned to camp. "You missed all the excitement."

James finished tying his captured horses in a pack line, nose to tail, and made sure his hands were steady before joining the others. He had acted without hesitation, almost as though he had practiced his move in advance, but when it was over, the trembling had started on the inside and worked its way out. He'd had to make himself busy with the horses while he brought it under control.

Catch The Bear gave him a congratulatory slap on the back. "Our cousin, Garrett, turned the Crows' surprise back on them, and two of them paid the price. But now we'd better move quickly, since our enemies may come looking for us."

"It's been a good hunt," Two Broken Arrows attested, and he looked at James. "You'll go with us next time."

James had been gone for ten days, and Kezawin had counted every heartbeat of every one of them. She had battled against despair, but with each passing day she lost ground. When the news came that the hunting party was on its way into camp, she ran back to their lodge, changed her dress, brushed her hair until it crackled and raced back outside to welcome her husband. The village rejoiced at the sight of fresh meat, but Kezawin's private joy was for James's safe return. In the midst of the excitement all she knew was that he was there, alive, whole and healthy.

The other men offered reserved greetings to their wives, but restraint was unthinkable for James. He saw Kezawin making her way through the snow to meet him, and he urged his horse in her direction. When she stood beside his knee and looked up at him as though he'd brought her a trove of treasure, he slid off his horse and caught her in his arms.

"You're all right?" she asked, almost as though she'd gone shy on him. "You're not hurt?"

"Not at all." She was an armful, bundled up to her chin in her wearing robe, and all he could do was shower her face with kisses. "I missed you. Oh, I missed you."

"Such a long, long time. I was afraid—"

"I'm fine." He took a moment to inspect her face. "Have you had enough to eat? You look tired. Is your father well?"

She smiled and took the reins from his hand. "I shall see to the horse." She had many things to tell him, but they would wait for a private moment.

"Horses." He grinned as he put his arm around her shoulders to keep her close as they walked. "They're Crow this time, not Brûlé." He saw all the anxious questions and the belated fear in her eyes, and he shrugged them off. "We had a little tussle with another hunting party. I ended up with a couple of extra horses." It was the explanation of a man who hoped his woman would never know how terrified he had been or how close he had come to being the corpse rather than the victor.

"There will be a victory celebration, then, and you will be honored."

"It isn't something I want to celebrate. It happened—you know, all of a sudden they were there, and it was either... I was lucky, that's all. I want to celebrate being home." He gave her shoulders a hard squeeze. "And I want to celebrate with only my wife."

But the community celebration was unavoidable. Three fur traders had stopped to trade in recent days, and they were invited to participate. There was not the jubilation of a summer festival, for the hibernating earth preferred not to be disturbed during the long winter's night, but there was feasting. In the wintertime, when the Lakota bands broke up into smaller camps, the council tipi at the center of camp was large enough to accommodate most of the people. Stories were told, first eagerly, then more leisurely until finally the children slept with their heads in their parents' laps and the tales were coming fewer and further between.

Pipes were passed, and James caught up on three-month-old news with the visitors from Missouri. There was a fever growing, they said, a fever to move West, and it wouldn't be long before the population spilled across the Mississippi. James found it hard to imagine, but it came from the mouths of the traders as a dire prediction. Settlers would undoubtedly threaten the fur business.

Could it be true? James wondered as he and Kezawin returned to their lodge. Could there be appreciable numbers of his kind edging closer to the great river? Surely this land, with its unbroken expanse of grassland and its formidable mountains, would not interest a nation of farmers. There was plenty of good land for them east of the Mississippi—land that had never been touched by a plow.

When the fire had warmed their tipi, Kezawin undressed her husband. He'd hardly spoken since they'd left the council lodge, and she knew he was troubled. She wanted to bathe him and caress the trouble away from his mind. He was content to give himself over to her and let her try.

Her hands eased ten days' tension away. He closed his eyes and willed that all thoughts and recollections be gone as he leaned against the willow backrest and absorbed the heat of the fire into skin he'd thought would never again be truly warm. The mint-scented water she used in washing him made him tingle all over. When he opened his eyes again, Kezawin was letting her dress slip to the floor. He watched her buff herself with the wet swatch of deerskin until her skin gleamed like burnished copper in the firelight. The long black hair framed her shoulders. Enchanted, he started up from his seat.

"Stay there," she ordered softly. "Let me make you more comfortable."

He gave her a lazy smile. "I don't think you can make me any more comfortable."

"I think I can," she said huskily as she straddled his lap. Then, as he eased himself inside her, she whispered. "It's good to have you home."

It was good to be home. It was good to taste her sweet breast, to tongue her nipple into a hard bead and then pull it into his mouth and suck gently and make her moan and hold her hips and make her move them against him and make her moan and make her take more of him, all of him, and ride him higher and higher and make her moan and moan and moan....

So good.

And then it was good just to hold her sweat-slick body against his chest and watch the fire burn.

Finally, it was good to be two in a sleeping robe again.

"Where did this come from?" James asked as he tugged on a red blanket that had been added to their bed.

"I got it from the fur traders. But I didn't trade food for it," she hastened to add. "Just a pair of winter moccasins."

"Your work is too good to trade away for blankets."

"Oh, I hadn't done much to those moccasins. And these blankets make good wearing robes, don't you think? Many of the people gave pelts for them."

"It's just a blanket," he said as his attention drifted toward the flames again. She remained silent, stroking the hair on his chest, and he knew she wouldn't ask, wouldn't coax him to tell her anything he didn't want her to know. He didn't want her to know the bloody details—the way a man looks when his face has been blown off or what it sounds like when someone hacks off the top of a man's head. Maybe she had seen it all before, but he wanted to believe she hadn't. He wanted to believe he could keep her from ever having to see and hear and smell such things.

Catch The Bear had announced at the feast that they had counted coup on the Crows and that James had handled himself like a true Lakota warrior. The song that had been sung in his honor couched his deed in poetic terms, and the details of the event had been discussed among the men. Kezawin knew what had happened, but James needed to confess it.

"I killed two men," he said tonelessly. "Two *more* men."

"The Crows."

He nodded without taking his eyes off the fire.

"They attacked you."

"They were ready to ambush me, but I made the first move. I was alone at the time, standing watch over the camp, and I didn't figure I had much of a chance unless I acted quickly."

"And you were spared."

"Again." He turned to her, and she saw the pain in his eyes. "I can still see them, Kezawin. Four of them now. Am I becoming some kind of an executioner?"

"No one kills without regret," she reminded him. "Even as you celebrate your victory, a part of you mourns because you have taken life."

"I must perform *inipi*," he decided. "Tomorrow. I must rid myself of this awful image of death—so much death."

"You did not seek this, but it came to you. You must regret it, then let it go. You have much to do with life." She turned her lips against his muscled chest, kissed him and whispered. "You have started a life where it was thought no life would grow."

For a moment James lay very still. "I have done... what?"

Kezawin took his hand and placed it over her firm, feminine belly. "You have done your sacred duty, beloved husband." She looked up to see the wonder in his eyes. "Your child grows inside me."

Chapter Eleven

Kezawin had reminded her husband that gathering wood and carrying water were woman's work, but he took a perverse pleasure in ignoring her protests. There was always a chance of finding some game near the spring, he said, but they both knew what a slim chance it was. He loved to walk the draw with her on mornings like this one, when the air was clear and crisp with cold. The winter sky was pale and delicate, like a bird's eggshell cast high overhead. The barren, windswept hills marked the shell's jagged edge, but the barely blue canopy was uninterrupted from horizon to horizon.

Tough slough grass poked its evergreen blades through the snow and ice in the bog below the spring. On the rise above, the morning mist hovered above a small pool, indicating the warm spring's location. Water seeped over a gentle grade and froze, creating a natural ice playground. The children were already out sliding over the gentle slope and on the glassy pond below it. The same bitter wind that had kept them inside for two days had cleared much of the snow off the ice.

There was wood to be found in the stand of cottonwoods on the high ground beyond the spring. It wasn't long before Kezawin had amassed as much as she could bundle up and carry on her back, but James's pile did not grow as quickly. The children were too delightful a distraction.

They laughed and shrieked at one another as they skidded on the ice, sliding over the little hill by the handiest mode—most often on their bottoms. James shivered as he watched, but even the toddlers seemed impervious to the cold as their older brothers and sisters dragged them over the ice on old hides or slabs of rawhide.

James forgot about the sticks in his hands as he watched one small girl's stubby legs slide out from under her several times. She picked herself up each time without a whimper. He imagined holding his arms out to catch a tiny version of Kezawin, and the image made him smile.

Kezawin's heart swelled when she glanced up from bundling her pile of sticks and saw the direction of her husband's attention. What a good day it would be when she presented this man with a child of his own. She made her rawhide loop secure and went to James, leaving her bundle on the ground. Together they watched one little boy slide across the ice and bowl his brother over. James laughed as he tossed a few sticks atop his own little wood pile. They exchanged a look that said, *Imagine this! We have a child coming.* He drew her closer, protecting his whole family within the warmth of his embrace, and slid his hand up and down her back as they stood watching the children.

"They must think you're a very strange man," she teased when they caught the brief notice of a pair of the boys. "Holding your wife as though you were a suitor with no courting robe."

At the sound of her voice, another boy looked up at them, then politely glanced away. James laughed and rocked Kezawin back and forth until she laughed with him. "We have a right to be strange," he reminded her. "It's expected. People would be disappointed if we were not."

"Then seeing that you also gather wood will keep them happy."

"They will say, 'It's just that crazy white man.'" He slipped his hand beneath her robe and laid it lovingly over her flat belly. "But when they see the reason for my strange behavior, this time they'll understand."

"They would understand the way you spoil me if I were heavy with child." Smiling up at him, she put her hand over his and squeezed it. He wore the badgerskin helmet she'd made for him, and the white center stripe ended at the bridge of his nose. Beneath the edge of the gray-and-white pelt his blue eyes twinkled at her. "But I'm still small," she said quietly.

"By summer you will be fat and irritable, and I shall be thin and anxious."

"I won't have you getting thin and anxious." She tucked her face into the warm hollow under his chin. The badgerskin touched his shoulders and made a little tent around his face, and she felt as though she had crawled inside. "Do all white men carry wood and water for their wives?"

"Only this one." To his knowledge, it was true. "You did all right, Mrs. Garrett. Crazy husbands are hard to come by."

"I know." She smiled. "As are crazy wives."

They tied James's pile of wood into a bundle, but he refused to let Kezawin carry even the smaller of the two burdens on her back. She protested his gallantry less this time and led the way to the spring. The winter sun cast sharp shadow images on the ice—a tall man with a bundle of sticks on his back, and a small woman, a bundle herself, who stood beside him. In blue shadow, they were a perfectly complementary pair. All around them the sunlight was caught, crystalized in the ice and snow, and the tiny rays of light winked at them.

Kezawin drew out the water bladders and lowered the first one into the small ice bowl full of continuously running spring water. As she watched, the air bubbles started doing a funny dance, while the ring of thin ice blurred into the water. She squeezed her eyes shut for a moment, and the ground seemed to tilt beneath her feet. She made a stumbling attempt to steady herself and lost her grip on the bladder's rawhide harness just as a strong arm kept her from falling into the sloshy snow.

"Steady, there. Did you slip?"

The rawhide string floated as the bladder slowly sank. "The water bag!" Kezawin started to reach for it again, but it dissolved before her eyes as she tried to regain her footing in the snow.

"Let it go." He caught her before she crumpled. "What is it, Kezawin?"

"Nothing. Just a little..." She used him as a mooring as she struggled to make muscles work in legs that seemed to be failing her. She managed a thin laugh. "A little craziness is all."

James slipped his arms out of makeshift straps and let the bundle of wood clatter to the ground. "Oh, no!" Kezawin cried as he swept her up into his arms. "Now they will talk. When they hear that I am growing strong with child, they will say that Double Woman Dreamer cannot carry a child the way other women—"

"They will say that Double Woman Dreamer married a man who will not let her carry his child alone." He knew that the buffalo robe accounted for at least half the weight he'd lifted. He had noticed how little she'd been eating in recent days, but if she'd been sick, she had succeeded in hiding it from him. He feared she might have done just that, for the Lakota word for pregnancy meant "growing strong," and sickness would seem a weakness to her.

"You see? I can easily carry you both."

"Oh, but it is for the woman—"

"Oh, but it is for the man, when the woman's head is light. I shall come back for the wood and water."

He carried her back to their lodge and laid her in their sleeping robes. She protested, but when she tried to get up, he eased her back down. "Stay put while I get a fire going. And then you'll stay here and get warm while I go back to pick up the wood."

"After the spectacle we just made, I won't have you carrying all my wood for me, James."

He tossed an arm load of wood next to the fire pit. "We may be in for our first marital spat, Mrs. Garrett." He took flint from the little strike-a-light bag Kezawin had recently quilled for him and built the fire as though he had eyes in his hands. Kezawin's complexion had taken on a strangely yellowish cast. There had been a time when he would have said, as any man would, let women take care of women's complaints, but not now. This was Kezawin, who never complained, and if she was inclined to do so now, she had no one to complain to but James.

She tried to lie still, but even when she closed her eyes, the lodge kept spinning. I shall not be sick in my husband's presence, she told herself. This will pass. The heat from the fire and the heat within her met and mixed, swirled and churned...

"What troubles you?" he asked gently.

She opened her eyes, found him hovering over her and wondered when he had moved. "It's the child. I shall brew a tea to clear my head and make my stomach behave properly. Then I shall finish—"

"I'll take care of the tea. And don't tell me—I know exactly what to put in it."

She closed her eyes and smiled only slightly. "You have stolen all my medicine, James Garrett. You have written my soul into your journals."

"Impossible," James mumbled as he arranged the boiling pouch on its tripod and maneuvered several stones into the hottest part of the fire. "Not even Will Shakespeare could find words to do you justice."

"Is he your *kola*, this Will Shakespeare?"

"He's one of the old ones, long dead, but we have saved his songs and stories in our books, and we—Kezawin, what is it?"

She was pulling at her clothes as he moved back to her side. "Too warm," she muttered. "Do not speak a dead one's name, James. Not now. Not ... with the child ..."

He cupped his hands around her face. She *was* too warm. He'd had little experience with pregnant women, but this worried him. Fever always worried him. "When did this start?" he asked.

"When we were at the spring."

"When was the first time? Has it always come in the morning like this?" He covered her with the red trade blanket and gently squeezed her shoulders. "Kezawin, when you're sick, you must tell me. I won't be—"

"I have not been sick," she insisted. "This was the first time. But I'm a strong woman, and I can bear you children, James. This will pass. I promise."

"It's just a little morning sickness," he assured her as he tucked the blanket around her. "You'll be fine if you'll stop trying to prove how strong you are and let me take care of you."

She closed her eyes and nodded. "I'll be fine." Her eyes felt like two small fire pits. "Please," she whispered. "I'm very thirsty."

"A little water, followed shortly thereafter by your own magic tea," he promised as he took up a pair of sticks and pulled one of the heated rocks from the fire.

"No magic."

"Fine. No magic." The water hissed as the rock hit the water with a plunk. "Just good medicine."

When the tea was ready, Kezawin wrapped herself in the red blanket and sat near the fire, using her willow backrest for the support that was more necessary than she wanted James to know. Her back ached, and the fire inside her burned as hot as the one James had made. Within her spinning thoughts there was one going round and round, telling her to cover her own fire. Smother it. Make it burn itself out. Douse it with tea. Make it go away. It must not touch the child.

James sat next to her and sipped tea from a wooden bowl. "It's normal for a woman to have sickness at this time." He glanced up and added quickly, "From what I've heard, I think it's normal. I've had precious little experience with these things, I'm afraid."

"You are a man," she said. Four words that explained everything. She was a woman, and she would have known about these things had it not been for her dream. She had treated women for menstrual difficulties, but no woman who carried a child dared get too close to one who had dreamed of the deer woman.

It was a woman's duty to protect the child in her womb, and Kezawin would do the same for her child. She was glad that James was there to treat the crippled ones, like Mouse Face Boy, whom she must avoid during the growing-strong-time. She would avoid eye contact with the *heyoka*, the one who had dreamed of thunder and was obliged to do everything he did in the reverse of the way it was normally done. The *winkte*, the man who wore women's clothes, must also be avoided lest she bear a son with the heart of a woman. Such a one was *wakan*, both respected and feared, and lived a lonely life.

Kezawin had known that life. She had accepted it, but now she had a husband, and a child was coming. She would not be sick, she told her spinning head. She wasn't certain whether this was normal, either, but it felt too much like weakness to her, and she would not permit herself to be weak. Not now. She would do all the right things. She sipped her tea. Douse the fire, she thought. It must not burn where the child was living inside her.

"I am a *strange* man," he reminded her. "*Wakan*. I behave as I please. I do what I want. And I want to help you grow strong."

She raised her heavy head with some difficulty and looked at him tenderly. "You already have," she said. "Now I must not disappoint you. I must—"

Her stomach rebelled and would not let her rest until its contents had been eliminated. James held her head and spoke to her quietly, telling her that he was with her and that all would be well. But the heat of her skin seared him with fear. This was something more than morning sickness.

Whatever his doubts about Lone Bear's medicine, James had the utmost respect for the old man's wisdom. He was a pipe-bearer, one of the *wakincuzas*, "the ones who decide." James knew that a man was neither expected nor permitted by the women to involve himself in life's exclusively female provinces, but Kezawin had kept no food down for two days. Herbal infusions had little effect on her fever, and she could not hide her pain. James had kept the two of them to themselves, but it was time to seek Lone Bear's counsel. If Kezawin suffered from influenza, others might have it, too. That was his first question.

"There are others who are ill," Lone Bear said after they had smoked together. "I heard of two yesterday and one today. Winter maladies, I guess. You must see that my daughter eats soon, and give her only fresh water." He wagged a finger in the air. "Do not let her drink stale water. If she has fever, a spirit must have built its fire near her. Have you been speaking of the dead?" James glanced away, and his father-in-law sighed. "Burn sage, and keep the lodge fire high. Perhaps a sweat would help to purge the evil."

"I would not have her get chilled."

"A little cold air makes the body stronger. No one shies away from the cold but those with weak blood, who cannot endure." He tapped James's thigh with a finger. "You have your *pejuta*, Garrett, your herbs and roots. Use them well. Let her sweat and pray. She will find strength. You'll see."

When James returned to the lodge, he found that she still slept. He added fuel to the fire and tossed a few sprigs of sage into the flames. He gathered all of the medicine bags in front of him and paged through his journal. He had tried everything. He had had some success with easing her headache—at least so she told him. Perhaps even in her illness she sought to comfort him. He had to find a way to control her vomiting. He chose dried prickly pear, willow bark and bee balm and reached for the water bag. Then he paused. Fresh water. When had he gotten water last? He couldn't remember.

He hurried to the spring, trotting most of the way. Squatting beside the little pool, he lowered the tawny translucent buffalo's bladder into the water and surveyed the late-afternoon sky while he waited for the pouch to fill. It had been days since any new snow had fallen, but there was snow in the air. A low gray cloud cover flowed overhead like a stream rushing from the western mountains toward the eastern rivers. Snow tonight, he thought. He popped the wooden stopper into the bladder, draped the rawhide strap across his chest and gathered a bundle of wood. By the time he got back to the lodge, his hands were stiff with the cold.

His heart leaped into his throat. There was Kezawin, wrapped in her red blanket and huddled near the fire, shivering like a small animal cornered by the hunter. He dropped the firewood and threw off his robe.

"Forgive me for being gone so long, love. Your father warned me against stale water, and he's right." He knelt behind her and surrounded her with his embrace. "I must be careful about the water," he said close to her ear. Her little body trembled in his arms, and he felt sick inside. "You're cold now?" he whispered. "I am, too. We'll be warm in a moment. Now that I'm here with you, we can both get warm."

She tipped her head back against his shoulder and closed her eyes. His cheek felt like a snowball next to her cheek, but it didn't matter. Her body was at once cold on the inside and hot on the outside, and he was all that was steady.

"Your hands are cold," she said. "Don't get them too close to the fire. They'll hurt."

"I need to thaw them out and get them working on some new medicine."

"Have you had a new vision?"

"No. Only a new idea."

"I trust you," she said, her voice raspy.

He shut his eyes tight and pressed his lips to her warm neck. "I know."

James made the tea and fed her small sips while he held her across his lap. She dozed in his arms, then awakened to ask him if he'd eaten anything. He told her he would, and she dozed again. He ducked outside and found that the gray afternoon had become an ash-white evening, luminous within a cloudy cocoon. Something was coming, and the camp waited quietly for the onslaught.

One thin, eerie cry rent the night. James was struck by this solitary night sound, in part because it was the voice of a child, and Lakota children never cried. Crying was discouraged from infancy. It touched him, too, with hollowness and hunger. He couldn't remember his last substantial meal. But there was something else in that cry, something elusive and frightening. Something was coming, riding in on the wind, and there was nothing to do but wait for it.

Kezawin was awake when James went back inside. He cooled her face again with his hands, and she made a smile for him that did not reach her eyes. "What have you eaten?" she asked.

"Nothing yet," he told her. "I've been soaking Cheyenne turnip and breadroot. And I've boiled some dried cherries. I thought you might try a little cherry soup."

"You must have meat."

"I plan to ask your father to stay with you while I go out hunting. There is *wasna* here and a little venison." He shrugged. "I cannot eat venison."

"I know. The *wasna* has only buffalo meat." She covered his hands with hers. "It's different being married to a white man." She thought it over again and shook her head. "Being married to *you* is different."

"Different from what?"

"Different from anything else. You do things differently. You must hunt whenever you see fit to hunt and not worry about leaving me. The others are close by."

He brought her fingers to his lips and kissed them. "Does 'different' mean better or worse than anything else?"

He had a way of not hearing what she said sometimes, but she smiled again anyway. "It's good being your wife. Your ways are different, but you love me well."

"You must let me have some of my own ways," he said, "even while I learn to practice some of yours. I will always be a white man, and there are those things I cannot change."

"And I will always be Lakota."

"Our child will look different from the other children," he told her.

"Our child will be beautiful, just like the others."

"But I shall be his father, and there will be things for me to teach him."

"And things for his grandfather to teach him."

"And his mother." He nibbled her fingertips again. "Or *her* mother. This child may have the best of both our worlds."

"I would have you do something for me," she whispered.

"Anything."

"Play the Big Twisted Flute for me." His eyes widened in a teasing suggestion, and she gave a wan smile. "I think the music will not have its usual effect tonight, but it would soothe me."

The music became part of the winter night, a melancholy whistling on the wind. From some distant corner of the camp came the slow, steady throb of a medicine drum. James remembered their wedding night, when his lilting music had entwined itself with the beat of the dance drum—two entities, like a man and his wife, becoming one. He played for his wife now, not to seduce but to comfort, because she was as dear to him as his own breath. He was tired and hungry, and his eyes rested on her and fed. In this moment, too, he was one with her.

The medicine drum stopped, and James put his flute down and dipped out a bowl of the cherry soup for Kezawin. He grabbed a handful of *wasna* from a parfleche and nibbled at it while Kezawin drank. The drumbeat resumed.

"Someone else is ill," she said.

"It must be some winter complaint that's going around. If we could rid you of this fever, I think you'd be back on your feet. I'm going to sponge you down."

"Mmm, I would like that," she said with a sigh. "Almost like music."

He took the red blanket from her and moved her closer to the fire. She helped him remove her soft buckskin shift, and he dipped a piece of chamois in warm water. He wished he had thought to add some aromatic herbs to the water as she had done for him. It was then that he noticed the rash of red spots on her chest. He glanced down and saw that her abdomen was covered, too. He could not draw breath as he touched her gingerly, his hands trembling with his disbelief.

The medicine drum threaded its rhythm through the steady howl of the wind as memory took him back.

A pale blond woman turned vacant eyes upon a child, and a man responded with a wretched groan.

"God, not this. God in heaven, not this."

Out of the corner of his eye he saw red, and the pieces fell together in his mind. With a predatory growl he snatched up the trade blanket and pitched it into the fire. The red wool smoldered, smoked, then lit up like a pool of oil.

"It had to be the traders," he muttered. "Damn their putrid souls, it *had* to be them."

Kezawin gripped a handful of curly buffalo hair and elevated herself on one elbow. She understood nothing but James's anger, for he spoke in English. As her head spun with nausea, she tried to make her burning eyes focus on the towering figure of her husband. "What is it, James?"

He took a deep breath and exhaled slowly, summoning some measure of reason. "I could be wrong," he said, but the words were devoid of hope. He knelt beside her and gathered the buffalo robes close about her as he examined the dark red spots closely. It had been a long time, but he had not forgotten how they had looked on his mother's skin—and his own.

Kezawin. This was Kezawin. He lifted his gaze from the swell of her spotted breasts to her face and read her question again in her eyes.

"This rash," he began carefully. "Have you seen anything like this before?"

Her dark eyes plumbed the depths of his. She did not need to look down. She knew what was there on her body. "It's a strange thing. I think it's a bad sign."

"I thought perhaps it was something you knew about," he suggested. "Something you had seen and treated before."

"It's something *you* know about. I see it in your eyes. Tell me what you know."

Tell her what? Tell her the word that was uttered in whispers lest it turn order into chaos? He had not learned the word in Lakota, and the only synonym he knew was death. "When I was a child, I suffered from an illness. My mother contracted it, too, and many other people also suffered from it. You see, when one person—"

"Your mother died."

He nodded solemnly.

"And the others?"

"Many...some recovered." He kissed her hand and pressed it against his chest so that she could feel his heartbeat. "I did, as you see. I'm healthy. But this disease is very... We call it smallpox." The word brought a bitter taste to his tongue. He carried her hand to his forehead and placed her fingers on the two small pits hidden beneath a sweep of tawny hair. "I wear the scars from the spots. They were like the ones you have now."

Lovingly she touched the small dents in his skin and thought of the child he once was, and then she glanced away. "This may be the same spirit that visited one of the Brûlé camps several winters past. We heard about it, but little was said. No one wanted to disturb that spirit again."

"It's not a spirit, Kezawin. It's a disease. Your father has told me that there are others who are sick, but the spots— a person gets sick first, and then the spots appear a few days later. That's how we know what it is."

"The medicine drum," she acknowledged.

"I think the traders may have brought the disease. If they did, it's in their blankets and every other filthy thing they palmed off on the people."

"I washed the blanket," she said, closing her eyes against the burning. Her mouth was dry, and she was tired, but she didn't want him to think that she would put a blanket on their bed that smelled of white traders. Everything that came from them had to be washed and flown in the air, even in the winter. The smell was... She opened her eyes and saw the blurred shape of her husband's white face, and she smiled a little. He was different. He was not a white man; he was James. "I did wash it," she repeated.

"It doesn't matter. If the traders carried the disease and the blankets were contaminated—"

"I don't understand." Kezawin shook her head and sighed. "Illness comes to the body, not blankets. It's an evil that dwells—"

He raised his hands in protest. "This thing comes from my world, and I know it well. We must burn everything they brought and keep the sick people away from those who are well."

"Why?"

"Because it spreads from one to another. I have seen this, and I know."

She pulled at the buffalo robe, trying to draw it closer to her chin. "Then you must leave here, James. You must take my father and the others who—"

"No." He touched her cheek, and she flinched, trying to draw back. "It's all right," he soothed, brushing her hair back from her face. "I've had the pox. I can't get it again. I'm the only one who should tend the sick."

"You must tell my father," she said. "You must tell the *wakincuzas* of your experiences with this pox."

"I'll tell them they must order the healthy families to move and put those who are sick together in—"

"James." She laid her hand on his arm and struggled with fading senses. "Don't tell them what they must do. They won't hear you. Tell them... what you know. What you have seen. Tell my father first. Let him... I'm so thirsty... so tired..."

He hated leaving her alone, but he had no choice. She had taken a little more soup and gotten sick again. She tried some tea, then slept while he sponged her with tepid water. The wind howled, and a fine cloud of snow swirled about him as he stood before Lone Bear's tipi and asked for admittance. Lone Bear was stretched out on his side, enjoying a smoke.

"I'm tired," he said. "There is too much work for an old man. The north wind brings on too many complaints."

James took his place to Lone Bear's right, but he left a six-foot space between them. Then he committed what he knew to be an unpardonable breech of etiquette by refusing the pipe. "Your daughter is very ill, Lone Bear. I cannot smoke with you. I cannot smoke with anyone."

"Is this part of your medicine now?"

"Yes." It was not untrue, although it was not part of his vision. Lone Bear had given him an explanation that would serve him well. "I must touch no one who is well now. I may touch only the sick, and I know that my wife is not the only one.''

"I have been in three different lodges just tonight," Lone Bear said. "It's too much for an old man. Buffalo Dreamer is busy, too. Something bad is afoot here."

"I know. I have seen it before, and I know what must be done."

Lone Bear saw the fear in his son-in-law's face. Out of respect for the young man, he turned his attention to the fire. "Is this a thing that comes from the white man?" he asked.

"Yes, I believe it is."

"Have you brought it here?"

"No. I had the disease when I was a child, and it will not come to me again."

Lone Bear considered the news and nodded. "That is powerful medicine."

"Yes, it is. And because I'm the only one who has this medicine, I must use it to help the people. And I must speak with the *wakincuzas* and tell them what I know."

Lone Bear looked at James again. "I remember your vision."

"Yes," James said softly. "So do I."

"They will listen to you because you have been to the hill. You need not tell them everything you saw there, but they must know that your *sicun* guides you in this matter."

Lone Bear instructed the *eyapaha* to announce a gathering of the ones who decide in the council lodge. Four men gathered, and James cringed as he watched them pass the pipe among themselves, but he said nothing. Lone Bear explained that James's medicine dictated that he keep his distance and refuse the pipe for the present time, and the explanation was not questioned.

"A number of people have become ill in recent days," James began. "They have fever, pain in the back and head, and they cannot keep their food down. Some may have spots." He passed his hand over his face and chest. "Dark red spots all over them. I have to come to talk with you about this illness."

"*Ohan,*" said Red Elk, the eldest of the four, nodding his approval as he lit a twist of sweet grass and laid it over a rock in the fire pit. "My grandson is sick."

"Then what I have to say comes all the harder. I have seen this illness before. My mother died from it. I suffered from it, too, but I recovered, and it will not plague my body again. The only way to prevent it from spreading throughout the camp is to keep those who are sick far away from those who are well."

James waited while the pipe was passed again. He wanted to say his piece and get back to Kezawin, but he knew that the deliberations would not be rushed. There would be no voting. The decision would be made by consensus, which took time. James rubbed his hand over his stubby beard and tried to recall his last shave.

"This illness comes from the white man, then," Meets The Enemy said. "It is the one that killed the Brûlés."

"I think it's the same one," James concurred, "although there are other illnesses that come with spots on the skin. My wife is a healer, and she has not seen spots like these. I think the traders brought it here."

"There is an evil among us," said Meets The Enemy. "Perhaps *you* brought it here, Garrett. You have been with the whites and the Pawnee. You married one who has dreamed of the deer woman. You killed my nephew."

"I have helped many others when they needed medicine, as has my wife," James said evenly. "All of you know what happened between me and Thun—the one you speak of. It was not my wish to kill him, but neither was it my wish to die."

The pipe was passed again before Cry Of The Crow contributed his thoughts. "Tunkašila would never protect us if we abandoned our sick ones."

"The new camp need not be far away," James said. "I would tend the sick, and those who are healthy would bring us food, water and wood. Everything that came from the traders must be burned, and nothing that the sick ones have used must be taken to the new camp. The illness abides in their bedding and on the bowls from which they drink.''

''I cannot think that I would leave my grandson and make a new camp,'' Red Elk said.

James leaned his elbows against his knees and stared at his own hands. ''When my mother and I were ill,'' he said, barely audibly, ''my father left us. I remember the sound of his footsteps as he walked away.''

''What did you do?'' Cry Of The Crow asked.

''My mother died, and I lived to hate him for it.'' He lifted one shoulder as if he could shrug off all those years. ''But I lived,'' He looked up. ''My father lived, and so did my older brother. There were many who died.''

''And so it will be,'' Red Elk said. ''Some will live and some will die, but the Lakota will stay together in all things.''

''You have separated into smaller camps for the winter,'' James pointed out, ''because it's easier to feed a smaller group and because... because survival—*our* survival—depends upon our doing what's best for all of us. We would have two small camps, close but not—''

''Everyone in one of the camps would be sick,'' Red Elk countered.

''Except me,'' James replied. ''I will not get sick.''

Meets The Enemy turned to Lone Bear. ''Did you interpret this one's vision?'' Lone Bear nodded. ''How do our people fall ill while this man does not? How does he avoid the deer woman's power? Is he a man of true vision, or does he trick us?''

''His medicine has grown stronger since he came to us,'' Lone Bear said. ''I have seen that he has a vision of the people, and for this I waved the horses' tails over him and made him a *hunka*. He would not deceive us.''

''I am *wakan*,'' James said. Hearing the words from his own mouth brought him a sense of inner strength. ''I know that now. Something brought me here. Perhaps this *śicun* my wife speaks about. I don't know. But I know now that I'm not lost. I'm here because I am supposed to be here. I have seen this in a vision, and I know that I have medicine. Beyond that, I bring the memory of an experience that no one seeks, but because of it, I can be useful to the people.''

"What you suggest is impossible,'' Meets The Enemy said. "If the traders brought this thing, I think you must be one of them. They will come back and murder the helpless in the camp you 'tend.' ''

James stared into the fire. "My wife is growing strong with child,'' he said quietly. "She is also sick with this disease.''

Again the pipe was passed, and the spark at the end of the slow-burning sweet grass glowed its last. "We must think about this,'' Red Elk said finally. "We must watch and wait. That is all I have to say.''

"Ohan," was chorused in agreement. Lone Bear only grunted. Red Elk tapped the ashes from the pipe, and the five men went their separate ways in the cold white night.

The more time they took to think about it, the worse things would get, James told himself as he trudged homeward. With his badgerskin over his head and his buffalo robe dragging behind him in the snow, he wondered at the strange figure he would have cut on the Harvard campus. How his life had changed in a year's time. Something had brought him here, he'd said. The real wonder was that he'd believed everything he'd said. He was not the same James Garrett who had walked the wintery streets of Boston in top hat and billowing black cloak a year ago. And the man he was now, no matter what the apparel, no longer belonged there. But Meets The Enemy—and there were surely many others—was not ready to grant him a place here.

The wind whistled in his ears as he bent to unfasten the lodge door, but as he pulled the peg, the sound of his wife's pain cut through all else. It was a breathlessly shallow, desperate grunting sound. He tore through the door and fastened it against the howling wind with unsteady fingers. His robe and his badgerskin hat crumpled in a heap on the floor. He tossed two pieces of wood on the fire on his way to her bedside.

"I'm sorry I was gone so long, but I had to..."

She saw a yellow beacon through the fog of her pain, and somewhere in the core of her brain she knew that it was wrong for him to be there. He was a man, and this was a woman's time. She tried to push him back with a trembling hand. "Go, James. When it's over—"

"When what's over? You're going to be—"

"It's the child," she gasped. "When it's over, then we shall grieve together, but now..."

He swallowed hard and glanced down, then away. The buffalo robe covered the length of her, but underneath that... Again she panted, voicing only the slightest hint of her agony with a low grunt. He took her hands in his. She squeezed them with more strength than he'd thought she had left.

"I'll make a poultice for the bleeding," he whispered.

"It's too late. The child has slipped from my body."

The pain subsided for the moment, leaving her dark eyes glazed with grief. "There will be more children," he promised. "You will grow strong again."

"But I lost *this* one."

"*We,*" he amended. "We lost him."

His eyes, once blue, now gray, were sorrow itself. That much she could discern through the mist that filled her head. "You must go," she said, rasping. "However different, you are still a man, and this is a woman's—"

I am your husband, his brain cried, but calmly he said, "I am a shaman, and I have learned much of what I know from a woman. You will not send me away."

The poultice he used was her medicine. The snowpack he put around her middle was his. The pain finally dulled, and the flow of blood became manageable. He cleaned up the bed, made some broth and got her to drink a little before she fell asleep. He was about to take some food when a voice outside summoned him to the council lodge.

There were only three of the *wakincuzas* there. James seated himself as he had before, and waited while the pipe was passed.

Lone Bear spoke. "Red Elk's grandson has died, and his wife and daughter are both sick. The *eyapaha* will announce the new camp at daybreak, and those who are untouched by the disease will move. We have decided upon a place on the far side of the ravine where there is windbreak."

James nodded. "How many would you say have become ill?"

"Maybe eight or nine."

"Move this lodge closer to mine. It's large enough to accommodate those and more." James sighed. "I'm afraid there will be more. Every person who is not sick must leave, but whoever becomes sick must return."

"There will be some who will not leave," Lone Bear said.

"But they must be ordered to leave. If they aren't sick, they must not be allowed to stay."

"Each person must decide for himself if someone close to him is ill," Lone Bear said. "I would not separate a mother from her child or—"

"If that mother has other children, she must think of them." James glanced from one wizened face to another, but none of the three would agree with him. "I hope you will explain to them what the consequences might be if they stay."

"We will tell them all that you have said. Red Elk has decided to stay," Lone Bear said. "As have I."

"Your daughter would not have you stay. I shall care for her and the others."

"It is too much for one man." He tapped the ashes from the pipe, and all four unfolded their legs and stood to leave.

"Lone Bear," James pleaded. "Please set an example for the others. Those who are well must look after themselves, and they must supply us with water and wood and . . . and offer prayers for this pox to leave us."

"I am not well," Lone Bear said quietly. "Meets The Enemy and Cry Of The Crow will go to the new camp. The *akicita* will collect those things that must be destroyed and see to the burning."

In the dim firelight James looked closely and detected the first sign—the yellowish cast of the old man's face. "I will bring your sleeping robes to my lodge, *Tunkanśi*," James said, calling him father-in-law. Lone Bear nodded. "There is something else," James added, turning to the others. "The corpses must be burned along with all that they have touched.

"That is not our way," Cry Of The Crow protested.

"In this camp, Red Elk and I shall decide," Lone Bear said. "When the time comes, we shall decide. But the four of us have agreed that you will keep no sick ones on the far side of the ravine."

Meets The Enemy's lip curled as he glanced at James. "How soon before everyone is back here, I wonder. Will the white man watch the last of the Lakota turn to smoke and ash?"

"I saw that some would die, and others would live," James answered. "But I did not see their faces. Already I have lost—" he turned to Lone Bear and gentled his voice "—my unborn child."

and they must supply us with water and wood and . . . and
offer prayers for this post to leave us."

"I am not well," James said quietly. Many, The
Plums and the Of The Crow will go to the new camp. The
warriors will collect those things that must be destroyed and
see to the burning . . ."

In my own tipi . . ." Lone Bear . . . and directed the
first one—the . . . woman . . . of the old man's face. "I will
bring your sisters . . . of . . . here now," James
said, taking him reluctantly. Lone Bear nodded. "Their
is something else," James added, turning to the others.

Chapter Twelve

Some of the people could not be persuaded to move to the
new camp and leave sick loved ones behind. Many Plums
was one who stayed behind with her sons, both of whom
had contracted smallpox. James knew that all he could do
for them was to treat the symptoms—the fever, the nausea, the pain—with herbal medicine and cool sponge baths,
and to try to get them to drink as much as possible. Red
Elk, who said that the years had tanned his hide and made
his skin too leathery to become spotted, spent nights as well
as days ministering to the sick. Lone Bear contributed
smoke, prayers and supplications until he collapsed in
James's arms and had to be carried back to his daughter's
lodge.

Kezawin continued to weaken, but each time James returned to the lodge to see to his wife, coax her to take some
tea or broth and tell her she was getting better, she re-
solved to live through the night to hear him tell her that the
sun had risen on another day. Then she would close her
eyes, and the deer woman's laughter would ring in her ears
and keep her from succumbing to a deeper, more restful
sleep.

When she rested that way, her breathing so slight and
shallow, James would hold her in his arms, listen to her
hallucinatory murmurings and chafe her fragile hand between his rough palms to remind her that there was life in

her limbs. "You cannot leave me," he would whisper, hoping she could hear him through her pain. "You once told me that I needed to discover what I value, and I have done that. It's you, Kezawin. You're my partner, remember? My teacher and pupil, my *kola*, my lover, my wife. It was not by chance that we found one another. You know that. We came together like two halves to become whole, and I will not become that pathetic fraction again. I don't know what I would do or where I would go if you left me now."

He pressed her hand to his mouth, willing her to feel the bonding between them. He wanted her to draw on his strength, his breath, his body's immunity. If ever such a thing was possible between two people, it had to be for them. Two halves of a whole. Two of the world's misfits, one concave with loneliness, one convex with unfulfilled promise. Across half a continent God—or *Tunkaśila*, who were one and the same to James now—had brought them together and found a perfect fit.

"You'll not leave me now, Kezawin." There was a hard edge to his softly spoken demand, as if he thought repeating it more firmly would make it be true. "If you go, I swear I'm going with you. I'll not stay behind to bury the dead. I'll not be the white man who shovels the dirt over the faces of the people. Let me be one with you, Kezawin. Stay with me. If I have a purpose, I cannot fulfill it without you. Stay with me," he muttered as he brushed his lips over her sweat-dampened temple. "Stay."

Each morning James met a messenger from the *akicita*, who brought wood and water, food if there was any to be found, and the newly sick. He stood at the rendezvous place and watched Catch The Bear approach this time, leading a horse loaded with wood and paunches of water. The morning's fog had lifted, and it floated overhead like a length of shimmering gauze, reducing the sun's power to a round soft glow. In his heavy wearing robe and his plush coyote cap, Catch The Bear mirrored James as the two men

faced each other across the established twenty-foot quar-
antine space.

"Can I hope that you bring me no new patients today,
my friend?" James asked.

"I bring only water and wood. Perhaps the end of this
nightmare is in sight."

"We need food here, Catch The Bear. Fresh meat. Some
are so weak—"

"I will bring the next kill. The snow is so deep, all the
creatures are sleeping or gone." He studied the length of
reins he held between his hands. "How is it with my wife
and sons?"

"I think Blue Heels has come through the worst of it,"
James said. "Many Plums . . . has fever now."

Catch The Bear nodded without looking up. "What news
must I take back to the others?"

"During the night we lost the mother to Runs His Horses
and Four Strikes's young son."

"I will tell them today's smoke belongs to them." He
raised his head, and James saw that the man's eyes glittered beneath the silver fur of his cap. "What of my son,
Mouse Face Boy?"

"Keep him in your prayers, my friend. He is very weak."

"It's hard being separated from them. If the *akicita* were
not needed here, I would cross over and die with them."

As he heard the anguish in his brave friend's words,
James remembered a similar vow he'd made to Kezawin
earlier. Catch The Bear would carry on for the good of the
living even if his heart crossed over to the camp of the dying. Would that he, James, could find such courage of his
own, he thought to himself. "I will care for them as I would
my brother's family," James promised.

Catch The Bear turned and trudged away.

Lone Bear was dying, and there was no help for it. James
had lost track of the days. Six, he believed, for Kezawin.
The spots on her body had turned to blisters. Three, he

thought, for Lone Bear. He had just broken out with the rash, but the fever had taken a heavy toll on the old man.

"No more," Lone Bear protested, shaking his head at the sight of the bowl in James's hand. "I cannot swallow."

"You must tell me what to do, *Tunkanŝi*. I've tried my medicine. Let me try yours. Tell me..."

Lone Bear lifted a bony hand and pressed his dry lips together. "When the time comes, you get the drum. You play slow... you play easy. I shall sing my death song."

"Your daughter still lives. Are you not as strong as she? Look at her." James knew that in his condition Lone Bear couldn't see that far. But it was for Kezawin's sake that he became angry with the old man. There she lay sleeping, her breathing shallow, but each time he brought her something, she drank. "She won't give up, *Tunkanŝi*, and I don't want her to wake up and find you gone."

Cracked lips stretched in a lurid smile. "I won't go far, you know. Don't speak my name."

"Don't try to scare me, old man. I'm not as naive as I once was."

"You've learned some," Lone Bear acknowledged. "When you have patience... when you have wisdom..." He closed his eyes, struggled with a few labored breaths, then surprised James with a faint dry cackle. "Then you will be as old as I am."

"I haven't time to become as wise as you. There are not enough suns and moons and summers to accomplish that."

"You know how to fill an old man's heart." Because he could no longer drink, he sucked at his cheeks, seeking enough moisture from within to finish out his life. "Think of this," he said. "There are some moments so packed full of life, like a woman nearing her time. They make up for a hundred summers. Those are the moments that make you... the man you are."

Surely this was one of those moments, and James searched for some important thing to say, something that would keep the old man there with him just a little longer. "I will dance this summer and gaze at the sun," he promised hastily. "I will pierce my breast. You must be there to see this, *Ate* to guide me, to show me the way."

The graying head rolled listlessly from one side to the other, but the thin smile was there. James had called him *ate*—father, not father-in-law—and Lone Bear understood. "You will know the way. You must make your vow...but not to me. *Tunkašila* will hear you. Say, 'All my relatives.'"

"*Mitakuye oyasin.*"

"Yes. We shall hear you, also. Rest assured." He opened his eyes suddenly and lifted a glazed stare toward a point beyond the smoke hole. "Welcome him," he intoned. "Welcome him. He comes. He comes."

James snatched Lone Bear's small medicine drum from its place near his bed and took up the beat of the old man's chant.

> "I am an old man.
> I have made much medicine.
> I am content to follow my relatives.
> He comes, *hey hunh*. He comes."

The chant became thready and weak, and finally it drifted on a trail of smoke toward the night sky.

Kezawin had listened to her father's death song, but she hadn't the strength to mourn him properly. She had seen tears standing in her husband's eyes, but she could not make them herself. Her body had been drained of the new life it had nourished and of the fluids that nourished her own life. Her body burned. Her father's inner fire had consumed him quickly, but hers burned slowly while her life evaporated. She had at least a dim awareness of everything around her, but it was all a part of the burning. When

James spoke to her of sorrow, she felt none. She hadn't the strength. She said nothing as she watched her husband take her father's remains from the lodge.

James carried Lone Bear's body to the little knoll that was already black with charcoaled wood and ashes. He arranged a bed of wood and laid the shell of the man, wrapped in his sleeping robes, to one side. Stalwart old Red Elk added the small bundled corpse of a child, and together they watched the past and the promise of the Lakota go up in flames. The heat from the fire seared James's eyes, and he let them be soothed by a gathering of tears.

It was not until he returned to the lodge that he truly saw how it was with Kezawin. The pulse beat in her wrist skittered against his fingers, and her breathing came in erratic puffs. She had held out this long, he thought, and if he could bring strength into her blood, she would survive. He had shared what food they had, and there was little left. He'd long since come to terms with his own hunger and made his peace with dried vegetables, but Kezawin needed fresh meat. Her people were hunters, and the blood of all prairie creatures flowed together in one communal vessel.

He offered her a sip of tea, but she refused. For the first time since she'd been ill, she turned the bowl away and curled up within herself. Panic pierced his gut like the hunter's lance.

"You have to try, Kezawin."

She seemed not to hear. Her lips were taut and unnaturally gray, and her eyelids were puffy. He adjusted his arm beneath her head and touched the bowl to her lips again. Her eyes and her lips remained closed.

"You can't die," he said flatly. "There's too much ahead for us. I know it. I can feel it. We have things to do, a life to live together. We have..."

The painting of the white deer claimed his attention. The light from the flames flickered over its stylized profile, the form he had not finished painting. The form itself was stiff and lifeless, but the cherry-hued eye gleamed with soft, unstinting compassion. Strange. He couldn't remember painting that eye. Perhaps Kezawin had finished it for him. But he had left other forms unfinished on the dew cloth. Why had she finished that one? And how did it come to look so...human?

He settled Kezawin back on the bed, rested his head in his hand and pressed his fingers against his eyes. Hunger and fatigue did strange things to the mind, he thought, but when he looked up again, the eye still looked down at him with the same haunting expression.

"Why?" he whispered to the painted form. "Did you bring me here to watch these people die? I'm no good to her. I'm no good to any of them now. Me and my kind." He stared steadily at the eye while he stumbled to his feet, the blood suddenly pumping through his body with growing, audible force. "Don't bring any more of us. Do you hear? Look what we've done!"

His head was filled with a terrible pounding, a sound and fury like the buffalo surround. Something compelled him to take up his robe and his rifle, even while he watched the painting, almost expecting it to move. He backed toward the door, taking a moment's worth of sanity to glance at Kezawin and see that she was sleeping. A moment's worth was all he had. He left the lodge without purpose or reason, his legs walking without direction. Something pulled him past the smoldering pyre on the hill and deep into the night. He heard nothing but the staccato pounding, the awful rush of pure energy. He saw nothing but black sky and white plains glistening, stretching into eternity. The Milky Way was the Lakota trail to eternity. Perhaps this was his journey.

He came to a grove of cottonwoods that stood beside a frozen creek. The roar inside his head faded away, and he heard the quiet of winter. He peered into the trees, but the grove was deep and dark as death. Then a breeze moved among the topmost branches, and they rustled like the medicine rattle. He took another step and stopped. Something didn't want him in the grove.

All right, he told himself. I'll wait here.

He watched, and as he waited, his mind was filled with the need for food. Not his own need, but Kezawin's and the others who were weak from the illness. He smelled meat, but he had no hunger for it. He saw himself as provider. Squatting in the snow, he loaded his rifle and balanced it over his knees, wondering how he'd satisfied himself on willow bark and calamus root. Perhaps he *had* become a brother to the deer. He pulled his badgerskin down over his forehead and waited—for what, he didn't know. He only knew that he was here, where he was supposed to be, and that something was coming.

The white deer, a shining, regal creature, stepped from the grove. James froze with his last breath caught deep in his chest. This area had been hunted and picked clean months ago. Where had this deer come from? His rump was round and ample, and his hindquarters were well shaped. He looked as though he'd been grazing in a cornfield all winter.

He could not be shot. No hunter would shoot such an animal, even if it meant that his family would go hungry. Even if James didn't believe that such a creature was *wakan* and that shooting it could bring about calamity, he knew that the albino was rare. He was enchanted by the wonder of the creature, who should not have been there at all. He should have fled the vicinity with his kind long ago.

James sat still and waited. The white deer sniffed the night air and took another step in his direction. Something spoke in his ears, telling him that Kezawin could not live another day without fresh meat. And there were others. Blue Heels, Mouse Face Boy and Many Plums. Poor noseless White Otter's Tail and old Whirling Water. All of them needed fresh meat.

Welcome him. Welcome him. He comes. He comes.

James gripped the barrel and the stock of his rifle, and his eyes became wide with horror as he watched the white deer approach. No! He could not do this thing. He stood abruptly and waved his hand. "Run!" he shouted. "Keep running till you reach the mountains!"

The deer stood still. James could see his eye now, soft with a compassionate gleam. "Run away," he whispered, his voice hoarse. "I can't shoot you."

Tears blurred his sight, and he heard the death rattle in the trees. His vision was no longer limited by his eyesight.

You are White Deer's Brother. You cannot use your brother selfishly, but he will share his flesh to help you feed your family.

"Send me something else," he pleaded as he shouldered the rifle. He trembled violently inside himself, but his hands were steady. "*Tunkaśila*, send me something else. Not this beautiful . . . prophetic . . ."

Welcome him. Welcome him. He comes. He comes.

The white deer stepped closer, then stood ready.

James aimed for a clean, quick kill and pulled the trigger. The deer dropped heavily in the snow. The tears that coursed down James's cheeks as he drew his knife were as much for those at home as they were for the brother who lay at his feet. They were for Lone Bear and Kezawin, Mouse Face Boy and White Otter's tail—all who suffered. He sang his apology in a surprisingly steady voice and knelt to gut the sacrifice.

James's stomach churned, but he knew that real sickness was not the cause. The odor of boiling venison made him queasy and spared him from any consideration of eating it himself, no matter how hungry he was. He cooled a bowl of the broth he'd made from the meat and one select herb. Sliding his arm beneath Kezawin's head, he prepared himself for her initial refusal, but not for her question.

"There is no more venison. Where did you . . . get this?"

He thought for a moment. He knew he could not lie to her, but to tell her what he'd done... "This was given to you by your *sicun*," he said.

"The white deer?"

James nodded, still holding the bowl for her.

"You did not... hunt him down."

"Drink this, and I will tell you how my brother provides for my family tonight."

She glanced at the bowl, and when she looked back up at him, he saw trust. She sipped at the blood of his brother.

"He must have been real," James said as he slid his leg beneath her back to lend support. "Meat cannot be made from dreams. Yet the whole time I was butchering, I expected it all to vanish into the frigid night air. I was led to the cottonwood grove," he marveled. "By what or whom, I don't know, but I simply followed... something. And he came to me. I couldn't chase him away. And that voice..."

It seemed strange to talk about it. Ordinary human words made the whole experience sound preposterous in his own ears. He'd killed the white deer, and that was that. Right or wrong, he'd done it.

"You knew the voice?"

She doubted nothing he'd said. He could see that in her eyes. The mystery was perfectly acceptable to her as a mystery. It didn't have to be solved. He was grateful for that, because she took the soup on faith, and there was no stronger case he could have prepared to persuade her to eat.

"It sounded to me like your father's voice, but, of course, he's very much on my mind, and I might have imagined, distraught as I was..."

"The soup is good," she whispered.

He smiled. A tight bud of hope began to open within him. "I don't know where he came from. He was as fat as a corn-fed calf."

"The Mandan had no corn to speak of this year. Perhaps he visited the Pawnee."

There was a spark in her eye, a light he'd not seen since the morning she fell ill. His heart soared. "I made a vow to pierce myself and gaze at the sun," he told her. "I told your father this, and I shall keep my word."

She nodded.

"You will recover now, Kezawin. You'll get strong again."

"And the others?"

"I'm encouraged by the fact that we have no new patients from the other camp. Red Elk has miraculously not been stricken. The fresh meat will help the others, at least some of them, I'm sure."

"You knew what to do," she said. "That's why you were brought here by my *sicun*."

"Perhaps." She finished the broth, and he laid her down and covered her with the buffalo robe. "Rest now and let the blood of my brother do its work."

Her eyes were drifting closed when she asked, "What was the herb you added to the soup?"

"That was the red root plant."

Mouse Face Boy was little more than a remnant of what he'd once been. His small crippled body had wasted away, having had no real muscle to feed on. Blue Heels had rallied, and he sat with his brother, trying to get him to drink some of the broth that the white shaman had made for the sick ones. But it was no use. The soup ran from the corner of Mouse Face Boy's mouth. He could not swallow. He muttered unintelligibly. Part of him had gone on its last journey already, and soon his breath would follow.

Blue Heels himself had been strong enough to partake of the meat of the deer the white man had killed. Over the course of the day his body had cooled, and the nausea had subsided. He had few spots on his body, certainly fewer than his mother, Many Plums, whose bed lay opposite her sons' on the woman's side of the lodge. Her breathing was labored. She, too, had been unable to take any nourishment. Not far from where she lay, Red Elk was making a bundle of White Otter's Tail's corpse. The woman without a nose. Perhaps she could be at peace now, Blue Heels thought. Surely she had paid the price for her bad behavior.

When the white man entered the lodge, Blue Heels stiffened. He held his dying brother's head in his lap, and he needed to be angry with someone. The traders had brought this evil upon his people, and the traders were white. Mouse Face Boy loved this man, but Blue Heels could not share in that devotion. He scooted back toward the dew cloth and glowered as the man approached.

"My brother is dying," Blue Heels announced defiantly, as though James might be getting his wish.

James knelt beside the frail little figure, took his pulse and touched his face. He sighed, hoping to expel the debilitating sense of helplessness he felt, but it was still there when he took another breath. He looked at Blue Heels and saw his anger. "You know your brother better than anyone," James said. "If you say death is coming to him, I believe you. How shall we prepare for this?"

"I don't want him to die."

"I know. Have you told him this?"

"I have told him, but I don't think he can hear me anymore."

James brushed the loose fall of hair away from the inert boy's face. "Perhaps not. Perhaps he is already at peace."

"It's the white traders," Blue Heels said. "And others like them."

James looked up, and this time he saw that the hatred was for him. "I'm sorry, my friend. You're right. I'm afraid we've brought trouble."

"I should kill you," Blue Heels ground out. Lightning sizzled in his dark eyes.

"If it would help Mouse Face Boy, I would say, go ahead." All the sadness he had known gathered in the grayness of his eyes. "I have killed, and I know that nothing is solved when the killing is done. It is a burden I would not wish upon a friend."

"I am not your friend."

"But I am yours." He touched Mouse Face Boy's cheek with the back of his hand. Another child, he thought. He remembered how hardy they had seemed as he'd watched them time and again, playing on the ice. Immune to the cold, but not the pox. "I lost the child my wife carried," he said quietly. "I lost my father-in-law. Years ago I lost my mother. All to this evil disease." Again James delved Blue Heels's dark eyes with his. "I grieve with you."

Finally Blue Heels permitted the pain, but he denied himself tears. "It should be me," he said. "The accident that crippled him many years ago—that was my fault. My brother should live in my body, and I should die in his."

The haunted darkness in the boy's eyes seemed worse than tears. James cast about for words, and suddenly they were there. "I have known this feeling you're experiencing, but what you suggest is not within your power. My father-in-law would tell you that there are other sacrifices you can make."

"What good will they do?"

"I don't know," James said. "We listen to those who are wiser than we are, follow their good examples, and then we watch and wait."

The next morning Blue Heels came to James's lodge. Out of respect he kept his eyes from the sleeping robes at the back of the tent as he took the crow that was perched on his shoulder and offered it to James.

"Since we must burn his belongings, we have nothing of his to give away except this bird. He would want it to go to you, James Garrett."

James nodded and offered his forearm as a perch.

"My mother is gone, too," Blue Heels said. "We're taking them up to the hill now."

"I shall join you there."

After the boy left, James found a perch for Sapa, the crow, on the top of his willow backrest. He added wood to the fire and gathered up his robe and his hat, all the while avoiding Kezawin's eyes. He had thought he could become hardened to all this after so much death, but he had not. If anything, it seemed he had gotten softer. Inside his chest his heart was breaking, and he could not look up. One look at her face would be his undoing.

"You must help me, James."

His resolve disappeared as he turned to find her sitting up in bed. She held her hair to one side, and with her skinning knife, she was sawing it off.

"Kezawin, what—"

"I would go to the hill with you," she said. "It is time I grieved, too."

In two long steps he was by her side. "You're as weak as a fledgling sparrow," he protested. "You can't even stand."

"You will help me," she said calmly. "If I falter, you will carry me. If you refuse, I shall proceed on hands and knees until I reach the place where they have all gone."

He watched the lovely black hair fall to the floor in discarded disarray. "He would not want this, Kezawin."

"He must be mourned properly. Four days, and then no more crying." She lifted her chin, and he saw the first tears he had ever seen standing in her eyes. "I have not yet had my four days."

"Please, love," he whispered. "You've been so sick. Have a care for yourself... for your husband."

"I do." She touched his soft, sleek, golden beard. "Your heart breaks, just as mine does. Mine will not heal until it has wailed in sorrow. And you must do what your way demands."

He dressed her warmly, but it was to no avail. Once they reached the bleak, white, windswept hill, she threw off her robe and scratched bloody furrows in her arms while she keened. Kezawin's voice rose highest above the crackling flames. Red Elk chanted, and Blue Heels, who had gashed his legs, covered his head with ashes and took a stoic stance. James allowed his heart its own expression. Tears rolled down his cheeks as he watched his wife rend her clothes and shower herself with ashes.

And the shrill sound of her keening echoed in the hills and became one with the wretched winter wind.

Chapter Thirteen

The long, cold, hungry winter was past. On the hide that bore Red Elk's winter count, the spiral of symbols through which he tracked the life of the band, it was memorialized simply as Smallpox Winter. The old man sensed that this would not be the last time the symbol was used, but he hoped it was the last time he would paint it himself. The measures they had taken to prevent the evil from jumping from one person's body to another's may have saved lives, but they had been unsettling. Children had been separated from parents. It was wrong to do this. People had been sent on their final journey without raising their bodies toward the sun. This was wrong, too, and Red Elk's instincts had shouted against it. But it was done to banish the evil, and soon after James had brought fresh meat, the evil had moved on.

For now, summer had come to the prairie once again. The deep snow had nourished earth's deepest roots and brought forth lush spring grass, and the early-summer rain had kept it green. The Hunkpapa journeyed southward. The small winter camps had come together, small creeks flowing into a larger stream. By the time the sun had reached its solstice, they would join the rest of their Lakota cousins in the sacred *Paha Sapa*, the Black Hills, where those who may have suffered less during the hunger moons would honor their cousins' endurance with gifts and songs.

There would be feasting and ceremony in celebration of the promise of life's renewal.

There were always many vows made during hard times, and this summer there would be many dancers who would gaze at the sun. Young men like Blue Heels would dance for the first time, and older men would seek new levels of vision. A few of the women would dance in behalf of people who were absent from them, but they would not be pierced. In all cases, the dancers had offered the pipe and made a vow. They journeyed now toward a rendezvous in the majestic pine-covered hills with, as they were wont to repeat ceremonially, all their relations, including those who had been and were yet to be.

James had made the vow as well, first to Lone Bear, and then in the formal, proper way. Kezawin lived, and in his mind the Sun Dance was something he could do to show his gratitude. Red Elk had agreed to sponsor him, to be the instructor that Lone Bear would have been to him. But as James rode beside his wife within the moving stream of people under the warm summer sun, he felt bereft by Lone Bear's absence and a reluctance to participate in the ceremony without him. The bird riding with him on the wooden perch he'd fashioned reminded him of another absence.

Kezawin sensed her husband's restlessness, and she knew that he would choose his time to speak his mind. They made camp, shared food and walked together in silence. There were women playing the plum pit game, girls wrapping strings around their fingers in a version of cat's cradle, and men swapping stories around camp fires. A young woman great with child ducked into her tipi when she saw James and Kezawin coming, but there were others who greeted them warmly. Catch The Bear, on his way to his Kit Fox Society gathering, stopped to suggest that James join Blue Heels and him for a hunt.

They walked beyond the camp toward the hills where the horses grazed. Kezawin had grown accustomed to the way

James would take her hand sometimes as they walked, especially once they had left the camp behind them.

"I found more red root plant this evening while you were getting water," he told her, breaking the silence.

"You seem to find it only when I'm not with you."

He'd never thought about it before, but he realized it was true. "Coincidence, I'm sure."

"I think it calls to you. Haven't you noticed?" The fringe of her dress tapped her legs softly as she walked. "It happens to me with some plants. My favorites, like food-of-the-elk."

"Maybe it does, in a way. I was watching a fight on the hill, and afterwards—"

"A fight?"

"A badger and a rattlesnake." He chuckled with the memory. "The snake was enjoying a nice warm rock and the badger's den must have been underneath it. You've never heard so much spitting and hissing. The badger puffed up like a billowing sheet, leaping into the air when the snake struck. Neither took his attention off the other as I crept up on them. I got pretty close before the snake fell back and slithered away."

"The badger won the battle?"

He nodded. "For the time being. He scooted under his rock to lick his wounds, I suppose, but the rattler had left him to his den. Then I found the red root plant, just down the hill near the creek bank. I went right to it."

"Your medicine bag is made of badgerskin. He shares his victory with you."

"A part of me said, this is interesting. I must observe. I must make notes. Another part said, this is significant. I must find someone who is wiser than I am and ask him what it means."

"What did you do?"

He shrugged. "I gathered some of the red root plant and came home."

"Some?"

"I left some to reseed, just as you always do. And I, uh, I made my apologies." He didn't know why he hesitated in reporting the latter. There was a feeling of rightness about making his peace with the plants.

They had walked into the privacy of the night, veering away from the horse herd, which was guarded by sentries. Crickets sang in the tall grass. "Shall we sit together in the cottonwood grove by the creek and talk of—"

"No, let's find another place. The other side of the hill, perhaps." Since the night he had followed his instincts to the grove where the white deer waited, he had not entered a grove of trees after dark. He remembered the strong feeling he'd gotten that the grove was inviolable, at least to him. It wasn't the thinking of an educated man, he told himself. Nevertheless, he hiked over the hill with his wife, and she took the blanket from her shoulders and spread it out for them.

The blanket created a cozy nest in the grass, a place to while away the night and enjoy the star-studded sky. He told her his names for the constellations and recounted Greek myths. She countered with her names for them and the legends the Lakota told. It surprised him that on opposing sides of the planet people had for centuries looked up at the same sky and seen the same shapes—bears, dogs, hunters, those who had dared to dream or dared to disobey.

"I'm afraid of the Sun Dance," he confessed finally without preface.

"It is a demanding ordeal," she said. "You must be prepared for pain."

"I'm not afraid of pain. I'm afraid of..." He searched the patterns of stars, looking for some hint. "I suppose it's all those things I haven't the capacity to understand. I'm afraid of being at their mercy, of hearing and seeing things that I cannot explain but dare no longer ignore."

"Don't white people have mysteries?"

"Yes, we have mysteries, but we feel compelled to solve them, and if we can't, then we just don't live quite so closely with them, I guess. We attend to them only on one day of the week."

"That seems very strange," she decided.

"Yes, it does...now." He turned over on his side and propped himself up on his elbow. "Kezawin, what if I don't belong here? What would happen if I were to see something or hear something while I dance that tells me I must not stay with the Lakota people?"

"Is this what you fear?"

"Yes. It is my worst fear."

"Where would you go?"

"I don't know. I'm not sure where I belong now."

"Would you take me with you?"

He let a moment of silence pass before asking gently, "Would you go?"

"I am your wife," she said. "We have starved together. We have shared the loss of our child, and whether we have another or not, I will be faithful to my husband."

He knew the full import of her vow. She would not marry again. "I would not take you from your people. They need you."

"Then you would throw me away?"

"No, never. I would never divorce you." He slid the backs of his fingers over her cheek. "I don't know what I would do. I keep thinking I should just leave well enough alone and not ask for any more visions. The last one was...so full of death."

"But it saved many lives, James. This smallpox came from the white man, and only a white man would know what had to be done to break its power."

"But what if there's more?" He rolled over on his back and considered the stars again. Half a continent away there were so many people. How many of them looked up at these same stars even now and wondered about charting a westward course for the chance at a better life?

He sat up, and she followed his lead. A bit of moonlight lit like a moth in her raven hair, which hung just past her shoulders now. He plucked a piece of grass and stuck the end of it in his mouth. "I told you once that I didn't think the white people would ever come here to live. They have their frame houses and their farms and cities, and I cannot think they would try to take this place with its ceaseless wind and flat, unforgiving terrain. But if they do, I cannot think that there will be anything but more trouble."

"But you are not trouble."

"All I wanted to do was study plants. Now it seems all I want to do is love my wife." He smiled. "And study plants and learn their special uses."

"The Sun Dance is a personal matter," she told him. "It is between you and *Tunkašila* whether you rescind your vow."

"What would you think of a man who rescinded his vow?"

"I don't know whether that's ever been done." She was quiet for a moment. "I would think that he knew himself and knew what he had to do."

He chuckled. "You refuse to be a nag, don't you?"

"A female horse?"

"A woman who is always reminding her husband to do this and that."

"Oho! Such a woman might find herself twinkling in the heavens as a reminder to the others. Perhaps the scars from my spots would become the stars."

He touched the twin spots that rode high on her cheeks, one on each side. "These beauty marks," he said. "They remind me that I don't ever want to come that close to losing you again. I need to be more wary. As you say, a white man should know the kind of threat the whites may pose."

"The Lakota are a strong people, James. If there is a fight—"

"This plague we had wasn't a fight," he said. "It was certain death for most of the clan if we had not quarantined the sick."

"What is certain death? Death comes when it comes. Even *Iktomi*, the trickster god, cannot trick death. James Garrett cannot trick death, either. Something *wakan* came to you, just as surely as something *wakan* came to me. We must listen and watch. The white deer is a powerful *ŝicun*."

"I shall honor my vow," he said with assurance, and then in a less confident tone, "I shall attend closely. Let come what comes. I want to know where I belong."

She laid her head against his shoulder. "I think tonight you belong in my arms."

He plucked the stock of grass from the corner of his mouth, and a grin slowly spread across his face. "What makes you think that?"

"Once the preparations begin, you will have to abstain."

"For how long?"

"Red Elk will determine that." She gave a flirtatious laugh as she sat up and looked at him. "I think it may be the hardest part of your sacrifice."

He pushed her hair back from her neck and murmured, "I don't doubt that," as he dipped his head to take a nibble.

"Returning to your wife will be a joyous occasion." With her promise she slyly slipped the knot on his breechclout thong. Her femininity responded even to the warmth of his breath in the hollow of her neck.

He moved his hands along her thighs, pushing her skirt up as he went. "I don't need a vision to tell me that," he whispered.

"But in your weakened condition, you may be unable to—" he groaned when she touched him "—make this warrior stand straight and tall."

"I shall trust him to you." He eased her down into their nest and moved over her.

Only from the vantage point of the hills, which protected the valley like the sides of a cradle, could the real circle be discerned. It was formed by a great multitude of tipis, almost as though they had been tossed into the outstretched hollow like a handful of sand. But the arrangement was prescribed by tradition, and each *tiośpaye*, or clan, had its designated place. Among the Lakota, everything was done in its proper way. When the people gathered for the summer ceremonies, there was a wealth of ancient tradition to be observed. At the center of it all was the Sun Dance, the most solemn and most essential ceremony, because it celebrated the wholeness of the people and made the connection between the flesh and the spirit of the Lakota.

The *eyapaha* rode among the circles within a circle of tipis and announced the choosing of the *can wakan*, the sacred pole. It had taken four days to prepare the campsite and four days for the medicine men to instruct the dancers. The third set of four would be devoted to the dance itself. Trusted scouts had searched for a worthy cottonwood tree and had made their report to the medicine men. The whole camp was abuzz with excitement, and all hearts pounded to the beat of the drum as men, women and children, some riding horses that were painted and draped with leafy chains, went out to bring the chosen tree back to the pit that had been carefully prepared for it.

The tree was cut down by those men and women who had been deemed worthy of the honor. With great care it was stripped of all but the fork and the uppermost branches and leaves before the procession escorted it to its place in the center of camp. There it was erected in the center of a huge circular bower, the Sun Dance lodge, which was made of poles and pine boughs to provide shade for the onlookers. A crosspiece between the forked branches at the top of the pole was outfitted with lengths of rawhide thong, one for each dancer.

For the rest of the people, the preparations had been marked by visiting with old friends and relatives who'd been distant over the long winter months. For those who had vowed to make the Sun Dance sacrifice, the time had been spent together in one lodge receiving instructions. Then came three days of solemnity throughout the camp as the Sun Gazers danced together as one from sunrise to sunset, blowing on eagle-bone whistles and pushing their bodies past the point of exhaustion. On the fourth day the dancers purified themselves in the sweat lodge and made ready for the final step.

James was certain that he had lost all the weight he had gained back after the first good spring hunt, but as Red Elk helped him dress for the climactic portion of the ceremony, he knew that he was ready, both in his mind and body, to meet unusual demands. His every sense seemed unusually keen, and he felt clean and strong. Although many of the dancers wore red skirts, Red Elk wrapped a blue blanket around James's waist to show that, as a wearer of the color of the heavens, he was engaged in a sacred undertaking. He carried a hoop covered with otterskin to symbolize the sun and the cycle of the seasons. He wore the deer amulet Kezawin had given him, and his medicine bundle was suspended around his neck. Arm bands and anklets proclaimed James's love, his strength and his cleverness.

He knew there would be pain, and he was prepared for that. Red Elk had explained to him that he must learn joy in pain and pain in joy, for such was life's greatest truth. After three days of dancing and purification, he had cleared his mind, and he was like the guileless babe who did not question whether the lesson he was about to receive was one he wanted to know.

The dancers followed the medicine men from the Sun Dance tipi to the center of the circular Sun Dance lodge.

Babies were brought to the circle, and the mothers called upon those men who exemplified courage and wisdom to pierce their children's ears. When a man's name was called, he stepped forward and told of his exemplary deeds so that all might learn from him and the infants might follow his precedent.

It was time for the piercing of flesh. James lay on the painted buffalo hide. Red Elk placed a piece of wood between his teeth, and James watched the gray head dip toward his chest. The first pain came of caring. Red Elk bit the flesh above James's heart to make it numb. Then quickly, surely, Red Elk pierced James's flesh with a sharp awl and inserted a sage stick and an eagle's claw, which were tied to one of the braided thongs. He moved to James's right, bit him again, and pierced him a second time. The pain became a dull ache, which throbbed with the beat of the drum.

James got to his feet, and Red Elk pulled him back to make the thongs taut. Blood streamed down to his belly. Catch The Bear helped Blue Heels to his feet and stood him next to James, who now faced the sun. The others, twelve in all, became one with him in this until they no longer needed to look at one another or harken to the sound of one another's presence. They were together, all "gazing at the sun leaning."

The thongs pulled the flesh away from his chest. James looked down at himself and saw two tipis, like a woman's pointed breasts. For a time he would be both man and woman. He remembered the way Kezawin had endured the loss of her child, her father, very nearly her life, and he hoped he could be female courage, as well as male, at least for this brief time. Red Elk put the eagle-bone whistle into James's mouth, and each breath became an offering.

The sun burned deep into his brain until the interior of his head was sheer brightness. At first it had seemed impossible to stare and keep staring, dance and keep dancing, but now it was impossible to look away. The beat of the drum kept his body moving, made his feet shuffle in the step that had become a part of him in the past few days. The singers' voices became distant as the shrill sound of his own whistle filled his ears. Red Elk was always nearby, reminding him to pull back, keep the thongs taut. The flesh would tear, he said. The brave man would bear the pain.

The bright light was filtered now through a soft haze of pain. Kezawin came to him, smiling. He saw that wonderful expression in her eyes, and he remembered she'd always looked at him that way whenever he'd brought meat for her cooking pot. She rubbed something soft over his sweat-streaked face. He could smell the pungent sage.

"I am permitted to clean your wounds," she said. "If thirst threatens to overtake you before you break free, call for water, and I will bring it. There is no shame in this. It is a sacred thing you do."

He knew she tended somehow to his chest, but he could not tell exactly what she did. Her touch soothed him, and he wanted to beg her not to take it from him, but he held his tongue. Afraid that he would disgrace himself, he said nothing while she daubed his face with grease.

"You endure this pain for me," Kezawin said quietly. "For I am one of the people, and you are one with us. You are our *hunka*."

"*Hunka. Hunka. Hunka.*" Another voice superimposed itself upon Kezawin's last word. The voice of the drum. The voice of a man. Not Red Elk. It was Lone Bear. James squared his shoulders and pulled back so that the old man would see his courage and be proud.

The sun blistered his brain, and from the blisters came rattlesnakes. Blue rattlesnakes with fangs that spat bullets faster than any rifle could shoot them. The badger flew from his rocky den and drove them back, but they doubled their numbers and came back to worry the badger from all sides. He bared his black claws and his flashing white teeth, bit off one head, broke the spine of another. But the rattlers struck and struck, hacking at the badger's silvery hide. He backed into his den, and the snakes surrounded him and kept him there.

Welcome him. Welcome him. He comes. He comes.

It would have to be a cool place. The sun blistered and scorched, and the cave would be a place of refuge. James stood at the entrance and asked for permission to enter. Kezawin appeared. "The badger is tired," she said. "He has tried everything, but they have no ears. They cannot understand. They make so much noise sputtering and hissing and spitting bullets. How do they hear *Tunkašila* when he tells them who they are and what they must do?"

"I don't know," James said. "I don't remember. I only know that the badger must not give up. If he does, they will consume him, and the hoop will be broken. There will be no children."

"No children? You must talk to them. You must tell them who we are." She stepped closer to him, and her hair caught the sun's bright rays and glinted, nearly blinding him. "You know who we are now, don't you? You know what makes us Lakota."

"I believe so."

"Then you must tell them."

"There are no words to tell them."

"You must try."

He nodded, and already he felt the badger's weariness creep into his bones, too. "Let me come inside. When they come, I shall meet them at the door. I shall tell them who you are."

Welcome him. Welcome him. He comes. He comes.

The face of the white deer waited for James. His cherry-hued eyes, full of compassion, beckoned. He was made of light, so bright that he made a man's eyes ache just to look at him. So beautiful that a man could not bear to look away.

"You are White Deer's Brother
He provides for your family,

The people at the center of the earth.
Welcome him. Welcome him.
He comes. He comes."

Filled with a sudden rush of power, James leaned back against his tether. His flesh broke away, and he fell back to the earth with a euphoric sense of absolute freedom.

James had a vague sense of the feasting and celebration that followed the Sun Dance, but his participation was minimal. He was grateful for food and water and the attention given his wounds. He sought the cool dark cave of sleep. When he woke, he found that Red Elk had cared for him. Like the other sponsors, he waited for the dancers to recover so that the medicine man could interpret their visions and the sponsors could see them home.

But in James's mind no doubts lingered. Lone Bear had seen him through his ordeal and let him know where he belonged. He spoke of it to Kezawin later when she tended to his bandaged wounds.

"*Tunkaśila* would not have me lose the part of myself that I have found," he told her. "I have work to do here. I am to be something of a bridge. If I cannot make my people understand when I speak with them, I will write it down, telling them what I have experienced, what I know to be true."

"You were not able to understand when you came to us, stumbling around the prairie looking for plants."

He laughed at the mental picture she painted of his former self. "I had to be changed," he said. "All the time that you were expecting to change into a deer, I was the one who was undergoing the transformation."

"Perhaps there are things that I have yet to learn about the deer woman. She gave me gifts."

"That she did." He could no longer doubt her. There were too many inexplicable mysteries, and for all his education, he was just beginning to understand what mystery meant. "But I think I am at peace with her. I don't think she'll harm me."

A grating screech sounded the warning a moment before a flapping black wing brushed James's face, and Sapa landed on his shoulder. "Impossible beast!" James grumbled as he slid his hand beneath the bird's breast and moved him back to his perch. "I'm speaking with my wife here. Wait your turn. I'll speak with you later."

"Sahhpahh," the crow intoned.

"Yes, I know. You are such a wonder." The bird reminded him of other news. "Catch The Bear spoke to me today of Blue Heels's wish to learn my medicine, which, of course, is *our* medicine. What do you think?"

"Blue Heels must have been touched by this wish while he gazed at the sun."

"Then he must have the opportunity," James concluded. "I may never be accepted completely, especially not by the relatives of the one I killed, but I think the people will grant me a place among them."

"You must certainly rid yourself of the burden of that one's death," she told him. "You must make restitution in the proper manner and be done with it."

"Is there a way?"

"Of course there is a way. There must be a way to put hard feelings and guilt aside. Without some way to release one another from these things, where would we be?"

Where, indeed? he wondered. Who dared call these people savages? "Show me the way," he said.

She smiled. "I shall. Tomorrow." Touching his wounds with feather-light fingertips, she asked, "Is it too soon for a joyous reunion with your wife?"

He returned a smile more mischievous than hers. "You are testing that question on the wrong part of my anatomy."

"Shall I ask the warrior?"

"He is most anxious to give his reply."

* * *

Kiciyuskapi, the Untying Each Other Ceremony, was announced throughout the encampment by the herald. James had performed *inipi* the previous night and expressed his need to release the burden of Thunder Shield's death. The following morning he and Kezawin waited near the council lodge while Red Elk went to Meets The Enemy, who was the eldest male in Thunder Shield's family, and told him that James was anxious to atone for the part he had played in his nephew's death. The relatives gathered at the council lodge before all the people. Red Elk lit the ceremonial pipe with a buffalo chip and handed it to Meets The Enemy.

"Take this pipe. In smoking it, bear no ill will toward anyone."

Meets The Enemy smoked, and then the pipe was offered to James with the same admonition. Red Elk then sent Catch The Bear and two other *akicita* members to lead the donated horses to the council lodge. James and Kezawin had pledged all but one of their horses to the cause of peace. Many of the horses had been given in payment for their medicine. Red Elk indicated that Meets The Enemy should mount one of the eight horses. When he did so, Red Elk led him back to his lodge, and the *akicita* brought the rest of the horses along. That done, Red Elk announced that the Untying Each Other Ceremony had achieved its purpose. "They are free," he said.

The Friends of the White Deer, a society of two, left the village together on the back of the one horse they had not given away, a stout buckskin. They were headed for an afternoon of gathering plants on the slopes of *Paha Sapa*, and they could be heard laughing as they went. It was unseemly for a man to ride his horse thus, with a woman sitting behind him. Unfitting, too, for a woman to laugh in such an unrestrained manner. But no one turned his head. No one sought out a friend to spread their names in gossip. It was Double Woman Dreamer and her husband, the strange white plant-taker. No one denied the fact that their medicine was powerful. Their behavior was sometimes odd, but like the *winkte* and the *heyoka*, they were *wakan*, and without them, the circle would not be complete.

* * * * *

Author's Afterword

Medicine Woman began as a personal challenge to write a love story about a Lakota woman and a transplanted white man—the reverse of my own situation—and set it in a time when the Lakota culture was dominant in the land that would be named North and South Dakota. The Dakota Territory was named in ironic tribute to those from whom the land was to be wrested by hook and by crook. The greater loss was not the land, but a way of life in which the individual lived in harmony with the environment and balanced the temporal and the spiritual aspects of life as a matter of course rather than design. The "noble savage" concept is as simplistic and ludicrous as any idea born of limited vision.

My research began with interviews, and continued with the tales my brother-in-law, Philip Eagle, told at a family reunion. He kept his audience entertained with stories of the *wanaği*, the spirits, interspersed with funny anecdotes, which were fast becoming local folklore. But the stories that interested me most were those of the deer woman. "I know of three," he said. "I didn't see them myself, but they said..." Intriguing stories, as was the story of the albino deer, which brought good fortune to the people as long as it was permitted to graze peacefully in the Grand River bottomland. I thank him and my husband, Clyde, for the soul of this story.

I researched this further with as many early interviews as I could find, realizing that most of the literature about Indians was written by non-Indians. Much is undoubtedly lost in translation, but late-nineteenth-century interviews recorded by apparently trusted non-Indians were the best source documents to be found. My aim was to bring as much authenticity to the Lakota in this story as I could. I apologize in advance for the degree to which I may have fallen short. In all fiction, there is an element of fantasy.

In my research I found precious little evidence of the kind of hero I wished to portray—a man whose mind was not too narrow to learn, not just intellectually but spiritually, from a native culture that was trivialized in his world. Happily, it seems that there were such people, though they were few and far between. There were those among the white immigrants who studied and transcribed the Lakota language, who pleaded the cause of justice for the Indian people before deaf Congressional ears, who photographed and recorded for posterity. There was even one case of a white man who stayed with the people through one of the many devastating bouts with smallpox. Such is the stuff that a cross-cultural romance may be made of.

Finally, the reader should know that the Sioux Nation has three branches and three dialects. The Santee, who speak Dakota, and the Yankton—as well as the Yanktonais—who speak Nakota, were located east of the Missouri River. The Teton, who speak Lakota, were west-river people made up of seven bands, or council fires: the Oglala, Brûlé (Sicangu), Miniconju, Blackfeet (Sihasapa; not to be confused with the Montana Blackfeet), Sans Arc (Itazipco), Two Kettle (Oohenunpa), and the Hunkpapa.

Lakota Words and Phrases

Lakota was not a written language until the white man applied the symbols of his alphabet to the cause. Hence, the spelling of Lakota words and the use of diacritical marks will vary from source to source. Besides the Lakota dialect, there are also the Dakota and Nakota dialects, and within each there are variations from band to band. When the U.S. government assigned people to reservations in the last century, Standing Rock Sioux Indian Reservation became the home of the Hunkpapa, one of the Lakota bands, but also of a small group of Yanktonais, who speak the Nakota dialect. To the government, they were all "Sioux."

I do not claim to be proficient with Lakota, but with the help of my husband's family and friends, I have gained some small knowledge of the language. I have used *Lakota-English Dictionary* by Reverend Eugene Buechel (Red Cloud Indian School Inc., Pine Ridge, SD, 1970) as my primary language reference. It is a language that is packed with connotative meaning, much of which is being lost as the language falls further into disuse, thanks to culture-killing educational policies that were implemented both by mission schools and the Bureau of Indian Affairs through the first half of this century. I hope that my attempt to describe the pronunciation of the words and phrases used in *Medicine Woman* and to list them here with admittedly limited definitions will help give the reader a feel for this wonderfully lyrical language.

akicita (ah-KEE-chee-tah)—policemen; a society of men who serve as peacekeepers

afe (ah-TAY)—father

can tarca winyela (chan-tarcha WEE-yay-lah)—the female white-tailed woods deer

eyapaha (AY-yah-pah-hah)—one who announces news to the village

Haho (hah-HO)—look at this!

hanble ceya (Hahn-BLAY-chay-yah)—to cry in prayer for a vision

heyoka (hay-YO-kah)—a contrary; a clown, considered sacred, who does everything in reverse

Hoka hey (HOH-kah hay)—Pay attention! Heads up!

hunka (HUHN-kah)—kin, relative; relative by ceremonial adoption

Iktomi (ick-DOE-mee)—a trickster spirit, generally evil

inipi (en-EE-pee)—purification rite performed by itself or in preparation for another ceremony; sometimes called the sweat bath

kiciyuskapi (kee-CHEE-yoo-skah-pee)—the untying each other ceremony; a ritual of putting aside guilt and resentment between two parties

kiniknik (kin-NICK-nick)—Indian tobacco made from such ingredients as pulverized willow bark

kola (KOH-lah)—friend

mahto (mah-TOE)—bear

mitakuye oyasin (mee-TAH-koo-yay oh-YAH-sihn)—all my relatives

mitawin (mee-TAH-wihn)—my wife, my woman

ŏhan (oh-HAHN)—Yes! (emphatic)

onśila (OHN-shee-lah)—Poor thing!

Paha Sapa (pah-HAH sah-pah)—the Black Hills

pannunpala (pah-HUHN-pah-lah)—milkweed plant; "two little workbags of women"

pejuta (pay-JOO-dah)—medicine; "grass roots"

pejuta wicaśa (pay-Joo-dah wee-CHA-shah)—man who uses herbs for healing; one kind of "medicine man," or shaman

pilamaye (pee-LAH-mah-yay)—thank you

śa (shah)—red; a very good thing is described as red

sapa (SAH-pah)—black

śicun (shee-CHUHN)—a spiritlike guardian, which may be derived or envisioned through the *ton*, the spiritual aspect of another being, especially an animal

taku (DAH-koo)—What?

tatanka (tak-TAHNK-kah)—the American bison, commonly called buffalo

Tiipaśotka Wakanśica (tee-ee-PAH-shoht-kah wah-KAHN-shee-kah)—Devil's Tower, Wyoming; "evil tower"

tiośpaye (tee-OH-shpah-yay)—band or clan

tos (dohsh)—yes; used only by women

tuki (doo-KEE)=Is that so!; used only by women

tunkanśi (tuhn-KAHN-shee)—my father-in-law

Tunkaśila (tuhn-KAHN-shee-lah)—grandfather; God

unci (uhn-CHEE)—grandmother; earth mother

unśica (UHN-shee-kah)—poor, pitiful

wahpehatapi (wah-PAY-yah-tah-pee)—lavender hyssop plant; "leaf that is chewed"

wakan (wah-KAHN)—holy, sacred

wakincuzas (wah-KIHN-shoo-zuh)—leaders of a clan, "the ones who decide"

wanaǧi (wah-NAH-chee)—spirits of the departed

wasicun (wah-SHEE-choohn)—white man

wasna (wahs-NAH)—pemmican made from pulverized jerky and tallow; dried berries might be added

waste (wash-TAY)—good

wicaśa (wee-CHA-shah)—man

wicaśa wakan (wee-CHA-shah wah-KAHN)—a holy man; the highest level of "medicine man," or shaman

winkte (WINK-dah)—a man who dresses and behaves as a woman, considered to be sacred

winyan (WEE-yahn)—woman, girl

Winyan he cinacaqupi (WEE-yahn hay chin-AH-chak-pee)—"He wanted that woman, so they gave her to him." Describes a marital agreement between families, based on the love between the two who are to marry.

Surely this scrawny,
half-drowned Englishwoman
—with a mark on her brow that matched
the one on his chest—
wasn't the bride he'd been promised by the
Great Spirit!

WHITE WITCH

Bronwyn Williams

Prologue

Croatoan, 1667

To the East, where the Big Water greeted the shore, Kinnahauk sat alone on a high dune, his golden eyes focused intently on a time that only he would be privileged to see. The sun stepped into its great house as he continued to invoke the spirits to be given the vision of manhood. Soon the evening star would rise above the clashing waters of the two great rivers that met off the point of land where the young boy waited.

The night was foreboding. Kinnahauk knew that it belonged to the spirits. Old Man Wind moved through the tall grasses, the dry whisperings making him think of the ancient bones of his ancestors even now resting in the Quiozon. He was strong for his years, and well formed, but even the strongest brave could not keep the moon from climbing and the sun from walking down. His youthful voice rose and fell as he chanted of Hatorask greatness.

All through the night he chanted, his voice growing rough but never quite fading. Just as the fingers of the sun showed in the eastern sky on the third day, Old Man Wind sighed once more, and his breath rose like smoke above the Big Water, and the smoke crept up toward the place where the young Kinnahauk waited, his golden eyes wide in fear and fascination.

Out of the grayness, mighty flames glowed suddenly, and the voice of Kishalamaquon rang out:

"Kinnahauk, son of Paquiwok, grandson of Wahkonda, blood of the mighty Manteo, hear these my words. In the time of the white brant will come to you an *oquio* from the land across the waters. This woman will be known to you by the fire mark on her brow. Join and cast your seed upon her. From this union will be born a *quasis* who will lead your people into the pathway of the setting sun. I have spoken, so shall it be."

Chapter One

England, 1681

Thunder rumbled overhead as Bridget crossed the stile and hurried toward her cottage. She frowned at the dark sky. Empty promises. Holding three eggs in her apron, she leaped across a dry streambed that was pockmarked by the hoofprints of thirsty cattle. If there was not so much yet to do, she would go past the millpond and wet her feet. But it had taken longer than she had anticipated to apply the poultice to Sarah Humphrey's festering foot. The old woman clacked like a guinea hen and could think of any number of reasons to keep her there. Both Bridget and her mother, Anne, had warned her against walking unshod where animals relieve themselves freely, but old Sarah was growing ever more forgetful.

Not that Bridget had minded visiting for a spell when she went to feed the cats and chickens. She had done so each day for the past week when she'd brought food and the poultices. Still there were others needing her help.

She was nearing the two-room cottage she shared with her mother when she heard the voices. At first she thought it was only the thunder that had teased them for so long, while crops died of thirst in the field and leaves turned brown before their time. But the piercing tones of Dodie Crankshaw were more like squabbling jays than thunder.

"'Er's the one, I be tellin' ye, did I not see the signs wi' me own eyes?"

Bridget broke into a run, sweat prickling her skin as she thought of her timid mother alone and unable to defend herself against the ill-tempered shrew. Anne had recently been stricken with an affliction of the throat that had robbed her of her voice, and so far, the bark of the slippery elm had done little to relieve it.

The air grew more oppressive by the moment. Not a whisper of wind stirred the faded leaves of the nearby trees. A pewter sky cast an eerie light over the neat bed of herbs that was Bridget's own domain, their pungent scent strangely intensified in the heavy stillness.

"'Er be a witch, I tell ye! Did not John's cow come up dry and me own old ma go lame wi' dropsy?"

Bridget dropped the eggs she carried with no thought for their fragile shells. She raced past the hollyhocks and rounded the corner of the tiny cottage. "Mother? I'm home, I've come—no! Please God, *no*!"

Unable to believe what she was seeing, she ran after the mob that half carried, half dragged, the mute and terrified woman toward the millpond. She tugged at first one, then another, pleading for reason and screaming for help with every other breath until Miller Godwin's lout of a son struck her on the side of the head with his forearm, slamming her against the trunk of a large oak, and knocking the wind out of her.

Facedown in the trampled grass, gasping for breath, she heard the splash and the ragged cheer. Struggling up, she fought her way through the mob, pleading incoherently. "Dodie, listen to me. Miller Godwin, please! Someone, pull her out!"

She was pushed to the ground, but she dragged herself to her feet, screaming all the while. "Mol, 'twas my mother who saved your little girl when her throat closed up, don't you remember? Oh, *please*, don't do this!''

She caught at the woman's sleeve but was slapped away. "Please, *please* listen to me, the rains will come any day now—John, your cow is too old—oh, no, please! Don't do this wicked thing! *Help her, someone, please, help her!* Let me go!''

Sobbing hysterically, Bridget kicked and clawed, but she might as well have been a kitten fighting a pack of wild dogs. There were no more sounds from the millpond, and a feeling of cold dread came over her. "God in heaven, why did you turn away?'' she pleaded, dropping to her knees.

For weeks now there had been mutterings. She'd seen the sidelong glances as she went about the village, but never had she dreamed anything would happen here. Not among people who had known her grandfather, who had been a kind and learned man. Her father had been a respected gamekeeper who had died rescuing John the smithy's simpleminded daughter from the frozen pond. There was not a family among them that her mother had not blessed with her healing herbs and her kind wisdom, accepting as payment their thanks, a sack of flour, an egg or a bit of meat for the table.

In shock, Bridget stumbled to her feet and pushed her way through the angry crowd that rimmed the millpond.

"Witch's brat,'' someone muttered.

"Cart 'er orf to Newgate, that's wot!''

Blinded by tears, she struggled to reach the water, knowing even as she did that it would be too late. If only there had not been such a drought these past two years! If only lightning had not struck Farmer Wedley's bullock last week—and her poor mother's voice failing her the very next day...

Bridget never even felt the blow that sent her crashing to the ground. When she came to, she was seated on a sack of flour just inside the mill, trussed up like a shoat on the way to market. She knew with a dread certainty that struck through her like a cold blade that her mother was beyond help.

Sheer hysteria made her trembling lips stretch into a rigid parody of a smile, which she had oft seen among the dead, it being no more than the tightening of muscles. In her tormented state, she wondered if she could have already died without knowing it.

"Aye, 'er laughs now, the witch's spawn, but 'er won't laugh long," someone cried, and someone else cheered in agreement.

"My mother was no witch, and well you know it!" Bridget cried out. She wasn't dead, then, for it was her own voice she heard, her own heart that was breaking. "You, Dodie Crankshaw, you've always hated my mother for being all that you could never be with your spiteful tongue and your wicked heart! It was you who threw the toads into our well to sicken us, I know it was, but not by guile nor wile nor gold shall you escape the wicked work of this day!"

Oh, how she wished she were a witch, for if it were in her power, she would cast them all into everlasting hell for what they had done.

"Mistress Anne, 'er went down like a millstone," one among them mumbled. "It be known that a witch can save 'erself from drowning."

"Aye, I'll not swing at Tyburn for the likes of a witch."

"Aye, but if Anne Abbott be'nt the witch," Dodie said slyly, "then this one must be, for there be a witch amongst us, else why do our crops wither and our cows go dry? Who called down the devil's wrath on Wedley's bullock? I say we take no chances!"

"I say we mark the girl as a warning to all God-fearing men of the evil that lurks in 'er soul!"

The cry was swiftly taken up. Bridget closed her eyes tightly and prayed to awaken from the nightmare that was too awful to be real. Surely the rising wave of voices was all a part of her dream.

It was the feel of intense heat that caused her to open her eyes to see the smithy's glowing hot iron moving slowly toward her face. Her scream was cut off sharply when someone standing behind her grabbed her by the hair and yanked her head back until her neck nearly snapped. As the iron touched her skin, she lost consciousness.

A chamber pot struck the sides of the cart, its contents trickling through the slats. Bridget opened her eyes and stared through a tangle of hair into the face of madness as a toothless crone patted her on the cheek with claws yellowed with age and blackened with filth. "Another one o' the gentry wot's been wrongfully did, dearie? Ye'll need sum'un to keep the ruttin' devils off yer, or ye'll not last out the week. Maudie'll be yer friend, dearie. Maudie'll look after ye an' 'andle the business end, ye might say."

The old woman cackled wildly, and Bridget shuddered. She raked a smear of human excrement from her arm and felt her stomach heave.

"Hark not to the likes o' Mad Maudie—she'll trade yer for a crust o' bread till you be as poxed as she be," jeered a sharp-faced woman whose features held remnants of beauty as she sat huddled near the center of the cart in a tattered and once-fine gown.

"Aye, Sudie, an' wot did his royal highness gi' ye fer yer favors this time, a pail o' pig droppin's?"

"Shut yer rotten mouth, ye—!"

The cart jolted over a heap of refuse, throwing its passengers against the sides and bringing about a rash of threats, each more vile than the last.

Bridget, her hair in wild tangles about her face, stared dully ahead, still in the thrall of this unending nightmare. Desperately she clung to the burning pain that radiated from her brow to all parts of her body, concentrating on that as if it could shield her from a far greater pain—the pain of remembering.

White Witch

But there would be no time for remembering, still less time to mourn. Herded through the dank chambers of Newgate like cattle to the slaughter, Bridget and the others were led down a long stone stairway made treacherous by an unbelievable accumulation of slime.

The air was so foul she was forced to cram her apron into her mouth to keep from gagging, yet the stench was not the worst of it. There were the sounds. And even those were only a prelude to what awaited her once the turnkey had gone, leaving the small group of newcomers huddled by the barred door of a cavernous room. Through the gloom of half light, figures of indescribable wretchedness moved toward the newcomers like a living, mouldering wall, some beseeching, some leering, others screaming virulent curses.

"Have we come to Bedlam? I thought 'twas Newgate," she whispered. "What do they want of us?"

The trull in the ruined finery, who called herself Sudie Upston, seemed not at all discomposed by the appalling surroundings. "What d'yer think?" she replied, her scornful gaze moving over Bridget's slight form and coming to rest on her brow, which, badly inflamed, appeared to have some sort of festering wound upon it. Turning to the mob, she raised her shrill voice. "Back wi' ye, gutter scum, or I'll see ye dance at Tyburn! Turnkey! Fetch th' turnkey, ye stupid lump!"

"Please, mistress," someone murmured.

Her eyes on the terrifyingly vacant face of an enormous creature who shuffled toward her, Bridget scarcely heard the soft voice at her side. Stunned, she cowered behind the strident Sudie.

"Please, mum?" The woman tugged at the sleeve of her gown, and Bridget looked down into a withered face that jarred a distant memory. "It be Mistress Bridget, be'nt it? The one that cured me old man o' the tetters?"

"Shut yer trap, ye rat-faced old bawdy basket, the dell's mine!" cried the harridan called Mad Maudie.

"Mistress Fitzhugh? Is it truly you? But how did you come to be in such a place?" Ignoring the dismal scene all around her, Bridget peered through layers of dirt and wrinkles, trying to recall the last time she'd seen Meggy Fitzhugh.

To her astonishment, her gentle old friend turned on Sudie Upston and struck away the fingers that bit painfully into Bridget's arm. "Let 'er be, trollop, or I'll turn Bedlam Billy on you!"

Sudie backed away with a wary look at the drooling giant, who offered her a toothless smile and began moving toward her, his enormous hands outstretched. She scuttled away. "Get 'im off me!" she screeched. "I warns ye, lay one finger on me and ye'll swing fer it. I got friends in 'igh places, I 'ave!" Snatching her stained skirts away, she renewed her demand for a turnkey.

With the throng momentarily entertained, Meggy Fitzhugh led Bridget to a corner where a few old women sat staring vacantly, mumbling softly to themselves. "Now then, child, tell me 'ow ye came to be 'ere, for surely there must be some mistake."

"Will he hurt her?" Bridget whispered, for even though she'd no liking for the one called Sudie, she would not willingly see her injured.

"Billy? Aye, 'tis true 'e be simple, but 'e be 'armless enough. Billy's me poor dead sister's boy wot lived wi' me 'usband an' me til 'e broke the neck o' Squire Jarman's mare. We'd no way o' payin', an' the young squire 'ad us put away, 'e did." Her face crumpled. Bridget could only wait until she composed herself once more. Wait and contemplate a scene more sad, more frightening, more degrading than anything she could have imagined in her worse nightmares.

Bridget's forehead throbbed abominably, yet she feared the time when the mark would become recognizable. As much as possible, she remained with the old women in the corner, a scrap torn from her apron wrapped around her head, partially covering her face. None of them had any bedding, or nearly enough clothing for it was ever cold and damp, seeming even more so for the eternal gloom.

There was scarcely any food at all—a few mouldy crusts tossed into the common ward for all to fight over like starving pigs in a pen. Billy was their provider, for none would willingly go within reach of his powerful arms. Each day he offered Bridget the largest crust, a worshipful look in his bright blue eyes, and she in turn divided her crust among the others.

As days grew into weeks and weeks into months, she lost all sense of time and all hope of ever leaving Newgate alive. With not so much as a ha'penny of her own, she could not even buy the ear of a gaoler to ask about her trial. The gaolers were like bustards, picking over the carrion for any scraps, and Bridget knew quite well that without Billy, she would have been passed from one to another of the wretched animals.

Meggy grew steadily weaker, wasting away for want of food and clean air. Not even Billy could provide what the poor old woman needed. Without her herbs to ease and strengthen Meggy in her last days, Bridget could only hold her like a babe, singing whatever scraps of song she could bring forth, for the sound of a familiar melody seemed to bring her peace.

Bedlam Billy hovered over them. To Bridget's amazement, he began humming along with her, his voice loud and uncontrolled but quite cheerful. Bridget had long since ceased to be frightened of him, for there had been two such naturals in Little Wheddborough, God's creatures whose bodies had long since outgrown their childlike minds.

More than once, it was only Billy's nearness that prevented her from being accosted by one of the lecherous beasts who, lacking privacy, tumbled such women as would have them or were too weak to protest, with no more sense of modesty than the animals of the field.

Sudie had quickly established her credentials with a whispered word in the proper ear and the few scraps of filthy finery she possessed. The day she left the common ward, Mad Maudie delighted in telling anyone who would listen that, despite her claims to gentility, Sudie Upston had been carted off to Newgate for stealing four guineas from a paying customer and selling his trousers to a passing palliard while he slept, so that he couldn't give chase.

The gentleman had evidently cared more for revenge than for his modesty when he awoke, however, for with his nether parts swaddled in a shawl, he'd caught up with Sudie as she stood bragging to a friend.

Oddly enough, Bridget missed the hateful shrew after she'd bargained with the gaoler for better quarters. Sudie's had been a familiar face, after all. To her relief, Mad Maudie had taken up with a group of old acquaintances and no longer bothered her, but there were days when it seemed as if she would never hear her own name spoken again in friendship, for Meggy was past speaking, and Billy had never learned.

As near as she could reckon, she had been at Newgate awaiting trial for nearly four months on the day that Meggy opened her eyes and began fumbling at the bosom of her stained and tattered gown. "Me silver," she whispered hoarsely. "Me silver be fer Billy. See 'at no 'arm comes to the boy, fer I love 'im as if 'e was me own." Her eyes, sunk deep in her head, gleamed with febrile brightness and then, before Bridget could reply, they faded.

By now inured to shock, Bridget continued to hold the pitifully frail corpse in her arms, for she knew not what else to do. Poor Billy sat and rocked, watching her expectantly as he waited for her to continue with the ballad of "The Three Ravens."

Death was a daily occurrence in the common ward. She knew well what would happen the moment Meggy's passing was noted. She couldn't bear to see her old friend stripped of her few poor possessions before she'd even grown cold. "Billy, go and fetch the turnkey," she finally managed to whisper. "Go now, Billy. Beat on the door, that's a good boy. Meggy needs the turnkey."

As gently as she could, without alerting those about her, Bridget smoothed the sparse yellowed hair and closed the faded eyes for the last time. Then, laying her flat on her own threadbare shawl, she straightened the withered arms, uncurling the clawlike fingers. It was then that she discovered the silver. Billy's inheritance—two shillings.

Tears sprang to her eyes, and she choked on the hard knot that rose to her throat. Slipping the coins into her own bodice, she allowed the tears to fall. She had not wept since the spring day when her whole world had ended. She wept now for poor, innocent Anne, for Meggy and Billy—for all, including herself, who were doomed to the living hell of Newgate.

What happened next came about so quickly, while her eyes were still blinded by tears, that afterward Bridget could never remember clearly what had started it. Two turnkeys had come for Meggy's body, yet Billy, not understanding, had blocked their way, grunting in that unintelligible way he had when he was disturbed.

"No, Billy, you must let her go," Bridget called softly, but the throng, sensing diversion had begun shrieking encouragement for one side or the other.

One of the oafish gaolers reached for Meggy's ankle, while the other began to clear a path. There was a wounded cry from Billy, and suddenly the turnkey was lifted into the air and thrown against a wall. The crowd screamed, half in terror, half in sick excitement. Bridget clutched the two old women nearest her and stared round eyed at the giant imbecile.

And then the second turnkey raised his club. Bridget screamed, there was a sickening crunch, and poor Billy lay sprawled across Meggy's body, his blood flowing over her gray face.

Bridget stared in disbelief. Huddled in the corner, she clutched the scrap of apron closer about her face. Even as she waited for death to strike her, too, the old women turned away from her, one by one, their eyes empty as their wavering old voices took up the familiar notes of "The Three Ravens."

It was only when she saw the way two of the more aggressive men were looking at her that she came to her senses. Prickles of unease rose along her spine, and her hand moved to the covering on her head, drawing it back. If need be, she must use her mark for whatever protection it could afford her, for without Billy, it would be only a matter of time before they would come for her.

And then what? Would she soon be like so many of the other women imprisoned, perhaps for life? First a victim, then an opportunist, trading her body for food, for a warm shawl, for a night free from the horrors of the common ward?

She *dare* not spend another night in such a hellish place! Billy was gone. Meggy's two shillings would do him no good. But for Bridget they could mean the difference between utter degradation and holding on to her sanity for a few more days. Two shillings would not buy her the light and air and privacy to be found in the part they called the Castle, but in the proper hand, it could buy up to a week in a healthier place than this.

The improvement was scarce two shillings worth, but at least she was able to discern day from night, and it was less crowded. One of the first to welcome her was her old acquaintance, Sudie Upston.

"I knew yer'd tumble sooner or later, Mistress Milk and Water," she said, mincing forward to drop her a mocking curtsey. "'oo lifted yer skirts, yer good friend, Bedlam Billy?" She laughed wildly, drawing all eyes toward the two of them. Bridget felt her face burn.

Slowly she reached up and drew off the rag that had covered her brow, taking malicious pleasure in hearing Sudie's gasp. "Ye be a witch?"

"I bear the mark," Bridget said calmly. She refused to be intimidated by the likes of Sudie Upston. She had bought a week in this place, and for Meggy's sake, she would not let anyone spoil it for her.

"Aye, and I bear the marks o' Newgate, yet I be as gently born as any fine lady. Have ye the power?" She seemed more fascinated than frightened, and Bridget turned away in disgust. There were those who would bargain with the devil himself, and it struck her that Sudie was among them.

The day before her week was ended, Bridget watched the gaoler unlock the heavy iron-strapped oak door. He was accompanied by a squint-eyed man with the look of a clerk about him, and she feared they had come to take her back to the common ward.

"'Old yer nose, sir, fer they be a stinking lot o' trulls," the turnkey warned his guest. He then threatened his charges with the removal of their tongues, bidding them hold and attend the clerk's words.

Bridget watched with hunger-dulled eyes as the inevitable exchange of coins took place between the two men. It seemed to her that gaolers and all who worked in this fiendish place must be among the wealthiest in the land, for they were ever being paid for one favor or another.

She failed to hear the opening words as the clerk began to read from a broadside. It was only when the stillness around her grew pronounced that her apathy began to lift.

"—any maid or single woman have a desire to go over, they will think themselves in the golden age, for if they be but civil and under fifty years of age, some honest man or other will purchase them for wives."

He then produced a list of names of planters and such men who had paid passage for a wife and instructed the women to make their mark against the name of their choice.

Fourteen stepped forward. Bridget was fourth in line, with Sudie two behind her. As it happened, Bridget could read, for her mother had been taught by her scholarly father, and had in turn taught her daughter.

As she looked down the list, the name Lavender stood out from the rest, putting her in mind of all that was clean and good and fair. David Lavender, planter of Albemarle, which was located in that part of the colonies newly called Carolina by the Lord Proprietors, had paid one hundred twenty pounds of tobacco for the passage of one healthy female on the bark *Andrew C. Mallinson*.

With the first glimmer of hope she had felt in months, Bridget carefully signed her name beside his.

Chapter Two

The London docks were aswarm with activity, for there were ships newly arrived and more departing. Cursing fluently, the wagoner inched forward, giving Bridget ample opportunity to examine the ship that would be her home for some six weeks. The *Andrew C. Mallinson* was far from being the largest ship in port, certainly far from the finest. Nevertheless Bridget felt her spirits begin to lift. Even the stench of the London waterfront was a welcome change from the stench of Newgate, for it was alive. Amidst noise and bustle, the rich scent of spices mingled with the smell of rotting fish and the ever-present effluvium of crowded humanity.

Alive and teeming with cheerfulness. A far cry from the clean pungent scent of her own herb beds or her mother's stillroom, yet it fairly bristled with activity, with freedom, with hope for the future.

"—naked 'eathen savages wot eats the flesh o' living mortals," someone in the cart whispered loudly. Bridget paid no attention. She'd heard the rumors. As soon as it was known that the fourteen women were headed out to the colonies, there were plenty who were eager to regale them with tales of the terror that lay in wait.

"I 'eared tell there be those that will pay gold just to tumble a woman. Why, a likely looking lass could find 'erself a fortune."

"Aye, or a slit throat."

"Shut yer eyes, Tess, an' maybe ye'll make yer fortune," Sudie taunted.

Hearing the young squint-eyed girl gasp, Bridget reached for her hand and squeezed tightly. She had taken the child under her wing, having met her the day she'd moved from the common room. Tess was a good girl, if exceedingly plain. She'd been badly used by someone she refused to name and imprisoned for stealing a rotten potato to keep from starving.

"Your sweet disposition is your fortune, Tess. Your planter will be more than pleased with his bargain," Bridget comforted. She only hoped it would be true. If all the planters were good and kind, she pitied the one who had paid passage for the shrewish Sudie, for she would soon take over all his possessions and send him weeping on his way.

Sudie Upston was the only one among them who carried anything resembling luggage. Bridget could have wished her intended had thought to provide her with a cloak of some sort, for the weather was damp and cold and promised to grow worse. However, he had secured her release from a living hell, and for that alone she owed him more than she could ever repay.

She only hoped he would find her pleasing. She was a good worker, for her mother had taught her well. Her health had always been good, her back strong despite her slight build. As for the mark on her brow, it would fade in time. There were potions that would help hide it, and she could arrange her hair so that it would be covered. Mayhap David would give her a comb as a wedding token.

And what would she offer him in return?

The bitterness and depression that had threatened for so long crept back, and Bridget made a determined effort to fight it off. She had much to offer! Was she not gently bred, if cottage born? Her grandfather had been the youngest of five sons of a poor but good family. He had possessed naught save a good mind and a gentle heart, both of which he had passed down to his only daughter, Anne, who had taught her only child in turn. How many women of seventeen could read and cipher?

Aye, she reminded herself, and how many good farmers needed a wife who could read the names of all the herbs and even a few words besides?

What David Lavender needed was a strong back and a willing hand, and he had paid for both. All her life she'd been taught that debt was a shameful thing. To owe a good turn was no dishonor. She'd often fed a neighbor's animals while he went to market, in exchange for mending a broken gate latch or some such. But to owe money was shameful. Such a debt must be repaid if it took a lifetime, and she had a lifetime to offer to the man who had paid her passage to freedom.

"Ahoy there, *Mallinson*, where d'ye want this cargo?" cried a rough voice from atop the wagon.

"Take 'em aboard! They be for stowage 'tween decks with the rest o' the varmints!"

"Ye heard 'im, ladies, move yer—"

"Keep yer bloody 'ands to yerself, ye gutter rat," Sudie snarled, yanking her soiled skirts away as the driver attempted to hurry them from the wagon.

Bridget's legs, stiff and cramped, threatened to give way as she stepped down onto the filthy cobbles. Clutching her tattered scrap of apron about her like a shawl, she hurried after the others as they mounted the worn gangway. All around her, men scurried about, hoisting casks and tubs aboard the ship, bellowing curses at anyone who got in their way. After months in the eternal dimness of Newgate, the brilliant sun was blinding. Her eyes watered, and the smell of salt fish made her stomach rumble with hunger. It was exciting, but overwhelming.

At the top of the gangway, a brawny sailor stepped forward just as Bridget reached the deck, blocking her way. His small, red-rimmed eyes moved over her with a slow thoroughness that made her flesh crawl. "Well now, mates, wot 'ave we 'ere? A bit scrawny, but I reckon I could share me 'ammock wi' 'er long's she don't wiggle too much." He reached for Bridget, catching her by the arm just as she would have tumbled into the incredibly filthy water below.

She tried to free her arm from his grip. No match for his bestial strength, she sank her nails into his fleshy hand and kicked out at the top of his bare foot. He yelped but refused to release her. "Ow! Blarst me if she ain't got claws like an 'awk an' 'oofs like an ox!"

Nearby someone laughed. A grizzled old seaman in canvas breeches and a striped jerkin was bearing down on them, a thunderous look in his eye.

Bridget was dimly aware that the passengers remaining on deck had paused to watch the byplay. Why wouldn't one of them help her? "Oh, please," she gasped, twisting in an effort to free herself from the frightening animal. His fetid breath made her gag, and she turned her face away, but grabbing her chin, he forced her head around.

"C'mon me pretty split-tail, gi' us a kiss, and I'll share me 'ammock wi' ye. Can't be fairer than that, eh, mates?"

There was a ragged cheer of approval from the seamen. Bridget, her panic suddenly overcome with fury, reached out and raked her nails mercilessly down one side of his leering face, feeling his skin tear and the warm spurt of his blood on her fingertips.

The sailor howled in pain. In one swift movement he grabbed a handful of hair and jerked her face upward. "Ye'll die for that, ye bitchin' 'ore!"

In the next instant he thrust her violently away. She went hurtling backward, clutching at empty air to save herself. Stunned by the impact of her fall, she stared up at her assailant through tangled masses of honey-colored hair, her gray eyes wide with terror.

The sailor's expression changed. His wide, boastful mouth grew slack, his piglike eyes bulging. "A witch! 'Er be a filthy, stinkin' witch!" He crossed himself vigorously.

"The mark be on 'er," he croaked, his face suddenly a dirty shade of gray as he pointed at her forehead.

Above and below, all sound suddenly ceased. Even the gulls that circled and screamed overhead seemed shocked into silence.

"Dougal, wot mischief be ye up to now?" It was the bos'n, the gray-haired seaman who had been making his way toward them from the quarterdeck. His opinion of the seaman Dougal was evidently somewhere below the bilge as he surveyed the bleeding scratches. "Looks to me like the lass is not the only one branded."

"I'll 'oist no canvas wi' the likes o' 'er on board, Tooly. A witch 'er be fer truth." With a filthy sleeve, Dougal smeared the red stripes across his cheek.

Tooly's bushy gray brows lowered in a fierce frown. "Ye'll do as I bid, or I'll peg yer cod to the fo'mast. See to the stowage o' those casks afore the tide turns. Move lively now!" Turning his attention to Bridget, the bos'n managed to moderate his ferocious roar. "Ye'd best go below, lass, or the captain will lay leather o'er both our backs. He be'nt a patient man."

Bridget, weak from months of starvation, attempted to get to her feet on the narrow planks that ran from wharf to deck and would have fallen had not the elderly seaman moved faster than she could have imagined. With an arm clamped around her waist, he led her aboard and then to the small hatchway that led down to the cramped passenger quarters. Faces loomed from the shadowy darkness along the way, and voices fell silent as they passed, the slight young woman and the grizzled seaman. Tooly's arms were the size of an average man's thigh, giving the impression of mountainous strength.

One man, more daring than the rest, stepped out from the shadows to block their passage. "We want no witch amongst us," he declared to a chorus of angry mutters. "We'll be doomed if the likes of 'er sails aboard the *Mallinson*."

Bridget learned then that for all his prodigious physical prowess, Tooly's real strength lay elsewhere. He looked the man in the eye for one long moment and then moved past as if he weren't even there. "I promise ye'll not be hurt, lass," he said softly, handing her the apron that had fallen to the deck when Dougal had first accosted her. "This 'ere's yer place, by the gun port. At least ye'll get a breath o' air, and in spite o' the cold that leaks in through the battens, ye'll be thankin' me afore long."

Sean Dooly, who'd been called Tooly so long he'd accepted it as the whole of his name, strode back the way he'd come, vowing silently he'd give the cat to anyone who dared lay a finger on her. Mayhap he'd been to sea too long, but all he knew was that one look at the lass's great gray eyes and frightened little face and he'd gone all soft inside, like the belly of a rotten bloater. He'd not give a quid for her chances of seeing the colonies, not with the likes of Dougal about, but he'd do his best.

"Toss 'er ashore, 'tis evil she be," someone yelled after him.

Tooly's mouth set in a grim line. Slowly he turned, his eyes like a wild animal's, seeing clearly in the gloom belowdeck. "The evil be in yer own mind, ye dung heap," he said softly. "I'll send the 'ole stinkin' lot o' ye to the bottom if ye so much as looks at 'er, d'ye ken my meaning?"

There were low murmurs of discontent, but no one else dared speak out against him. From the far side of the low, cramped space, Bridget watched her mentor stride away. Drawing herself up into a small bundle, arms wrapped around her knees, she watched warily to see if his words would have any effect on the angry passengers. She was so discouraged, so frightened and so weary at this point that she could almost wish she'd gone with her mother and Meggy. She was too tired to fight anymore. Hope had been born anew, but before it could take wings, it seemed to shrivel up into a small knot in her chest.

A bead of perspiration trickled down between her breasts. The heat belowdecks was stifling. Her head throbbed, and she longed for a drink. Physically and emotionally exhausted, Bridget lowered her head to her knees and slept.

Like an uncaged bird, the *Andrew C. Mallinson* took flight. Acres of heavy canvas billowed out from her yards as she set sail for Plymouth, the last stop before they took to the open sea. Bridget had slept heavily, slipping uneasily in and out of troubled dreams. The image of a man's face flashed through her mind and was gone before she could grasp it. She was left with no more than the memory of a dark sky filled with large white birds and a pair of golden eyes that seemed oddly... compelling.

If the dark sky was her past, then the white birds must represent her freedom, the white sails billowing overhead that would bear her away. But the golden eyes? Frowning, Bridget pondered the meaning of those. Gold had been mentioned by the clerk who had come to Newgate, and there had been some mention of gold by one of the women on their way to the docks.

But what matter? Dreams were only dreams, and a dream of gold did not mean riches. Just the reverse, in fact, for gold was the color of the tobacco David Lavender had paid for her passage. Never in her lifetime had anyone in Bridget's family owed such a debt. It would take forever to repay it.

Pushing her hair aside, she sat up and looked about her. There seemed to be more than a hundred people crowded like swine into a space no larger than three good-size carts. They had left a small circle of space around the gun port where Bridget lay, for which she could thank her witchmark. Or perhaps Tooly's warning.

Sudie was nearby, her sallow skin stretched more tightly than ever over her pointed features. Evidently the sea air did not agree with Mistress Upston, Bridget thought with the first glint of amusement she had felt in many a day.

Sudie's only saving graces were a pair of dark eyes that missed little, and a quick mind that wasted few opportunities. Her garments were tatters of squalid finery which had been acquired by nefarious means and used skillfully at Newgate as a passport to gentility.

In the days that followed, Sudie wasted no time in establishing a pecking order. The paying passengers, among whom she included herself for reasons that escaped Bridget, ranked well above the indentured, and the indentured above the common prisoners.

And all of them looked down on Bridget.

Rough weather struck only days after they left Plymouth. Bridget quickly learned why Tooly had secured the space by the gun port for her, for the air grew fetid with the constant heaving of those poor souls who were ill. She grew accustomed to the sound of rows of creaking hammocks, to the constant retching, the moans and prayers and the occasional muttered references to the witch on board.

Out on deck, it was better. Tooly made her a place that was out of the way, sheltered by several casks of salt fish that had been taken aboard after the bulk of the cargo had already been secured. They had been lashed to the railing, and provided her with a small corner all her own.

Bridget grew to love the wildness of the sea, the salt spray and the creak of rigging as it strained under mountains of wet canvas. Masts that were twice as large around as her body, looked as if they might snap under the strain. She heard snatches of song from the hardworking seamen, and now and then caught bits of gossip and tales of adventure that made her flesh crawl.

"Aye, them savages be a cruel an' barbarous lot, they be. Did ye hear tell aboot the man wot was flayed alive and then set fire to?"

Bridget shuddered, glad they were bound for a more civilized place.

"Got knives sharper'n any ye ever seen, and I 'eared tell they whack off a man's cod and—"

Fortunately a cry from the bos'n sent the speaker running up the rigging, and his mate hurrying toward a flapping line.

Soon after they had set sail, Tooly had used his knife on Bridget's hair so that now it fell in a soft fringe over her brow, obscuring her shameful mark. She had been touched by his kindness, though it had helped little, for everyone knew the mark was there. The fact that she had been allowed to leave London instead of being burned or hanged said little for her innocence, with Sudie there to whisper of favors bought and paid for.

On the day when it was discovered that the remaining food stores were tainted, Tooly hurried her up from between decks and hid her in the forecastle among tons of musty-smelling canvas until the mutterings ceased. Not a week later a new cask of water was broached and discovered to be brackish.

All eyes turned toward Bridget, some accusing, some merely curious. The fact that she had been as sickened as the rest by the rancid meat, that she gagged on the water like the others, and had got into the habit of striking a beam with her ship's biscuit to knock out the weevils before eating it might have helped save her.

Whatever the cause, despite Sudie's constant efforts to discredit her, there were some who no longer shunned her. And some, like young Tess, who never had.

"Jealous, that's wot she be," declared Tess. "I know 'er sort."

"That's foolishness, Tess, for I've naught to make a church mouse jealous." Bridget smiled at the unlikely idea.

"Aye, that may be fer now, but Sudie 'eared tell from a man that went out to the colonies two year ago that the place where 'er man settled be off by itself, and like as not swarming with bloody savages."

"Tess, there be no savages in the colonies now, surely."

Crossed eyes gleaming earnestly, the young maid bobbed her head. "Aye, there do be, Mistress Bridget, leastwise outside the towns and settlements. Fierce, too, they be, wi' knives and clubs and such wickedness in their black 'earts as you never seen!''

"But Albemarle—?"

"Oh, Albemarle be a fine place, I 'eared, wi' markets an' land so rich it don't even need droppin's,'' said the younger girl with the authority of one who had access to all the ship's gossip. "If your planter be from Albemarle, then you've naught to worry about, save mayhap Sudie stealin' yer man."

That was the least of Bridget's worries. Her name had been signed beside that of David Lavender, not merely her mark as the other women had done. The captain had the manifest, and their planters would be there to greet them when they stepped off on the dock. The journey was almost over. They had come through the worst of the storms without losing too much canvas or being blown too far off course, although Tooly did mention something about a dangerous shoal that reached out from a sandbank to bar the way of the unwary.

Nay, her luck had finally come about, Bridget told herself. If she could stomach the foul provender for but another few days, she would soon begin her new life.

Chapter Three

Croatoan

Kinnahauk was aware of Gray Otter's presence long before he felt the light touch along the back of his thigh. He
had heard her quiet footfall, smelled the thick sweetness of
the muskrat from the oil she rubbed into her skin.

He was not pleased to have her here, for he had deliberately sought out this place so that he could be alone. In the
olden days the boldest warrior would fear to pierce the sol-
itude of Kinnahauk, chief *werowance* of the Hatorask
People of Croatoan.

For a woman to tickle him below the tail clout with a
head of grass spoke more clearly than words at how greatly
the world had changed since the coming of the white-eyes.
His people had once filled two towns on the island of Croatoan. Now they could scarce fill one. Many among his
brothers the Paspatank, the Poteskeet and the Yeopim wore
the dress of the white-eyes and mimicked their foolish ways.
His people had not done so, yet their numbers had dwindled steadily from the white man's sickness. Of those who
escaped the sickness, many had been afflicted with the
madness brought on by their whiskey, until Paquiwok had
forbidden his people to go among the white man. He had
ceased to welcome the white-eyed visitors to the shores of

Croatoan, but not soon enough to save him from their killing sickness.

Kinnahauk had been but a youth then. Now the white tide had swept across all the best hunting ground on the mainland. When Kinnahauk had become chief, he had tried to hold his people to the old ways, but one did not swim against the tide forever.

Aiee! Not since the Hatorask had come from the Land Where the Sun Sleeps in the Time Before the Grandfathers, to build their *oukes* on the sands of Croatoan between two great waters, had they been so threatened. Many times had the Great Spirit sought to test their courage by making the waters sweep across the land until they covered all but the highest hills, yet they had not weakened. Many times had He sent His cold breath down upon the waters, making them grow hard until a man could walk where the fishes swam, yet could not catch them. They had survived. He sent strong winds to bend the corn, and rain to beat it into the earth, and sands to cover where it had once stood. Yet they did not starve, for He sent the fish of the sea and the animals of the forest and the birds that filled the air so thick that the face of the sun was hidden.

Aiee, and did not the white-eyes come in their winged canoes to take the fish and fowl to feed their own? Did not they burn clear the hunting lands, and build walls around them? Did they not dig up the seed that had been hidden for the next Planting Moon, and frighten away the fowl with their noisy thunder sticks?

Kinnahauk despised the white-eyes. Honor had compelled his people to come to this place in the Time Before the Grandfathers to await the coming of men from across the Big Water, but the prophesy of the ancient ones had been fulfilled.

As he stared out across the Inland Sea toward the land the white-eyes were now claiming as their own, Kinnahauk's face revealed little of his thoughts. His golden eyes, pale eyes that were a heritage from an English maiden some hundred years earlier, gleamed fiercely for a moment before the spark was extinguished.

He was beset by problems. Many of his people lived across the Inland Sea in scattered villages. For many years they had wanted a *werowance* of their own. Each time Kinnahauk joined the other chiefs at council fires, one of their numbers would speak before council asking that Kinnahauk leave Croatoan at each Song Moon and dwell with the mainland Hatorask until the Moon of the Falling Leaves.

Again he felt the caress of soft grass on his bare leg, and with a grunt of displeasure, he turned his thoughts to another problem that had been pressing him greatly. Gray Otter was too bold by far, her ways unseemly in a maiden of her years. His friend Kokom would have his hands full when he finally tamed her and took her to his lodge.

"Do you never grow weary of your childish games, Gray Otter?"

"The games I would play with you are not childish, Kinnahauk. Sweet Water loses patience with a son who only stares at the water and thinks of the wicked white-eyes when he should be making many strong *quasis* to follow in his moccasins. Some day our people will need a new *werowance* to lead them. When the white-eyes go away, the Hatorask will grow strong again."

The white-eyes would not go away. Kinnahauk felt the truth in his bones, but he allowed himself to be distracted for a moment. Raking the tall, beautiful woman with a stern look, he said, "It is you who should be making babies, woman, for you are no longer young. Soon your hair will be white and your back will bend with the years. Then who will warm your sleeping mat when the Cold Moon rises over your *ouke*?"

Leaning her slender body into the curve of a tree, Gray Otter smiled slyly, her black eyes sparkling. "Perhaps you will hobble to my poor lodge if your ancient bones will carry you, Kinnahauk. For if I have waited long, surely you have waited with me?''

''*With* you, woman, but not *for* you. You have led poor Kokom a fool's journey these years. It is time you put an end to his misery.''

''Kokom is a fool. He thinks himself a maiden's dream, and wishes to have them all,'' Gray Otter retorted. ''I do not want a fool for a mate. Kinnahauk knows I would make a better wife to the chief than any of the unmarried women. If you want to know just how good a wife I will be, you have only to take me to your sleeping mat tonight.'' With a sway of her hips meant to stir his manhood, Gray Otter left him there.

Kinnahauk permitted himself a sigh. She was right. He had waited long and would wait longer still, he feared. He had sought three visions in his life and been given two. In his first vision he had seen the skies covered with the wings of many white brant. They had followed the shore and then turned toward the place where the sun slept. Beneath the sky, the Big Water was filled with many white wings, and these, too, followed the path of the sun.

From this vision he had taken his name, Kinnahauk known by the sign of the White Brant. It was his own father, Paquiwok, who had cut the symbol high on his chest, but Kinnahauk himself had painted it on his first childish shield and on the flanks of his first pony.

The dream had returned many times since, bringing with it a feeling of great sadness which he did not yet understand. Still, he knew that his vision had been true, and when he was wise enough, the Great Kishalamaquon would open his mind.

It was the second vision that concerned him most often now, for he was a man, and a man's needs were strong. Surely the time had come? Surely he was not meant to burn forever, his seed wasted on fallow ground? There were maidens both here and among his friends across the Inland Sea who made him welcome in their lodges and on their mats, for he had early shown an aptitude for the game.

Gray Otter would be only too willing to bring her mat to his lodge, but something in him would not allow that to happen. The Voice that Speaks Silently had whispered that they were too much alike in many ways, both being bold and strong-minded, but too different in others. They were of an age, and his friend Kokom had long coveted Gray Otter for his own.

In his heart Kinnahauk knew that he was waiting for something more. He could have taken a first wife and made the waiting more comfortable, yet he did not. Each time the leaves fell and the cry of the wild geese could be heard overhead, his blood grew heated as he thought of the promise made so long ago.

One day his mate would come to him. She would be beautiful, his special woman, with eyes as dark as acorns and hair that glistened like the wings of a blackbird. There were many such women among the Poteskeets and the Paspatanks, and one widow among the Yeopim who had shared her mat with him after many council fires.

His *oquio* would be more beautiful than any of these. Kinnahauk would pay whatever bride-price her father asked, and then he would offer his token of promise—his arm band and a sprig from the *yawaurra* tree. He would take her deep into the forest, high atop the Great Ridge, and there he would build her a skin lodge and spread it with a fine red wolf robe. He would say sweet things to her, for women softened to words as they did to a gentle touch.

Many times would he prove his prowess as a man, with the roar of the Big Water and the song of the wind to cover her cries of joy.

Kinnahauk knew his worth. A mighty hunter, he knew the mind of his quarry. Skilled among fishermen, he could sense unerringly where to set the weirs. He was in demand among the women of many villages, for he was a man who knew well the secrets of a woman's body.

His *oquio* would be the envy of many, for was he not the chief of a great people, as well as a lusty warrior? She would be young, the maiden who bore his mark, without knowledge of such matters. He would take great pleasure in teaching her how to please him, weaving fragrant blossoms through the midnight darkness of her gleaming hair, rubbing her dusky skin with the finest of oils, paying special attention to those parts that made a woman writhe in ecstasy. Soon she would beg and plead with him to take her, to end the sweet torment.

"Sleep now, my promised one, for it is late," he would whisper that first night. "Perhaps I will lead you farther along the pathway after we have both rested well."

He would not be led by his man part, as so many men of his age were. From the beginning he would prove to her that he had control over all his weapons, his spear no less than his bow and blade.

A ragged flight of white brant passed over his head, bound for Chicamacomick to the north, and Kinnahauk breathed in deeply, then allowed his broad shoulders to sag. This mighty *werowance* and brave hunter would do well to stop wasting time and go in search of meat for his mother's lodge, for the signs gave notice of a fierce winter. They must prepare well for the coming months, or go hungry.

Bridget awoke with hot sunshine beating down on her eyelids, cold water swirling about her feet and an uncanny sensation of being watched. Eyes closed tightly, she fought against awareness, for with awareness would come pain. But there was no denying the incredible ache in every part of her body, nor the raw torture of every breath she drew. Her throat felt as though it were on fire and someone had laced her bodice much too tightly across her chest.

As the hungry surf dragged at her limbs, she forced herself to think through the sequence of events that had brought her there.

She remembered hearing the lookout cry, "Land ho!" after the sudden storm had abated, and being fair trampled by her fellow passengers as they rushed topside for a look at their new homeland. She remembered the pushing and tugging by those who still had enough strength, the cries and curses of those weakened by endless weeks of sickness.

Bridget had hung back, ever mindful of her friend Tooly's warning to stay clear of her fellow passengers whenever possible. She had waited until the first rush was past before making her way closer to the rail, for the seas were still rough, the decks too wet for safe footing. The storm had sprung up out of nowhere, taking them all by surprise.

"Where away?" had cried a voice from the crowd. "I see naught but these infernal seas!"

"Yonder, see the dark smudge on the horizon? 'Tis Albemarle, God's truth! We be saved!"

"'Tis but another of these bloody reefs and shoals," grumbled a man more distrustful than the rest. "Show me a church spire, and I'll show you a town, and not some floating patch of seaweed."

"Aye, Adam be right, it be naught but another trick. A witch's trick, most likely, for didn't I hear the captain say that we be blown far off course by all these unnatural storms?"

Bridget had paid no heed. For the past weeks she had heard the threats and accusations until she had grown hardened to them. Once ashore in Albemarle, she would leave this miserable company behind, and good riddance! She was sick of being a pariah through no fault of her own! The only two people worth more than a grain of salt on this accursed vessel were Tess and Tooly.

Pushing her way to the rail, she had shaded her eyes against the late October sun that had finally broken through the clouds to splinter diamonds across the tossing seas. A new land. A new life, a new home—even a new name. Bridget Lavender. Aye, it had a ring to it. She dimly recalled now thinking some such high-flown nonsense as she had stood at the rail and strained her eyes against the brilliance of the westering sun.

"Ware the shoals!" the lookout had screamed from his vantage point in the rigging just as someone had jostled against her.

Everything seemed to happen at once—the frightened cries as they'd felt the keel snag bottom, the loud report as a mast top snapped off, snarling rigging and shrouds, and the crush of hot, stinking bodies all around her. Something had struck her hard between the shoulders, and the next thing she'd known, she'd been flying over the side. Just before the water had closed over her head, Tooly's curses had rung out.

"'Ang on, lassie, 'ang on tight! Dig yer fingers inter the rim and 'old on to the cask! She'll carry ye ashore if ye keeps yer wits about ye!" Something had struck the water nearby, catching her with its spray, and blindly she'd reached out.

Somehow she had managed to grab the bobbing cask. It reeked of salt fish, and dimly she had recognized that it was the salt that kept it buoyant despite the drag of her heavy clothing. With every bit of strength she possessed, she'd hung on, swallowing half the sea as wave after wave had carried her shoreward to hurl her finally onto the sloping bank, more dead than alive.

Once again Bridget felt a prickle of awareness that told her she was being watched. Had the ship truly wrecked, then? Had others come ashore? Were they even now planning to burn her for a witch because she hadn't had the grace to drown? She would be dead of the cold by nightfall unless she found shelter quickly; even so, she didn't fancy a stake and a bundle of fagots to keep her warm.

Something touched her forehead, brushing her hair aside, and she stiffened. It was a fleeting touch—she might almost have imagined it. Eyes shut tightly, she pretended to be unconscious. Perhaps if her tormentor thought her dead, he might leave her alone.

"Ungh!"

The grunt of disbelief seemed to come from high above her head. Carefully Bridget slitted one eye against the painful glare that beat down on her face. At first she saw only a shadow. One of the crew perhaps, risking her witch's curse to hoist her skirts while she lay helpless?

She lifted a hand to push him away, shocked at how slow her limbs were to obey the commands of her mind. It was all she could do to open the other eye, for her lids seemed weighted. For all she was freezing to death, the sun beat down with a fierceness she had seldom known.

Through a thicket of brown lashes stiff with sand she peered upward, her eyes stinging with salt. The first thing that caught her gaze was the glint of metal. A blade of some sort, and something more—a band of copper around a naked arm. She blinked to clear her vision and tried to make sense of what she was seeing.

A knee? It was hardly the first knee she'd ever seen, but never before had she seen one quite like this. Surprisingly well formed, it was attached to a long, muscular thigh, and both upper and lower limb glistened like polished wood in the harsh light.

And then her senses cleared, and she felt her heart leap into her throat. Dear Lord, she had fallen into the hands of one of the godless savages who made sport of torturing their victims to death!

Fragments of prayer ran through her mind for the first time since she had seen her mother murdered before her very eyes. Had she once thought of giving up? Never! Not while she had breath to fill her lungs and the wit to escape this naked heathen. She had come too far and endured too much to be defeated on the very day of her deliverance!

Before he could slit her gullet with that wicked blade of his, she sat up. Pain slammed into her head. She ignored it. The aborigine was evidently startled by her sudden movement, for he stepped back quickly, and Bridget took advantage of his sudden look of surprise to roll over onto her hands and knees.

Briny foam swirled about her. No wonder she was freezing—she was still half under the water, and though the water itself was not so cold, the wind blowing over her wet body chilled her to the bone.

The savage began to circle like a wild dog around a wounded calf, his lean, tall body glinting in the sun. Against the light, she could make nothing of his features, but they would be fierce, with hideous paint and sharpened teeth for tearing at flesh. Oh, yes, she had heard the tales, never dreaming that one day she would have one of her own to tell. If she survived to tell it.

Warily, she eyed the savage. Just as warily, he eyed her back.

Kinnahauk had been trailing a great buck for hours when something had startled his quarry. Flashing the white of his tail, the creature had lifted his head and looked toward the shore before bolting into the dense woods.

Instead of following the buck, Kinnahauk had turned toward the shore, curious to discover what had alerted the deer. His own ears, for all their keenness, had heard nothing.

Swiftly he had moved through the wind-stunted cedars that dotted the flat expanse between the Great Ridge and the line of dunes that held back the Big Water, his golden eyes alert as they skimmed the horizon. From high overhead, the plaintive cry of the great white brant had risen above the deep voice of the sea. Kinnahauk had run with a long, easy stride, his bearskin moccasins proof against the sharp spines of prickly pear and sandspur alike.

He had leaped easily to the top of the grassy dune, his gaze still on the distance, and it was then that he'd seen the hull of the Englishmen's ship, the tip of one stick dangling and its white wings filling with wind as it skirted the deadly shoals.

The ragged flight of brant had passed directly overhead, their hollow voices echoing in his mind as he stood poised at the top of the dune and watched the crippled ship disappear over the horizon. Like an answering call, had come a voice from the past. "In the time of the white brant will come to you an *oquio* from the land across the waters. You will know her by the fire mark."

She had come!

Proudly he had traced the small pattern of scars high on his chest. His strong white teeth had flashed in a rare smile as he readied himself to go forth to meet his mate. Standing atop the dune, he had scanned the shore, and his man part had grown hard and tall at the thought of what lay ahead. Aiee, his stallion, Tukkao, would quickly grow fat and lazy, for soon Kinnahauk would ride another throughout the long winter nights.

It was then that he had seen the dark crumpled form at the edge of the sea. Swift as the plunge of a fish hawk, he had covered the distance, slowing only as he neared the thing cast ashore by the tide. And then his shoulders had drooped, his rising flesh had fallen. Once more he had misread the signs, for it was but a poor creature drowned and washed ashore.

A woman. A white-eye woman. He would ask his Great Spirit to offer a prayer to her own gods before he buried her body, for she had no one to sing her Song of Sorrow.

He bent to drag her out of reach of the water, and she rolled onto her back, a pale arm flung over her head. Frowning, he stepped back, just as a playful finger of wind lifted her hair from her face. His eyes widened with disbelief.

The fire mark? No! It could not be. She was English, her skin the color of a cooked crab, and speckled like the egg of a wren. Her hair was more like the dead grass of winter than the glossy wings of the blackbird. Tall and comely?

There was scarce enough flesh to cover her wretched bones. In truth, he had never seen such a pitiful creature.

His *oquio*? He had misread the signs. Or perhaps he had misread the vision of so long ago. In his youthful eagerness he had mistaken the cry of a loon for the voice of the Great Kishalamaquon.

Yet the mark on her brow was clearly his own. Using the point of his knife, Kinnahauk lifted the hair away as she stared up at him in terror. He studied the mark she bore, and then he touched the scar on his own chest.

Both were the symbol of the flying white brant. Both were the same. The white-eye woman bore the mark of the woman; Kinnahauk the mark of the man. Plainly they were made to fit as a woman was made to fit with a man.

His fists curled painfully into his hardened palms as he lifted his eyes to the darkening sky. How could such a creature bear his sons? He doubted his seed would rise for such as she.

Chapter Four

Bridget's mind worked feverishly. Hampered by the weight of her sodden garments, she could scarce outrun him, but she had no intention of staying where she was while he decided which part of her to lop off first. It took all the strength she possessed to rise, but pride would not allow her to crawl like a dog before any man, much less a heathen. She had faced death and worse often this past year and been helpless to save herself or those she loved. She had little else to lose.

It was as if the very thought set her free. The pain in her head was naught, the tremors that racked her body still less. Burning with the fire of determination, she rose to her feet, unaware that she was swaying like a reed in a high wind.

"I'm not afraid of you," she rasped. To her own ears, she sounded bold and unafraid, but her voice was scarce above a whisper. "I know all about what you do to your captives." She was interrupted by a hacking cough, but she continued as soon as she caught her breath. "Heed my warning. If you lay a finger on me, David Lavender will hunt you down like the animal you are, and—"

"*Sehe!*" roared the savage.

Bridget froze. "Don't speak to me in that heathen tongue! I have no intention of—" She broke into another fit of coughing and grasped her throat with both hands for fear it would split wide open.

"Hush, *oquio*! You know nothing. Speak no more."

Bridget's mouth fell open. She was dreaming. Of course she was dreaming, for savages did not speak her own language, and certainly not with such arrogance, their heads held as proudly as any fine lord. "What is this place? I must reach Albemarle quickly."

With that, he set loose another barrage of that strange tongue of his, the likes of which Bridget had never heard. She could feel her strength flowing out the very soles of her feet, yet the moment she showed fear, he would be on her like a feral dog. She opened her mouth to demand that he take her to David Lavender, or at least point the way, but before she could utter a word he reached out and touched the mark on her brow.

"*Oquio*," he said once more.

So now she knew her first word of the heathen tongue. *Oquio*. Did that mean witch? She swallowed painfully, wondering what the savages did to witches. It could hardly be worse than the treatment witches were afforded in her own land. But if she did not want to learn firsthand, she had best be planning her escape, for the wicked creature watched her like a hawk with those great golden eyes of his, ready at any moment to pounce.

Head flung back with a boldness she was far from feeling, Bridget took a step backward. First one and then another, never breaking contact with his eyes. It would be fatal to show any sign of fear or weakness.

Another step backward. The savage hadn't moved so much as a muscle, his gaze never leaving her face. What strange eyes he had, she noted abstractedly. There was something about them . . .

She yanked at her drenched skirts impatiently. Her gown was ruined, her petticoats no better. There was no way she could lay claim to so much as a gram of dignity, and for the first time in months, that seemed somehow extremely important. Her wet hair was filled with sand and all manner of grasses, and she seemed to have lost both her shoes and her stockings.

Mayhap it was best that she look so unappetizing. Some aboard ship had whispered of the wicked things the savages did to their women captives before boiling them alive. She had no intention of ending up either as sport or feast for some naked savage, no matter how tall and haughty he appeared.

Two more tottering steps carried her out of reach of the waves. Bridget watched warily, afraid to look away even for a moment for fear the wicked devil would pounce. It came to her that he was not quite so hideous as she'd first thought. His teeth had not been filed down, nor was there a bone through his nose. Indeed, there was a strength and a symmetry to his features she deemed rare among men. His limbs were like the trunks of strong young saplings, shapely and smooth, and his dusky body appeared to be both manly and quite clean.

Far cleaner than the stinking, sweaty bodies that had been packed so tightly between the decks of the *Andrew C. Mallinson*. For all it was nearing winter, his only garment was a small leathern apron that covered his privities both front and back.

Bridget was mildly surprised to discover that for a moment she had been thinking of him as a man and not a beast of the forest. It must be this infernal headache, she thought, shoving her hair away from her burning face. "How odd that a beast should appear so noble, while in the guise of humankind there be devils who would take the life of an innocent woman and call it their sacred duty," she murmured wonderingly.

The man frowned, as if trying to understand her hoarse words, and she shook her head. Her gaze encountered a small mark high on his smooth chest, a scar of some sort. It looked almost familiar, yet she could not recall having seen its like before.

She fell into another fit of coughing, and the savage reached out as if to catch her with his hands. Bridget stepped back quickly, nearly losing her balance. She must trick him into leaving somehow, for she could never out-run him. But how?

Her attention strayed back to his eyes. They were the color of a bright new guinea, golden as the eyes of a hawk, and with the same constantly shifting light. His face, too, put her in mind of a hawk, with its proudly arching nose and the angular planes of his lean cheeks.

Yet there was a gentle look about his finely shaped mouth. Faith, he didn't look cruel at all, but to her sorrow Bridget had learned that looks could not be trusted.

In a flash of inspiration, she decided to risk her modesty in trade for her life. "I beg your pardon, for I have need of a moment's privacy behind yon hillock. If you will wait here, I will be but a short while."

Her gaze never faltering, she took a step away, and then whirling about in blind panic, began to run. She had not gone twice her length before she stepped on the torn hem of her gown and staggered.

Moving with lightning speed, Kinnahauk caught her before she could fall. He ignored the small flailing fists as easily as he did the mosquitoes that swarmed over the island whenever the wind fell. His *oquio*! He could have taken a woman to his lodge many winters ago. He could have taken three women, yet he had waited. For this!

Stung with anger and disappointment, he held her tightly in his hands, letting his fingers bite into her thin arms. Only when he saw her eyes go blank with terror did shame over-come him. Was he no better than a starving wolf, to pounce on a bone cast ashore by the storm? Kinnahauk, *wero-wance* of the Hatorask of Croatoan, did not frighten help-less maidens until their hearts ceased to beat in their breasts. He had shamed the blood of his ancestors by such behav-ior.

Slowly his fingers eased their grip. His arms fell to his sides, yet still she stood, like a bird caught in the spell of a snake. Deliberately he broke that spell, shifting his gaze to stare at the inland woods so that their eyes would no longer bind them together.

Without turning, he knew when she ran. He was aware of each step she took as she blundered clumsily across the sand toward the highest dune. She could have taken the easy path between them, but blinded by her foolish fear, she passed it by in favor of the steepest slope.

White-eyes. Would he ever understand their ways?

Chapter Five

"*Ho, waurraupa! Wintsohore!*"

The words meant nothing to Bridget as she raced for the dunes. Not until she had gained their dubious sanctuary did she pause to look over her shoulder, her heart pounding, her lungs fit to burst. He had made no effort to follow, but she didn't trust him, not for one moment. The thought of those strange eyes of his moving over her, lingering on the mark on her forehead, brought a rash of gooseflesh to a body that was already chilled.

What would a heathen know of witches and witchmarks? Let him look! Let him dandle her between his two hands like a pup being looked over to see if it be bitch or dog. At least he wouldn't call her a witch's spawn as her own people had done.

What was it he'd called her in that heathen tongue of his? Winter-something? If that meant food, he would have to catch her first. If she could reach the woods, she could hide until he grew weary of searching.

Odd that he could speak her own tongue, she thought, panting as she stumbled over the soft sand. Parroted phrases learned, no doubt, by hanging around the townspeople, though his voice held a resonance that fell pleasantly on the ear. Her own had sounded more like the creak of a windlass drawing water from a deep well.

Thinking herself shielded by the tall grasses that grew on the dunes, Bridget paused to catch her breath. She peered up and down the shore for signs of wreckage or other survivors, but there was naught save the tall figure that stood by the water's edge, the setting gun glinting from the blade he wore low at his side.

If the *Mallinson* had truly foundered, there could be others saved by the same kindly current that had borne her ashore. Perhaps if she cried out, someone would hear her and come to her rescue.

To a witch's rescue? Not likely, she thought bitterly. If she were to escape death at the hands of savages, she would have to manage on her own. Any moment now he would tire of playing the game of cat and mouse. She had surprised him and thus gained the advantage, but she must not rest until she reached a town, or at least a passing farmer who would give her a ride in his cart.

If only she wasn't so exhausted and so infernally hot! Hot one moment, freezing the next. If that was an example of the weather in this fair clime, she'd perish before she ever met her intended. Her head was splitting, and there was no telling how far she'd have to travel before she came to a settlement where she could inquire as to the whereabouts of David Lavender.

At that moment the savage started after her. Wasting no more time, Bridget snatched up her skirts and ran for the cover of the nearby woods.

How very strange, she thought, that for all her head felt as if it were soaring o'er the treetops, her feet seemed to drag behind, stumbling over every tussock of grass.

She had gained less than half a furlong when something stabbed her foot with a pain so intense it brought her to her knees. To her horror, she found herself surrounded by great fleshy leaves bristling with long, sharp needles. Whimpering, she tried to pluck out the one that had pierced the side of her bare foot, only have another spine jab her hand.

What could she do? The wicked things were everywhere, even clinging to her skirt. The one in her foot was so deeply embedded she feared she would not have the strength to remove it.

One swift look told her that the savage was much closer, his measured tread frightening beyond belief. The arrogant devil! Knowing that she was held captive by this army of needles, he felt no great need to hurry.

With renewed determination, Bridget tugged the evil plant from her right hand, leaving the needle behind. This she grabbed with her teeth and managed to remove it, spitting it to the ground. Wriggling forward, she edged toward a clearing in the thicket of needle plants, hoping to avoid collecting still more. She removed one from her other hand and several from her skirt, taking extreme care not to impale herself again. Even where they had been removed, the thorns left behind a burning pain, as if they had been touched with poison.

Her foot ached abominably. She could never run in this condition. Glancing nervously over her shoulder, she saw that her pursuer was drawing near, easily treading the perilous path as if nothing could hurt him. With a thoroughness learned only in recent months, she cursed his ancestors and vowed vengeance on their offspring as she renewed her efforts to remove the spur that went deep into the side of her foot.

A swarm of black midges descended on her, and she waved them away impatiently, only to discover that they were not midges at all, but dark spots dancing before her eyes. She was ravenously hungry. Perhaps her mother would coddle the eggs that old Sarah Humphrey had given them, if only she could remember where she had left them ...

A shadow fell across the sand where she sat cross-legged, staring at her injured foot with a puzzled frown on her flushed face. She glanced up quickly, and her foot slipped off her lap, jarring her injury so that she cried out.

The savage dropped to his knees beside her, and her head cleared instantly. "Get away from me, you black-hearted knave, let me be!" she warned, her voice little more than a whisper.

"*Mothei.* Give me your foot." His hand descended to the handle of his wicked blade, and he drew it from the band about his waist.

Bridget cringed. "I would rather keep it, please, sir."

With an expression of disgust, he knelt and reached for her ankle, drawing her leg across his knee. Bridget was paralyzed by fear when, drawing back his lips to reveal a set of flawless white teeth, he lifted her foot to his mouth.

At that moment, everything she had ever heard about the savages and their unholy appetites condensed into one hard lump of determination. Merciful heaven, did he mean to gnaw on her like a bone? She kicked out, catching him on the jaw. He grunted in surprise and fell backward, righting himself easily with one hand. Bridget, hampered by her wet and sandy gown, snatched at her chance, however small. Taking care to avoid a sprawling cluster of the devil plants, she rolled away from him and struggled to gain her feet.

He was on her instantly, pinning her to the ground with the full weight of his body, his face to her feet, her own head trapped between his two muscular calves. The coolness of his bare skin and the sweet, smoky scent of his flesh affected her oddly for a moment. It was like nothing she had ever known before. She felt something warm and wet licking at the side of her foot and shuddered as her consciousness wavered. Fresh terror attacked her, bringing a spate of trembling deep inside her body.

A moment later a piercing pain shot all the way up to her groin. He had bitten her! The devil was eating her raw— feet first!

Not until she twisted around, small fists flailing at anything in reach, did she realize that the savage had but removed the needle with his teeth and spat it to the ground. The weight on her back eased, and once more she attempted to escape, but a wave of dizziness assailed her. Before she could fight it off, he had lifted her up and was carrying her toward the wooded hills.

Bridget wriggled her toes experimentally. Her foot still hurt, but it no longer throbbed. She might have a flock of the devilish things clinging to her gown, only waiting a chance to leap into her skin, but for the moment there was little she could do about it. The wild creature was prodigiously strong. He could snap her bones easily if she angered him.

Surrendering to exhaustion, she breathed in the oddly pleasant scent of wood smoke and some sweet herb that seemed to cling to his skin and his glistening black hair. His tread was even, and her face rubbed rhythmically against his sleek, naked chest. She would await her chance and leap from his arms as soon as they reached the woods, she told herself....

Through half-closed eyes, she watched their progress, then watched the steady rise and fall of his broad chest: the oddly formed scar, like a sprawling letter *M*; the flat brown disc of his—

Quickly she twisted her head away, her heart slamming against her rib cage in a fresh burst of horror. It was then that she caught a drift of another scent, one not nearly so pleasant. The rank smell of old fish seemed oddly familiar. Now that she thought of it, she had been smelling the same vile odor ever since she'd come ashore. Evidently the whole place reeked of oily, rotting fish.

Just as she was growing resigned to her fate, the savage halted and lowered her to the ground. The sand still held the remnants of the sun's warmth, but without the heat that had unexpectedly been kindled by the close bodily contact, Bridget shivered.

Warily she studied him, searching for a clue to his intentions. He could have killed her outright several times over, yet he had not. Could it be that he meant her no harm after all, but was merely carrying her to the nearest town? His face revealed neither anger nor friendliness—nor even curiosity.

"Where are you taking me?"

Ignoring her as though he could not understand her words, the savage knelt beside her with a gracefulness that would have put the finest courtier to shame, and lifted her skirt. Gathering up a handful of petticoat in one hand, he reached for his knife with the other and began hacking at the bedraggled ruffles.

"Stop that! What are you doing?"

He continued to ignore her. Then, grasping her legs, he pulled them out from under her. Stunned, Bridget could only sit where she had landed and watch as he tore the ruffle clean off her stoutest petticoat and ripped it into two equal portions. As she looked on in amazement, he proceeded to bind each of her feet, securing the ends with a knot.

Then he stood and held out his hand to her. For one endless moment they stared at each other. Neither of them spoke. Ignoring his hand, Bridget clasped her arms for warmth. She was determined not to be the one to drop her gaze first, but it took all the strength she possessed just to hold her head up.

What an arrogant devil he was, looming over her with those burning eyes of his and his shameless nakedness! What was he waiting for, a coin? A trinket?

Ignoring the outstretched hand, she struggled to her feet, swaying dangerously. She really must find an inn shortly, for she was weak as a day-old chick. It would pass, of course, once she had a decent bite to eat. There was no telling how long she had lain on the shore, more dead than alive, but 'twas long enough for her belly to have grown hollow. She would give anything for a pot of strong tea and one of the weevily ship's biscuits, or even a mouldy crust from Newgate.

But first she must get away from the savage.

Lowering her gaze from his wild, proud face, Bridget looked down at the shoes he had fashioned for her. Savage or not, he had done her a kindness, and she owed him a debt of gratitude. "Thank you for these," she said, with no hope that he would understand her words. Likely the few he had repeated were all he knew, yet she must try. "You have been most kind. If you would be so good as to tell me where lies Albemarle, I must be on my way."

Still without a flicker of expression on his lean, handsome face, the savage lifted an arm and pointed to the densest part of the woods that followed the shoreline as far as she could see.

There was no break in the wall of foliage. Still, she had little choice but to heed his words. Mayhap once inside the woods she would see the town, or at least a road that would make traveling easier. "Thank you kindly," she said in her croaking voice. Lifting her skirts above her ankles, she began trudging up the sandy slope toward Albemarle.

Kinnahauk watched her awkward progress with no sign of emotion. His *oquio*. How had he so displeased the Great Kishalamaquon that He sent him such a one as this for a mate? She had the strength of a wet mosquito, the wisdom of a rabbit and the voice of a rattling gourd.

"Albemarle," he spat out in disgust. "White-eyes and their stinking houses and their stinking bodies and their dishonorable ways!" Let her go to Albemarle if that be her will. Let her cross the three ridges, the two great pocosins and the broad Inland Sea. Let her go past the villages of the Roanoaks, past Pasquinoc, where his friend Taus-Wicce dwelled, past the lands of the Paspatank and the Yeopim, all the way to Metockwem, where the Moratocs and the Chowanocs met. He had not spoken falsely, he told himself. The settlement called Albemarle did lie in the direction he had shown.

His *oquio*! Paugh! He would sooner take a swarm of bees into his lodge. There were times when honor and duty were a heavy weight upon his heart, yet he knew he must

follow to see that no harm befell her. Many moons had
passed since the Hatorask had made their way to this place
to welcome the first white-eyes to come to their shores. The
Great Spirit had placed this obligation upon them in the
Time Before the Grandfathers, and He had not yet released them from its bondage.

With her bandaged feet, Bridget was able to move faster, but the forest that had looked so near when she had set
out seemed to grow ever more distant. She was breathing
heavily, her throat burning with every labored gasp, yet she
could not stop to rest, for the devil was as persistent as a
shadow.

Stepping on the torn hem of her gown, she stumbled and
nearly fell. In some part of her consciousness, Bridget realized she was ill, her fever mounting. Plans tumbled about
in her mind. She would be no match for the silent cat who
pursued her if he caught her again, but it was fast growing
dark, and darkness was her ally. Once inside the forest, she
might be able to elude him. With the lights of the town to
guide her, she could make her way to Albemarle and David Lavender.

Her skin burned, yet she was freezing. Wicked insects
swarmed about her face, and she swatted wildly, almost
losing her balance. What would Mr. Lavender think if he
could see his bride now?

What would he think when the *Andrew C. Mallinson*
arrived at the docks without her? Or had the ship been
wrecked, all hands and passengers lost? Would she never
see Tess or Tooly again? Had it not been for Tooly's quick
action, she might even now be floating amidst the sea
wrack, with fish nibbling on her toes and fingers.

Tears prickled at her eyes, tears of self-pity, weakness
and fear. She wiped them away impatiently. Time enough
for weeping when she had got herself back to civilization.
For all she knew, the dark woods that loomed ahead might
be crawling with savages like the one who followed.

Water. Oh, what she would not give for a sup of cool water. She was perishing of thirst!

Stumbling into a wind-shaped cedar, she mumbled an apology. No longer did she even trouble to look over her shoulder, knowing he would be there, his powerful legs moving tirelessly, the mark on his chest—

The mark on his chest? No, she was confused. This infernal fever! The mark was on her brow, not on his chest. Did she not still dream about it in the night, the glowing iron moving closer, searing her flesh four times to form the misshapen *W*?

An osprey circled high overhead, its enormous wings outstretched to catch the unseen currents. Its voice fell sweetly on her ears, like the piping of a baby bird. Tilting her head to the sky, Bridget frowned. "I keep trying to tell you, I am no witch," she explained patiently, wishing it would go away and stop watching her with those strange golden eyes.

Her gaze settled on the tall figure who followed, his measured pace easily keeping up with her slow progress. "Why do you torment me this way?" she rasped softly, her throat a raw agony. If he planned to kill her, she would almost rather he do it quickly and be done with it. She was so tired, so tired....

Turning away, she staggered onward until she gained the top of the ridge, where wild grapevines made the going even more treacherous. The pungent smell of salt air and rotting fish was gradually overlaid with the sweet earthy scent of the forest, and she breathed deeply, bending over to brace her hands upon her thighs for a moment. She did not dare lie down for fear of never rising again, but she did take time to pluck a handful of the small, thick-skinned grapes. She ate her fill, savoring the rich, musky taste of them, all the while watching nervously over her shoulder.

Momentarily revived by the moisture and sweetness, she felt a renewed burst of energy. Seeing no sign of any habitation, she plunged deeper into the woods, leaving behind the last gleam of the setting sun. It was much darker under the canopy of trees. From time to time she paused to listen, hoping to hear, if not the sound of voices, at least the bark of a friendly dog.

Something . . . some sign that she was not alone in this strange and bewildering place. Bridget decided that she would walk until she could no longer tell one tree from another, and then she would lie down and rest until the morrow. Come daylight, she would search out grapes to breakfast on and see what nuts this forest offered. Mayhap she would even find a cherry tree or an alder for bark tea. All the salt water she had swallowed had left her throat in a sorry state.

It did not occur to her to wonder what she would use to brew the tea, nor how she would boil the water. Shoving aside a swag of vines, she stepped forward, only to find herself slithering down a gully made slippery by a blanket of leaves and pine straw. With a low cry, she flung out an arm to save herself and struck a tree, bruising herself but doing little to slow her descent to the bottom of the ravine.

Winded, she closed her eyes. A few moments to catch her breath and she would go on until she found a decent place to rest for the night.

How strange to feel hot and cold at the same time.

With a sigh, Bridget turned onto her side, savoring the feel of cool damp leaves beneath her burning cheek. All around her, sounds that had ceased abruptly when she had come tumbling down the hillside began again. Rustlings, snappings, the hum of insects. Somewhere nearby, a bullfrog croaked once and broke the surface of the water with a noisy splash.

Kinnahauk gazed down on the sleeping woman, his face revealing little of his feelings. He had followed her, taking care not to come close enough to frighten her, for he had known beasts of the forest to take fright and run blindly until their hearts burst.

His *oquio*! He might have taken her where she wished to go, except that she was too ill to survive without care. If he took her to his village, all would see the mark and laugh, for they knew well his feelings toward the white-eyes. Had she been stronger, he might have sold her or traded her for corn to feed his people, though she was but a weak and stupid white-eye woman. Yet in all honor, he could not leave her to stumble into a pocosin and die unsung.

Kneeling reluctantly beside her, Kinnahauk touched her brow, tracing the shape of the mark he knew so well. She burned! He heard her soft whimper, felt her stir restlessly at his touch and closed his heart against pity.

The English had shown no pity toward his young brother. In his foolish youthful pride, Chicktuck had taken a gold coin from among those that Kinnahauk and Kokom had found after a storm had broken the back of an English ship and cast it upon the shore. Drilling the soft metal, he had worn it around his neck to impress a certain young maiden, but before he had reached her village he had been set upon by a group of white-eye hunters and murdered, the gold stolen and Chicktuck's body thrown into the water.

No, it was not pity but honor that caused Kinnahauk to lift the slight form in his arms. He wrinkled his nose at the odor that arose from her. He had learned the source of the stench when he had seen the wooden cask that had carried her ashore, and now his own skin smelled like rotting fish where he had touched her.

Moving easily in a forest that kept few secrets from him, Kinnahauk bore the woman to the shelter of a spreading live oak, treading firmly to give warning to any rattle tails and white-mouth snakes. He lowered her to the ground, waving away the swarm of insects that followed.

A grim smile shifted his features. Her tender flesh would provide a feast for many such insects before the sun awoke. Still, she would be safe from the worst dangers. In the light of a new day, she could go or stay, he cared little. It was in the hands of the Great Spirit.

Kinnahauk stood and wiped his hands on a bundle of pine needles. He sighed in disgust. His *oquio*. The virgin mate sent to him by the gods. They must be rocking the heavens with their laughter now, he thought sourly. One poor Hatorask brave, called *chief* by a people whose numbers had dwindled until they were fewer than the horses that roamed the island. Truly, such a one deserved no more than this poor speckled rabbit.

He gazed down on the woman at his feet, the darkness no hindrance to one whose eyes were accustomed to it. She was small, her bones as delicate as the hollow bones of a bird. Even now her hair seemed to glow with a strange radiance, not unlike wild winter grasses under the light of the moon.

Half kneeling, he reached out to touch her, but drew back his hand. He would watch over her this night to see that no harm befell her while she slept. When the sun lifted above the water once more, it would be time enough for him to consider what must be done with her.

By morning Bridget's fever had abated, as was the way with fevers, but she was weak with hunger and parched for want of water. Finding herself alone in a tidy shelter, she blessed providence for having led her to bed down in such a place. She had been so exhausted she could not even recall closing her eyes.

There were acorns on the ground all about her, small shiny nuts still wearing their caps. Ignoring them, Bridget reached for those nearest her on the overhanging branches. The meat was rich and sweeter than any she had known before, and she ate her fill, hoping they would give her the strength to go in search of water. Without it she would surely perish.

Maddeningly enough there was water all around her, dark and sluggish streams of it twisting through the moors. To her great disappointment it tasted even worst than it smelled. Fearing the unsavory quality of it would make her even sicker than she was, she wet her mouth, splashed some on her face and throat and set off once more. There must be good water *somewhere* in this infernal place, else how could the savages survive?

Kinnahauk had no trouble keeping her in sight, for not once did she look behind her. He watched her move in circles like a fear-crazed rabbit. The bindings he had fashioned for her feet were soon lost as she scrambled through the forest, and he winced to see her tread on poison vines and all manner of prickly leaves. With no oil to protect her against insects, she was already showing great red lumps on her face and throat.

She traveled as if she were dazed by whiskey or the juice of certain berries. Twice he had saved her from the vicious temper of the white-mouth snake, yet in her blindness she had not even known he was there. Such a woman would surely perish without his care, and much as it pained him to admit it, she was his responsibility.

Kinnahauk had known many disappointments in his four-and-twenty winters, but none so great as this. For many moons he had dreamed of soft, dusky skin, of flashing dark eyes and sweetly scented hair as glossy as the wings of a crow.

And the gods sent him this! Speckled skin the color of raw venison, hair the color of dead grass, eyes like a summer storm, and the smell . . . !

Aiee, he had known many English, for they were thicker than ticks in the forests of the mainland. But for some trappers who lived more like the red man than the white, few were friends. Many were dogs, none were wise. It seemed to him that when white men met, all talked and none listened. The women of his own people talked more than enough, their tongues like dried beans rattling on the vine. He had known no white-eye women, but surely they would be even worse.

He shook his head in disgust. Even if he could bring himself to bed such a one as this, he would have to stop his

ears with grains of corn to keep from being driven senseless by the clatter of her tongue.

No. He would take her to his village and have Kokom
carry her up to the settlement at Albemarle. Then he would
seek a new vision.

Chapter Six

Bridget's head fell forward. It had been hours since she had caught sight of her pursuer. Or had it been days?

She shivered and burned at the same time. Were it not for the savage who trailed her so relentlessly, showing himself each time she would lie down for a moment's rest, she might have given up before now. All she had left in the world was David Lavender and a chance to start afresh, and she could not give up her last hope so easily.

So she plodded on telling herself that Albemarle could not be much farther. Already the trees were beginning to thin out. Once she reached the top of the hill she would surely see the town.

Catching the dangling tentacles of a rough, hairy vine, she dragged herself up the remaining few steps, her breast heaving as her lungs fair burst from the final exertion. The ever-present midges swam before her eyes, and she waved them away. Then she crumpled to the ground with a cry of despair. There was no clearing, no Albemarle—not even a trace of a road.

With a sob she turned away, only to catch a gleam of copper melting into the shadows. "Be dammed, you wicked heathen," she cried out in frustration. "If you wait for me to die, then you'll have a long wait, for I'll live to spite you!" Defiantly she lifted a fist, but the gesture went unfinished as she pressed her aching temples. If only she could lie down and rest a moment! Leaning back against the broad trunk of an oak, she closed her eyes. Just a few moments to regain her composure and she would be on her way again.

Kinnahauk sat on his haunches in a small clearing where deer had bedded down, and he watched the woman sleep. She needed his care, yet she had been frightened of him when he had found her on the shore. Her eyes had gone to his knife as if she expected him to remove her skin for a sleeping mat. As if the thin, speckled skin of such a creature would be of any value.

Honor left him no choice. He would take her to his mother's lodge. Sweet Water still grieved for the son slain by the English dogs, yet this small spotted one had not been to blame. She could not help it if her skin was ugly and her eyes were the color of rain clouds. Since the coming of the first white-eyes, many of his brothers had been born with pale skin, their eyes blue or gray, yet they were men of honor.

Since she had awakened and left her shelter the night before, he had directed her footsteps, guiding her in the direction of his village and keeping her from harm while he awaited the Voice that Speaks Silently. The Voice had spoken. He must wait no longer to take her to his mother's lodge, where she would be cared for until she was strong enough for the journey beyond Roanoak, beyond Pasquinoc, to the white-eye settlement.

But before he fouled his mother's lodge with the small, stinking white-eye, he would wash the smell of rotting fish from her skin. One of his favorite bathing places lay nearby. The sun would have removed the chill from the water. He would take her there, and while she bathed, he would prepare food, for he would not have her faint away from hunger before they even reached his village.

She was after all, his *oquio*. Weak, foolish and exceedingly plain, a great disappointment to him after all the years of waiting for his own special woman to come to him from across the Inland Sea, yet he could not deny that she bore his mark. She was his to do with as he wished. He might send her away. He might take her for a second wife to help with the work, or he might offer her to one of the old ones who had need of a woman to cook and to warm his sleeping mat.

It occurred to Kinnahauk that the mark was not always visible under her tangled hair. If none should see it, why then all the better. His mother would know—and Soconme, for the medicine chief knew all, but he would just as soon the knowledge stayed within his mother's lodge. If all knew of the mark she bore, Kokom would never cease laughing. Gray Otter would double her efforts to secure for herself a place in his lodge and on his sleeping mat, and he was not ready for that.

While Bridget slept, Kinnahauk gathered grapes, acorns, grass nuts and the meat of the prickly pear. This he peeled and cut into small bits, placing all beside her on a fan of palmetto. Cutting another frond, he cupped the center and wove the ends together to form a drinking vessel, which he filled from a nearby artesian well that had flowed since Time Before the Grandfathers. The water was not sweet, but it would do her no harm.

Placing it with the food beside the sleeping woman, he moved away, lifted his face to the sky and gave the haunting broken cry of the great white brant.

Bridget awoke with a start and sat up, her mind racing through the past until the present caught up with her. She had wasted too much time; she must hurry on.

Wearily she struggled to rise, and in doing so tipped over the water, which spilled over the small store of food, washing it off the fan-shaped leaf and into the sandy soil. She noticed none of this as she searched the woods for a glimpse of the beast whose cry had roused her from her sleep.

At first her fever-dulled eyes moved past without seeing him, until some deeper instinct drew them back. Her spirits plunged. There leaning up against a gnarled tree, his mighty arms folded across his chest, stood her savage. For once, that stony face of his spoke his thoughts quite clearly, nor were they pleasant ones.

Kinnahauk tightened his lips against the words that would have poured forth. Would he curse the sparrow for not being a hawk, the muskrat for not being a deer? She was naught but a poor foolish rabbit who ran in circles, blundering from the poison-leaf vine to the cat-claw vines, to the sharp thorns of the toothache tree. Gray Otter would have taken his gift, eaten half, saved the rest for another time and then cunningly asked for more.

No, his poor foolish rabbit was not so bold as the sleek otter. Yet she had faced him bravely and told him she was not afraid when fear had darkened her eyes like night shadows. She had threatened him with something called a *davidlavender* before she had fled. And in truth she had scorned the plentiful berries of the yaupon that were fit only for the birds and taken her fill of the grapes and ripe acorns, wisely choosing those ready to fall over those on the ground that were riddled with small worms.

Passing a blackberry thicket, had she not plucked the withered leaves and rubbed them into her arms as she stumbled along, as if knowing of their soothing properties?

How could this be? How could one be so ignorant and yet so wise?

Turning away, Bridget began to move.

Water.

With great effort she managed to focus her mind on her most immediate goal, forgetting her persistent shadow. With single-minded determination she blundered on through the forest, picking herself up when she tripped over fallen branches.

When she came to a small pool of clear brown water shallow enough to reveal a white, sandy bottom, she knelt and sniffed, hardly daring to hope it would be sweet. She sniffed again, the tip of her nose touching the still surface and then greedily began to drink. Only after she had drunk her fill did she stand and begin removing her gown.

Watching from a safe distance, Kinnahauk felt something stir inside him. The white-eye woman was stronger than he had expected, he thought with an unconscious touch of pride. Kinnahauk could journey for many moons and many suns without growing weary, but he had expected this small, weak creature to give up long ago. Aiee, his *oquio* hid her strength well, for there was not enough of her to stand against an evening wind, yet each time she had fallen, she had risen again.

Her own gods must have led her to this water, but even in her weakness she had known it to be good. That pleased him in a way he did not seek to understand. On Croatoan there were pools of salt water and pools of fresh water, and sometimes not even the fish could tell them apart. She was not quite as stupid as she looked, his small *oquio*.

Kinnahauk watched curiously from the hill above as she shed her ugly garments and stepped cautiously down into the shallow water. The flesh on her back was as pale as a winter moon, except for the red spots on her buttocks and thighs where all manner of insects had feasted on her most tender parts. There were long red streaks where her skin had been torn by thorns, and a dark bruise spread over one arm. Her small feet were too filthy to be seen clearly, but he knew they would be sorely damaged.

Her back remained turned toward him, but as she entered the water, her shoulders swung around so that he could see the sides of her breasts. He stared with unabashed interest. She was his, was she not? Even if he wanted none of her. Though for all her scrawniness, she carried more womanly flesh than he had supposed, her small breasts rising from her body and her hips flaring sweetly from a waist he could easily have spanned with his two hands.

In all the parts that had been touched by the sun, she was the color of a crab that had roasted over a bed of coals.

Already those parts of her were beginning to shed like a snake. Under the splotchy surface he could see the same small brown spots he had noticed on many other pale-skins. Her winter-grass hair was matted about her head and filled with leaves and twigs and the webs of all the spiders left homeless by her careless blundering.

Kinnahauk continued to watch, his lips curled in an unusual display of feeling as she lurked in the shallows, too timid to venture further. Was she afraid to rid herself of the rank odor that clung to her skin? Did she hope the foul scent would keep away the biting flies and the small vermin of the forest?

Were that so, then he would have perished long ago, for since birth, his own skin had been anointed with the clear oil of the black bear, which had no scent at all. Now his skin was as smooth and supple as the finest pelt, and he did not feel the cold or the worrisome bite of the insect.

Paugh! The English could not long survive in this land, for they would not learn to live with it in harmony. As soon as she was able to travel, he would send her to her own people and go in search of a fine strong woman of his own kind.

Yet in spite of his derision, Kinnahauk's man part began to stir. He turned away impatiently. It had been many moons since he had known the pleasure of sharing his body with a woman. Perhaps he would not wait too long after ridding himself of this unwanted burden before he went in search of a suitable mate. It was not wise for a man to save his seed when there were women who would welcome him to share their sleeping mats.

Hearing a splash behind him, he leaned his hips against the sloping trunk of a hornbeam tree, deliberately forcing his thoughts to the large buck that had escaped his arrow, and the need to build another storeroom before the Cold Moon.

But such thoughts would not cling to his mind, for his body spoke more clearly. He reminded himself that he was no young brave, to be led about by the needs of his man part. If he could not rule his own flesh, how could he hope to rule his people?

Unmindful of the cool breeze that tossed the tops of the trees about, Bridget lowered her body into the refreshing water with a sigh, allowing her head to fall back until the water covered all but her face. The throbbing in her head dulled, and illogically she felt the rise of hope once more. Now that she had eaten and found water to drink, she would surely regain her strength. *Had* she eaten? She no longer felt the pangs of hunger, so she must have filled her belly with something. If only the buzzing inside her head would cease for a while, she would not forget so quickly.

If she were not afraid of worsening her fever, she might rinse out her gown, but the sunlight was already growing weaker, which meant that day was drawing to a close. If she did not reach Albemarle before nightfall, she would have to sleep in her wet gown. That would never do. She needed warmth and rest, a nourishing broth and tea made of herbs that, for all she knew, might not even grow in this land.

A graceful white heron settled over the pond, then swept up again on seeing her there. Bridget sat up, taking in the beauty of her surroundings for the first time since she'd set foot in this strange land. For all its wildness, there was a loveliness about this terrible place that quite enthralled her.

A small familiar-looking fish darted past, followed by an awkward creature that scuttled across the bottom. Bream were found in many freshwater ponds at home, but surely the blue crab was found only in salt waters? What a strange heathen land was this, where even God's creatures knew not what they were about. Bream abiding with blue crabs, savages abiding with civilized townspeople....

Her feet made idle patterns on the sandy bottom. On hearing a splash, she searched the near bank. There were frogs in the millpond back home in Little Wheddborough, but the thick black head moving toward her like a stubby thumb belonged to no frog. Nor did the sinuous body that followed it!

Scrambling onto the bank, Bridget snatched up her clothes and backed hurriedly away from the pond. Her body felt oddly heavy after the weightlessness of the water, yet she hardly noticed. Nor did she notice the smell of rotting fish that surrounded her once more as she hurried to climb the nearest hill.

Hearing the crackle of brush behind him, Kinnahauk turned. He groaned inwardly as all his mental discipline came undone. Why did she not cover herself with those stinking rags she clutched? Did she not know it was unseemly for a maiden to show herself this way? For all she bore his mark, he had not claimed her. No bride-price had been asked, none paid. Therefore she should not present herself this way. Gray Otter possessed more boldness than all the other women of his village, and many of the men, yet even Gray Otter would hesitate to display herself in such a fashion before her chief.

And then, seeing the flushed cheeks, the overbright eyes, it came to Kinnahauk that the poor witless creature had not known he was there, did not see him yet. He had made no effort to hide himself, yet so skilled was he at moving silently through the forest, blending with the shadows, that she could not see what was before her very eyes.

Without moving a muscle, he watched her push the thick dripping mass of hair back from her face so that the fire mark stood out clearly in the fading light. Terror drained slowly from her eyes. They were strange eyes. He had seen them darken with fear, like the wrath of the storm gods. He had seen them grow pale as moonlight on the water when she did not know he watched.

Her lips, which were full and curved, were dry from fever. He thought of the sweet oil his mother would stroke on them to ease their tightness, and the hand that rested on his thigh grew tense, the fingers curling against his hard flesh.

Seeing her standing there, halfway up the hill where he waited, with the sun streaming at an angle across her slight body, Kinnahauk told himself grudgingly that her hips just *might* be broad enough to ride a small brave. And perhaps bear his son. Her breasts just *might* be full enough to suckle a babe. And a mate, as well. They were small—he could easily cover each one with the palm of his hand—yet they rose proudly, their tips the color of the wild pink mallow that brightened the pocosins instead of deep brown, which was the only color he had ever seen.

Kinnahauk told himself that she was not quite the *ugliest* creature he had ever seen. An Englishman might even find her suitable as a mate.

But then his eyes widened as they encountered yet another part of her body that was unlike anything he had ever imagined.

The people of Kinnahauk's tribe kept their bodies plucked scrupulously free of hair, save that which was covered by a brave's tail clout. In truth, there were times when he wished it were not so, for there were places on a man's body where the hair grew thicker and faster than he could remove it. Nor was it pleasurable, even when he was assisted by a willing young maiden.

His *oquio* was not plucked. Yet the small golden fleece in the shadow of her slender thighs was not at all unsightly. To his great amazement it stirred him in a way that the smooth, sweetly oiled bodies of the dusky maidens of the Paspatank and Roanoak had never done.

His hand dropped unconsciously to adjust the fit of his single garment as he watched her dry herself with her stinking garments before putting them on again. What good had it done her to bathe? She smelled as rank as before. He could not take her to his village in such a condition, for she would be an affront to his mother's senses.

Sweet Water, like all the people of his village, was scrupulous in her habits, bathing frequently in all seasons and making good use of sweet herbs in her bedding. The lodges of his people were swept daily and rebuilt after each storm, unlike the small, stinking boxes the English built for themselves that gathered all manner of filth.

Kinnahauk sighed with resignation. He must wash her again and destroy the wretched rags she wore before she could foul her skin with the stinking oil that clung to them. He waited until she was covered to step forward, saddened to see the fear leap into her eyes. For a moment he thought she might try to escape, but instead she sighed and pressed her hands to her eyes, as if they troubled her.

"Sit, *waurraupa wisto*. You must rest now." When he had first found her, he had called her *yauta wunneau*—red crab—after the color of her skin. As the *yauta* color faded, her skin became more like the rare white-speckled fawn. "I will take you to my village."

Bridget watched him warily. Did he possess some magic that he could suddenly appear out of nowhere? If he had meant to harm her, surely he would have done so before now, for she was ill with fever, weak from lack of food and exhausted from battling the wretched creatures that inhabited this wonderful new promised land.

If she could have got her hands around the windpipe of that lying clerk who had blathered on so about the golden age, she would leave him whistling for air! "Are we near the town, then?" she asked, hardly daring to allow herself to hope again.

Kinnahauk ignored her question. "Rest. No harm will come to you in this place."

Bridget needed no urging, for as evening had approached, her fever had burned hotter. For a long moment they stared at each other. Bridget surrendered first. Swaying on her feet, she made her way to a place well above the pond and was asleep almost as soon as her head touched the ground.

The moon had not yet risen when Kinnahauk returned. He stood over the slight form, his heart softening in spite of his determination to remain untouched. Burning with the fever, she whimpered and moved restlessly, but did not awaken. Poor *waurraupa wisto*. Bedeviled by dreams in her sleep, pursued by a wicked savage when awake. He knew well what lies the white-eyes told of his people, of killing and torturing, of burning and flaying alive. Red-skinned savages they were called, yet their skin was not so red as the poor wretched English who burned in the sun.

Savages? He had known far more savagery from the white-eyes, with their endless greed for gold and land and their hunger for power. Yet between this one small white-eye woman and one troubled Hatorask brave who was called *werowance* by his people, these matters were of no importance.

His lean face unguarded, Kinnahauk studied the sleeping woman, recalling the way she had looked with the sun touching her nakedness, lighting the small golden nest where her thighs met. He had once gazed on an unplucked woman from a lesser tribe and felt no great rise of interest in her dark woman-hair, but never had he seen such a thing as he had seen this day.

Kneeling, he laid aside the doeskin he had brought to cover her and placed his hand on her foot. How pale her limbs were, how angry the wounds from the briars. He ringed her ankle with thumb and forefinger. She was so delicately made, even for a woman. Once again he felt a strange stirring deep within him.

His nostrils quivered as the scent of fish rose on a wave of body heat. Was it truly only those wretched garments? He would soon find out, for when they reached the pond nearest his village, he would scrub her himself and then dress her in the sweet-smelling skin he had brought with him.

If after that, she still reeked of dead fish, fevered or not, he would send her on her way to Albemarle with the first white-eye to come to Croatoan. Then he would seek another vision from the Great Kishalamaquon, for surely not even the Great Spirit would expect him to foul the air of his village with such a one?

Chapter Seven

Dreaming of the chill depths of Newgate, Bridget was unaware of the eyes that gazed down on her, and the gentle arms that lifted her up and carried her along a narrow trail that led across a ridge, beside a broad pocosin and through a stand of oaks so mighty that it would take five men to reach around the trunks of the greatest. Wisps of pale moss trailed from the thick boughs that spread from each tree to tangle with those of the next, weaving a canopy that shadowed the white sand beneath with a lacework of silvery light.

Kinnahauk moved rapidly, but his smooth gait did not jar the sleeping woman in his arms. He could feel the fever burning in her, and it smote his conscience. He should have taken her directly to his mother's lodge when he had discovered her on the shore, for even then she had been fevered.

"David," she muttered, her parched lips moving against his chest in a way that affected him strangely.

Clearly her mind wandered. Perhaps it was wrong of him to want to wash away the foul odor before he took her to his village. Pride was a good thing in a man, for without it he was nothing. Too much pride could lead one to foolish and dangerous acts.

She was sleeping now. Sleep was healing. He would wash her quickly by the light of the moon in waters still warm from the sun. Sweet Water would have done the same, cooling her body so that it would accept the potions of old Soconme, who would be summoned to work his healing spells. Kinnahauk would not offend his mother's nostrils by dropping this stinking scrap of a woman at the door of her lodge.

Just as he neared his destination, Bridget awoke, and finding herself being transported, began to struggle. "Where is the town? I see no houses, I see no people. Where are you taking me?"

"Be still, foolish rabbit, for I mean you no harm!"

Kinnahauk, whose great patience had lured the blue crab into his hands and the small yellow finches onto his shoulder, found himself very short of that commodity. He took a tighter grip on her flailing limbs. Surely he had done nothing to deserve such a fate! The White Brant Kinnahauk, son of Paquiwok, grandson of Wahkonda, blood of the mighty Manteo, was being tested yet again to prove his worthiness to lead his people. With the Voice that Speaks Silently, he asked for the wisdom to overcome this greatest of trials.

"Be still. Lift your face to the wind and smell the cooking fires as they burn low. The old men sit outside smoking their pipes even now while the children beg to be allowed to stay and listen to their stories. The women put away the food and ready their lodges for sleeping. Can you not hear their voices? Can you not feel their nearness?"

At his words she grew still, allowing Kinnahauk to complete the journey to a small clearing that lay hidden within a crow call of his own people. She would have been even now under the tender care of Sweet Water and old Soconme had she not been so foolish.

Kinnahauk knew that sickness had caused her footsteps to wander and stumble, yet if she were not so foolish as to jump at shadows, she might even now be sleeping peacefully in his mother's *ouke*.

On reaching the clearing, Kinnahauk lowered his slight burden to the ground and stepped back, waiting to see if she would try to escape. Swaying on her feet, she looked around her, as if expecting to see one of her own kind. In the silvery light of the moon, he saw her small shoulders sag and her face grow sad.

"Are you going to murder me now and throw my body into the sea?" she asked in a hoarse whisper that showed more curiosity than fear.

A whippoorwill called softly from the base of a nearby tree. Small rustling noises told of the passage of raccoons and opossums, who moved about when the sun slept and slept when the sun was in its great house.

Kinnahauk reached for the last shred of patience. "Woman, before I soil the blade of the knife given me by my father, who was the great *werowance* Paquiwok, I would scrub the stench of rotting fish from your ugly, speckled hide! You offend my nostrils. You offend my eyes. The least of my warriors would count no coup from wearing your colorless hair on his spear!"

Arms hanging limply at her sides, Bridget regarded the haughty figure before her. She had almost—*almost*—come to trust him, but even with her head pounding so that her thoughts no longer made sense, there was no mistaking the meaning of his words. He despised her. As she had given him no reason to dislike her, and he did not seem put off by the mark on her brow, she could only conclude that he had no liking for Englishwomen.

They continued to stare at each other, and Kinnahauk began to regret allowing his tongue to run away with him, for it was not usually his way. This small wretched creature seemed determined to test him in ways more devilish than even the devious Coree could invent.

In her filthy rags, with her head thrown back, she held his gaze as if daring him to do her harm. He knew from her unsteadiness that her muscles cried out with the waiting, yet she would not break.

Aiee, why had he been tempted to go in search of that which had frightened the big antler-bearer? The buck would have made a good hide. Even now his mother would be preparing the meat for drying.

For Kinnahauk, the joy had ever been in the hunt and not the kill. As a boy he had learned to cast his mind into the body of his prey, which had brought him much success as a hunter and fisher. Yet in doing so, he had experienced the fear of the hunted. Each time he killed, his heart was saddened, even as his belly rejoiced.

With wide gray eyes she continued to look at him gravely, as if she were waiting. Few women would gaze into the eyes of a brave in such a bold manner, being too modest by nature. This one did not know the meaning of the word! Her ugly garment was rent almost to the waist, and caked with the mud of many stagnant pocosins. Her face was mottled where insects had feasted on her flesh, her nose spattered with small brown markings. But for the pale color, her hair resembled the nest of a squirrel.

Neither of them spoke. Kinnahauk understood that it was difficult to look into the eyes of pale-skins and read what was in their hearts. Yet somehow he sensed that this one was not deliberately hiding her thoughts from him, nor was she laughing at what she saw as ignorance and savagery.

He could wait no longer. "Woman, you burn with fever. You must wash, or the wounds on your skin will grow angry and turn inward. Your smell will drive away the game of the forest, leaving our people to starve. The water in this place is not fit to drink, but it is sufficient for bathing. Go now! I have waited long enough."

He reached toward the band at his waist, and thinking he reached for his knife, Bridget flinched but made no move to escape. "If it be my life you want, then take it, for I no longer have the strength to stop you, but I'll not wash to make the killing of me more pleasant for any heathen savage."

Anger flared in his eyes. For a moment she thought he would strike her down on the spot. Instead he only muttered something in his unintelligible tongue and lifted his eyes to the moon.

Too weary to defy him further, Bridget sighed. Her hand went to the fastening at the neck of her dress, and she turned toward where the water glimmered like hammered silver through the trees along the shore. Mayhap a cool bath would ease her feverish body.

"Not there, little rabbit. Come, I will show you."

Impatiently he led her a short distance from the shore to a low swale where a small pond lay, its white-sand bottom gleaming palely in the moonlight. "The water captures the heat of the sun and holds it for a time. If you wash quickly, you will not take a chill."

He turned away and left her so that she could perform her bodily functions without embarrassment. The English had less modesty than did his own people, for they were ever boastful of matters that the Hatorask would never speak of, yet they were strange in their own customs.

Kinnahauk waited on the shore as he listened for the sounds that would tell him she had entered the water. He gazed up at the knotted skein of clouds drawn across the face of the moon. The sign of the mackerel fish. On the morrow, before the sun reached its great house, the cold rains would come.

Not far away, Bridget lowered herself gingerly into the water, welcoming its coolness.

Once the initial shock was over, she relaxed, her head resting on a root that protruded into the water, her feet floating to the surface. The water held more than a bit of salt, yet it felt soothing to the skin.

A bit of her mother's soap, made from tallow and wood ash and sweet herbs, would not come amiss, she thought as her eyelids drifted shut. Inhaling deeply, she could almost smell it. At least she no longer smelled rotting fish. Perhaps the stench only lingered on the opposite shore, and had not followed them through the forest.

"Are you not done yet?"

Startled, she opened her eyes to see a pair of darkly gleaming tree trunks, one on either side of her head. She blinked, and the tree trunks became two legs of remarkable length and straightness. Her gaze moved upward, but the savage knelt to grasp her head between his hands, dunking her three times under the water before lifting her sputtering to the surface.

Bridget felt as if her head would burst like an overripe melon. Closing her eyes against the pain that throbbed at her temples, she felt his hands leave her. "I have not the time to prepare the roots of the spear plant, but clean sand will do well enough," he said gruffly. With that, he slapped a handful of dripping wet sand on top of her head and began scouring.

Bridget howled, abrading her raw throat. Her headache was nothing compared to the agony of having his fingers comb through the tangles of her hair as his strong fingertips covered every inch of her scalp with sand. She exhausted her small store of shipboard profanity, then fell into a fit of coughing, and still he did not cease.

Not content to torture her poor head until she was sure she was bald as a gourd, he commenced on her body, working his way down from her neck. "The minute I can find a way," she vowed fiercely, "I intend to hammer splinters of wood under your fingernails and set fire to them. Then I'll peel the skin from your body like the skin of a grape and feed it to the ants, and then—" Once more, she began to cough until all she could do was lean her head against his supporting arm as he scrubbed her back with a sandy palm.

"*Sehe*—hush, for I only do you a kindness," Kinnahauk murmured. "Would you have a rutting buck sniffing after you? Or is it the polecat you seek to attract?"

The wicked heathen was laughing at her, yet Bridget felt her defensiveness begin to slip away. Even though her head ached until she could scarce sort out her own thoughts, much less his words, she sensed that he meant her no real harm. "I've been ill," she said with what small dignity she could summon.

Sitting waist-deep in a brackish pond, subject of the rude attentions of a naked savage, with only a few stinking rags for her dowry, it was small indeed. The savage himself made a better showing. His braided hair, of a shade less than black, yet darker than brown, held all the colors of the rainbow trapped in its sleek depths. His skin gleamed with a sheen that reflected both cleanliness and good health, and his breath, when he'd knelt over her head, had been sweet as meadow grass.

Her back scrubbed raw, he turned her in his arms and picked up another palmful of sand, plastering it on her chest. The moment Bridget felt his hand touch her breast, she squawked hoarsely and began trying to twist and kick.

"Quiet, foolish one, your cries will drive the fish hawks from their nest." Yet even as he spoke, Kinnahauk felt his body respond to the feel of the small, slippery woman in his arms. He had dropped his tail clout before entering the water when it became evident that he would have to scrub her himself. How could he have known that his man part would stir to life for such a wretched creature?

"Stop that, you foul savage, or I'll—" Bridget reached for one of Tooly's colorful threats, few of which she'd ever understood, although they had proved effective against the most sluggardly seaman. "I'll crack your walnuts with a marlinspike!"

His reaction was the last one she expected. When he threw back his head and laughed, she could only stare up at him, thinking she must finally have succumbed to delirium.

"Even the rabbit has teeth," he said with a chuckle. "I would do you no harm, small one. Let us finish here quickly. My mother awaits in her *ouke*, where she will care for you until your body grows cool and your throat no longer rattles.''

Bridget was confused still further by the reference to his mother. The thought of her own mother still brought a pain too great to bear, yet she gained an odd sort of comfort from the thought of *someone's* mother caring for her. It was what mothers did best of all, though she would never have thought of such a man as having been born of a woman, like civilized mortals.

''What is this—this wicky where she waits?'' she rasped.

''*Ouke?* It is the thing you English call a house, but not the same.''

That told her something, but not much. She was in no condition to pursue the matter, yet one other thing bothered her. ''How did you come to speak the King's English?''

For a moment she thought he would not answer. It hardly mattered, she thought wearily. Yet it was curious that a naked savage spoke two tongues, when she, a civilized woman who could read and cipher, spoke only the one.

''Some of my ancestors could talk from a book. They valued themselves highly for their affinity to the English.'' The note of bitterness that entered his voice was not lost on her, even in her weakened state. ''It is dangerous to remain ignorant of the tides when there is a tide that rises higher with each moon.''

Bridget tried to follow his talk but soon gave up. No matter. At least he could understand her when she told him he must take her to Albemarle and deliver her into the hands of David Lavender.

Her small store of defiance exhausted, she lay still in his arms as he gently rubbed her shoulders, her neck and her arms. But when his hand once more slipped under her arms and slid down over her breasts to her stomach, she stiffened. No man had ever touched her body! ''No! Please, you mustn't. I'll wash the rest of me." It occurred to her that she was thinking of him more as a man than as a savage, and she cursed the fever that kept twisting her thoughts into such strange patterns.

"What manner of man would go naked into the autumn, save for a scrap of hide to cover his privities?" she whispered wonderingly. "What manner of man would adorn his body with a scar in the shape of..." Tentatively she touched the mark on his chest, her eyes lifting to his with a puzzled look. "Are you truly a warlock?"

Kinnahauk had continued to scrub her body, his touch like a feather on her breasts. With his fingertips, he stroked the pink tips until he was certain no fish oil remained, and now his hand moved slowly down the hollow of her pale belly, as if seeking the place that had stayed in his mind since he had first seen her unclothed. His breathing grew labored, his hand unsteady. When he felt the brush of her soft fleece against the tip of one finger, he grew still for a moment, willing his body to behave.

"Warlock?" he repeated, his voice sounding as strained as her own. "I do not know this word. I am of the Hatorask people."

"The Hatorask." Bridget tested it on her tongue, finding it strange, but oddly pleasant. She knew of the Spanish and the French, yet she had heard naught of the Hatorask.

Slowly Kinnahauk brought his hand back up to her waist. "You are of the English, my *oquio*. I have called you *Waurraupa Wisto* for the white fawn. I have called you Speckled Rabbit, for the rabbit has little wisdom. Yet in your weakness, you have survived, knowing which seeds and berries to eat and which to leave untouched. I watched as you rubbed the leaves of the blackberries on your skin, yet you walk blindly into the vine that blisters. In truth, my *oquio*, I know not what to call you."

Bridget frowned. Again that strange word, o-*kwe*-oh. She had thought it meant witch, but perhaps it meant friend. "My name is Bridget Abbott," she said, wondering at the strange new fever that seemed rooted deep in her belly and grew worse at the touch of his hands. What manner of man was this who held her thus and talked so calmly of seeds and berries and rabbits?

What manner of woman was she who lay naked as a newborn babe and allowed a man such liberties! If indeed he were a man, for truly, he must be a warlock to have addled her wits so.

Finding one last burst of strength, she stirred herself from the lulling comfort of his arms and sat up. "Please thank your mother for her hospitality, but I must ask to be taken to Mr. David Lavender in Albemarle," she said with a firmness that was agony to her throat.

"The settlement you speak of is two days' journey by canoe. First you must eat. Then you must rest in my mother's *ouke*. When you are strong enough, we shall see about this Davidlavender you speak of."

Kinnahauk was not pleased. Davidlavender was a man, one of her own kind. He must think on what to do now. It was true that he had not found her to his liking. Still she bore *his* mark. She had been sent to *Kinnahauk* and not to some white-eye called Davidlavender in the place the English called Albemarle after one of their own chiefs.

He did not dare bring the wrath of the Great Kishalamaquon down on his people by turning away from the woman who bore the fire mark, yet he did not want her for a first wife. Perhaps he would take a woman from the village of his friend, Taus-Wicce. When the small speckled rabbit was stronger, she could come to his *ouke* as his second wife to help with the work. The choice was his to make, yet the more he thought on it, the more trouble he foresaw.

With a reluctance of which he was hardly aware, Kinnahauk put her away from him. "Finish your washing, Bridgetabbott. I will bring you a new doeskin to cover yourself, and we will leave this place."

He said her name as if it were all one word: Bridget-abbott. She noticed he did not stumble over the syllables. 'Twas not a fevered dream; there was intelligence as well as kindness in those strangely colored eyes.

The hope that had been so painfully crushed again and again, rose once more. She was ill and weak, but she was still alive, was she not? And her golden future lay but two days' journey away.

"What am I to call you?" she asked as her savage friend rose from the water. Moonlight bathing his wet body in runnels of liquid silver, he stood unashamed on the bank and fastened on his single garment.

Without meaning to, she stared. Surely there could be no evil in the heart of one so beautiful. Bridget knew little about the male body, yet she knew that this primitive creature was more finely formed than even the handsomest of the men of her own village.

"Kinnahauk," he said in the voice that brought fresh chills coursing down her body. "I am called Kinnahauk, known by the sign of the White Brant."

Chapter Eight

Bridget had to be shown how to fasten the soft doeskin around her body. She was horrified at the amount of skin revealed after Kinnahauk had wrapped it around her, overlapping the front and fastening the ends behind her neck.

"I can't go into town dressed like this! It's—it's shameful!"

"Shameful, Bridgetabbott? Is it not more shameful to offend the nostrils of all who go downwind of you? Come, we will go now, for you are fevered and the night air grows cold."

As if in response, Bridget began to cough. Not waiting for further argument, Kinnahauk swept her up into his arms once more and proceeded along a trail that only he could see, moving at a swift pace.

But no matter how smoothly he ran, Bridget's head registered every footfall. She could only cling to his shoulders, burying her face against his throat, and pray for the journey to end. If the townspeople were accustomed to seeing the savages dressed in next to nothing, why then perhaps they would not be too horrified at seeing one of their own kind covered in no more than a scrap of leather. An extremely soft scrap of leather, she had to admit—one that smelled sweetly of a fragrance that was not familiar to her.

In fact, now that she came to notice, the smell of rank fish no longer permeated the very air she breathed. Had it truly been she who had smelled so foul? After her long swim yesterday—or was it the day before? After that it was a wonder she was not the cleanest mortal alive. The shore had been little more than a blur on the horizon when she had felt the shove between her shoulder blades and gone sailing over the rail.

Had not Tooly tossed down that salt fish cask to cling to...

"Oh, no," Bridget moaned softly, finally realizing the source of the odor that had followed her for days. She must have been soaked in fish oil, which had left a film on her skin that had ripened in the sun. Small wonder he had found her offensive.

Kinnahauk approached the village carefully, pausing at the edge of the woods. Instead of turning toward the *ouke* where Sweet Water lived alone, he turned toward his own lodge, which stood on a high knoll apart from the others. He was not ready to share this thing that had happened with everyone in his village. It would be difficult enough to explain to Sweet Water and Soconme, for he could well imagine the old medicine chief's delight in telling all who would listen of the fire mark on Bridgetabbott's brow. Even the wisest among his people were not without fault. Soconme's greatest failing was his wagging tongue. Unfortunately it was a failing that Kinnahauk's mother, Sweet Water, shared.

A group of old ones still sat outside their lodges, talking quietly among themselves. From the nearby shore came the sound of Kokom's cheerful boasting. Gray Otter's sharp retort was swallowed up in the laughter of several of the young ones, with the giggle of Sits There ringing out quite clearly.

Moving as silently as darkness, Kinnahauk approached the front of his own *ouke* and lifted the flap of hide that covered the opening. It bore the mark of his family, which was the Great Turtle, the mark of his office, which was three cut feathers with their tips dyed red, and his name mark. He looked down on the sleeping woman in his arms, the woman who bore his name mark, and his heart was troubled.

Kneeling, he held her across one knee while he unfolded his sleeping mat over a bed of moss and sea grass, sweetened with the leaves of the waxberry bush. She did not awaken as he carefully lowered her to the mat, covering her with another of the many soft skins his mother had prepared for his use. Bending over her, he frowned in the darkness as he heard the labored sound of her breathing. He could not wait until the others slept to summon his mother. Already he had waited too long.

With gentle hands he smoothed her wet hair as best he could so that it covered the mark on her brow. "Rest well, Little Rabbit," he whispered.

The moment he stepped outside, a shadow detached itself from the nearby trees and came to join him. Gray Otter ran the tip of one finger up his arm in a teasing manner. "After such a long hunt, it is good that you do not return empty-handed, Kinnahauk. But will such lean bones nourish a hungry man?"

"I do not know of what you speak, woman."

"I saw you creeping into our village, O mighty chief. Tell me, have you taken a captive? Will you trade her to her own people for much corn? Or will the Hatorask now join with their brothers and fight against the lying fish-bellies? Have we not fulfilled the prophesy of our ancestors? We are called coward by those who are not afraid to fight!"

"*Sehe!* You shame the ancestors of which you speak! You are free to leave this place if you do not like our ways. Go and fetch my mother, and do not arouse the whole village, or you will feel my wrath on the part of your miserable body that sits atop your horse!"

The tall Hatorask maiden stepped closer to lean against Kinnahauk, her black eyes laughing as she gazed up into his taut features. "Oh, what sweet promises you make, my bold chief. If only you meant them."

"Go! No—I will go myself," he grumbled, but the woman stayed him with a hand on his arm.

"I will fetch Sweet Water for you, but one day soon you will repay me, Kinnahauk. I will see that you do."

Kinnahauk felt torn, as he often did in dealing with the woman he had known since they crawled together on the sandy shore, tasting every shell and bit of driftwood they encountered. He did not like leaving Bridgetabbott unguarded while he went to Sweet Water's lodge, not when Gray Otter knew she was there.

"No, stay. But you will not enter my *ouke*, Gray Otter. I have not called council for many moons. Disobey me in this matter and you will go before your elders."

The young woman tossed her head angrily. She might safely taunt Kinnahauk the man, but not even she dared disobey Kinnahauk the chief. Having loved him since her twelfth winter, she found it sometimes hard to remember his great office.

Resentfully she watched him stride across the expanse of moonlit sand toward Sweet Water's lodge. If only Kokom were more like Kinnahauk. The two men's mothers were sisters, so they were much of a similar build, their features not unlike, although Kokom's eyes were black like her own. Kinnahauk wore his hair braided, the ends bound with strips of soft deer hide, while as often as not, Kokom's fell unbound to his shoulders.

Kinnahauk was more serious, especially since the death of his father, when he had become *werowance*. There was a depth to him that sometimes frightened Gray Otter, but she was ever drawn to things she could not easily understand. Kokom was like a shallow, sunlit pond. She could have had him anytime. When it pleased her to do so, she allowed him to share her mat, but always she pretended it was Kinnahauk who made love to her, Kinnahauk who whispered in her ear and made her body soar with the eagles.

Kinnahauk had dismissed Gray Otter from his mind as soon as he turned away. He was troubled by how he was going to explain the presence of the woman in his lodge to Sweet Water, for in spite of the peaceful ways of his people, Kinnahauk's feelings toward the white-eyes were well-known.

Why had he taken her to his own *ouke* instead of to his mother's? It was as if a night spirit had guided his feet, turning them from the path he would have walked.

Outside the small rush *ouke* where Sweet Water slept, he breathed deeply and then spoke in a low voice. "My mother, I have found an Englishwoman who needs your care. May I enter your lodge?"

Sweet Water, a widow of many years, had taken no other husband after the death of her beloved Paquiwok. After her eldest son Kinnahauk had been given his name-vision to be tattooed on his body and painted on his war shield, he had built his own lodge as was befitting a young brave. For a time Sweet Water had shared her lodge with her younger son Chicktuck, a laughing child who had delighted in playing pranks, but then Chicktuck, too, had been taken from her.

She appeared now, a woman of some forty-four winters, in the doorway of the lodge, her face serene and unlined for all her hair had gathered the snow of age. "You have been gone long, my son."

Kinnahauk stood outside the *ouke*, which was constructed of bundles of rushes that had weathered with sun and salt air until they blended with the muted colors of the live oak grove. Courtesy would not allow him to enter the lodge of another until he was made welcome, for their smallness provided little privacy once inside.

"A woman of the English was cast ashore, and I followed her to see that she came to no harm. When she grew too weak to go farther, I brought her to you. She is in my *ouke*."

"Why did you not bring her to me, my son?"

It was the first of many questions. Kinnahauk answered only those he felt necessary while he waited for his mother to gather the things she would need. He almost wished he could have hidden his small captive in the woods until she was healed. Or at least until he knew what he was going to do with her. Once her fire mark was discovered, there would be more questions than there were stars in the sky. In the way of all women, his mother would talk, and the other women would listen. Then they in turn would talk.

In the way of all men, the braves and old men would hear and pretend they did not. They, too, would talk. Soconme would be among the worst in this respect.

Moving with a surprisingly graceful step for one of her age and stature, the older woman led the way to her son's *ouke*, with Kinnahauk walking behind her, burdened with skin sacs and pouches and three earthen jugs. He barely suppressed a groan when he saw that Gray Otter and several of the others had gathered near his doorway.

"Leave us, for we have need for quiet," he said sternly.

"Sweet Water will need me. I have helped her many times in caring for sick children. Perhaps I can help your poor rack of bones." The last words were spoken so that only Kinnahauk could hear. To his chagrin, he knew there was a grain of truth in her claim. Gray Otter had indeed aided his mother many times. More than once, Kinnahauk had called himself ungrateful for doubting her true purpose.

She would have slipped in behind the older woman, leaving Kinnahauk to follow with his burden, but he barred her way.

"Stay!" he said sternly.

"Paugh!" the maiden replied irreverently, giving Kinnahauk little hope that she would obey his command for long.

The first thing Sweet Water did was to begin scolding. "Quickly, build up the fire. If I am to care for this poor creature, I will need to see. Even now she trembles from the cold."

"Mother, she was burning when I brought her here," Kinnahauk defended.

"Stupid one, why did you not bring her to me as soon as you found her? The poor child is suffering—my lout of a son takes time to go hunting while her fever worsens!"

"I hunted *before* I found her, Mother, not *afterward*," Kinnahauk explained. He had been dealing with this woman's stinging words for four and twenty winters. He knew well they were only a defense against a heart that had loved greatly and suffered much.

Kneeling beside the sleeping figure, Sweet Water smoothed the hair away from Bridget's brow, testing the heat of her skin. It was only after she lifted her hand that her eyes fell on the mark. Her gasp was audible. She lifted a dark, impenetrable gaze to the similar mark on her son's chest, and then to his face. "You thought I was blind, that I would not see? Or perhaps it is you who did not want to see that this white-eye woman wears your mark."

Her gaze held his for a long moment before she turned her attention to the restless figure on the mat. She placed the back of her hand against the flushed skin. "The child burns with fever, my foolish son. Why do you stand there like a great gawking heron when she needs care? Bring me my things. Go and find Soconme and send him here. You need not return, for I will not need you again this night."

"Is she very ill, Mother?"

"Ill enough, thanks to you and your dawdling ways," scolded Sweet Water as she began to smooth a thick ointment on the fire mark. "You should have brought her directly to me. Go now, fetch Soconme! Bring water, for I must cool her."

"Mother, I—" Kinnahauk thought better of confiding in Sweet Water. Sooner or later she would wonder how the white-eye woman came to be wrapped in one of the skins she herself had prepared. Kinnahauk could wait. He had had enough questions for one night.

"Cherry bark and willow, and perhaps witch hazel," Sweet Water muttered as she selected from among her store of healing herbs.

Moving away, Kinnahauk said diffidently, "She will need something for the weeping and itching on her arms and legs, for she has touched the poison vine. Perhaps blackberry leaves or—"

"My son has studied with Soconme? Kinnahauk has decided to become a great medicine chief instead of a great leader who will not even give his people a son—a great hunter who brings home nothing for the cooking pot? Go! Do my bidding before I lose my temper!"

Kinnahauk backed toward the opening, recognizing his mother's sharp words for what they were—a sign of worry. He had delayed too long, he thought as he gazed helplessly down at the small figure lying so still on his sleeping mat. "I will bring Soconme, and then I will bring you fish, for she has not eaten."

"An old rabbit would make a stronger broth."

"Or a squirrel," he said quickly. Somehow Kinnahauk was certain that many moons would pass before he again hunted the rabbit.

"Where do you go now?" Gray Otter asked the moment he stepped through the door.

"Who is she?" asked Kokom.

"Will you keep her for a slave, Kinnahauk, or sell her back to the white-eyes?" someone else chimed in. "She would be worth much corn."

Kinnahauk was saved having to answer their questions by the approach of a small man dressed in many skins worn like shawls about his withered body. In a face as lined by the years as the stump of a sea-washed oak, gleamed a pair of eyes as blue as the sky in the time of the ripening corn.

"You have need for me, Kinnahauk?"

Kinnahauk did not have to wonder how the old medicine chief knew. Little that went on in the village escaped him. "Soconme, my mother would have you look at a woman who lies ill with fever in my *ouke*."

The old shaman's eyes sparkled with some inner amusement that Kinnahauk could only guess at. Whatever the cause, it made him greatly uncomfortable. After Soconme had disappeared into the *ouke*, Kinnahauk shoved an earthen pot into Gray Otter's arms. "My mother needs water."

Gray Otter pushed the pot back. "Then fetch it yourself. Is that not all you're good for, to do the work of a woman while our brothers fight to hold back the white tide that floods our shores?"

Speaking through clenched jaws, Kinnahauk said, "Kokom, if you would take a woman to your *ouke*, why then I ask that you consider Yauta's daughter, Sits There, who is sweet of temper and fair of face. If you would take a white-mouth snake to your sleeping mat, why then, Gray Otter is to be highly recommended for her venom."

Kinnahauk strode off into the darkness to the place where good water came up from the ground with the sound of Kokom's laughter and Gray Otter's anger ringing in his ears. He returned quickly, relieved to find that they no longer lingered outside his lodge.

They were inside.

"Leave this place, you are not welcome here!" he hissed as the Hatorask maiden cast him a look of triumph. Sloshing water from the jug, Kinnahauk shoved her toward a grinning Kokom.

Sweet Water looked up from where she knelt, her expression stern. "*Sehe!* You are worse than small squirrels, chattering and shoving! Kokom, stir the fire! Gray Otter, make yourself useful." She handed the young woman a shallow bowl of water and several small scraps of soft doeskin. "We must cool her body, for the fever rises too swiftly."

Kinnahauk had never felt more useless in his life. There was something for all to do except him. He did not *want* Gray Otter touching this woman! He did not want her in his *ouke* at all, for well he knew that his mother had encouraged her to believe that one day he might turn to her. Gray Otter had boasted to him of their closeness, hinting that Sweet Water longed for the strong grandsons that would come of such a joining.

Old Soconme muttered incantations as he readied the fire to receive his offerings. Already the odor of red cedar berries permeated the smoky enclosure. Soon the whites of the Englishwoman's eyes would be as pink as those of any redskin.

From high overhead came the cry of a flock of white brant. Kinnahauk thought it must be the laughter of his ancestors as they looked down on this poor brave. Helplessly he stood and watched as Kokom rushed out to fetch more water. Gray Otter and Sweet Water continued to bathe the slight body above and below its single garment, while Soconme, now wearing his full regalia, circled the fire, chanting incantations as he sprinkled a gray powdery substance on the flames.

It was too crowded. There was no need for all these people to be here, Kinnahauk told himself. *He* could have brought water. *He* could have helped with the bathing. Anger began to grow in him as he watched Gray Otter slap the wet dressings on the face of his *oquio*, paying no attention as water puddled in her eyes and at the corners of her mouth.

"Aiee! Do you wish to drown her?" he whispered fiercely when he could stand no more. Stepping forward, he reached for the bowl of water. He would do this thing himself!

Sweet Water, who had been preparing a strong decoction that would cool fever and ease congestion of the chest, moved to stand directly in front of her tall son. The look she gave him was not one to be taken lightly. "Go and walk on the shore, my son. You are not needed here," she said firmly.

Kneeling beside the sleeping mat, Gray Otter cut him a wicked look. "Kinnahauk fears for his ugly white slave. He should learn to choose his captives with more care. Next time you go hunting, O mighty Kinnahauk, bring back a slave who is strong enough to rebuild my *ouke*, for the winds already find their way inside and my sleeping mat is cold."

The word Kinnahauk uttered was not one he had ever used in the presence of his mother, but Sweet Water only smiled and nodded knowingly.

"A white-eye man, Kinnahauk," Gray Otter persisted. "One of the big stupid ones with a broad back. This bone of a *tauh-he* has no more strength than a *weekwonne*." Lifting one of Bridget's small wrists, she let it fall.

"It is you who are the bone of a dog, woman! The *weekwonne* is strong enough to build your *ouke*. It is wise enough to bend before the wind so that it does not break!" Head tipped back, he glared down the length of his proud nose at the black-eyed woman. "Better the *weekwonne* that grows tall and free than the poison vine that clings and entraps and spreads its evil venom on all who come near!"

For reasons of her own, Sweet Water had covered the fire mark with a band of doeskin after anointing it with the pungent salve. Kinnahauk rejoiced, for if Gray Otter had seen the mark, her tongue would have been even more vicious.

"Children, children!" Sweet Water scolded. "Kokom, we will need you no more this night," she said, dismissing her sister's son. When he had left, she knelt and prepared to unfold the single doeskin that covered her patient's body.

Kinnahauk could stand no more. Taking Gray Otter by the arms, he lifted her away from the sleeping mat, glaring down at her. "Nor you!" he said angrily. "It is not fitting that you should enter my *ouke*!"

Gray Otter tossed her head proudly. "I was invited to enter by your mother."

"Kinnahauk invites you to leave."

"*Quauke?*" she asked coyly, inviting him to go with her.

"Leave, woman, before I lose my patience!"

"*Yauh-he noppinjure,*" she taunted, swinging her hips in one final gesture of disdain as she ducked under the flap and disappeared.

Kinnahauk wiped his brow, which had suddenly grown damp. He would rather be called an Englishman's cow than to suffer such a one in his *ouke*. Kokom could have her! Kinnahauk would seek his own first wife from among the Roanoak, the Poteskeet or the Paspatank, where a maiden early learned to please her man by doing his bidding quietly and quickly.

Ashamed of having lost control of his temper, Kinnahauk sought his mother's eyes, only to find her laughing silently at him. This did not improve his temper at all. "The woman has a wicked tongue," he said defensively.

Sweet Water grinned widely, revealing a perfect set of teeth save one, where she lodged a pipe for a quiet smoke now and again with her old friends. "Yes, my son. The otter is fierce to defend her territory against all enemies."

"Enemies! We are not enemies. It is just that we have known each other for too many years." His gaze strayed anxiously to where Bridget rested more easily now, half hidden in the thick vapors that filled the lodge.

"Yes, my son," Sweet Water agreed meekly, her eyes dancing with merriment.

"The small white-eye woman is no enemy, for she can no longer even hold up her head."

"No, my son."

"My mother, I asked Gray Otter to leave only because it is not good to have so many people in one small place. The woman cannot rest with the clacking of so many tongues."

"Yes, my son. Now go and fetch my sleeping mat, for I will sleep here this night. You may sleep in my *ouke* if you wish." Her smile was the smile of one who knew him far too well. "Or perhaps you would rather sleep outside so that the night wind can cool the fever that disturbs you so."

Chapter Nine

Bridget came awake slowly, afraid of opening her eyes for fear of finding herself half-naked in the middle of Albemarle town, surrounded by strangers all pointing to the mark on her brow. It was a fleeting thought, yet a vivid one. At least her head no longer felt as if seven kinds of devil were fighting to get out.

"Teetche-wa waurepa."

At the strange words, spoken in a guttural voice that sounded more like the grunt of a pig than the words of a man, her eyes flew open. Bending over her was an apparition more shocking than anything she had beheld in all her eighteen years. It seemed to rise from the clouds of scented vapor that swirled around her, a figure more ancient than time itself, and more hideous than her worst nightmare.

"Yecauau te Kinnahauk."

A single word emerged from the gibberish. *Kinnahauk!* Was not that the name of the man who had promised to take her to Albemarle and then brought her to this place instead? "Where is Kinnahauk?" she demanded.

The apparition began to cackle. Through the curtain of swirling fog he moved closer. Bridget cringed in fear for her life, her fingers curling into a surface that was both soft and strange. She dared not take her eyes off the creature long enough to examine her surroundings. "Not one step closer,

I warn you," she croaked in a voice so deep she hardly recognized it.

Frantically trying to remember how she came to be here, Bridget eyed the wizened figure suspiciously. A short cloak bearing all manner of strange symbols covered a shrunken body similarly adorned. He seemed to be covered with scars and tattoos, his head shorn, save for a cockscomb on top, from which dangled a long feather dyed blue on the tip and dotted with yellow. Draped about his wattled neck were several necklaces made of what appeared to be teeth and small bones, with a skin pouch of some sort dangling from the center.

Bridget swallowed hard, feeling her stomach lurch. Was this to be her fate, then? Her bones and teeth to be rendered up for a bauble to grace the ugly carcass of some wretched godless savage? The creature moved closer to lean over her, and her heart leaped to her throat, quivering there in stark terror.

"*Te reheshiwau?*" he crooned in a voice surprisingly strong in one so ancient.

Stricken speechless, Bridget stared up into a pair of eyes that were as blue as the sky above Wicken Fen. "Please—what have you done with David Lavender? Where are all the townspeople? Where is Kinnahauk?" she whispered.

"*Ne te reheshiwau.*" The old man continued to babble his heathen sounds, and Bridget wondered despairingly if she had lost her hearing, or lost her senses—or both.

Firelight flickered as fingers of wind reached through the mat walls of the lodge. Through the swirling mixture of steam and smoke, she watched as he turned away and began to prepare a potion of some sort, dipping gnarled fingers into one earthen jug after another. Her heart stopped. He was planning to poison her! She clamped her teeth together until her head began to throb once more. If only she could attract someone's attention . . .

Kinnahauk? He had betrayed her once already. Had he not brought her to this place after promising to take her to

Albemarle? Or had he mentioned a village? How was she to know how many towns and villages there were in this benighted land?

Even so, she wished he would return. He had frightened her, but he had never treated her unkindly—unless offering her up as a gift to this evil old creature might be called unkind.

A current of cool air stirred through the room as a small plump woman entered. Bridget turned to her in desperation. "Please help me," she pleaded. "I will do your bidding for as long as you wish. I can cook and wash and write and cipher, and I am well versed in the healing arts—only don't eat me. Don't let that wicked old man poison me—please!" she whispered hoarsely.

"*Sehe, Wintsohore woccanoocau,*" the woman said gently.

Bridget grasped at two familiar words. The *winter* thing, and the one Kinnahauk had said to her most often, which sounded like *say-hay*. She repeated it questioningly.

The woman grinned broadly, her black eyes almost hidden in plump cheeks. "*Sehe.* Hush," she said quite clearly. "Child of the English, you speak too much with angry throat. Hush and let Sweet Water make you good."

Weak with relief, Bridget realized that her hostess could also both speak and understand her words. There followed a short interchange between Sweet Water and the wrinkled old man. Bridget understood none of it, yet she was almost certain that they were discussing her fate.

Kinnahauk, Bridget wailed silently, why did you bring me here to these strange people? You promised to take me to David Lavender. You *promised*!

No, she thought, a frown creasing her sun-parched brow. He had promised to take her to his mother. Oh, it was so hard to remember! Why was she so very confused?

The woman called Sweet Water brought her a steaming drink, and she sniffed it suspiciously lest it render her unconscious so that the old one could do his wicked deeds while she lay helpless. Mint. Of a variety she did not recognize, and those were clearly bits of wild aster floating about on the surface. For all her caution, she could not detect any other substance.

The pretty, plump woman waited patiently, her round face without expression. "Drink. Make you good," she said firmly, and Bridget, uncertain whether the draft was intended to make her feel better or taste better, supped cautiously.

Mint and aster tea. It would do well enough until she was strong enough to prepare her own decoctions. Her head no longer ached quite so fiercely, and the pungent steam had eased her cough, but it would take time to regain her strength. Meanwhile she must learn as much as she could from this seemingly friendly woman so that as soon as she was able, she could escape.

There followed a period of time during which Bridget grew daily stronger. She had lost weight she could ill afford to lose, and her fever returned each evening, only gradually loosening its hold on her frail body. Sweet Water nursed her as lovingly as if Bridget were her own daughter.

"Are you the mother of Kinnahauk?" Bridget asked one day after her voice had returned to normal.

The woman beamed, nodding vigorously. "First son. Big chief. Good hunter. You like?"

"Where is he?" she asked with a careless air that would have convinced few. As her strength slowly returned, she remembered puzzling bits and pieces of the time just after she had washed ashore, and the man who had rescued her, followed her and eventually brought her to this place.

She had been terrified at the time. She was no longer frightened, but as each memory slipped into place, she grew more and more embarrassed. Had she really smelled like rotting fish? Had he truly held her naked body in his arms and bathed her, or had that only been a feverish dream?

"Kinnahauk go to make council with our people near Dasamonquepoc. Many trouble come to our people who live on mainland. Many trouble, aiee!" she finished softly with a look of sadness.

So Kinnahauk had left her here and gone to another place. Did that mean she was not to see him again? Oddly enough, Bridget found the notion unsettling. Not even the thought that she would soon be strong enough to continue on her journey to Albemarle and David Lavender seemed to lift her spirits, and she remained listless, sleeping all day and then dreaming restlessly at night.

Finally her fever left and did not return. Sweet Water, for all her kindness, was a stern caretaker, and Bridget grew daily stronger on a diet of thick, savory broths made of meat and roots, flavored with wild onions. She was offered a thick mush made of fermented acorns, which she refused, but the flat cakes made of ground corn and spread with wild honey were as tasty as any her mother had ever made.

There had been cold rain for a time, but as soon as the winds blew warm again, she was allowed to sit in the sunny doorway each day. Old Soconme, the wizened, blue-eyed creature who had frightened her out of her wits when she had first seen him, became a regular visitor, telling her much about the Hatorask people and their legends, and teaching her some of the words.

It seemed he was an apothecary of sorts, and for a heathen, surprisingly well versed in the art. They had many fine arguments over roots versus bark of the different trees and shrubs, elixirs over decoctions, and the merits of one potion over another for treating certain ailments. Soon they were comparing notes as Bridget had once done with her mother, and she did not even remark on the strangeness of it, for it had all come about so gently.

Lying on her sleeping mat, across an expanse of clean white sand from Sweet Water, Bridget told herself she would have much to relate to David Lavender about her life with the aborigines when she eventually reached his side.

The village, though quite different from anything she had ever seen, was not unattractive, lying as it did on a sandy bluff overlooking a great river or sea. The houses, which they called *oukes*, were small, yet surprisingly roomy. Instead of stone and thatch, they were constructed of peeled poles and bundles of rushes and woven mats, with sometimes a large tanned hide on the side where the cold wet winds blew fiercest.

They were kept scrupulously clean, the air made ever more pleasant by the use of a fragrant shrub called waxberry bush that seemed to keep the worst insects at bay. Though there was a fire bowl inside for heat and light, much of the cooking was done outside, where racks of meat dried slowly, and fish that had been impaled by the gills were roasted, sending off the most delicious odors.

The people of Kinnahauk's village were by far the most generous people she had ever known, for whatever they had, they offered freely, knowing that she had naught to give in return. She wore a dress fashioned of soft skins that was quite lovely, and moccasins on her feet, as well as a shawl of fringed doeskin for warmth.

Save for one, a beautiful woman called Gray Otter, the people were exceedingly friendly, as well as quite handsome, being tall and well formed. Both their hair and eyes for the most part were black, though some few had hair that was more auburn and eyes of blue or gray. None save the one had eyes of that peculiar golden hue.

Kinnahauk's name was often spoken, but he was nowhere to be seen. Somehow Bridget could not find the courage to ask after him. If Sweet Water wanted her to know more about her son, she would tell her. Still, she wondered. He lingered on her mind far more than any of the others, even old Soconme, who had become her good friend.

Bridget was especially taken with a girl of about her own age called Sits There. Like the others, she spoke a mixture of English words and the Hatorask tongue, which she took great delight in teaching, although the lessons often dissolved into fits of giggles over Bridget's pronunciation.

And gossip. "Has Kinnahauk offered the bride-price to your father? Was it acceptable to you?" Sits There asked one day as they sat shucking acorns to be made into the vile-tasting *pawcohiccora*.

Bridget, while not fully understanding the question, saw it as a means of learning more about the elusive man who had brought her to this place and left her in his mother's care. Sweet Water had lost no time in transferring Bridget to her own lodge after that first night, for as Bridget had since learned from the one called Gray Otter, it was not seemly for a woman to sleep in the lodge of the chief until they were promised.

"What is this bride-price thing, Sits There? I have heard others mention it."

The young Hatorask maiden cast her a teasing look. "It is what your father demands in payment for you. At first no one thought you would be worth more than a few poor summer skins, for you were weak and much ugly to look on, but now your skin is smooth, and your hair is like the white man's gold, and Gray Otter is afraid you will find great favor in Kinnahauk's eyes."

Bridget's mouth fell open, but no words emerged. Finally she managed a snort of disbelief. "I have never heard such foolishness! I have no father, and if I did, he would not sell me to anyone. And as for finding favor in..." In stunned disbelief she shook her head. Truly, these people were strange. Were they all pranksters like the one called Kokom? She was beginning to think so.

"Kinnahauk took you to his *ouke*," Sits There reminded her slyly.

"I was ill. It certainly did not mean—he would never—! I have not seen Kinnahauk since he brought me here," she snapped. "You may tell Gray Otter she has nothing to fear, for as soon as he returns, he has promised to take me to Albemarle."

"Why go you to this place Albemarle, Bridget? Have you a brother there? Do you stay in his lodge until the bride-price is paid?"

"I have no brother, Sits There. There is no bride-price! At least, there is, but it was paid by someone else," she explained patiently. "A man called David Lavender."

"You would have two husbands?" The younger girl burst into another fit of giggles, and Bridget shook her head helplessly. "Aiee, that is a fine custom I would like well. Among our people, a man may take two wives, one for the sleeping mat and another to help the first wife with the children. Second wife only shares her husband's sleeping mat when first wife is in the women's *ouke* or large with child. I like your way best. I would have Kokom to make me laugh, and Kinnahauk for my protector, and Crooked Stick to warm my sleeping mat, and—"

Laughing, Bridget shook her head. "That's not what I meant at all, and I suspect you know it. You're a big tease, Sits There."

"I speak true, Bridget. A brave can take many *yecauau*—many wife. A woman may share her sleeping mat with any man before she promises herself to her chosen one. When promise is made, our chosen one take us to his *ouke*, where we lie together as *yenxayhe*—as brother and sister—until bride-price is paid."

They had been joined by several of the younger women of the village by this time, and Bridget thought it as well to set the matter to rest. She had often seen them staring at the mark on her brow, had herself seen the marks on Kinnahauk's lodge and on his body. They were not at all the same, yet there was a certain similarity about them that seemed to have some meaning to these people.

"Kinnahauk does not want me for a wife," she assured them all, suspecting that many of them had cast desirous eyes upon the handsome brave. "He brought me to Sweet Water only because it was his bad fortune to find me after I had fallen from the ship on my way to Albemarle." There—she thought that should put to rest any speculation until she left this place.

Her remark brought forth a fresh burst of giggles, and she sighed in surrender. They were like children playing games, she thought. At least their teasing was friendly, and even Gray Otter had not been openly hostile.

As she strolled back to Sweet Water's *ouke* with her basket of acorn meats, munching as she went, her thoughts ranged back over the past year and all that had happened to her. Her whole life had been ruined, her mother's life stolen, by the very people they had always considered their friends. As to what lay ahead ...

Bridget did not know what manner of man she had sold herself to. His name had sounded so sweet and noble when she had first seen it written, yet treachery came where one least expected it.

As did friendship, she admitted, for she would never forget the gentleness and the unfailing courtesy of these people who had taken her in and nursed her back to health. With few exceptions they were kind and helpful, and she would miss them greatly when she left this place.

Popping another acorn into her mouth, Bridget looked up to see one of the exceptions barring her way.

Gray Otter, her doeskin gown and moccasins bleached to a creamy shade of white and skillfully beaded in the pattern of a wild lily, confronted her, hands on her slender hips.

"Why do you wear the mark of Kinnahauk?" she demanded. "Did you think to trick him into taking you as his wife? He would never want such a woman as you. Do you not know how he despises your people? They killed his father with their filthy diseases. They killed his brother in their greed for gold. They steal our land and enslave our brothers with their strong whiskey. Soon they will come here. They will drive us into the water to live with the *ya-cunne*, for there will be no more forests for us to hunt, no more land for our village. Paugh! You are not wanted here, white-eye!"

Bridget reeled under the attack. "Gray Otter, I mean you no harm. I know nothing of whiskey or disease. And certainly nothing of gold." She ventured a smile that trembled and died. She had heard of the brave souls who had sailed forth to the colonies—who had not? They had been men and women of good character, farmers for the most part, God-fearing folk who would plow and plant and not be inclined to fight with anyone, much less such a kind and gentle people as the Hatorask.

For a long time the two women stared at each other. Bridget refused to lower her eyes, for she had done nothing of which to be ashamed. If a few Englishmen had caused problems, she could hardly be blamed.

Finally Gray Otter shrugged. Reaching into the basket Bridget carried over her arm, she helped herself to an acorn and promptly spat it on the ground. "Paugh! *Wintsohore eppesyau* does not know ripe acorn from green!"

Bridget knew the word for English was *Wintsohore*. The other, she suspected, she would be happier not knowing. "A few are underripe, mayhap, but these are for *powcohiccora*, not for bread."

Gray Otter's disdain showed quite clearly in her beautifully carved features and her dark, lustrous eyes. Perhaps Sits There had not been teasing when she had implied that the Hatorask maiden was jealous.

Bridget made an effort to smooth over her ruffled feathers. "I did not come here by choice, Gray Otter. Kinnahauk brought me to this place when I was too weak to protest."

"Why do you wear his mark?"

"It is not his mark! I was mistaken for a witch by the ignorant among my own people, and branded as such."

"What is this *witch*?"

Bridget shifted her weight to the other foot. She was tired, and this whole discussion was bothersome, yet as long as Gray Otter showed signs of becoming more friendly, she could not simply walk away. "A witch is—well, it's something like what you call a *shaman*. Only different. My people fear witches. Your people hold *shamans* in great esteem."

"Yet Kinnahauk took you to his *ouke*."

"And Sweet Water removed me to her own as soon as I could walk. If you have fault to find, then find it with Kinnahauk, for I have no doubt he can tell you his reasoning. I cannot."

"Kinnahauk will soon take me to his *ouke* as his first wife. I could have you as my slave if I wished."

Bridget stiffened. "I fear that will not be possible," she said in as haughty a tone as she could summon. "As soon as Kinnahauk returns, he will take me to Albemarle, where I am to wed a planter." Aye, she added silently, and if he did not soon return, her planter might give her up for dead and send for another bride. "David Lavender has already paid the bride-price," she declared, which was more, she suspected, than Kinnahauk had done for this overweening wench!

They were joined on the path to the village by the others, and Wattapi held up a withered plant. "Is this the flower you spoke of, Bridget?"

Bridget, glad of the distraction, examined the wilted thing. "It looks the same, but without the blossom I cannot be sure. In my country, 'tis a sure cure for the swelling that comes with a woman's monthly flux."

Gray Otter paused in the act of nibbling another of Bridget's acorns. "Then it is true? You are a *waurraupa shaman* among your people?"

From the low murmur around her, Bridget discerned not fear but respect. Did they not know of the evils laid at the door of those called witches?

Waurraupa shaman. White Witch. Soconme was called *shaman*. Although Bridget considered him something of a windbag, with his dancing and endless chanting, she had to admit that the old man was knowledgeable when it came to the use of herbs and cures. "I was called witch, but I am only an apothecary, practiced in the art of healing, as was my mother."

"The *Waurraupa Shaman*," said Wattapi reverently. It occurred to Bridget that the girl was easily impressed.

"So that is why Kinnahauk turned up his nose at you, Gray Otter," taunted Sits There with a wicked grin.

Gray Otter's eyes flashed. For once, Bridget wished her friends were not so quick to tease.

Both Bridget and Gray Otter were silent as they entered the cluster of lodges. The others laughed and chattered, soon lapsing into their own tongue.

Sweet Water appeared in the opening of her *ouke*, her round face trying hard to look stern. "Come, Bridget-abbott, it is time to rest your ears. These noisy children have no more sense than a lump of mud!"

"Sweet Water, Bridget said that the blossom of—"

"Sweet Water, did you know that—?"

The older woman planted her hands firmly on her hips and gave them a look of mock anger. "Did I know that Bridgetabbott was a *waurraupa shaman*? I am not a foolish *yicau*. Did I know that you chatter like crows until my ears ring with your foolish talk? I was not born *yottoha*. Go and help your mothers with their work, *tontaunettes*, or when the Cold Moon comes, you will rub your empty bellies and cry yourselves to sleep!"

But she was smiling, and none could take offence at her sharp words, certainly not Bridget, who found her strength still limited so that she needed rest after the midday meal.

"What awful thing did you call them this time, Sweet Water?" asked Bridget with a tired laugh.

"*Tontaun*—? Ah—the lazy ones. But they not lazy, they good children. Soon they make good wives. Come, my child, we prepare you for return of my son, who has been sitting council with our brothers across the Inland Sea. Kinnahauk not be pleased to find his *oquio* wilting like a plucked blossom. I promise him I make you strong before he return."

Strong! Bridget felt anything but strong as she allowed herself to be undressed as if she were a mewling babe. Indeed she was growing strangely breathless as she was shoved none too gently onto a mat, given an earthen basin of water made fragrant by an infusion of dried blossoms, a handful of the strange soap made from the root of the yucca plant, and a comb that had been cleverly fashioned from the bones of a fish.

She was washed and dried, her skin rubbed with an unguent seasoned with some sweet herb that left it soft and supple. Her hair, which had been washed in the pond only the day before, was first combed and then smoothed with a scrap of doeskin that left it hanging in pale, gleaming waves about her shoulders.

Only then did Sweet Water profess herself satisfied. Clucking like a broody hen, she walked around and around her bewildered guest, nodding her head, flicking a bit of fringe so that it fell another way, and nodding again.

"Now we wait," she announced finally.

Chapter Ten

The sun was walking down, its flames reaching out to touch the waters, when Kinnahauk pulled his narrow log canoe up on the bank some distance from his village. For several long moments he rested there, head bent, back curved, arms hanging loosely at his sides. He had traveled far across the water, his mind troubled by what he had seen and heard.

Now he must restore himself before greeting his people, for he would wear the three eagle feathers denoting his rank, and the war shield bearing his sign that he had carried with him to the council fires.

Because the Hatorask were so few, Kinnahauk hunted and fished with the others, but even there he was reminded of his responsibilities, for the white-eye came to gather food from the waters around Croatoan. Their cattle roamed the island beyond, separated only by an inlet that grew more shallow with each moon. Soon they would spread to Croatoan, browsing on the tender leaves of the forest until the deer went hungry, grazing on the swales until there was no grass for the horses. Many trees would fall as the white-eye built their ugly boxes and called this land their own. Sometimes when he could not sleep at night, he raced his stallion along the beach, letting the wind work its healing spell on his mind and body. But not even his swift Tukkao could outrun the future.

Now he had come from a great council fire. He had heard the elders of those Hatorask who had crossed the Inland Sea in the Time of the Grandfathers. He had heard the elders of the Roanoak, the Yeopim, the Poteskeet and the Paspatank. They had spoken of the changes. They had spoken of the troubles and the sickness of the spirit that had infected many of their people.

He had not spoken of the white-eye woman who had come among the Hatorask. If he had learned that such a one bearing a fire mark on her brow had been lost and was sought by her people, he could not say how he would have acted. He was not ready to accept this woman, yet he could not let her go.

Now he must ready himself to greet his people. It was known that he had returned, and that he would present himself. First he must prepare by bathing and renewing his spirit, for there would be much feasting and many tales to be told. His body was rank from the long day's journey across the water. In the old days, his father would have taken three canoes each bearing three braves.

Now there were too few fighting men left to defend the village, and though they had few enemies other than the white-eye and a few renegades who had heard tales of the gold coin that had brought death to his brother, Chicktuck, Kinnahauk had chosen to travel alone.

Stripping, Kinnahauk plunged into the frigid water of the shallow pond, releasing his frustration in a long, seething exhalation. Aiee, he needed this time to refresh his body and restore his mind! Not all his troubles had been left behind on the mainland. He would wash the scent of the wretched white-eyes from his skin. The very earth was beginning to smell of their towns. Their houses, their fences were everywhere. They did not know the land belonged to all men; they called it their own, driving out all others.

In the days of his father the skies had been dark with fowl. Now the sky was dark with the smoke and fire from the English guns, so that even the *auhaun* and *atter* grew

wary. Lands where once his people had gone to hunt the
deer and the bear were now planted and fenced.

Rolling over in the shallow water, Kinnahauk floated
facedown as the last light of the dying sun painted his back
with flames. He thought of another time when he had
bathed in this place. The light of the moon had shone down
on the small clearing then. He had held the woman in his
arms, the pale, ugly creature who bore his mark. His body
had responded to her even as his mind had rejected her.

It was good that he had gone away, for she had cast a
spell that had distracted his thoughts greatly. Now that he
was prepared, he would keep her from infecting his mind
until he had decided her fate.

Scooping up two handfuls of sand, he scoured every inch
of skin, taking pleasure in the abrasiveness, for even now
his traitorous body threatened rebellion as the image of
pale, flower-tipped breasts and a small golden floss arose
to torment him.

Splashing noisily, he rinsed the sand from his body and
climbed out of the pond, his face grim as he struggled back
into his tail clout. He should have spent more time on the
sleeping mats of willing maidens and less time seated
around the council fire hearing his friends speak of their
grievances against the English. The white dogs had taken
much from his people, leaving only disease and desolation
in return.

Kinnahauk's lips thinned in a cold smile. He would repay their wickedness by taking something of theirs. Why
should he return the yellow-haired woman to her own kind?
Would they have returned one of his own women after
taking her captive? Bitterly he thought of the treatment
Taus-Wicce's daughter had received at the hands of the
English whiskey-maker, who had used her until she was too
weak to do his bidding and then thrown her out to die.

He thought of the treatment the white-eyes accorded
their own women who had lain with one of his people.

Poison meat, they called them, deeming them less than *wastomug*, the carrion refused by even the buzzards.

Aiee! He would keep this one small thing that belonged to them. Perhaps he would use it as he wished until he tired of it. Then he would see if her people wanted her enough to beg for her return.

Surely that had been the meaning of his vision-quest of so long ago? A maiden would come to him from across the waters, and he would cast his seed upon her and send her back to her own people, where she would bear up his children among her own kind, their punishment an atonement for all the evils of the past.

Kinnahauk fixed the three feathers in his hair and then his shoulders sagged. He was weak. He did not deserve to be called *werowance*. He could no more send away his own sons to suffer for the sins of their white-eye ancestors than he could cut out his own heart.

Bridget heard the sudden hush outside the lodge where she waited, followed by a joyous outcry. She had grown tense with the waiting, and her tension translated itself into quick irritation. From the way they shouted his name, one would think he was a king, at least, if not a deity. Chief, they called him. *Werowance* or some such in his own tongue. Often they used both terms, the English and the Hatorask together, as if they would honor him in all the tongues of the world.

Soconme had told her about the first Englishmen who had come among them so long ago, explaining that the Hatorask had been sent to Croatoan to care for the powerful chief, Raleigh's, people. They had heeded the words of the Great Spirit and taken the white-eyes in, and many of the tribe still spoke the King's English, the elders more than the children. Many of them also had light eyes and auburn hair. So, why did Gray Otter claim they despised the English? And if they all hated her so, then why had they treated her so kindly?

There was no time more to ponder, for from the sounds outside Sweet Water's lodge, the greatest hero of all time had just entered their midst. Mayhap he had walked across the water, she thought bitterly. If he had carried her with him, as she had wished, why then she might even now be serving her husband his evening meal in a house of her own, instead of waiting timidly in a drafty, smoky hut on some godforsaken sandbank in the middle of two great seas!

"Bridget, will you not come to greet Kinnahauk who is just arrived from the council fires of many great chiefs?"

Hearing Sweet Water's summons, Bridget sighed. She wasn't certain whether she preferred to greet her captor-savior in private or to confront him with all the village looking on. To be sure, it made little difference. Taking a deep breath, she stepped outside before Sweet Water could come and drag her out.

He was even taller than she remembered, with three feathers standing above the white band he wore around his neatly braided hair. She was struck anew by his sheer physical perfection, for this was a proud man, and justly so, his skin gleaming like newly polished copper in the last rays of the setting sun.

Bridget swallowed with great difficulty, her mouth having suddenly gone dry. His mark was everywhere, the sign of the flying white brant—on the dark leather shield he wore on one arm, on the flap of his lodge beyond and high on his broad chest. She found it strangely fascinating, as if it held some ancient power that could enslave one who grew careless.

Tearing her gaze away from the tattoo on his chest, she found herself impaled by the cold gleam of those strange eyes of his. She had forgotten their impact.

"Bridgetabbott," Kinnahauk said in a deep, uninflected tone.

"Mmm—ah, Kinnahauk. I bid you welcome. For Sweet Water's sake, that is," she added hurriedly as hot color rushed to her face. Who was she to welcome a man to his own mother's *ouke*? House, that was. 'Strewth, she was beginning to sound like one of these heathen people! Old Soconme and his wicked chanting and his powders and potions—he had cast a spell on her!

Standing away from the small group of people who had gathered to welcome their chief, a woman watched silently, her eyes smoldering with resentment. Gray Otter turned to Kokom, who was never far from her side, even though he was ever teasing the other maidens.

"Are all white-eyes so skinny? No wonder the English men seem always in a sour state."

"Ho, Gray Otter, have you been eating unripe persimmons that your tongue curls so wickedly?"

"My fingers will curl wickedly about your *yauta* neck," she threatened carelessly, to which Kokom gave the gabbling cry of the wild turkey he had been accused of resembling.

After a moment, Gray Otter asked almost wistfully, "How could any man find such pale skin to his liking? It is like the belly of a fish. It is like the—"

"Like the sweet, juicy meat of the *yonne* fruit," Kokom finished.

"Paugh! All hard, wrinkled stone with a thin covering of bitter flesh!"

Kokom only laughed. As Gray Otter flounced away, he gave the turkey cry again, but his eyes, as he followed the figure of the tall shapely maiden, were not laughing.

Kinnahauk had returned to his people.

A feast had been prepared when the chief's canoe had first been sighted. Fish had been smothered in the leaves of the sweet bay tree and placed on the fire. A layer of oysters and clams had been spread around the edges of the bed of coals. Young women set to grinding maize from the small store of grain that had been traded for on the mainland; the old ones to seasoning the stews they had prepared for their own families. The men, both young and old, now sat cross-legged around a large central fire and spoke of many weighty matters.

Their chief had returned.

Bridget was set the task of caring for the younger children while their mothers rushed about preparing food. There was a festive air about the whole village. The children were infected by it, and Bridget had her work cut out for her to keep them from getting underfoot. She gathered them around her, holding the youngest on her lap, and commenced singing the song of "The Three Ravens." Unexpectedly, tears appeared in her eyes as she thought of Meggy Fitzhugh and poor Billy. She blinked them away and kept on singing, her voice soft and clear on the cold evening air.

There were stories to follow, some she remembered from when her grandfather had taken her on his knee and some she made up as she went along. Soon, all but the babe, who had long since fallen asleep in her arms, were leaning forward, their bright faces eager to know more of the wings that captured the wind that turned the wheel that ground the wheat, and the fox that saw his own reflection in the stream and lost the fat hen he had caught for his evening meal.

More than once she looked up to find a pair of golden eyes fixed on her face. Even when her own eyes were on the children, she fancied she could feel them burning over every inch of her body.

That notion was fanciful indeed. Kinnahauk had spoken scarce a dozen words to her, and those heard by all the village. Why should she now imagine that his eyes spoke a different message, one for her alone?

The night seemed endless. Bridget and the other women had served the men first, which was their way, but Kinnahauk had bade them sit and partake, for he had much to relate and would have one telling do for all.

Even the children grew silent under the spell of the young chief's deep, melodious voice, for indeed it was like music as he told of his visit to the Hatorask who had gone across the waters many moons ago to plant crops.

"The Chief of England is named Charles, and this chief has given over our lands to some few of his favored brothers, calling it Carolina in his own honor. He bids them build their towns from the Chesapeake to the land called Florida by the *Waspaines*, from the Big Water they call the Atlantic to the Western Sea.

"The one called Whittie and the one called Carteret, who came in the time when my father was chief to the place the white-eyes call Colleton, destroyed the land and went away. The great white-eye chief called Samuel Stephens brought his *noppinjure* to Roanoak until there was no food for the deer, no cover for small animals to hide from their enemies. Even now their great winged canoes come and go through the waters of Roanoak Inlet, carrying more of their people to spread through our land."

No one spoke throughout this recital. The old men nodded, drawing deeply on their pipes. The young braves sat stoically, their eyes never leaving the face of their leader. The women quietly moved about, taking away mats of oyster shells and fish bones before the biting black flies could swarm down on them. In many villages the chief did not speak before women. On Croatoan there were few people, and all were valuable to Kinnahauk. All must be made aware of the changes that were taking place, for one day those changes would come to this island. They must not be unprepared.

In Bridget's arms the babe slept peacefully, the other children having been carried in to their sleeping mats by their mothers. She allowed her senses to be filled with the man who spoke so impassively of the wrongs done his people by hers. Was it true? Had the English really come to this land and stolen it from these people?

Oh, she had heard talk of the great new land across the sea, of the riches to be found there, the fertile land for the taking. If she had thought about it at all, it would have been about who was taking the land, not about the ones from whom they were taking it.

The fire had burned low, and a cold wind had sprung up, making Bridget wish she had thought to bring another skin to cover her shoulders. Kinnahauk and the other braves showed no sign of feeling the cold. Kinnahauk continued to speak, after gravely accepting a pipe from the most ancient of the men, blowing smoke in four directions, and then passing it on.

"There is a man called Robert Holden who is appointed to take possession of all wrecks, ambergris or other projections of the sea. He will come to our village and question our people whenever there is a rumor of a shipwreck along these banks." His gaze settled on Bridget, seeming to linger on her hair, which was touched by the light from the rising moon and the glow from the dying fire. "It is as well that there have been no ships cast upon our shores since the time of the great storm." It was after that storm that he and Kokom and Chicktuck had found the pouch containing four gold coins, called guineas by the white-eyes.

"It is as well," echoed several of the old ones gravely.

"It is as well," Kokom repeated quietly.

Bridget's back was aching, and her arm felt as if it would break. Many Toes' son was only seven months old, but built as heavily as one twice his age. Among the Hatorask, children seemed to belong to all the people, eating with whatever family they wished and being watched over by all. It was as though the few children were a precious gift to be shared instead of being hoarded selfishly by a few.

"Come, you have stayed too long in the night air, Bridgetabbott. I would not have your fever return," Sweet Water said, coming quietly up behind her. "Give me the boy. Many Toes will need him beside her tonight, for it is still too soon to be taking a new husband to her mat."

Bridget handed over the sleeping boy, glancing at his mother as she did so. The comely young widow had lately been casting looks toward one of the older braves, the one called Yenwetoa, who was also called Face of a Horse. Indeed his face had the long, narrow look of one of the horses that roamed freely throughout the island. She only hoped he also had the strength of a horse, for he would soon need it to handle the strapping child.

Within moments the clearing was empty of all save Bridget and Kinnahauk. He stood and came around to where she still sat, her arms clasped around her for the warmth. She had changed much since he had left her in his mother's keeping. He looked on her hair, which was no longer the color of dead grass, but of the sweet yellow flower that climbed the tallest pine trees. He looked on her face and saw that it had grown soft and clear, her cheeks flushed with the color of the flowering mallow. He looked on her lips and found them full and soft and sweetly rounded, and then his gaze moved to her eyes and lingered there.

Kinnahauk felt as if the sand had shifted beneath his feet. He told himself it was weariness, for he had just returned from a long journey. He had smoked the pipe and drunk the fermented juice of the scuppernong grape. This woman was nothing to him, even though she bore his mark. Her eyes were too clear. They made him uncomfortable. Why did she not hide her thoughts from him, like the others of her kind? Did she not know it was dangerous for a maiden to look on a man in such a way?

"Sweet Water has cared for me well," she said, her voice little more than a whisper.

"And old Soconme? Have you worked your white man's magic on him that he calls you *Waurraupa Shaman*?"

Bridget wished he would sit down, for towering over as he did put her too much in mind of the first time she had laid eyes on him. She had thought him a wild, heathen savage and been terrified for her life. Had he changed so much since then?

Or had she? "I have no magic," she said faintly, addressing his moccasins.

"You steal the magic from the moon that makes your hair glow like the inside of the mussel shell? Or from the *yoccoweeho* that scents the night air so sweetly?" When she did not reply—could not reply, for he had fair robbed her lungs of wind—Kinnahauk continued. "The fire mark is hidden from my eyes by the band you wear, yet I know it is there. Do you seek to deny it, Bridgetabbott?"

"I do not know what you mean." She touched the soft band of white fur taken from the belly of a rabbit. It had been Sweet Water who had given it to her, shown her how to wear it, when the hair Tooly had cut with his knife had grown long enough to be bothersome.

"I have thought about you, Bridgetabbott. At times when I should have been listening to the problems of my people, trying to find a way to bring them together again, I found my thoughts scattering like a flock of *auhaun* that you call geese. How could this be, unless you cast some spell over me before I left you? This has not happened to me before. It puzzles me greatly, for I cannot explain it."

Bridget said nothing. His words had left her feeling weak and disoriented. Her fingers bit into her arms as Kinnahauk bent over her, and then his hands closed over her shoulders, and he lifted her to her feet.

"I do not want to feel this way, Bridgetabbott. You are the enemy of my people. Only a weak man allows himself to be distracted by the enemy, and Kinnahauk is not weak. He must be stronger than two men, for his people are divided, yet all have need of a *werowance*."

"Kinnahauk, I have never been your enemy."

Ignoring her, the tall brave continued to speak. "My people are called coward by their brothers, who would fight to drive all white-eyes from our shores. Since the Time of the Grandfathers, my people have welcomed your people in this place. No more. The vision is ended. It is done. My sons will not live in the Time of the Grandfathers. They will live under dark clouds. The sun will not long shine on my people. This was said to me by the Voice that Speaks Silently.''

Caught up in the spell of his rich voice, his strange eyes, Bridget forgot to breathe. It was almost as if she could see the visions he spoke of, hear the voice that spoke in his heart.

"I have borne this burden, Bridgetabbott. I have been called 'yellow dog' by my brothers who were given a different vision by the Great Kishalamaquon. This I have done that I do not dishonor my father and the spirits of all those whose bones once rested in the *Quiozon* before they were destroyed by your people.

"But this I will *not* do. I will not let you weaken me with your woman's magic. I will not listen to your soft words and touch your soft skin and think of the golden treasure you guard with your thighs. This I will not do."

Bridget could feel the warmth from his body, could smell the clean, wood-smoke scent of his skin. Suddenly she wanted more than anything in the world to walk into those arms and feel them close around her as they once had.

Bridget watched as the tall young brave disappeared into the shadows, his proud head with the three clipped eagle feathers held high. He did not look back.

Why did his coldness hurt her so? He meant nothing to her, no more than any other stranger who had done her a kindness. If he would not take her to Albemarle to find David Lavender, then she would ask someone else.

All the same, she found it impossible to put the young chief from her mind as she turned and slowly made her way to the *ouke* she shared with Sweet Water.

Chapter Eleven

A drift of tobacco smoke rose above the two graying heads as Sweet Water and Soconme sat outside Sweet Water's *ouke* talking, enjoying the first warm day after a siege of cold, rainy weather. "Aiee, old blood runs cold," said Soconme, drawing one of his many shawls about his scrawny shoulders.

"Young blood runs hot," Sweet Water responded, watching the son of her sister as he set his horse to dancing for the amusement of Sits There, Wattapi and Bridget. "Kokom knows well that Gray Otter watches. What devil drives him to tease her in such a way?"

"A devil I have long forgotten," mused the medicine chief.

From across the clearing, where several braves worked to build a new storehouse, Kinnahauk glared at the laughing women. "My son follows the young *Waurraupa Shaman* with angry eyes," Sweet Water observed.

"The young *Waurraupa Shaman* follows your son with eyes that are not angry, but hungry."

Sweet Water's face grew troubled. "She is not like the others of her people. My son's hatred for the English makes him blind."

"He is green. In time he will ripen."

"Paugh! In time my bones will ripen under the sands. I would hold a grandson before my spirit takes wing."

"Be patient, old woman. Before the death song is sung over your bones, you will see your grandsons grow tall and straight. Kinnahauk feels the winds of change. They are like the white winds that bite at the fingers and gnaw at the long bones until the weak cry out and even the strong feel much pain. He would prepare his people."

"Kinnahauk's eyes no longer smile."

"The eyes of our young chief see more clearly than most. They see that the sun walks down for our people. They see that the Great Spirit grows weary of watching His children tread the old paths and would mark new paths for us to walk. Kinnahauk sees this. It falls like a shadow over his soul, for he knows he must lead his people in a new way if they are to survive."

"My son has much pride," Sweet Water acknowledged sadly. "It is hard for such a one to bear the scorn of his brothers for a covenant made in the Time Before the Grandfathers. Even our friends the Yeopim, the Paspatank and the Poteskeet look with pity on us for our peaceful ways."

"When the white trapper brought the body of your younger son to his people in the year when the corn failed, all were saddened, but Kinnahauk most of all. He still mourned his father. As leader of his people and head of his family, he felt that he had failed."

"Aiee," cried the woman softly. "My heart bled for both my sons, for Kinnahauk wounded himself grievously so that his blood would be buried with his brother. After the death songs were sung, he took his canoe and went across the water, and I bade Kokom follow to see that he came to no harm. The moon rose many times while my son walked with his sorrow. Kokom said Kinnahauk did not speak. He said he did not eat. He said he walked unarmed in the white-eye villages, seeing their lodges, seeing their fields, seeing their children. Kokom followed after him, yet Kinnahauk's eyes did not see his friend. He said that when our great friend Taus-Wicce of the Poteskeet would have taken

Kinnahauk to his lodge, Kinnahauk walked by him as one
blind who could not hear.''

Soconme drew deeply on the comforting *un-coone*,
which the white man called tobacco. ''Many thoughts are
at war within the mind of a young man who must be strong
for his people. It is not easy to stand like the oak and bend
like the rushes. It is not easy for the old ones, whose sap
rises slowly. It is harder still for one who has not yet seen
five and twenty winters.''

The old medicine chief pressed his yellowed fingers to the
hollows above his eyes. ''My head bone tells me the white
horses will ride across the water before the sun awakens.''

''I am sorry, old man. When the cold wind blows from
the land of the sleeping sun, it brings pain to many old
ones.''

''Perhaps we have need of pain to tell us we still live, for
our bodies offer us little pleasure.''

Sweet Water's face softened with sympathy. She, too,
knew what it was to feel old and alone, though she was not
so old as Soconme and she was not alone. She had Kinnahauk, and now the young white-eye woman to care for.
''My sleeping mat is big, Soconme.''

''Your heart is big, Sweet Water. You are a good friend.
I have something to release the devils, but I would save it
for worse pain than mine. The white-eye medicine is strong,
and I have little left, for it is no longer easy to trade across
the water.''

Sweet Water nodded, cradling her tiny pipe in her cupped
hands. ''In the old days my father had but to cross the water with five canoes filled with oysters to return with five
canoes filled with corn. Now the corn grows behind English fences, and our brothers who once traded with us have
hardly enough to fill their own bellies. I have not been to a
feast on the mainland since Kinnahauk lost his small teeth.
Aiee, so many changes. Why cannot things remain as they
were?''

* * *

Bridget was learning to ride in the Hatorask manner. Kokom had used a whistle to summon one of the shaggy ponies that roamed the woods, and he bade Bridget to sit astride the bare back of the animal.

"Kokom, how can I sit on that great beast with my bare limbs hanging down on either side? It's shameful!"

"Shameful? You would have your limbs hang *up*?"

"No, you great buffoon, I would have them decently covered!"

"Ho, you English are strange creatures. You cover the bodies given you by your gods as if they were something to be ashamed of. We Hatorask are not ashamed of the gifts of our Great Spirit Kishalamaquon." Holding out his arms on either side, he turned slowly before her, a teasing grin on his handsome face. "Should I be ashamed of such a bountiful gift?"

"Be ashamed that you were not equally blessed with the gift of humility," Bridget teased. Perched uneasily atop her high-strung mount, she grasped the thick, flowing mane with both hands, dismayed as she felt her short deerskin skirt climb even higher on her thighs.

"Bridget, do not bury your face in Yauta Youncor's hair!" called out Sits There, who seemed to guide her own mount by some mysterious means known only to her and the pony. "Do not lie on her as if she were a sleeping mat."

"Are you sure Red Wind knows I am supposed to be here?" Bridget replied nervously. "I think it tried to bite my foot when I got on."

Kokom leaped onto his stallion and set the shaggy beast to dancing around her, kicking up the wet sand. "She only wishes to know your smell so that she will know who guides her."

"My smell is of sweaty horse," Bridget replied, doing her best to relax her grip on the thick tangle of dark hair that spilled over the head and neck of the red pony. "And I think she knows which one of us is the gui-*eeede*!" She must have inadvertently given a signal of some kind, for the mare took off at a gallop, leaving her rider bouncing helplessly.

Racing after her, Kokom scooped Bridget off before she fell. Sits There halted the runaway mount with a single sharp whistle, and Bridget, panting, clung to Kokom's broad shoulders as the ground raced by beneath them. Roaring with laughter, he seemed determined to carry her all the way back to the village.

"You c-can put me d-down anywhere, Kokom! I'll walk home."

Still laughing, Kokom shook his head. "I promised you a ride on one of our horses. Kokom is a man of his word."

With Sits There following on her pony and Red Wind trotting obediently behind, they entered the village. As if fearing she would leap to the ground the moment he halted, Kokom held her tightly about the waist with one powerful arm, his unbraided hair tangling with her own as the stiff northwest wind struck them in the face. He was grinning broadly, his dark eyes teasing her as she struggled to pull her gown over her knees.

In the shelter of Sweet Water's lodge, several women were mixing fat with dried berries. Gray Otter was directing three young girls in tying bundles of rushes for the storehouse that was being built under Kinnahauk's direction.

All turned to watch as Kokom slipped off his mount and carefully lifted Bridget to the ground. Her knees trembled so from her first riding lesson that she could hardly stand, and she clutched at his arms to keep from falling.

Kokom was well aware of Gray Otter's frown. He slipped an arm about Bridget's waist and murmured a few consoling words in her ear. "The morrow we try again, my pale-haired friend."

Bridget sent him a quelling look, aware that everyone in the village had seen her undignified arrival. All were smiling, some were laughing. A grudging smile quivered on her lips. "The morrow I may not be able to move, my black-hearted friend."

"You said you knew horses," Kokom chided gently.

"Aye, I know them well." She did not bother to add that the only horse she had ever sat atop had been a plodding farm animal. Besides, not even the ladies who had ridden Squire Jarman's fine mounts would have dreamed of riding astride.

"The morrow?" Kokom prompted.

She rubbed her backside, which had been severely pounded. "The morrow," she sighed, determined not to retire in disgrace.

"*Kittapi*," Kokom agreed, grinning broadly. "The morrow."

Fingers suddenly bit into the hollow between her shoulder and her neck, causing her to wince with pain. "Bridgetabbott, if you would learn to ride, have one of the children teach you. Kokom has more important things to do." Kinnahauk spat out the words like grape seeds while Kokom departed with a look of apology.

"If you do not pry your talons from my shoulder, you great fish hawk, my arm will fall off," Bridget seethed. She was not at all happy at the way her heart leaped whenever Kinnahauk was near. It was unseemly. While she had come far from her first belief that the natives were all bloodthirsty heathen savages, it would be folly to pretend they were not vastly different from the English. These people worshipped gods whose names she could not even pronounce, and as for their courts and their royalty, why Kinnahauk, a man who wore naught save a scrap of leather to preserve his modesty, was called Lord of Croatoan and all the Hatorask!

Kinnahauk's fingers eased their painful grip. He stroked the injury, a look of shame on his face. "I spoke too sharply, Bridgetabbott. It is not your fault that Kokom would make a fool of himself over every woman he sees. He is a fine brave, but he is not for you. If you would learn to ride, I will teach you myself."

"I know how to ride!" Bridget's anger swiftly eclipsed her embarrassment. Kokom had shown her nothing but kindness. He had made her laugh when she thought nothing would ever bring a smile to her face again, and this great gloomy creature with his golden eyes and his harsh manners wanted to keep even that small pleasure from her. "It's only that your horses are not at all what I'm used to. And there are no trappings to make it easier—no reins to steer with. And it's been a while since I've been on top of any beast. I don't need to be taught," she said sullenly.

"Do not speak untruths. It is no shame to learn."

"Fine! Then I will not be ashamed to allow David Lavender to teach me. If you can spare Kokom to take me to Albemarle, I will burden you no more with my *untruths*!" The accusation had hurt, for Bridget had never knowingly lied to anyone.

Kinnahauk seemed to grow taller before her very eyes, and more like a thundercloud than ever. Grasping her by the shoulders, he marched her to the edge of the live oak forest that surrounded the village. From there they could look out over the limitless expanse of water that beat upon the shore, flinging creamy spume high into the air. "Can you not see how angry the water is, woman? Do you wish to spend many days and nights in a small canoe riding such waves just so that you can lie in the arms of your David-lavender once more? Paugh! You will stay here until I tell you you can go! I will not risk a good dugout canoe and the life of one of my brothers just to take a weak, selfish white-eye where she wants to go! Kinnahauk has spoken!"

Bridget placed another earthen container of sunflower seeds in the new storehouse. They would be ground to make both bread and broth during the winter. According to old Soconme, there would be many days when the hunters could not hunt, for rains would come down so hard that one could not see an arm's length ahead. There would be days when the wildfowl ranged far out on the reefs, out of reach of the strongest bowman. For three moons the fish would sleep at the bottom of the sea, according to Soconme, who had taken to spending much time with her since Kinnahauk had turned his back on her. They had talked of many things, and he had told her that unless they prepared well, filling many storehouses, there would be hunger before the Planting Moon returned. And even if they filled all the storehouses, marauding animals and sudden storms could ruin the winter's food supply without warning.

Gray Otter's behavior grew increasingly strange. At times the woman seemed almost friendly, although she always managed to look as if she were laughing at some wicked secret known only to herself. She was no longer openly hostile, at least when they were with the others, though her coolness grew more pronounced when they were alone.

Still, many women were subject to strange moods, Bridget reminded herself. Even she had been moody of late, her spirits rising and falling with the going and coming of one man.

Kinnahauk.

Sealing the lodge securely, Bridget gazed out at the men who were setting a sort of fence that was supposed to capture fish to be smoked and dried for the winter. Two men stood out among the others, and one above all. Kokom and Kinnahauk were much alike, yet her breath never quickened when Kokom came near. Her heart always beat placidly in her breast even when Kokom steadied her on her mount before releasing her to ride alone.

Bridget had taken pleasure in her one small defiance. She had learned to ride, almost daring Kinnahauk to protest. He had said no more, but she had been aware of his eyes on her as she returned to the village with the others and released her mount to return to the swales and forest.

Sometimes when the day's work was done, she joined the other young women as they cut through the woods to the ocean beach in search of shells for decoration and trade. Sometimes they stopped to watch the men racing their own mounts along the flat stretches left by the falling tide. As the days grew increasingly short, however, there was little time for play. The women worked to smoke and dry the meat brought in by the men, and to scrape and tan the skins in the dark water from certain ponds hidden in the oak groves.

Now and then there were visitors from other tribes. Bridget had come to recognize the different manners of dress, and although she was learning the Hatorask dialect, she could make little or no sense of the other languages. For reasons she could not understand, it pleased her that the Hatorask were in all ways finer than these others. It was as if they knew themselves to belong to some chosen group and stood taller because of it.

Many times she saw sails that could only belong to her own people, but each time they turned away before reaching Croatoan. No more was said of her going to Albemarle, and she dared not ask again, for indeed, the weather seemed determined to thwart her, the winds being constantly from the direction in which she would have to travel.

"Ho, Bridget," greeted Soconme from the mat outside his lodge.

"Ho, Soconme," Bridget returned. "Is your head still hurting?"

"It comes with the winds. Pain is but another sea for the mind to sail upon."

Bridget knew that she could ease the ache in his head, if not the pain of his knotted joints, yet she could not bring herself to offer for fear the old man would be insulted. The beliefs of the Hatorask were different from hers. She could easily offend without even knowing it.

"May the sun's warmth bring you ease," she said, having heard Sweet Water use the same words many times.

Soconme watched as the young *waurraupa shaman* made her way into the *ouke* of his friend. He had grown fond of the young Englishwoman, for they had much in common. Both had met many foes and had overcome them. This was no bad thing in itself, being but another test sent by the Great Spirit. The small *waurraupa shaman* walked proudly, though at times there was great sadness in her eyes. She had suffered great pain. She had suffered great loss. She had not bowed her head before these things, but had crossed the Big Water in the great canoe with the broken wing to find Kinnahauk.

Soconme had looked into the heart of Gray Otter and found much strength, yet the coldness of winter. He had looked into the heart of the *waurraupa shaman* and found great strength with the warmth of summer.

The young chief had chosen well. The small *waurraupa shaman* would temper his haughty pride with the fertile warmth of summer. Her strength was that of the reed that bent with the wind and survived. His was that of the oak that withstood the mighty winds, but could not bend.

Yet even now, storm clouds gathered across the Inland Sea. The young *waurraupa shaman* would be tested once more. When the storm broke, Kinnahauk would not be there to shelter her with his strength.

Chapter Twelve

Albemarle

Sudie braced her elbows on the rough table and stared at the man she had just killed. Her skirt, made of material bought from a trader from Virginia, for she refused to spin and weave, was stained with the blood that even now thickened at the back of his filthy head.

The stinking whoreson! She had told him to leave her alone when the moon was wrong, but in his usual drunken condition, he had ignored her. This morning she'd vomited until her sides were sore, and she'd known. Oh, it wasn't the first time she'd been caught. Had she been in London, there were women who could have helped her, potions she could have taken to rid herself of her unwanted burden, but here in this bloody awful stink hole, she had no one to turn to.

Damned drunken bastard! She had flown into a rage, her belly still heaving, and he had laughed at her. *Laughed* at her!

Screeching obscenities, she had thrown a bowl of cold stew at him, but when she had tried to kick him, he had snatched at her foot, jerking it so that she had fallen hard. Straddling her prone body, he had belched loudly and ordered her to feed him his breakfast.

The very thought of food had gagged her. The thought of Albert Fickens had sickened her even more. He had kicked her halfheartedly and collapsed into a chair, tipping his jug to take a gurgling swallow. Sudie had reached for the table edge to help pull herself up, and when her fingers had encountered the handle of a cold iron skillet, she had acted instinctively.

She had no idea how long she had been staring at him while she waited for her belly to settle down. He was not the first man she had sent to his reward, nor would he be the last if all the men in this rotten desolate wilderness were like Albert Fickens.

The tangy-sweet smell of whiskey mingled with the stench of spoiled food and unwashed bodies. The white-corn whiskey Albert made out behind the cabin trickled across the floor, soaking into the grease-stained bricks. In swinging her skillet, she had knocked his jug to the floor and broken it. The odor sent her stomach into a fresh revolt.

"Whoreson," she muttered dully. "I'll teach ye to plant a snivellin' brat in me belly, ye bleatin' boar." She swallowed down the sour taste in her mouth. She was in trouble again, but then trouble was nothing new to the woman who had been born in a Lime Street bawdy house. From some fine gentleman twenty-six years before, who had come a-liftin' skirt in London's less savory district, she had inherited the brains to get herself out of there when she was thirteen and into a house where she serviced only the gentry instead of every scurvy palliard and seaman who could find halfpence to toss her way.

Newgate had been no new experience for Sudie. She had seen the inside of that hellish place more than once. Give her a shilling or two, and she could make her way up to the Castle in the wink of a cat's eye, for she had always found the most prestigious part of London's infamous prison to be as fine as any gentleman's club for making arrangements.

Aye, she had bloody well arranged herself *this* time, all right! The wife of a fine planter, she was going to be. Mistress Fickens, with fine feather beds and servants and all, in this golden land of promise!

She had known the moment she'd laid eyes on what was waiting for her on the docks of Albemarle that she had made a mistake. Albert had stood apart from the others. Or mayhap they had moved upwind from him, for even then, without the flies settling on his stinking carcass, he had not been a savory prospect.

Sudie had made up her mind on the spot to take the name of Bridget Abbott. It was no fault of hers that she had tripped and fallen against the little doxy just as they had struck the shoal. If the mort be a witch, why then she would have saved herself. If she be ought else, why then, mayhap she had sprouted wings and flown away.

Sudie had waited until near all the gents had claimed their baggage. The last to go had been squint-eyed Tess, who had landed herself an old gray-bearded goat with a wicked gleam in his eyes. He had come by boat, stinking of fish and a foul-smelling pipe, and led her off along the wharf. Aye, she'd not be laughing now, Sudie vowed, for instead of a rich planter, she had landed herself a doddering old fisherman too poor even to hire a carriage.

There had been two men left standing on the dock, one tall and fair, though a mite liverish for her tastes, the other this ugly lout she had just hastened to his reward. Sudie had brushed a wrinkle from her skirt, mentally repeated the name Bridget Abbott several times so that it would roll off her tongue. She had just started across the rough timbers, reeling slightly from having been at sea for so long, when the captain had cut across in front of her.

That cold-eyed devil, with his fist full of papers, had looked her over as if she were a joint of maggoty pork and directed her to the lout, Fickens. "There be your husband, mistress." He had glanced down at the manifest, running his stubby forefingers down the list of names. "Albert Fickens, tradesman."

"Oh, but I be—"

"That'll be Mr. Lavender, come for the poor child that went over the side."

Both men were converging on them by then. David Lavender was tall and almost gaunt looking in a black wool suit faded purple, his colorless hair hanging over a pale, high forehead. His lips were too thin for Sudie's taste, for she knew the look of a pinch penny. Albert Fickens's face had been red, his hair black and greasy, and his clothing, if it had ever had style or color, had long since lost both. His expression was that of a starving man being led to the trough.

Thus Sudie had learned that she had gambled and lost the day she had made her mark at random beside one of the names on the clerk's list. The clerk had read her the name of the man who had paid her passage, but she had scarce paid attention. Freedom was what she had heard. Freedom and the chance to climb as high as her wits would carry her.

Well, they had carried her to the top of the dung heap. Now it was up to her to use her wits and get herself out of here before those bloody savages came sniffing around, bringing their stolen corn to trade for more of Albert's whiskey.

He'd made good whiskey, Sudie was bound to admit. She had even developed a taste for the sweetish beer he'd made of bruised and boiled cornstalks. He'd been a stinking, brutish lout, but she had to admit he'd been a good businessman, trading a skinful of alcohol for all the corn the redskins could provide. Of course that meant the place was ever swarming with the grunting heathens, for they had such a great weakness for the drink that they robbed the fields of white and redskin alike, and then fell down dead drunk so that they were easy prey for the angry planters.

Aye, but she hated them! If she had her way, every stinking, grunting one of them would be butchered. She didn't know which she had hated more—the savages or that devil she had wed!

Sudie dragged herself up from the table, one hand going to the small of her back, where too many hours of back-breaking work had left a permanent ache. She was not licked yet, not while she had a noggin on her shoulders. First she must find where Albert had hid the gold she knew he possessed. That done, she would set fire to this place, and any who found the remains of his battered skull would think some heathen, tired of being cheated, had dispatched him with a blow from a club.

Before the smoke could even be seen from the town, she ought to be well on her way. She could take the cart and claim Albert had sent her into town for supplies, somehow finding a way to remain there until he was discovered and the red heathens blamed. Only then could she afford to settle back and accept the comfort due a new widow.

A new widow with a brat in her belly, Sudie thought bitterly. The rutting boar! Well, she had been knocked off her feet before, and she might be again, but she knew enough to make the most of what she had, which was more than could be said for many. She would need a protector. Women were scarce in this new land, with many a planter needing someone to run his household.

There was David Lavender, for instance. 'Twas said in town that he had built a new house for his bride, and cleared more acres to be planted in corn and tobacco. 'Twas said he was a remittance man, one sent to the colonies and paid to stay out of England. A man of good family, then, a family that might someday relent and allow him to go back home. With his wife.

Oh, aye, such a man needed a wife to look after his fine home and order about all the house servants, and there had scarce been enough time to fetch a new bride out from London or Plymouth.

Sudie brushed a rough hand over her lank hair and began to smile, her dark eyes taking on a sparkle that had been missing for some time. Her blue linsey-woolsey was flattering. A bath, a bit of rice powder on her nose and a splash of rose water, and she could still catch a man's eye. If she moved fast, before she began to swell, there was no reason why poor Mr. Lavender should have to do without.

She would have to go to Boris Hoag, the trader, for she could not go directly to Lavender without his thinking something amiss. Nor could she throw herself on the mercy of any of the mealymouthed women who lived in the scattered houses near the river, for she had lost no time in letting them know what she thought of them.

Hoag would be the one to ease her into the Lavender household, for a man in his position would know everyone on the Albemarle. It had not taken Sudie long to recognize the trader as the type she knew best, a man who had climbed out of the gutters of London by wits and wickedness. Unless she had lost her touch, she would have him crawling on his knees and whining to get under her skirts.

Aye, he could take his pleasure, all right. For a price. And her price would be setting her up with David Lavender as a poor widow woman in sore need of protection in this wild, wicked land.

Cackling, Sudie dropped to her knees and began testing for loose floorboards where Fickens might have hidden her inheritance.

Chapter Thirteen

Croatoan

The furrows between Kinnahauk's brows grew more pronounced as the Cold Moon grew fat. Two of the old ones had died, leaving behind much sorrow. A youth, thinking to prove his manhood, had entered a tavern and demanded whiskey. He had been badly beaten and thrown into the marshes, where he would have died except for a white-eye fisherman who brought him to Croatoan. Kinnahauk had rewarded the man with a basket of oysters and six fine deer hides. He had asked the youth why he had not chosen to prove his manhood in the old way, and was told the old ways were for the old.

Crooked Stick had gone among the Matchepungo to hunt and trap, for the father of Sits There was asking five bearskins as a bride-price for his only daughter. Many Toes had taken Face of a Horse into her lodge. Kinnahauk had reason to believe that by the Moon of the Great Wind, the Hatorasks would be blessed with another small brave.

Troubled, Kinnahauk watched as his *oquio* opened the hearts of his people and made a place for herself there. The children followed her around, begging for songs and stories, and even old Soconme had fallen under her spell. The old *shaman* claimed that her healing hands could drive out the devils that hammered inside his head when the wet wind blew, and that she had knowledge of many strange and wondrous herbs that even he had never heard of.

He saw the sun strike her hair and turn it the color of the white-eyes' gold. He saw the band of white fur from the belly of a rabbit that she wore around her brow to cover the fire mark. Was she ashamed to bear his mark? Was it not a sign of honor to wear the mark of a chief?

He watched the supple movement of her body as she went about her tasks, the way her small breasts brushed against the soft doeskin when she moved quickly. A smoldering fire was kindled in his loins, and no matter how many hours he spent counseling his people, how many nights he spent racing his stallion along the shore, it continued to burn with a steady flame.

After a long swim in frigid waters, Kinnahauk had leaped upon Tukkao's back and ridden until the village was far behind him. He was resting his mount near the shallow waters of Chacandepeco Inlet when Kokom approached from behind.

"I would not care to be the one who brings the thunder to your face," said the young brave. He hooked one knee up before him on the bare back of his mount and grinned at his friend and chief.

"Ho, Kokom. I did not hear you."

"Be glad I am not one of our renegade brothers across the water who would dangle your ugly hair from his coup stick. What troubles you, my friend? Is it that the fish are sleeping and our nets go empty, or is it the storm that even now approaches? My ears tell me the birds have left this place. My eyes tell me the wind gods are chasing the small clouds from the skies."

"The voice of the Big Water has changed. It speaks of the winds that will come and tells me not to fear this storm. The birds move deeper into the forest. They do not desert us. The Voice that Speaks Silently tells me that the waters

will eat more of our shore, but they will not cover our island.''

''Then why do you not rejoice?''

''It is a more deadly tide I fear, one that reaches even the
highest hills.''

''The English,'' Kokom said quietly, staring out across
the inlet.

Both men looked toward the shoreline that stretched as
far as the eye could see on the other side of the shallow inlet of Chacandepeco, beyond the oak forest of Pasquinoc,
to the point of land the English called Cape Kendrik, which
grew smaller with each season of storms. Once all had been
a part of the lands of the Hatorask, the farthest village being called Hatorask after the people.

Then the English had come, first with their guns, then
with their cattle. The Hatorask had turned south, joining
their brothers at a place near Chacandepeco and in the village where Kinnahauk's people still dwelt, leaving the land
that had belonged to them since the beginning to the white-
eyes, whose great winged canoes had come in ever-
increasing numbers.

''The English,'' Kinnahauk repeated gravely.

''Aiee, the land sinks under their weight, and still more
come with each passing moon. Soon we will be driven into
the Big Water. Will you not fight, Kinnahauk?''

''You know I cannot, my friend. In the Time Before the
Grandfathers, our people were told in a dream-vision to
come to this place and await the coming of men from across
the waters. This we have done. We were told that a small
group of white-eyes would come to our shores, guided by
one of our own blood. This came to pass in the time of
Manteo, whose mother was of our people. We were told
that we must take these white-eyes into our blood, for they
were the way of the future. This, too, we have done, as
witness the sky-eyes among us.''

''And the yellow eyes,'' Kokom added dryly, knowing his
friend despised the sign of his own mixed heritage. ''I say

we have fulfilled the dream-vision, Kinnahauk. I say the time of the future is upon us. I say if we do not soon fight, there will be no future for our people.''

Sitting cross-legged atop the shaggy beast he had first captured and tamed as a youth, Kinnahauk studied the man who would indeed be chief if Kinnahauk were to die without sons. Among their people, leadership came down through the women unless there were no daughters. Neither Sweet Water nor her younger sister had given birth to a daughter who would have chosen from among the braves the one best suited to lead. Thus had Kinnahauk become chief. Thus would Kokom become chief at his death unless Kinnahauk took a woman to his *ouke* and bore sons or daughters.

Thus the old ways came to an end.

Kokom would rule differently, Kinnahauk thought. Beneath his teasing ways, there were depths to this son of his mother's sister that would have surprised many. ''I like the filthy English savages no more than you do, my friend, but I am the son of Paquiwok, the grandson of Wahkonda. I am bound by the honor of my people to uphold the law laid down in the Time Before the Beginning. So it will be.''

''Then the tides will wash over us,'' said Kokom, his voice without emotion.

''Does not the earth support the tides that cover it? Then who is superior, earth or tide? Who came first when the Great Kishalamaquon shaped a ball of mud, spat upon it and gave it life?''

''Kinnahauk has been smelling the foul stuff old Soconme sprinkles on his sacred flames. His soul has grown as hard and dry as a side of venison left too long over the fire. I say to you, Kinnahauk, that every outgoing tide carries the great winged canoes from the place called James Towne Port. They are filled with *un-coone* that the white man calls tobacco. The incoming tide brings them back again, and they are filled with guns and black powder and still more English.''

"It is another tide I must prepare for now. Let us go back to the village, Kokom. There is much to be done before the full face of the moon blows the waters high upon our shores."

Bridget, hearing the talk of the storm, was inclined to dismiss it, for surely no sky had ever been so blue. The shallow waters nearest the village were calm, and even the sea on the far side of the island beat with a slow and steady cadence. Only now and then did a large wave strike the shore with a boom like the voice of a cannon.

Had she not feared Kinnahauk's wrath, she might even have asked him to take her to Albemarle while the calm weather held, but for reasons she did not care to dwell on, she dismissed the idea.

Laughing and calling back and forth, the women and children began carrying all food stores, as well as anything that could blow or wash away, deeper into the forest to a place where the trees had grown into a thick canopy that would shelter them from wind and rain. There they quickly erected a small village of pointed tents made of slender poles and hide, still with much teasing and laughter.

The men, who numbered far fewer than the women, carried the canoes high up onto the shore. They, too, exhibited an air of excitement that put Bridget in mind of the fairs and market days back in Little Wheddborough.

Many times as they went about the work of preparing for the storm, Bridget passed Kinnahauk. Each time, their eyes seemed to meet and cling. He alone among the men looked troubled, and Bridget thought of the weight of responsibility he bore. She told herself it was no wonder he had little time for her now that she was fully recovered.

The third time they passed, Kinnahauk bearing an enormous bundle of rushes on his back and Bridget with both arms filled with Soconme's precious hoard of herbs, Kinnahauk halted directly in front of her, blocking her way.

"Ho, Bridgetabbott. You have done enough. I would not have you weak with fever again."

Bridget tilted back her head, pride warming her cheeks. "I'm no weakling, for all you once called me a scrawny rabbit."

Kinnahauk's eyes slid away. He had not known she had understood his words. "Truly, I did not mean—"

"And speckled, too," she added testily. "'Tis a pity we are not all blessed with a fine dark hide such as yours! Some of us must make do with a less hardy covering, one that easily spots in the sun."

"The Cold Moon robs the sun of her power," he said thoughtfully, for indeed, her skin had grown soft and fair, inviting his touch. Though his expression did not change, amusement began to dance in his eyes. "Your hide is as soft and unblemished as the finest pelt, my small rabbit. You would bring many bushels of corn in trade."

Corn? He would trade her for *corn*? Bridget stared after him as he strode away, carrying on his back twice the burden borne by any of the other braves. Why had her heart begun flopping about like a crippled bird when he'd looked at her that way? He had shown her naught but a careless sort of kindness, and even that was touched with haughty disdain, as if she were the savage and he some mighty nobleman.

By the time all that could blow away or wash away was removed to the safety of the hills, a thick skein of clouds had covered the sky. The wind had picked up, and the water had grown choppy, flinging spray high up on the shore.

"Aiee, the fish hawk will go hungry this night," said the old *shaman* from the opening of one of the pointed tents Bridget had helped Sweet Water construct. There would be no cook fires this night, Bridget knew, for such a wind would reach even into the woods, and fire was ever an enemy to be feared. Two of the women had spent the morning making cakes of ground sunflower seeds and dried berries for all, which would be eaten with cold meat.

"Soconme, I do not understand," Bridget said now. "If there is really a storm coming, why does everyone laugh and talk as if this is all a children's game?"

"Would you have them weep and slash their arms?"

"I should think they would worry."

"They have done all it is in man's province to do, my daughter. Their fate is in the hands of the wind spirit. Weeping will not change that. Laughing will not change that. Go and laugh with them, *Waurraupa Shaman*, for it is good to laugh when the work is done. When the sun shows her face once more, I will offer up a special prayer for your child."

For her child? The old man must be suffering, for he had confused her with Many Toes, who had confided in her just that morning that it would be many moons before she would again see the *ouke* set aside for the women's monthly confinement.

Frowning, Bridget turned away to see what more Sweet Water would have her do. Everyone seemed to be busy, the women making their small tents ready for the night while the men ate the meat and cakes and talked of other storms. Kinnahauk sat apart from the others. More than once, Bridget felt his eyes upon her.

"Sweet Water, shall I bring in more moss for the sleeping mats?" she asked after they had shared their evening meal.

"You will not be sleeping in my *ouke* this night, Bridgetabbott. Soconme will feel the storm in his twisted bones before the moon walks down. I would give him comfort."

"But I—"

"It is time, my daughter. A seed planted in a storm will grow strong and true. Kinnahauk will take you to his mat this night."

Bridget's mouth fell open. She continued to stare at the woman who had been her friend, who had taken the place of her mother in caring for her these many months. Surely she had misunderstood?

"You gasp like a *cunshe* newly taken from the water. Did you think to wear the *weehewac* to cover your fire mark until my son grew tired of waiting and turned to Gray Otter? Paugh! That one—she grows bitter on the vine. Bridgetabbott bears his mark. It is for Bridgetabbott to be his first wife. Go now."

"But Gray Otter said— But I could not—"

"Go now," said the older woman, shoving her none too gently out into the darkness.

Bridget pulled the soft, tanned deerskin more closely around her as she waited for her eyes to grow accustomed to the dark. Wind howled about her, shrieking like a soul in torment. She could barely make out the small huddle of tents she had helped erect on the sheltered hillside, and there was not a living creature to be seen.

Where had everyone gone? There had been dozens of people going about their business when she had ducked into Sweet Water's tent to escape the wind for a few moments. Now everyone had disappeared. The sound of the wind drowned out any voices that might have set her mind at rest.

'Twas a nightmare. Any moment now she would wake up and tug the warm robe over her shoulders, snuggling deeper into the comfort of her sleeping mat.

Her sleeping mat! Where was she expected to sleep? How was she expected to stay warm? Surely Sweet Water had not seriously expected her to walk into Kinnahauk's tent and ask to share his sleeping mat! Why had she been cast out? Had she done something to displease her new friends?

A drop of rain filtered through the canopy of trees, and then another. She turned back toward Sweet Water's tent. Her chin quivered, and she drew her shawl up over her head.

"Come Bridgetabbott. It is time," said Kinnahauk quietly.

Bridget swung around, her night vision taking in the tall man who stood before her. *It is time*. Those were the very words Sweet Water had used, as if Bridget herself had nothing to say about her fate.

She thought of all the sly looks, the pointed remarks she had received before Sweet Water had shown her how to cover her witch-mark with the band of rabbit skin. Even Kinnahauk had hinted at some significance, but she had paid it no mind.

"No, Kinnahauk," she said decisively, her teeth chattering from the cold. "It is *not* time. I don't know what you and all the others expect of me, but I will not be offered up in some—some pagan rite to placate your storm gods, no matter what you say. This has gone far enough. The moment this storm is ended, I insist that you take me to David Lavender."

For all her fine show of bravery, Bridget knew she stood little chance if all the Hatorask turned against her. She could hardly imagine such a thing. Yet where were her friends when she stood in need of them? Where was Sits There? Where was Kokom?

She made up her mind that as soon as the storm ended, she would steal a canoe and set out alone. She would hail the first English boat she met and ask directions. It had been only the name of David Lavender that had given her the courage to hang on. After months of degradation on the ship, barely escaping death, she had come thousands of miles to find the man whose name she clung to like a talisman.

Well, just because she had been cast ashore in this forsaken wilderness; just because she had been rescued by this handsome savage; just because his people had been kind to her, had made her well, treating her as one of their own, that did not mean she must forget David Lavender and give herself over to whatever pagan rites these people practiced. Sweet Water had even hinted at some sort of union between Bridget and Kinnahauk.

Union? There could never be any union with a man who talked of first wives and second wives. It was purely heathen. Ignoring the sudden weakness that assailed her, Bridget lifted her head proudly and said, "You can stand there demanding all you wish, Kinnahauk. I am not one of your women, to roll sheep's eyes at you and put herself in your path in hope that you might notice her."

She saw the flash of his white teeth as her remark hit home. Let him laugh, the arrogant savage, although she wished he were not so magnificent. It would be easier to remember the debt of honor she owed the man who had paid her passage if this creature with the golden eyes and the sweetly curved mouth was not staring at her in such a way that made her throat grow tight and her breasts draw up into tight little buds.

Chapter Fourteen

A drop of rain struck Bridget on the forehead and trickled down into her eye. She blinked. Kinnahauk continued to watch her silently. The wind dropped to a whisper, and there came the sleepy murmur of voices from a nearby tent. Was everyone else asleep? Or were they only hiding to discover if she would meekly follow this arrogant bellwether into his tent like some witless lamb to the slaughter.

In the distance she could hear the roar of the ocean beating against the far shore. It sounded cold and threatening, as if it might cross the hills and moors to seek out their small haven. Several more drops of rain struck her face, and she shivered. Never had she felt quite so alone, halfway around the world from all that was dear and familiar. She felt the strangest compulsion to move closer, to rest her cheek against that smooth, broad chest and allow those powerful arms to close around her, shutting out the storm.

She stiffened against the momentary weakness.

"Come, Bridgetabbott, we will talk of this matter. I cannot leave you standing here in the rain, and no one else will take you in."

"Of course they'll take me in," she countered instantly. "Any one of them would give me shelter if they knew you were about to—if they thought you meant to—"

"Go to them, then," Kinnahauk said quietly. "Ask Sits There if she will take you into her small tent with her father and her mother and her two young brothers. Ask Face of a Horse to go out into the night so that you may share the mat with Many Toes and her child."

The rain was coming down in earnest now. Even under the sheltering cloak made of unscraped deer hide, her dress and moccasins were growing unpleasantly cold and slick to the touch. She possessed nothing else but the pitiful rags she had worn throughout her long ordeal. Sweet Water had scrubbed them often, but then she had hidden them away, wrinkling her nose with such distaste that Bridget had dared not ask for them.

Her heart sinking, Bridget knew it would do little good to ask any of her new friends for shelter. These were Kinnahauk's people. They had been his friends for a lifetime, hers for only a few short months. They would never go against the wishes of their chief for the sake of an outsider.

White-eyes, they called her people. Stinking pale-skins. English devils. Oh, never to her face, but she had heard the younger braves talking among themselves. She knew that they feared and despised the English who had come to their land. If only a few of the tales she had heard were true, she could scarce blame them. Before she left this place she would ask old Soconme the truth of such accusations, for it stung to think that her own kind had been less honorable in their dealings than those she had once called savages.

A trickle of icy water ran down her spine, causing her to stiffen. No matter what had gone before, she refused to give herself over into the hands of any man in payment for the sins of some unknown ruffians who might or might not have mistreated a few of his relatives. If only he did not look so... If only he were not so...

"I grow tired of waiting, woman. Come!"

"I grow tired of being ordered about like a disobedient child," Bridget retorted. "Since you have seen fit to turn

my friends against me, I will make a tent of my cloak. I am
no treacle tart to melt in a bit of rain.''

''As you wish. Were I such a fool as to turn away from
shelter in a storm, I would seek to spread my cloak where
the serpents cannot crawl. On Croatoan they do not sleep
soundly throughout the Cold Moon as they do in other
lands. When the water rises over their homes, they go in
search of high ground.''

Bridget's eyes widened. She swallowed hard, glancing
into the impenetrable darkness around her. ''Oh, but
surely...''

''Come, Bridgetabbott,'' Kinnahauk said again, his deep
voice gentle, almost as though he pitied her. ''I have a soft
mat and warm skins to cover you. You may sleep alone if
you wish, for I would not take a woman against her will.
Come now, before your chattering teeth awake the spirits
of my ancestors.''

It was only because she had always feared serpents,
Bridget told herself, allowing Kinnahauk to lead her to his
tent. Only because the rain threatened to beat the leaves
from the trees and the cold wind cut through to the bone,
and she had nowhere else to go.

There was no warming bed of coals in the center of the
tent, but it had been tightly constructed to withstand the
storm. Bridget dropped down onto a pile of moss and dried
sea grass that had been covered with a soft buckskin. She
preferred the pine needles herself, for the sweeter scent, but
the sea grass made a finer cushion once the small creatures
had been plucked away. ''Take off your wet clothing and
cover yourself with this.'' Kinnahauk handed her a thick
robe made of many soft pelts.

''My clothes are not so very wet,'' she lied through jaws
clenched tight to prevent their chattering.

There was scant space. Kinnahauk stood over her, making her feel small and exceedingly vulnerable. The fact that
she was rapidly turning to ice did not help, but she was not
about to remove her clothing while he towered over her like

some great beast of prey. Not for one moment did she doubt that he could see in the darkness.

"I have skinned many rabbits, Bridgetabbott. One more will be no great task. Would you like my help?"

Shivering uncontrollably, she retorted, "I would like for you to stop calling me by that silly name!"

"You are not called Bridgetabbott?"

"Not the way you say it," she muttered, drawing the fur over her wet clothing, which was no help at all.

Gently Kinnahauk removed the robe from her stiff fingers. "I seek to honor you by calling you your name, yet still you find fault." He wrested the dripping deerskin cloak from around her shoulders and his hands went to the bottom of the simple one-piece garment that fell below her knees. "What would you have me do?"

"I would have you leave me be! You promised me I could sleep alone."

"You are not sleeping."

"Of course I am not sleeping! How can I sleep when someone keeps trying to remove my clothes? I know what you want, Kinnahauk—your mother told me about planting seeds in a storm, and—and first wives and such. I don't hold with such heathen practices!"

Kinnahauk eased off her wet moccasins and chaffed her small feet in his hard, warm hands. Then, stroking the moisture from her legs, he reached the bottom of her sodden garment and shoved it up as far as it would go. Shivering with more than the cold, Bridget pushed at his hands, but he ignored her as he would have ignored a bothersome insect. Lifting her up, he tugged the clinging doeskin over her head and tossed it aside.

Her heart felt as if it would leap out of her breast. She was grateful for the darkness, although she suspected it offered scant protection from eyes such as his. Before she could protest, she felt the heavenly warmth of the thick robe close around her. She drew up her knees, tucking her feet under the supple folds as she tried to come to terms

with the strange weakness that seemed to assail her whenever he was nearby. Whenever he touched her.

"It is no dishonorable thing," Kinnahauk informed her
stiffly. She could fair see his eyes glittering, the proud tilt
of his head. "The men of my village once took many wives,
who lived as sisters to each other. Once we numbered as the
trees of the forest. We lived in peace, growing old among
our grandchildren and their children. When the white-eyes
came they called us heathen. They called us savages. They
taught us the meaning of those words."

Bridget felt a rise of gooseflesh as the deep, smooth voice
flowed over her, even though she was warm and no longer
feeling quite so threatened.

"We greeted these people as brothers, bearing them
many fine gifts. They turned to our brothers the Roanoaks, who also gave them gifts. They took all our gifts and
demanded gold and pearls. They were given seeds. They
were taught how to hunt, for they were but planters. They
were taught how to fish our waters. The seeds were not
planted. Our ways of hunting and fishing were strange to
them, though they claimed to know all things. They would
not learn from us when we would have taught them. In their
search for gold, they did not think of preparing for the future. They wasted much and demanded more. In the time
when the Rain God turned his face away from us, there was
little corn among our brothers across the Inland Sea. All
our people were hungry as the Cold Moon approached, but
my brothers opened their storehouses to ease the hunger of
these new friends. Still their greed was not satisfied. They
raided our storehouses, destroying what they could not
carry away. Our brothers the Poteskeets, the Roanoaks, the
Paspatanks and the Yeopim saw their *oukes* burned, their
women and children killed. We were called savage, yet what
man of honor would kill a woman or a child?"

As a gust of wind caused the lashed poles to creak overhead, Bridget shivered and drew the robe closer around her.
She was puzzled. Kinnahauk spoke as though all this had

happened only yesterday, but surely it had not. Surely the law-abiding citizens of these colonies would not suffer such injustice to take place.

Outside, a branch crashed down. She edged closer as Kinnahauk began to speak once more. "The depth of our sadness was great, for we had learned that the words spoken by these people came only from their tongues and not from their hearts. Much blood was shed. Many women wept. Many great chiefs and many brave warriors came in honor to sit in council with the leaders among your people, only to be met with treachery. The blood of the great *werowance* Pemispan of the Roanoaks and Granganameo, his brother, was spilled, their bodies desecrated by those who wore fine clothing and called themselves lords."

The leaders among *your* people, he had said. *My* people, thought Bridget. She wanted to believe that her countrymen could never be guilty of such wickedness, yet had she not known murder, torture and disgrace in her own land? Had she not suffered at the hands of her own kind?

Had the things he had spoken of happened yesterday or a hundred years ago? Time itself seemed strange and different in this distant, windswept place, ordered not by days of a week or weeks of a year, but by tides and seasons.

Drawn to his warmth, Bridget had gradually moved closer until now she could smell the clean, smoky scent of his body even though she could not see him. As the wild winds howled through the treetops, causing the skin to sag between the poles, she was grateful for his nearness.

"Is that why you despise my people, Kinnahauk? Why you hated me even as you dragged me from the water and chased me across your island? Because of what my people have done to yours?"

"I do not hate you, Bridgetabbott. I cannot, for it is not in my power to hate a gift from the Great Spirit."

"A gift from the Great Spirit?" Her astonishment was obvious.

"Yes." Kinnahauk's amusement was just as evident.

"That's foolishness. From the very first, you have looked on me as if I were some poor creature cast up on the shore by an unfriendly tide. Surely you would not treat a gift from your Great Spirit with such lofty disdain." Warmer now, she felt secure enough to tease him a bit.

"And were you not some poor creature cast upon my shore?" he countered with indisputable logic. "I have known carrion dropped by feeding seabirds that smelled sweeter."

Remembering only dimly the smell of fish that had permeated her nightmares that first day, Bridget turned away, huddling under the robe. The sound of Kinnahauk's soft laughter did not help to restore her spirits. "If all you say is true, why did you bother to bring me to Sweet Water? You could have left me to wash away on the outgoing tide. I would scarce have known the difference." She was not aware of the way her breath grew still as she listened for his answer. When it came, she only knew she felt a great sense of disappointment.

"My blood is tainted with the blood of your people, Bridgetabbott. I cannot hate you, even as I hate the wrongs your people have done to mine. By many I am called coward because I choose the way of peace. It is enough to fight the tides that cover our island, and the fierce winds that blow without ceasing for many days. It is enough to see that the bellies of my people are filled, for corn does not thrive in sand. There are many hungry mouths, but too few hunters."

Bridget grew warm under the cover of the robe, her fears lulled by the deep, resonant voice that shaped familiar words in a thrillingly unfamiliar way. She had seen many sides to this complex man, yet this was the first time he had spoken to her of such things. She felt as if a door had been opened to her, one that lured her ever closer, even though she was half-fearful of entering.

"I say these things to you so that you will not fear me, Bridgetabbott. I would not willingly shed the blood of any man, but my people have not forgotten how to fight. We fought our way through many lands in the Time Before the Grandfathers. One day we may fight our way back to the land of our beginnings. Until that day, we will paint our faces only if we are threatened, for we do not seek to gain by coup that which belongs to another."

"But who would threaten you? There's no one on the island but your own people."

"Soon your people will bring their guns and their cattle to our village, Bridgetabbott. Our fighting men are but few, the guns of the white-eyes many. Who will care for our women and children if our blood stains the sand? Who will bring food and warm skins to their *oukes*? When the English tide comes, it will cover the highest hilltop. Where do we go, Bridgetabbott? To the sea? Back to the land where the sun sleeps? Even now, your people spread over that land. Do we fly with the white brant as do the spirits of our ancestors, to return each year at the time of the falling leaves?"

What could she say? She knew not who was right or who was wrong, she only knew that at this moment, she would have given anything in her power to ease the burden of this troubled man who must keep his people safe against such great odds.

Reaching out in the darkness, her fingertips brushed against bare skin. Thinking it to be an arm, she cupped her hand around it, only to discover that she was fondling his knee. Before she could draw back, he covered her small hand with his own much larger one.

"Do not be frightened, Little Rabbit, for I mean you no harm."

"It seems I have heard you speak those words before," she said with a nervous laugh.

"And have I ever harmed you?" he taunted gently. His hand felt warm and hard, his touch gentle.

"Only if you do not count scaring me half out of my wits. The first time I laid eyes on you, I thought you were going to skin me and eat me alive."

"Your people tell wicked tales, not all of them untrue. Many of my brothers are far from peaceful."

"And many of your own braves wish you felt the same way," Bridget ventured. The young men sometimes spoke more freely than perhaps they should, for they had grown used to seeing her among the other women and now paid her no mind.

"Aiee, Bridgetabbott, be done. I would speak no more of such weighty matters, for my back is weary from carrying rushes to rebuild our village, and my mind with questions that have no answers. We will sleep now."

"Will you—do you..." She did not quite know how to frame the question she would ask. "Where will you sleep?" she blurted finally.

"Alone. My sleeping mat and the red wolf robe are yours."

There was scarce enough room to unfold one mat, let alone two, Bridget thought guiltily. "Have you another blanket?"

"You rattle on like the seeds in a dried gourd," Kinnahauk grumbled. She could tell from the sounds that he had moved away from her, turning his face to the small opening of their tent, his back to the soft cushion of sea grass with its deer hide covering and warm fur blanket.

With a heavy sigh, she snuggled down in her cozy nest and tugged the wolf robe down over her back where a finger of cold wind had found her nakedness. The tent was secure from all but a trickle of rain, but the wind had increased until it seemed determined to find a weakness. In a gale such as this, it was not a difficult task.

Even though her body welcomed the rest, her eyes remained open in the darkness. Had Kinnahauk no covering at all? 'Strewth, the men of this place wore little enough and seemed not to suffer from cold, yet Bridget could not help but wonder how it would feel to lie before a loosely tied flap of hide, wearing naught but a tail clout, a pair of low moccasins and a brief vestlike garment that seemed more for looks than for warmth. And were not all those soaked from rain?

"Kinnahauk," she whispered.

He grunted.

"Kinnahauk, my conscience pains me. Please come and share the sleeping mat. Surely it's wide enough for two to sleep in comfort."

Bridget was aghast at her own words. Had he misunderstood her? "I only meant—well, at least, take the fur robe." Sitting up, she reluctantly handed it across to where she knew him to be. The cold damp air immediately bit into her tender warm flesh like the teeth of a ravening beast, and she tucked the thin covering of the sleeping mat about her. "If you catch the fever from sleeping in wet garments, who will lead your people? I would not have you on my conscience, Kinnahauk."

"Keep the thing, woman," he growled, flinging it back to her.

"I will not have you turning into a block of ice before you can take me to Albemarle as you promised. *You* take it!" She flung it back. "I can use the deer hide."

Suddenly she was not alone. He was kneeling beside her, his hard palm closing over her shoulder as he pressed her down onto the soft mat. "We will share both. When my mother asks on the morrow if I have taken you to my sleeping mat, you will speak truly, for I grow weary of her constant nagging!"

Kinnahauk thought the gods must have stolen his mind away in the darkness. He could hear them laughing in the voice of the wind as he arranged his lean body on the far edge of the mat, his back to the woman, his knees drawn up and his arms crossed over his chest in an effort to stave off the cold. The red wolf robe was not so large that it would reach over a man and a woman who were determined to sleep apart and yet together.

Let her have it. He did not need the comfort of a robe, nor the soft cushion of sea grass beneath him. He had slept under the stars with naught but his own skin for warmth half the nights of his life, for it was only thus that he hardened his body against its natural enemies. He did not know why he had even listened to the foolish creature, but that her constant wagging tongue would have kept him awake all night.

His *oquio*! Surely the gods were laughing. They gave him for his own a land which would not grow corn. They plagued him with questions that had no answers. And the final irony—for his comfort, they gave him a woman he had despised when he first cast eyes upon her!

The wind shifted to another quarter, driving rain against the front of the tent. Bridget drew her feet higher up under the robe, and her knee brushed against Kinnahauk's backside.

She caught her breath. He froze.

Nor had the gods finished with him yet, for they had devised an even more fiendish torture, Kinnahauk thought as he sought a position that would relieve the growing pressure in his loins. His exquisitely sensitive nerves could feel her soft warm breath against his back. His nostrils flared as he caught the scent of her body. Above the sweet musk of her own womanliness, he picked out the separate scents of the sweet herbs and the leaves of the waxberry bush she had mixed with the yucca root for her bath.

She was restless. The mat whispered as she turned over, her back to his. Kinnahauk followed her move, turning and moving closer until he could feel her warmth along every inch of his body. A strand of her hair tickled his face, and he caught it between his fingers, marveling at its fineness. Had he once likened it to dried grass?

Long after the sound of her breath told him she slept, Kinnahauk lay awake, thinking of the woman who shared his mat. She belonged to him. She wore his mark. The whole village knew of this, yet he had not taken her to his *ouke*, for he had been sorely disappointed after years of waiting for his vision-quest to be fulfilled. She was not pleasing in the way of his women, yet he had come to see in her a beauty he had found in no other woman. She was of the people he despised, yet had she not shown herself to be kind, to be loving and gentle, to be a friend to his people? Had she not proved herself honorable by seeking to go to this man who had paid her bride-price?

Yet she belonged to Kinnahauk. Not by right of bride-price, but by right of his vision-quest. Perhaps if he sought out this man Davidlavender and paid an even greater price for her, both his honor and hers would be satisfied.

Kinnahauk's fists knotted in the darkness. If his mind gave him little rest, his body gave him still less, for his man part reached out to her in the darkness with a will of its own. It was not the way of his people to take an unwilling woman, for in such a deed there was more shame than pleasure. Yet there was no pleasure at all in burning.

Closing his eyes, Kinnahauk sought to direct his thoughts to a higher place. He listened for the Voice that Speaks Silently to give him direction, but there was only one voice to be heard above the crying of the wind. The voice of his own fierce need.

He would hold her against him. He would hold her and make no move to take her, and when his man part grew tired of waiting, it would sleep. Then he would rise quietly and walk down to the village to see how it had fared against the tides.

Thus he drew close, fitting his body around her back, his arm around her waist. He buried his face in the soft warmth of her hair and breathed in its sweetness, the groan that passed his lips losing itself in the song of the wind. His rebellious man part sought a resting place between her thighs, stealing pleasure from the soft pressure, which satisfied for a moment even as it fed the flames of a ravening hunger.

Kinnahauk swallowed with great difficulty, for his mouth had grown dry. There had been many times in his life when he had suspected he was lacking in wisdom, but never so much as this moment.

Under his breath he chanted the words of an ancient war song, one that brought courage to those about to face the enemy on the field of battle. "Courage, courage, all will pass away, all will return."

His hand brushed against hers, and he captured one small finger. With thumb and forefinger, he began to trace its contours, keenly aware of the increasing heat as he neared the valley between her fingers. He reached the joining, and with a sensitive touch, stroked it gently, his thoughts on another joining.

Lips parted as he tried to quieten his breathing, Kinnahauk allowed his hand to spread over her small belly. His thumb settled in the hollow of her navel, and he bit back another groan. Memory was a vicious foe, bringing visions of a small golden floss. His shaft, already hard and seeking, began to stir restlessly. Tormented by the hunger in him, he slipped his fingers downward until they brushed against a feathery softness.

By the Great Spirit, man was not meant to suffer such torture!

One of her legs, the lower one, straightened out, tilting her body downward so that his hand was pressed between her flesh and the deer hide mat. The thighs that had harbored his aching man part so snugly had now parted, leaving that poor creature exposed and vainly seeking the source of her womanly heat.

She murmured something under her breath, and Kinnahauk froze. But it was only sleep talk. She had not awakened, then, for all her breathing was growing heavy and quick.

For a long moment he did not move. Honor battled with the fierce demands of his body. He did not *want* to hear. He would not *listen!* This woman bore his mark. She had been given to him. Honor demanded that he not refuse such a gift.

She stirred, and he felt the tip of her breast brush against his arm and grow hard. This time he could not suppress the groan. Slowly he lifted his hand from her belly and brought it up to her breast. He cupped her in his palm, marveling that flesh could be so firm and yet so soft. As he traced the small beaded tip with his thumb, he remembered the way she had looked standing bare before him, the strange beauty of her pale coloring exciting him even then.

Drawing air in through his teeth, Kinnahauk lowered his face to the downy softness of her hair. Cautiously he brushed it aside with his chin until he felt the hollow at the back of her neck, which he touched with the tip of his tongue. Never had he known a woman's flesh to be so sweet! Never had he hungered so for the taste of a woman's body! What would happen if she awoke and found him so close beside her? Would she turn to him and take him into her body? Would she scream and run out into the storm? How could it be that she bore his fire mark, yet another man had paid her bride-price? Such a thing had never before happened to his knowledge.

Kinnahauk knew he should wait and ask the council of the old ones, yet he did not want to wait. Cautiously he moved his hand over her breast and downward, seeking that which had haunted his memory for so long. His own body was an agony of need by the time he finally buried his sensitive fingertips in the damp petals beneath the golden floss.

She stirred against him in her sleep, and he pressed himself gently against her soft hips, wishing he dared awaken her. Instead he remained still until she rested quietly once more, his palm cupping her mound, one finger savoring the heat of her sweet, narrow valley. He recognized the small changes in her woman flesh that told him she was not without awareness, even though she slept.

Unable to help himself, he began to caress her, his heart pounding as he felt her growing arousal, the swift dampening that told him she was his for the taking. Her thighs trembled and grew slack, and he knew she would spread them for him if he turned her onto her back. It would be so easy. So good....

Her body is yours this night, O mighty chief. You have taken it by stealth and cunning. But what of her spirit? Will she come to you willingly on the morrow?

Kinnahauk hardened himself against the Voice that Speaks Silently. Why was it that the Voice heeded him not when he sought its wisdom, yet cried out loudly when he did not want to hear?

Why should he not take what had been promised him in his youth? The woman was in his lodge, she slept on his mat, she warmed to his touch, her body as hungry as his. Would the Great Spirit not be pleased? Was it not said among his people that seeds planted at the height of a storm grew tallest and hardiest?

Was it not said that Kinnahauk was a man of honor?

Reluctantly he stilled his fingers. She shifted uneasily in her sleep, murmuring softly, and he touched the vulnerable back of her neck with his lips. "This much I can do for you, my woman. One day you will ask for more."

Finding what he sought, he began to touch her gently, to stroke and caress until she began to whimper. If she were to awaken now, he promised himself, he would take her.

She did not. Instead she pressed herself against his hand, until she shuddered, moaning in her sleep.

Kinnahauk sighed. He allowed his palm to cup the downy nest for one long, aching moment. Then, slipping his hand from beneath her, he touched his own flesh with her dew. "Not this night, my bold warrior," he whispered.

Silently he eased himself from the mat and drew the robe closely around her shoulders, gazing down through the darkness at the sleeping woman. Then he slipped outside, where he stood for a long time, buffeted by the winds, chilled by the rains, his thoughts more troubled than ever before.

Chapter Fifteen

For three days the wet wind blew. Where once a circle of *oukes* had stood, now there was only clean sand, littered with the gifts of the storm gods. Sweet Water had found a wooden bucket that had sailed across the Inland Sea, and the son of the widowed Running Fish found a coat of blue cloth with one sleeve missing. This he put on, whooping and dancing in circles on the shore to the great amusement of his friends. In his mind, the small brave counted coup against the enemy for the death of his father, Three Horns, many years ago.

But the coat was eventually cast back out to sea, for all knew of Kinnahauk's feelings on the matter. While their brothers on the mainland took up the white-eyes' ways, wearing their uncomfortable, ugly clothing, eating their food, living in wooden boxes, falling senseless with their alcohol, the Hatorask stood apart. Had it been in Kinnahauk's power to reshape the past, the eyes of blue and gray and even of gold would change in an instant to black.

Sweet Water kept her bucket. "In the Time Before the Beginning, our people ate their meat without cooking it," she argued. "Would you have your stew red, your fish meat pink? Aiee, my stubborn son, you cannot keep the sun from walking down."

After the night of the storm, when Bridget had dreamed so vividly—dreams that had brought heat to her face for days afterward—she had gone directly to Sweet Water and asked to be allowed to return to her tent. "Sweet Water, I'm sure Kinnahauk is a good son and a fine chief, but what you wish can never be."

The older woman had examined her closely, her face long with disappointment. "No seeds planted? Is it the moon flow? We did not think to build a separate place for those women among us who—"

"No! I mean—it's nothing like that, Sweet Water." How could she explain when she didn't fully understand herself? She had lived among these people too long, for she was beginning to see things through their eyes. At times she almost wished she had been born among them, for then her duty would have been much clearer. "The man who paid my passage—my bride-price—will be waiting for me," she explained gently. "I would have gone to him long before, but at first I was too weak, and then the men were so busy with the hunting and fishing, and then the weather..."

There had been many fine days. The men had not been busy *all* the time. And she had healed rapidly under the tender care of this woman. In her heart Bridget knew that had she but tried a bit harder, she might have persuaded someone to guide her to Albemarle. It had been too easy to say, "Wait until the weather clears, wait until the warm winds, wait until the Planting Moon...."

Their Planting Moon would be well into spring by her reckoning, and that was by far too long to make poor David wait for his bride. "Mr. Lavender paid a big fortune for my passage, Sweet Water. How can I simply turn away from him and be happy here, knowing that surely he must think me lost and his fortune wasted?"

The older woman shrugged. "He find another woman."

"He paid one hundred twenty pounds of tobacco for me. If I stay here when I could go to him, that makes me no better than a thief."

"Kinnahauk has pay bigger bride-price. Did he not lift you up from Big Water? Did he not bring you to my *ouke* when you were *waurepa caure* with fever? Without my son, you go with Great Spirit, walk no more this place. I say this Davidlavender no have Bridgetabbott. I say Bridgetabbott sleep on mat of Kinnahauk." The older woman's eyes grew crafty. "*Waurraupa Shaman* not find Kinnahauk pleasing to the eye? His skin too dark? He not smell sweet to your English nose? The sound of his voice make bad to your ear? His touch make your throat grow sour with bile?"

Sweet Water's grasp of English tended to slip when she became emotional. Bridget hurried to reassure her that her son was indeed exceptional among men. "How could any woman not find him attractive? He is more handsome than any man I have ever known. He's strong and wise, and gentle, and—and his touch and his smell and—and the sound of his voice please me well enough," she finished in a small rush.

In truth, they were beginning to please her entirely too much. The dreams that had filled her head as she had slept beside him were but foolish fancies, to be forgotten quickly. As hot color swept up her throat to cover her face, she blurted, "Sweet Water, please—I am not ready. Take me into your tent again, and let Soconme share Kinnahauk's tent."

Sweet Water studied the flushed young face with great interest, seeing something there that seemed to restore her good spirits. At her slow smile, Bridget felt a touch of unease, but at least she had her way. She was taken back into Sweet Water's tent until the village could be rebuilt.

All day long Bridget intercepted swift, curious glances from the bustling woman who went about her work humming and singing. Bridget built a small fire, and Sweet Water made the corn cakes called *appones* to soak up the juice of the salty oysters Kinnahauk had opened for them. As always when they were not having some sort of ceremonial meal, women, children and men ate together in family groups. Often the children visited one another, taking bits of food from this pot and that one, and there was much friendly calling back and forth from one group to another.

Including Bridget, there were four at Sweet Water's fire, for old Soconme took most of his meals there, as well. With Kinnahauk's gaze on her more often than not, Bridget grew increasingly uncomfortable. If she had thought she had to share his sleeping mat again that night, she would not have been able to choke down a morsel of Sweet Water's delicious oyster stew, *appones* and yaupon tea.

Casting him a quick glance once while his attention was on a tale old Soconme was relating, she thought again of Sweet Water's words. *Was* his skin too dark? Sooner ask was her own too pallid, for indeed copper skin and all, he was more pleasing to gaze upon than any man she had ever known. Did his scent offend her? How could anyone be offended by the scent of wind and rain and sunshine, mingled with the heady scent of leather and wood smoke? As for the sound of his voice, had she not seen him lull a bird from the topmost branch of a tree until it flew down onto his shoulder?

And his touch, she thought wonderingly. How could she say it displeased her when, long after his hand left her, her skin tingled where his fingers had rested?

Sighing deeply, she gazed into the glowing coals. If she thought Kinnahauk could read in her eyes the wicked dreams she had dreamed about him, she would simply walk out into the water until it closed over her head and never come up again.

With a fickleness Bridget had come to expect, the weather changed from wild and wet to warm and springlike almost overnight, though it be mid-January as nearly as she could reckon. From the far side of the island, the sound of the ocean pounding against the shore could still be heard, like the heartbeat of a sleeping giant. On the landward side, a neat cluster of *oukes* had sprung up quickly once the wind had shifted, permitting the storm tides to subside. There the looking-glass surface of the water nearest the shore reflected the images of stalking herons and soaring gulls against a background of cloudless skies.

Leaning over, Bridget saw and was amazed at the changes in her own reflection. Instead of milky white, with a scattering of freckles, her skin had taken on the color of the palest honey, with a flush of pink that came from spending much of her time out-of-doors. Her hair had grown longer and seemed to glow with new life, flowing down over her shoulders like a cape.

Perhaps she should braid it and tie the ends with a scrap of soft hide, as the others did. Kinnahauk sometimes wore his dark hair loose, as did Kokom even more often, but for the most part, men, women and children alike wore their hair neatly braided to avoid having it snarl in the wind.

"Would you go with us along the shore to gather sea grass, Bridget?" called out Wattapi from the group of unmarried young women who trailed down to the shore.

"Paugh! The white-eye woman is too busy admiring her sickly pale face in the water. She has no time to work. Leave her be, we do not need her. She is weak, as everyone knows." With that, Gray Otter strode off ahead, carrying a net slung across her shoulders.

"Do not mind Gray Otter, Bridget. It is just her way," apologized the gentle Sits There, hurrying past. Gray Otter was recognized by all as the leader of the women. Despite her sharp temper, she was clever and bold, her bright eyes missing little of what went on in the village.

Bridget could not like her. She stared after them, anger burning in her chest. "Weak, am I? And how would you have fared in my place this past twelvemonth, you dark-eyed viper?" she muttered under her breath.

Everyone in the village, Bridget included, had worked hard to rebuild the homes and the storehouse, using the rushes the men had cut before the tides had flooded the lowlands. Bridget's hands were still raw from tying countless bundles of the long grass to be laced onto a wooden frame.

Two of the canoes had been lost, and the men had felled and stripped a large cypress, splitting it in half and shaping the ends. They set coals to burning along the center of each half so that they could later scrape away the burned wood, leaving only the solid shells. Face of a Horse had claimed a small end of the same log and was using fire to hollow out one end, for Many Toes was in need of a new mortar to grind the corn for their *appones*.

Smoke from the village cook fires drifted down to where Bridget stood, and it mingled sweetly with the burning logs that were being tended by two youths. She felt her anger slip away. Gray Otter had meant no real harm. She was merely tired, having worked long hours directing the placement of each bundle of rushes and the layering of the fan-shaped fronds that would keep the rain from soaking through.

They were all tired, for the work was hard and constant, even without having to rebuild the village. It would be so much easier were it not for that stiff-necked pride of Kinnahauk's that would not allow his people to borrow the English ways. An iron cooking pot on a trammel over Sweet Water's fire would be much more efficient than an earthen pot buried in coals and likely to crack when least expected. And surely there could be no great sin in wearing a cloak made of fine wool instead of a drafty bit of buckskin? The braves all wore their blades of steel strapped to their sides, to be sure, but the women must do without.

Men! Even the poorest among her own villagers had been able to purchase ha'penny's worth of flour already ground. Bridget thought of the giant waterwheel that turned the stones that ground the wheat back in Little Wheddborough. She thought of the deep millpond. She thought of her mother, and the . . .

"No! Oh, no," she whispered. Sometimes she went for days without thinking of that. With the passage of time, the harsh memories had grown more distant until now she

thought mostly of the days of her childhood. But at times
when she least expected it, something would release her
mind, and the terrible events would all rush back, as though
they had occurred only yesterday.

Forcing the painful past behind her, she began to run
along the shore after the others. She could heartily recommend the freedom of a short buckskin shift over layers of
long, sweeping skirts and tight binding waists and sleeves.
"Wait for me!" she cried out.

She caught up with them on a wide stretch of white sand
where weathered tree roots projected starkly from the sand,
mute evidence of a long-dead forest. Sits There cast her a
teasing look. "Did you come to work with us, or did you
come to play the game, *Waurraupa Shaman*?" She and
Wattapi burst into a fit of giggles.

With a snort of impatience, Gray Otter pointed to a
mound of gleaming, wet sea grass. "The white-eyes do not
play our games. She can busy herself by picking the live
creatures out of this pile and setting it out to dry. Hush your
foolish laughter and come, there is more to be done if you
would sleep in comfort."

Bridget knew that the wet sea grass had to be carried
higher up on the shore and spread out atop the tall grasses
to dry in the sun. It would be turned frequently throughout the day, and with each turning, more sand and shells
would winnow away until it was dry enough to be taken into
the lodges, mixed with the crushed leaves of the waxberry
plant, which kept away all manner of insects and lent a
sweet smell.

Bridget was left to her task. When the others returned,
she was all but done. Wattapi and Sits There carried a net
between them, filled with a load of dry sea grass that had
been prepared the day before. Gray Otter hung back,
glancing over her shoulder at a group of riders that had just
rounded a wooded point.

"The game begins, Bridget," cried Sits There. "Quickly,
come stand with us!"

Suddenly all the women were huddling together as if terrified for their very lives. But these were but men from the village, not some pillaging hoard of savages bent on rape and destruction. Mystified, Bridget looked from the women to the men, who were now bearing down on them at full gallop, waving spears, shouting loud enough to wake the dead.

A game? All the women playing at being terrified maidens, the Hatorask braves whooping and shouting like small boys at play? It was something the foolish clown Kokom might do, for he was forever playing pranks to make people laugh, but surely that was Kinnahauk in the lead—and just behind him on the ugly dun mare was Crooked Stick.

Bridget glanced swiftly at the tight knot of women. To the left of them was spread all the sea grass she had carefully laid out to dry. To the right of them was a narrow band of white sand that bordered the water.

Not about to risk treading on her neat beds of grass, she moved warily to the very edge of the water, out of the way of the wild-looking army bearing down on them. She watched in growing amusement, curious to see how far the mock war would go. She could scarce believe that Gray Otter would shed her dignity so far as to join such childish frolick—but then, Gray Otter, among all the women, was not laughing, her opaque eyes following Kinnahauk's every move as the snorting animals were suddenly reigned in.

With careless skill, the bare-chested braves began guiding their mounts into the cowering group, the steeds tossing their small heads and taking short, mincing steps as if they, too, found pleasure in such antics.

One by one, the women were cut from the group, much as a herdsman might separate his flock. Bridget watched while Crooked Stick skillfully herded Sits There apart from the rest, leaning over the side of his mount to sweep her up in his arms.

Was this the game, then? Or was there more to come?
Was it all a part of a ritual that would end in a feast or a
dance—or mayhap a celebration of another sort?

Kinnahauk's great shaggy stallion stood apart from the
others until there were only two women left standing. Gray
Otter, standing near the beds of dried sea grass, and
Bridget, cowering beside the water. Now, with great deliberation, man and animal began stalking.

And then Gray Otter was there beside her, crowding her
onto the wet sand. With an arrogant toss of her head, the
Hatorask maiden stepped forward, planting herself in front
of Bridget. With no visible direction from his rider, the
stallion Tukkao danced sideways to move between them.

Kinnahauk's muscular leg, gleaming in the late-day sun,
touched Bridget's shoulder, searing her with its heat. The
smell of sweating horse was strong in her nostrils, and instinctively she stepped back, only to feel icy water seep into
her moccasin. Momentarily distracted, she glanced down
just as Kinnahauk leaned over, his arm outstretched.

What happened next was never quite clear to her. Later,
Sits There whispered that Gray Otter, looking as if she
could spit fire, had slapped Tukkao on the rump, causing
him to rear up. Bridget only remembered stumbling backward to escape the flailing hooves, and then the water was
closing over her face. Numb with shock and cold, she found
herself strangling for air.

It was over in an instant as, breathless from her unexpected bath, she felt herself being lifted up out of the water. The numbness left her, leaving in its wake a stinging
cold that struck clean through to the marrow. Dimly she
was aware of Kinnahauk's voice, sounding even more cold
than the water. "No, she was not struck by Tukkao's
hooves. Move away! Kokom, see to your woman!"

Bridget was thankful for Kinnahauk's warmth. He held
her tightly against his chest, lending heat to the parts of her
he touched, the rest of her body feeling all the colder in
contrast. The others fell back, their faces filled with con-

cern. Someone—she thought it was Crooked Stick—gave
him a buckskin, which he wrapped about her. Someone else
offered to run ahead and fetch Soconme.

"I d-d-don't need Soconme," Bridget chattered, bur-
rowing deeper into the comfort of Kinnahauk's arms as he
strode back toward the village. "All I need is a change of
clothing. I have b-b-bathed in colder water than that." That
was not true, for the pond where the women bathed was
shallow and warmed by the sun. It was only the hardiest
among the men who waded out into the freezing salt waters in the winter months to gather oysters, all others using
canoes and long-handled forks.

Hearing a loud snuffle, she glanced back to see Tukkao
plodding meekly behind, his head drooping as if he were
aware that he had displeased his master. Meek or not,
Bridget was just as glad Kinnahauk had not attempted to
put her up on the horse's back. Her small mare, Red Wind,
was almost more horse than she could manage.

"My new *ouke* is warm and tight, Bridgetabbott. You
know the warmth of my red wolf robe," Kinnahauk said
softly.

But it was the spicy warmth of his breath that disturbed
her as it caressed her brow. Her head resting on his shoulder, she remembered another time when he had carried her
through the woods. Was she fated to be rescued by this man
each time ill fortune befell her? This time he had been
partly to blame, but Bridget was in no mood to chastise.

"Come, my *oquio*, will you not return to my sleeping
mat? It was not kind of you to send old Soconme in your
place, for he snorts in his sleep like a wounded bear."

Bridget glanced back to see if the others had heard. They
were following, two atop each horse, all save Gray Otter,
who had run into the woods, with Kokom three paces behind.

"Kinnahauk, please don't ask me that, just take me to
your mother. She understands that I cannot sleep in your
ouke. I—there's David Lavender."

The dark centers of his eyes became blazing pinpoints, the angled planes of his cheekbones taking on a sharper aspect. "And if there were not?" he demanded stiffly.

Knowing she had dealt his pride a blow, Bridget could only admit to the truth. "If there were not, why then I would be honored to share your lodge." *Honored!* Was it honor that caused her heart to beat faster whenever she caught sight of this man? Was it honor that made her forget to breathe when he touched her? Afflicted with feelings she was at a loss to understand, she buried her face in his shoulder. "Truly, you seem always to be coming to my rescue," she whispered, praying that he could not read her foolish thoughts. "Kinnahauk, I owe you more than I can ever repay, but I have nothing—no way to thank you for all—" Stealing a glance at the hard set of his handsome young features, she broke off in confusion. His arms tightened painfully around her until she feared she might break.

"You speak of payment," he muttered harshly. "Perhaps I will take this payment you say you owe me!"

Mesmerized, she watched the dark pinpoints expand until they all but eclipsed the gold of his eyes. Her lips parted as her gaze fell to his mouth, a mouth that was beautifully curved for all it uttered such angry words.

As she watched it move closer, a pulse began fluttering somewhere inside her, making it near impossible to breathe. The familiar scent of leather, wood smoke and something that was essentially masculine, essentially Kinnahauk, heightened her senses until her head reeled. Held high in his arms, she lifted her face in the way of a flower seeking the sun.

"What have you done with her *now*, you foolish, impatient boy? Must you forever pluck unripe fruit? Can you not wait for the harvest when it will fall into your waiting hands?"

They had reached the edge of the village, and Sweet Water was hurrying to meet them, scolding every step of the way. Kinnahauk blinked once and then glared down at his small wet burden. "I do not want your thanks, English-woman!" he rasped just low enough so that Sweet Water could not hear. "One day I will take what I want from you!"

Those harsh words were the last ones he spoke to her before practically dumping her inside his mother's *ouke*. Bridget was given a steaming hot beverage made of something not even she could identify.

"To keep away the bad spirits," according to the bustling woman who scrubbed her with warm water well laced with horsemint until she feared she would have no skin left. She was rubbed all over with heated oil, forced to eat until she could eat no more, and then, wrapped in a soft robe of rabbit pelts, she was told to sleep.

As if sleep would find her this night. As if the events of the day were not tumbling over and over in her mind like squirrels at play. Why had she been so foolish as to let herself be trapped between the water and that great, ugly beast, Tukkao?

But more than that, why had Kinnahauk grown so angry when she had tried to thank him? It was not as if the Hatorask knew nothing of courtesy, for they were among the gentlest, most courteous people she had ever known, their manners consisting more of thoughtfulness than of empty phrases.

Perhaps that was it. Instead of simply saying "thank you," she should offer him some gift. She had heard talk aboard ship that those brave explorers who had first come to this place a hundred years before had brought many gifts for the natives as a means of making friends and showing their good faith.

He spoke of taking, but she had nothing to give. Was she not beholden to others for the clothes on her back, for every morsel of food she put into her mouth? Bridget was shaken to realize that she would have given him the night sky filled with stars if be within her power. She would have given him a ship filled with corn and cucurbits to feed his people, and peace of mind to ease the frown that oft cut a furrow between his brows.

There was naught else for it; she must stop making excuses and get herself on to Albemarle. One way or another, no matter how her heart ached at the thought of leaving this place, she must go to David Lavender and commence paying her debt. Marriage was no longer possible. She could no longer tolerate the thought of sharing a marriage bed with a stranger, no matter how sweet his name.

Many who had crossed with her on the *Mallinson* had been indentured, some for two years, some for four, a few even longer. Bridget had no way of knowing the value of one hundred twenty pounds of tobacco, but she was a strong and willing worker, with more talents than many. She would work out her passage, and a bit more to clear her conscience.

Her mind made up, she closed her eyes and sought sleep. Aye, she would repay her debt, and then she would return to Croatoan.

"Return to see Kinnahauk's sons grown tall, his daughters working beside Gray Otter," a nagging voice whispered, causing her eyes to open wide in the darkness.

"'Strewth, I do believe my brain has turned to cheese," she muttered, flopping over onto her belly and willing herself to forget those wicked, wonderful dreams that had tormented her of late.

The sun was shining brightly when Bridget opened her eyes again. She had been awakened by the sound of a familiar voice outside—a voice that brought a familiar flutter to her pulses, a dryness to her mouth.

"Have you seen Gray Otter, my mother? Each time I approach her, she seems to melt away."

"She took the path that leads to the green pond, my son. If you follow after her, you might have your bow ready. I grow weary of oysters and birds and would have fresh venison."

Bridget dressed hurriedly in the buckskin dress Sweet Water had put out for her until her own was rid of salt, dried and softened once more. She tried not to care that Kinnahauk had come to his mother's lodge without once asking if Bridget had suffered from her dunking. She tried not to care that his thoughts had all been for Gray Otter, for after all, that was as it should be. Her own future had been set the day she had signed her name beside that of a certain planter, whether or not she wed him. Just because she had entertained foolish dreams, just because her mind wandered along forbidden paths now and then . . .

Gray Otter would make a good wife for that arrogant young chief, for she was every whit as strong, as stubborn and as maddening as he was. Bridget told herself it mattered naught to her, for once she reached the towns and cities of the colony proper and lived among her own kind, she would quickly forget any foolish notions about golden eyes and sweetly curved lips and hands that held magic in their touch. How on earth had she come by such thoughts?

"Shall I go and turn the sea grass, Sweet Water?" she asked a short while later as she munched on a cold *appone* dipped in dark honey.

"Let the children turn the sea grass. I would go to the ridge for acorns this day, but my knees grow as knotted as the ancient hornbeam tree. Aiee, my gullet was all set for a bowl of *pawcohiccora*."

Bridget knew there was nothing wrong with Sweet Water's knees, nor did she herself care for the dish made of ground and fermented acorns, but if her friend wanted an excuse to sit in the sun and gossip with the other women while she worked on her new moccasins, Bridget would be more than happy to oblige. "Shall I fill your acorn basket then?"

Sweet Water cast her a sly glance. "The wind has stripped the trees bare. You must go deep into the woods, all the way

to the far side of the second ridge, to find the place where
the wind does not reach.'' She smiled her lovely, gap-
toothed smile and selected a large pine-straw basket from
among those that hung just inside the *ouke*. ''Take this one,
and if you find a persimmon tree the opossums have not
robbed, shake it. The sweetest ones will drop into your
hands.''

''Onto my head, more likely. Which path must I take?''
Bridget asked, praying that it would not be the one that led
to the green pond.

''That one.'' Sweet Water pointed in the opposite direction. ''Go past the big toothache tree, through the blackberry thicket, near the place where the fish hawks nest.
That ridge. That path. Walk swiftly, my daughter, for
Kinnahauk has gone for venison. We will feast this night.''

Chapter Sixteen

With a short, distinctive cry, a fish hawk skimmed the tops of the trees, a wriggling trout clutched securely in his talons. Crows scolded, chasing one another from branch to branch, leaping into the air and settling down again as if at a secret signal. Though it was only midday, the winter sun rode low on the horizon as Bridget trudged up the second ridge. Despite the chill, she felt perspiration bead her brow. For all the land seemed so flat, the ridges that meandered through these woods were surprisingly steep.

Bridget skirted the edge of still another pocosin, its tall reeds rustling like parchment, its dark waters choked with lily pads. From a thicket of winter-brown bracken came the sound of some small creature scurrying to hide lest he end up in the cook pot, surrounded by squash and potatoes and savory herbs. Shadows moved across her path as wind swayed the curtains of wild vines that clung to every branch of the tall pines, the graceful bays, the sprawling oaks.

Gaining the top, she paused to catch her breath, delighted to discover that from such a lofty vantage point she could view both the Atlantic Ocean and the Pamlico Sound, or as the Hatorask would have it, the Big Water and the Inland Sea. It struck her for the first time how very isolated and vulnerable was this crooked, splinterlike sliver of land, surrounded on all sides by water as far as the eye could perceive.

She shifted the basket to her other arm and commenced picking her way down the side of the ridge. There was all manner of greenery and even a few small yellow blossoms sheltered in this small Eden, out of the reach of the fiercest winds. It would be a perfect place to grow the tenderest herbs. Oh, for cuttings from her own beds! If she was going to dwell here for any length of time, she must seek to find— But she would *not* be dwelling here, Bridget reminded herself forcefully. There would surely be a place on David Lavender's land where she could cultivate potherbs as well as medicinal ones, mayhap selling the surplus to those whose thumbs were not so green as her own. The notion had merit, she told herself, eager to get on with purchasing her freedom.

Halfway down the hillside, she paused. Was that the cheeping of the fish hawk again or the sound of voices? Canting her head, she listened until she heard it once more. A woman's voice? Mayhap someone had fallen or stumbled into a honey tree aswarm with bees, for surely that was the cry of a mortal in pain.

Sweeping aside a curtain of vines, Bridget felt the air leave her lungs as surely as if she had run into a large, hard fist. The basket fell unheeded and rolled away, coming to rest in a bed of partridgeberry. Pain seared her with its white-hot flames, as, unable to look away, she stared in disbelief.

Even in the throes of passion, Gray Otter's sharp voice was distinctive. Those were unmistakably her legs wrapped around the lean waist of the man astride her, for no other woman wore moccasins bleached and headed with the wild lily. And surely the shell bracelet on the wrist of the hand that cupped that proud dark head belonged to Gray Otter, for Bridget had seen it on her many times.

The man. Inevitably Bridget's gaze moved to his broad, sweat-polished back and powerful arms before straying downward to the fiercely pumping buttocks. How oddly pale they were in the place usually covered by his tail clout, she thought distractedly. His face hidden in the throat of the woman beneath him, he was completely unconscious of all save her.

For an endless moment Bridget continued to stare at him—at the copper arm band, at the toed-in moccasins that bore the shape of his long, narrow feet well marked on their bottoms. Cool sunlight set blue highlights to dancing in his dark hair, hair that had been released from its usual bondage to flow about his shoulders.

Suddenly he stiffened. From his throat came a long, guttural exclamation, and then he slumped over his mate. As if the sound of his triumphant cry had released her limbs, Bridget spun away, battering her way through the vines. Eyes blinded by tears, she was not even aware when she strayed from the narrow path. Branches whipped at her, but she fought free and stumbled on. Briars tore at her flesh, roots caught at her feet, and still she ran heedlessly, cutting across trail after trail.

Fragments of incoherent thoughts bedeviled her as she fled. She heard Kinnahauk's voice asking, *Have you seen Gray Otter, my mother?*

Sweet Water's reply sounded strangely mocking to her now. *Follow after her, follow after her!*

Once more she heard Gray Otter's voice taunting her. *I will be Kinnahauk's first wife, useless white-eye woman!*

"How *could* he!" Bridget cried, the words lost between sobs. Inviting her to share his mat, claiming the witch mark on her brow somehow tied her fate to his, yet all the while he was panting after that—that female viper! Only yesterday he had held her in his arms and gazed at her lips as if he would touch them with his, and now he met with that sharp-tongued woman so that he could bury his lustful flesh in hers, as if he had never asked Bridget to share his lodge, to join him on his sleeping mat!

"Ooohh," Bridget howled as shock gave way to fury and fury to inexpressible pain.

She had been right all along—they were worlds apart! She was an Englishwoman whose grandfather had been a clergyman, whose father had been a well-respected game-keeper, whose mother had been beloved by all who knew her until . . .

While *he*, she thought angrily, throwing herself on a bed of pine straw, too weary and lost and miserable to go far-ther—*he* was nothing but a rutting animal! A savage who roamed the wilderness in naught but a scrap of leather, brandishing knives and uttering curses in that heathen tongue of his, sowing his seed on any willing field with no more thought than a—a buck rabbit! First wives and sec-ond wives, indeed! Fourth and fifth, as well, more likely, for what would such people know of love and faithfulness and cleaving only unto each other?

Would that she could cleave his scalp with a hatchet!

She scrubbed her eyes dry, only to burst into another spate of weeping. How could he hurt her in such a way? Why did it feel as if her heart were breaking?

She had thought him her greatest friend, and he had be-trayed her trust. It was a sneaky, wicked thing to do, res-cuing her when she would have washed back out to sea with the next tide, carrying her in his arms when she was too weak to walk and delivering her to his mother to be cared for as one of their own. How could he do all that and yet betray her this way?

And does a true friend not have title to his own life, to seek pleasure where he will? The question formed in her mind before she could stop it. In all honesty she was forced to admit that she had no claim on him. It was not as if they were bespoken, for what would a savage know of such things?

Lying facedown on the ground, she wept until she was drained of tears, cleansing her body with a few deep, shud-dering sighs. Gradually she became aware that the sun no longer shone down upon her. She would soon grow cold, yet she did not look forward to confessing to Sweet Water that not only had she failed to find the acorns, she had lost the basket, as well.

Still lying on her stomach, her face cradled in her arms, Bridget began gathering her resolve for the long trek back to the village. She sat up, brushed away the pine straw and smoothed her hair back from her damp face, dimly aware that she must find a stream and bathe away the signs of her distress, or Sweet Water would badger her until she confessed to more than a lost basket.

How could she speak the real reason for her misery when she scarce knew it herself? It could hardly be the thing called lovesickness, for how could she be in love with a man so different from herself? Such a thing as love scarce happened among her own people, for all their sweet words and proclamations. Need was behind most matches, greed behind the rest, all save a few, and even in those few, the sweet words and languishing looks seldom lasted once a woman grew ungainly with child.

Shivering as the heat of emotion drained away, she drew up her knees, wrapping her arms about them. It had turned cold and damp, for all it had been so pleasant when she had set out. Or mayhap she had reached the windward side of the ridge.

Taking note of her surroundings for the first time, Bridget saw nothing at all that looked familiar—no landmark tree or pond. Could she somehow have wandered off the trail? In such a wilderness, without so much as a decent cart track, 'twould not be hard to do. Even the birds had fallen silent.

Bridget sniffled one last time. With the back of her arm, she smeared her tears across her cheeks. Time to forget what she had seen and set about finding her way back to the village. On the morrow, she must make arrangements to leave this place once and for all, before her mind became further afflicted with fanciful notions.

Later she would wonder what had alerted her, for there had been no sound, not so much as a whisper, yet she had

suddenly sensed that she was no longer alone. A deer, perhaps, resenting the intrusion into its realm? Surely nothing
more frightful. She had heard tales of the English coming
in their shallops to take oysters and clams from the waters
near the inlets. She had even heard of a few Spanish who
had been shipwrecked and made their way ashore for a
time, yet they would hardly be wandering about in the
woods.

She had heard still more tales of bloodthirsty men from
other towns who came silently in the night in their canoes,
robbing, raping and slaying for the joy of it, but according
to Soconme, that had not happened for many years. Unlike the towns and settlements on the mainland, Croatoan,
by its very location, was guarded from all save the elements.

Yet her scalp prickled. She could *feel* the presence of
another person, could almost hear him breathing. Every
muscle in her body tensed as she gathered herself to jump
and run.

"Bridgetabbott, why are you alone so far away from the
village? It is not wise, for there are many paths. You could
lose yourself."

Stunned, Bridget twisted around, staring at the man who
stood at the edge of the clearing, his coppery body blending with the trunks of the pine trees. How many times had
her eyes passed over him without seeing him?

"Kinnahauk?" she whispered. Had he come to mock
her, then? To crow over his prowess? To show her that he
no longer had need of her to share his sleeping mat?

"Why do you look at me with round eyes? Do you not
know your old friend?" He stepped out from among the
shadows, and Bridget scrambled to her feet and backed
away.

Seeing him there, so magnificent with his golden eyes and
his proud bearing, the pain returned unexpectedly, and she
fought it with the only weapon she possessed—anger.
"Friend? I would not call you friend!"

Kinnahauk was puzzled. He had cut across the base of the second ridge on his way back to the village, but hearing the sound of weeping, he had eased the buck from his shoulders and crept closer. He had stared in disbelief at the sight of his *oquio* lying on the ground, far removed from any of the well-known paths. It had taken but a moment to discover that she was alone and crying as if something pained her greatly.

Yet how could this be? He had seen her frightened, fevered, her skin assaulted by all manner of thorns and spurs. He had seen her when her poor head was so bedeviled with pain that she held it between her hands and rocked back and forth, moaning softly. Yet she had not wept.

He moved closer. Watching her eyes grow wide as if in terror, he saw her back into the prickly trunk of a devil's walking stick. "I would know what troubles you so, Bridgetabbott," he said in the tone he used to soothe a wild animal.

"You *know* what troubles me," Bridget cried. She yanked her skirt from the clutches of the thorny tree, heard the sound of tearing doeskin and bit her lip in frustration. "No, it doesn't trouble me, it disgusts me!" she corrected, and then with a sigh, she shook her head. "No, not even that, for it matters naught to me who you tumble. I'll be gone from this place the moment I can make arrangements." Hearing her own rash promise, she vowed that one way or another, she would keep her word.

Kinnahauk had approached quietly until he was almost within reach. He was deeply concerned, yet he knew he must allay her fears before he sought answers to his questions. Why was she here? Why was she speaking as if they were strangers? How could she speak of "tumbling" in such a way? Had her unexpected dunking in cold water brought back her fever? Surely it must be that, for why else would she look upon him as if he were a drunken dog who preyed on women?

"The sun walks down quickly. The moon will hide her face behind the clouds this night. I would not leave you to find your way back to the village alone." Her skin was prickled with gooseflesh, her eyes still swollen from weeping. Kinnahauk's arms ached to hold her. He would share the warmth of his body with her; he would bathe her face with his kisses, tasting her salt tears as if they were the sweet nectar of the honey vine blossom.

"I can follow the path. I found my way to—I found my way here well enough," she amended quickly, unwilling to speak of the place where she had seen him with Gray Otter.

"The trail that leads from this place is used only by the muskrats. It will carry you to their mud *oukes*, where you can ask the chief among them how to find the village of Kinnahauk."

Bridget's lip trembled, and she bit it and struggled for control. It should not hurt this way, truly it should not! She must not allow herself to care, for there could be no future in caring for such a man.

Moving with the speed of a striking snake, Kinnahauk caught her to him, holding her tightly until her struggles ceased. "Now you will tell me what has made you so angry, my small rabbit. We are friends. We are more than friends, for you wear my—"

"Don't *say* that!" Bridget protested. She struck out wildly, only to have him capture her hand and tuck it under his arm. "I wear only the mark of a witch, and that means nothing, for I am no witch! Look for your mark on the body of some other woman—perhaps you brand them all so that you can take your pick! I'm surprised that Gray Otter doesn't wear your mark where all can see. Where did you brand her? On her buttocks? On her—" She wrenched herself against his arms, only to be squeezed until she thought her ribs would crack.

"What is this you speak of, woman? Have you been tasting the *yau ejau*? What is this about Gray Otter?" He sounded truly puzzled.

Recklessly Bridget rushed on. "I do wonder how you could leave her alone so soon after—"

"Leave her alone?"

Bridget twisted, succeeding only in tightening his hold. Tears she had thought finished began again, and she kicked out, but with her soft moccasins, the blow did little damage other than bruising her toe. "How can you go from her to me this way? I *hate* the smell of her on your skin! Truly I hate you as I have hated no man on God's green earth! I wish I had never come to this terrible place!"

Crying uncontrollably, she felt him lift her up and carry her a few steps, where he lowered her to the ground out of reach of the wind. She thought longingly of escape, but then the chance was lost, for he was beside her, gathering her onto his lap and cradling her head in the warm hollow of his shoulder.

"Ah, my small yellow flower, please do not weep so, for it pains my heart to see you so unhappy," he crooned, swaying with her as he would a small child.

"Then your heart must b-be the size of a pumpion, to have room for so many."

Kinnahauk nodded slowly, a motion that Bridget felt rather than observed. "This is true," he said thoughtfully, eliciting a fresh burst of tears.

Sliding her from his thighs, Kinnahauk eased her down and then settled next to her, lying on his side with one arm over her, holding her close. And then he sat up again. "It is a foolish hunter who would lie down with a quiver of arrows strapped to his back," he said, an undercurrent of humor in his deep, rich voice.

Exhausted by the surfeit of emotions, Bridget lifted swollen eyelids to see him ease the strap from his shoulder and lay his arrow sac aside. At the same time she noted that his hair was neatly braided, the ends carefully bound with strips of red-and-white dyed rawhide.

She blinked and tried to remember. . . .

Kinnahauk lay down once more, gathering her to him. "What great sadness sends the rain flowing from your storm cloud eyes, Bridgetabbott? If it is within my power to heal this wound, you have only to ask."

"Where have you come from, Kinnahauk?" she ventured, one hand absently tracing the distinctive tattoo just below the base of his throat. How oddly similar they were, his mark and hers—one the reverse of the other.

"Tukkao carried me along the shore toward Chacandepeco. From there I followed the tracks of a large buck into the woods, trailing him until I came upon him browsing near the green pond. My mother will have fresh venison."

The green pond. Bridget had only the haziest idea where it lay, for the trails twined and twisted so, there was no way of telling in which direction one traveled. "Did you see anyone there?" Her fingers left the tattoo and strayed over the firm flesh.

"Yes, I saw Gray Otter. I spoke to her sharply for her misbehavior yesterday, but I do not expect her to heed my words, for she is willful. Kokom will have trouble with that one when he takes her to his *ouke*."

Kokom. It had been Kokom and not Kinnahauk who lay with Gray Otter! Relief washed over Bridget in great waves. Her fingers curled into his chest, brushing over one of his flat dark nipples and causing it to harden instantly. "Kokom," she whispered aloud. "I do believe it will not be long before he takes her to his lodge, for not long ago I saw them together, and they looked—ah, pleased."

Understanding came to Kinnahauk, swelling inside him like a ripe seedpod. So that was the way of it—she had mistaken Kokom for himself, and it had angered her. No woman could be so distressed without reason. Perhaps he would not sleep alone after this, though he must be patient

for as long as it took to tame her if he would have her come
to him willingly. If he took her body before she offered
herself freely, he could never be certain he held her heart,
as well.

Kinnahauk grinned. "I would not prepare for the wedding feast so soon, Bridgetabbott. It is our way for a man
and a maid to lie freely with each other until the heart is
given. After that, there must be no more straying, for there
is no honor in taking that which belongs to another. Kokom is ready. Gray Otter will play her fish for a time before she closes her net."

Bridget allowed herself to be gathered close to the
warmth of Kinnahauk's body, and when one of his legs
covered hers, she felt a surge of heat streak through her.
"Then Gray Otter is still—uh—free to share any mat she
wishes?"

With her head tucked beneath his chin, Kinnahauk
smiled to himself. "Does that bother you, my *oquio*?"

"No. Yes. Truly, it's no concern of mine." Feeling a stick
beneath her hip, she squirmed to ease the pressure and was
swiftly made aware of another, one that pressed the soft
hollow of her belly with relentless masculine force. She
swallowed hard and made an effort to remain exceedingly
still.

The wind soughed in the treetops overhead. The light was
fast waning, and soon it would be difficult to see the trail.
One part of her wanted to remain here forever, held in the
arms of this strong, gentle man, this magnificent creature
who brought such strange and wonderful feelings to her
that she even dreamed of them.

Kinnahauk found her breast. Through the covering of
doeskin, she felt the heat of his palm, felt her own flesh
swell and harden in response. One of his hands caressed the
back of her neck, and she writhed against him, causing his
heartbeat to drum visibly in his throat. Tilting her head, she
touched the place with the tip of her tongue, tasting for the
first time the sweetness of his flesh.

His response was stunning. His arms tightened about her, his man part leaped, eagerly probing beneath the flat of his tail clout, and he groaned. With one hand he lifted the apron, leaving only the soft pouch to contain his aching male flesh. In all honor he could not take her until David Lavender no longer stood between them. Still he could not bear to release her. What harm could there be in prolonging this sweet agony for a moment more before he led her back to the village?

Stroking down her slender thigh to the fringe of her skirt, he drew it upward until it was caught between them. Swiftly he yanked it free and pressed himself to her, seeing in his mind's eye the golden floss that nestled his spear, sheathed though it still was.

There would come a time when he would bury his spear in the sweetest sheath of all. Soon. Soon . . .

Bridget was panting, twisting in an effort to ease the intolerable ache that burned inside her. Never had she known such sweet anguish, never such a fierce craving! "Ah, please," she whimpered. "I don't know how to make it stop!"

There were many ways, and Kinnahauk knew them well, for he had burned and quenched the fire many times since he had come to manhood. Yet never had he burned so hotly! Could such a one as she put out this raging fire that robbed him of his senses?

"I could make it stop, my golden blossom, but on the morrow, you would not thank me."

"*Please*, make it stop, for it drives me wild!"

Closing his eyes briefly, Kinnahauk allowed the struggle between flesh and wisdom to proceed for a moment more, knowing there would be no victory this night, for the time was not yet arrived. Then he opened his eyes and gazed down on the small, flushed face of this woman who had stolen into his heart and made it her own. Her lips were swollen from crying. He had yet to taste her, for he had somehow sensed right from the beginning that, like the sweetness of honey, once he partook of her own special taste, he would seek it again and again.

She would own his soul. If he took her now, only to have her go to the man who had paid her bride-price, a part of him would die. He must go slowly. Honor must be upheld, the proper payments settled. And even then she must come to him willingly.

His lips settled on hers as lightly as the wings of a butterfly, brushing softly with a teasing touch. Then they grew still, caught in the thrall of a spell more powerful than any *shaman* could cast. His lips parted. They slid over the moist, gently curved surface, exploring, tasting, moving as cautiously as a hummingbird in search of nectar.

And then, like the hummingbird, he plunged. Spearing her with his tongue, he parted her lips and sought the secret depths of her sweetness, even as his hand moved between their two striving bodies. He eased himself off her, aching with the loss, yet he would not leave her wanting when he could give her the ease she sought.

Restlessly she moved against his hand, instinctively seeking that which she hardly understood. Kinnahauk felt his heart touched in a way that he had never before experienced, to know that it was within his power to bring her a magnificent gift.

She was a maiden still, his *oquio*. Had he not been promised such a one? The night when she had lain with him on his mat, he had touched the veil and known that before he could tear it away, he must win her trust in such a way that the pleasure would overcome the pain.

He cupped the soft mound, allowing one of his fingers to settle between the petals of her womanhood. Gently he began to stroke, even as his tongue stroked hers. Soon she was writhing, and he allowed her to set the pace. When she began to whimper, bucking against his hand, he moved down and suckled her breast through her shift, wishing she was lying bare beneath him, her sweet breasts beading to his touch.

In agony he braced himself not to give in to temptation, for he could have taken her at this moment, and she would have thanked him for it. But when the morrow came and her flesh grew cool once more, would she thank him then? Or would she again throw down the name of Davidlavender between them, a barrier against which he had no ready defense?

She collapsed, panting in his arms, her face flushed with the sweet color of passion. Kinnahauk gazed down in sorrow at his own thrusting steed, knowing it must suffer yet another night of loneliness. If he were of another tribe, he might have taken her as his slave and kept her until he tired of her, selling her to another brave when he was done.

Aiee, it was the hateful strain of English blood that flowed in his veins! He could not look on her as a slave. When he took this woman for the first time, he would have her spread her thighs wide in eagerness for him. Only then could he plant his seed, knowing that together they would nurture his sons.

Had he not been promised as much in his vision-quest? She would give him a *quasis* who would lead his people long after his own spirit had slipped away to fly with the white brant.

Chapter Seventeen

The pungent scent of tobacco drifted high on the still evening air. From inside the *oukes* came the murmur of sleepy children. Soconme had labored long in the *ouke* of old Tumme Wawawa to prepare her spirit to fly away. Many spirits had joined the flock of white brant that returned to these islands each year after the Moon of the Falling Leaves. Soon there would be no more. The white-eye would spread over this island with his *noppinjure*, laying waste to great swales of grass so that no other animals could exist. Many tall trees would die to create his ugly *oukes*. With his thunder sticks, he would kill many deer, eating few, wasting much, taking neither hide nor bone nor sinew. The white-eye did not save the meat by drying or smoking, but slaughtered more when their bellies grew empty.

That time would come. In his heart Soconme hoped that when it did, his own spirit would be free to fly away on borrowed wings. He could not live under the rule of the white chief called Charles who sent his people across the Big Water to take that which was not theirs.

"The ways of the Great Kishalamaquon are strange," he said ruminatively. "For the spirits of *webtau* old ones—" he held up five gnarled fingers "—he gives us back but *num-perre.*" He folded back three, leaving two. These he studied as if to divine the purpose of such an unfair trade.

"Yet we have done his bidding. We have made welcome his lesser children with their pale skins and their strange ways."

"Before the Moon of the Great Wind we will have three new spirits, old friend, for Many Toes carries the child of Face of a Horse," said Sweet Water.

"The child will wither unripened on the vine."

"Aiee!" she wailed softly, covering her face with her hands. "Do not say such a thing!"

"Through the sacred smoke, I asked the Voice that Speaks Silently if the spirit of old Tumme Wawawa would return to us to walk in the moccasins of Many Toes's child. The Voice says Tumme Wawawa will not walk with us once more until the time of our great-grandchildren. The Voice says Many Toes's child will soon leave her mother's body, for no spirit has joined to her flesh. Many Toes will follow. My medicine will not hold them here. This the Voice told me to be true."

Sweet Water gazed stoically out over the still water. A streak of light along the horizon cast its silver reflection. All above and below was dark, for the clouds had crept up from the land of the Mattamuskeets. Soon the rains would come.

"Once I thought my son would take Gray Otter to his *ouke* to bear me many fine grandsons," she said, following her own thoughts. "She is a strong woman. She would have strong babies."

"Gray Otter stands tall, like the pine tree. She is of much value, yet she would not stand before the powerful winds to come. Such a one will break before she will bend."

"She does not like *Waurraupa Shaman*."

"You speak the truth." The old man nodded slowly.

"The young *waurraupa* woman would be a good daughter to me, for there is great kindness in her heart. She has suffered much, yet her suffering has not turned inward to eat at her soul. Her ways are more like the ways of our people than those of her own."

The old medicine chief drew on his foul-smelling pipe and nodded thoughtfully. "Your son is blind to the fire mark on her brow, seeing only the color of her skin."

"My son thinks of his father, an honorable man and a great chief, who was killed by the pale-skins's sickness. He thinks of his young brother, Chicktuck, who was slain by a pale-skin's thunder stick and brought to me with no face at all. The pain has burrowed deep inside his heart where it no longer shows, but it does not go away."

"Have patience, old woman. Kinnahauk is no stranger to pain. Did he not prove his manhood by walking the storm when he was but twelve winters, fasting from the first signs, binding his eyes and baring his body to the storm gods? Did he not find his way alone from the Inlet of Woccon to the Inlet of Chacandepeco through angry tides that covered all but the highest hills? Did he not escape the weapons hurled by the wind gods, who destroyed many trees in their effort to strike him down and made the waters to rise up and walk upon the land? I say to you that your son is stronger than the white tide that approaches. He will not bow down before the white chief Charles who has stolen our lands for his brothers by making his mark on a piece of skin. At Kinnahauk's side will stand *Waurraupa Shaman*, for she is like the oak whose roots go deep, whose boughs are sturdy, yet giving."

"She is but a small thing, no bigger than a *week-wonne*."

"The *waurraupa* shaman is stronger than the winds that will shape her. This Kinnahauk knows. The Voice has told him many things about the young white-eye woman. His body turns to her as the yellow *wittapare* flower turns to the sun. Soon his heart will follow."

"Aiee," Sweet Water moaned softly. "My grandsons will be half bloods."

"Better a babe that is part Hatorask than no babe at all. Too many spirits have flown, too few have chosen to return to us. Kinnahauk must plant his seed before it grows too old to sprout. I will speak to him of this.''

The wind changed direction during the night, clearing away the rain clouds and sending fish into the nets. Bridget, her fingers hooked in the gills of a croaking fish, stared at the sails that appeared off the island to the north of Croatoan.

"Wintsohore," grunted Long Ears. Bridget knew the word meant Englishmen.

"Tontarinte?" asked old Too-Cona, who had lost his sight when he had stared at the sun for five days after his family had died of the weeping-skin disease.

"Nam-mee," replied Kinnahauk.

Two Englishmen, Bridget translated. Or was it three? Sits There had been teaching her to count, but she always confused the words for two and three.

Bridget hardly noticed when the other women began slipping away into the woods. She carried her scored and gutted fish to the smoking rack, moved a branch of green bay farther into the fire and returned, washing the slime from her fingers with wet sand and water and rubbing them with the crushed leaves of the spicy waxberry bush to rid them of the smell.

At the edge of the water, the men stood silently. Bridget watched as the small shallop tacked cautiously across the shifting shoals that made Chacandepeco Inlet too treacherous for all but the smallest vessels. As it slowly beat its way along the shoreline, she found her attention straying to the men who watched its approach. There were two sets of broad shoulders, two sets of narrow hips and long, muscular legs that were much alike. Kinnahauk and Kokom. Both wore copper bands high on their right arms, although Kinnahauk's was wider and bore some sort of design.

It was no wonder she had mistaken the one for the other, seeing only his back. Then, too, Bridget reminded herself, he'd been kneeling at the time. More or less, she amended, hot color suffusing her face as she recalled the scene that had sent her fleeing from that small sheltered Eden.

She darted a look at the flap of leather that covered Kinnahauk's buttocks. Would he be paler there, too? The first time she had gone with the women to bathe she had been surprised that they were much lighter beneath their shifts, though still much darker than her own pale skin. They had marveled over her own coloration, making much of the hair that covered her privities, their own being plucked.

At first Bridget had been mortified, having been taught modesty from the cradle, yet she could find no evil in the innocent merriment of the women. In their own fashion they were more modest than her own kind, for their dress was cut for comfort and usage, and never to tantalize the eye of a man with a narrow waist or a glimpse of bosom.

What would the fashions in Albemarle be? More like those of Little Wheddborough than London, she hoped, or else she'd make a poor showing in naught but moccasins, a buckskin shawl and a threadbare gown. David Lavender would most probably turn away in disgust, which was just as well, as she had no intent of wedding the man.

Shading her eyes, Bridget watched the shallop's cautious approach. Kinnahauk had offered her one excuse after another each time she had asked to leave Croatoan. If these men would carry her to their own town, why then she would make her own way to Albemarle and settle her debt once and for all. She had been sorely troubled of late, her feelings torn twixt going and staying. She must listen to her head, for surely it was wiser than her heart.

She had taken but three steps when Kinnahauk turned and saw her. "Go quickly, woman! Hide yourself in the woods!"

"But I would—"

"Go!"

"No!"

Closing the distance between them, he scooped her up and slung her over his shoulder, carrying her into the woods, where he dumped her unceremoniously on her feet before Gray Otter.

The women glanced up. They were seated on the ground gossiping idly as they worked at twisting limber vine into rope or softening dried sinew, the children playing a quiet game with acorn caps and a circle drawn in the sand.

"Stay here with the women and children until I return for you. Speak only in whispers or be silent." And then he was gone, leaving Bridget furious at having missed her chance to escape and embarrassed at having been treated in such a manner before her friends.

"Why am I—?" she began, only to be shushed by Gray Otter.

"Kinnahauk must think he can bargain for you the better if he keeps you hidden, for truly you are not much to look at," she whispered.

"Bargain for me? For my passage, you mean?"

Gray Otter smiled, her dark eyes glinting in malicious delight. "And the return passage of a bushel of corn or a fine sharp blade."

"He would *trade me*?" Bridget exclaimed, forgetting the need for caution. Fury gave way to an inexplicable ache beneath her breast.

Sweet Water struggled to hoist her small round form up from the ground. "Ho, Bridget, perhaps my son did not explain to you that—"

Gray Otter broke in to finish the statement. "That if the English dogs knew you were here, they would think you a captive and take it as an excuse to wipe out our village."

"No! You only say that to hurt me." Bridget turned to Sweet Water, seeking the truth. Gray Otter had a way of wounding with smiling words; she would not listen to her.

But the old woman nodded sadly. "She says the truth, my daughter. Not all English are so wicked, for some have shown our people kindness, even seeking to share their gods with us, yet even the noblest of them think us no more than the animals of the forest, to be tamed for their use or driven from the land."

Bridget sank down to the ground, clasping her arms across her breasts. Gradually the talk among the other women resumed, with even Gray Otter joining in the soft laughter as they teased Sits There about the lovesick brave who followed her around like a tame pelican waiting to be tossed a fish.

The next few days were gray, even though the sun shone brightly. Kinnahauk had gone with the men in the shallop, who had come from Corrituck Banks seeking water to replenish their supply, which had leaked from faulty casks. They had made no provisions to catch the recent rain.

"Kinnahauk will show them how to find good water in the ground," Kokom told her when she sought him out. "They see our forest. They know we have good water. The water on the other side of Chacandepeco is not so fine."

"Then it's the water they were seeking, not an English captive."

Kokom's smile was sad. "Gray Otter spoke falsely. She sees the way Kinnahauk looks at you, and it poisons her mind. She is not a wicked person, it is only this wrong feeling she has for Kinnahauk that makes her act so."

"She loves him," said Bridget, wondering why the words tasted so bitter on her tongue. "She told me she would wed him soon."

Kokom's eyes blazed. "Paugh! She is foolish. It is Kokom she needs. I have loved her since we were children together. Am I not as great a hunter and a fisher as Kinnahauk? Paugh! It is only because Kinnahauk is chief that she will not come to my *ouke* as my woman."

Reaching out, Bridget placed her hand on his, searching for a way to offer him comfort. He was all that he claimed and more, and any woman would be proud to have him for a husband, she told him.

"Come, ride with me, Bridget, for I need the comfort of a friend, yet I cannot say these things to Kinnahauk."

With her newly developed skill, which never failed to delight her, Bridget whistled for the mare she called her own. Soon they were galloping along the sandy shore, past the tall wooded dunes that marked the end of the forest, and out onto the low flat plain that stretched to the distant woods that lay to the south and west.

They talked for a long time that day, and Bridget tried to distract him by telling him of her own home and of London, where she had twice gone with her father when she was a small child. She did not speak of her mother's murder, nor of her own last trip to London to await trial for witchcraft.

Kokom listened, but it soon grew obvious that his mind was elsewhere. He spoke of Gray Otter with longing and frustration, and Bridget searched for a way to help him.

"She shares my sleeping mat, yet she will not come to my *ouke* as my woman as long as there is a chance that Kinnahauk will take her for one of his wives." He smote his thigh with a fist. "I need a wife, Bridget! I would have sons before I grow too old to prepare them for the name-quest and the vision-quest and the walking of the storm."

As they rode their horses back toward the village, Bridget sighed in sympathy. She knew of this last rite, for old Soconme had told her of the ordeals a young man must endure to prove his strength, not to the others so much as to himself, so he would know no fear in the face of great dangers. He had told her that Kinnahauk's storm had been the greatest storm in any man's memory.

"Speak truly, Bridget, am I not as handsome as Kinnahauk? Am I not as brave?"

Even as she agreed that he was indeed as handsome and as brave, Bridget knew the words were not true. No man could be as handsome or as brave as Kinnahauk. "You play the buffoon, Kokom. We all laugh at your antics. Gray Otter, too. Perhaps she cannot take you seriously because she thinks you're jesting with her. You must seek to show her that you are serious in your feelings.''

Near the village, they slipped down from their mounts. Kokom slapped both beasts on the rumps, sending them off to join the other horses, who ran free until summoned by a distinctive whistle.

"You have helped me much, Bridget. I will do as you say. No more pranks. With sad eyes and a long face, I will seek to prove my love to Gray Otter." But even as he spoke, laughter danced in his eyes, for his was a merry disposition.

Bridget's attention was caught by a movement at the edge of the clearing. Gray Otter, her expression stormy, turned away and disappeared into the trees.

She turned to Kokom. "Not *too* long a face, my friend, for I think Gray Otter needs your cheerful spirit more than she knows.''

Chapter Eighteen

It was unlike Kinnahauk to ride Tukkao to a lather, but when Gray Otter had told him upon his return the following day that Bridget and Kokom had spent much time together, and even now were riding toward the lower woods, away from prying eyes and wagging tongues, he had not waited even to greet his mother.

It was no great distance to the lower woods. He had walked it many times as a youth, hunting wildfowl that fed in the shallow bays. The land was not a good place for a village, for it was low and often flooded, yet it was a pleasing place, being sweet with the breath of many cedar trees.

Suddenly he shifted his weight, checking the speed of his stallion as he saw the two mounted figures some distance ahead near the shore. There was no mistaking that flow of golden hair, even from a distance. To think that his true friend, who was blood of his blood, could so betray him!

With a hardening of his features, he touched Tukkao's flanks with soft-shod heels. Not until he was nearly upon them did he give voice to the ancient war cry that had been used by his people as they made their way through the lands of many enemies in the Time Before the Grandfathers.

The two guilty ones moved apart. Kokom's mount danced backward, but Bridget could only stare, her eyes widening in fear when it seemed that Kinnahauk would ride them down.

"Ho, Kinnahauk, what has passed that you—?" Kokom began.

That was as far as he got. From Tukkao's broad back, Kinnahauk launched himself at the other man, knocking him to the ground. Kokom's horse screamed and shied away, while Tukkao rose up on his powerful haunches, pawing the air.

Red Wind danced sideways, tossing her head, and Bridget clutched her mane, too startled to do more than cling. What had happened? Was this another of the strange Hatorask rituals designed to prove a man's worth? If so, it was barbaric! The two lifelong friends were now on their feet in the soft sand, crouched and circling, their knives glinting in the sunlight.

There was a kind of deadly beauty in the dance, and Bridget stared in horrified fascination. Kinnahauk was clearly dominant, his face a mask of vengeance. Kokom laughed in an attempt to break the unnatural tension, but the laughter faded quickly when Kinnahauk feinted with his blade.

"What great wrong have I done Kinnahauk that he seeks my scalp?" asked the younger man.

Kinnahauk snarled. With lightning speed he moved in. Kokom tripped on a root, going down, and Kinnahauk followed, landing astride him. Then suddenly, Kokom's blade flashed upward. Bridget screamed as a fine crimson line appeared on Kinnahauk's chest.

The sound of her cry was too much for her skittish mare. Red Wind bolted. Bridget felt herself bouncing like a sack of flour. It was all she could do to hang on, for there was no saddle, no bridle, naught save her own voice and the pressure of her thighs to guide the beast.

The mare was beyond guidance. Terrified, Bridget felt herself begin to slide, and she snatched at the long, tangled mane. She struggled to regain her balance, but she was no match for the short-barreled mare, who was determined to rid herself of her clumsy burden. Knowing she was falling, Bridget tried to jump clear, but there was no time. One moment she was clinging to the damp, slick side of the panic-driven animal, the next moment she was in among the wildly flying hooves.

She landed awkwardly. Before she could roll away, she was struck a glancing blow on the back of the head. There was a single moment of blinding brilliance, then the light winked out like a snuffed candle, and she was aware of only the muffled thunder of hooves, which became mixed in her mind with the muffled thunder of the surf. And then there was nothing.

After a time she felt herself being borne along on the turbulent surface of the sea. Was she back aboard the *Andrew C. Mallinson*, then? Or had she been set adrift again, to be tossed about like an empty cask?

Whispers. Were the voices in her head? She was afraid to open her eyes, afraid to discover that she was alone, cast up on the shore of some strange wilderness. Had that really happened to her once before, or had she only dreamed it?

"No, my mother, she will remain here." The voice was familiar. Deep and resonant, it made her feel warm all over.

"What if she does not recover? Such a blow to the head could have robbed her of her senses. Would you burden yourself with a witless wife? Take her to my *ouke*, my son. If her mind returns to her body, then I will give her back to you. If it does not, I will care for her as if she were my own newborn babe."

"Would you burden yourself with a witless daughter, my mother?"

"A daughter is no burden, be she witless or wise, for a loving heart knows no such matter."

"You speak true, my mother," said the familiar voice. "The heart knows only that it is compelled to love. I will care for her here. You may send Soconme to my *ouke*."

"You will not—"

Bridget made a small sound, and Sweet Water's words went unfinished. Mother and son stared down at her so intently that Bridget closed her eyes. She struggled to sort out the meaning of all she had heard. Had Sweet Water really offered to care for her like a daughter, not knowing whether or not she would ever recover? She could hardly comprehend such generosity. They had spoken of love, but surely Kinnahauk had not meant...

No, of course not. There were many kinds of love, and many words with subtle differences. Liking. Loving. Caring. She was constantly making Sits There laugh by confusing one word with another in the Hatorask tongue, calling a panther skin a rat, or the wind a fish.

Sweet Water knelt beside her, concern in her large dark eyes. "I would take you to my own *ouke*, child, and care for you there, but this son of mine tells me you are not to be moved from this place. If you say it, I will have Kokom remove you. Kinnahauk is my son. He is my chief, and his word is valued in council meetings, yet I say to you there are times when no man is fit to make judgments."

Bridget's gaze was drawn to the tall man who stood silently near the opening of the *ouke*. Smoke from the bed of coals near the center masked his expression, but it did not hide the thin red line that crossed his chest. Dried blood. Blood drawn by the knife of his friend and hers. What had happened to turn Kinnahauk against his lifelong friend?

"Where is Kokom? What have you done with him?"

The golden eyes seemed to blaze with light at her question. Kinnahauk turned to his mother. "Go now. I would speak to my woman alone. Say to Soconme that we do not need him at this time. I will come for him if I have need of him."

With a smile that whispered uneasily across Bridget's nerves the way a light breeze whispers to the surface of the water, Sweet Water ducked under the flap, leaving them alone. Bridget looked after her longingly, wanting to call her back, knowing it would do no good. Whatever it was that Kinnahauk wished to say to her, he would say it, whether or not she wished to hear it. From the angry look on his face, it must be something dreadful.

She tried to rise. If she must deal with any man's anger, she preferred to be on her feet for the small measure of dignity it afforded her, but she had underestimated her own weakness. Even sitting was too great an effort. Her bones seemed to have turned to water, and every muscle in her body ached. For all she knew, she could be badly injured, not that anyone but Sweet Water seemed to care.

Churlishly she demanded, "What is it? Did I not bring as much in trade as you had hoped? Do you regret keeping me here to fatten me up for market? Take me to Albemarle, then, and ask David Lavender for corn! Not even the poorest farmer expects to receive London prices for his wares without going far from Little Wheddborough."

"*Sehe*, woman! Do not speak until your senses have returned."

"My senses are in wonderful order, you great red savage! 'Twas not I who waved a blade about like some madman, frightening horses with wild whoops and threatening the lives of my friends."

"No, it was *you* who waited until I left this place to spread your thighs for the first man who—"

"Oh, is *that* what I am accused of? And will you brand me with another mark?" Shoving her hair away from her face with an angry gesture, Bridget jabbed her cheek, which was already stained with a patch of angry color that stood out starkly against her pallor. "Here? Or mayhap here?" She touched the other cheek, so furious she was barely able to contain herself. "My brow, as you can plainly see, already bears the mark of my trade. Oh, I have earned many such fine marks, my lord and chief—what an honor 'twill be to have another to add to my collection!"

Kinnahauk saw tears rush to fill the wide gray eyes. Was he so very fearsome that she could not look on him without weeping? He saw her pale lips tremble, and his heart tightened into a painful knot. Why was it that he could do nothing right where this woman was concerned? He knew many ways a man could bring smiles to a woman's face and joy to her body, yet with this woman who had been sent to him by the Great Kishalamaquon, he could do nothing right. If he held back, it was wrong. If he pressed forward, it was also wrong.

He knelt beside her, steeling himself to ignore the way she flinched from his nearness. Somehow he must make her understand. "We both say things we do not mean, Bridgetabbott. Our worlds are far apart, the ways of your people and mine very different. There are no words in your language for many of the things that have great meaning to my people." Drawing a deep breath, he began the task of claiming what was his. "You have heard me call you *oquio*."

"And rabbit," she said sullenly. "And speckled fawn, and stinking fish keg, and white-eyes, and pale-skin and white witch."

Kinnahauk smiled, and she was struck by the rare beauty of it. "*Waurraupa Shaman*. My people named you the white witch for your skill and your knowledge. It is a name to wear with pride. Hear me now, my own *Waurraupa Shaman*, for I would have you know what is in my heart. When a youth of my people approaches his fifteenth winter, he must seek guidance in those things that will become a part of his life as a man. When the time came for me to go on my vision-quest, I fasted for many days. I anointed my body with sacred oil and walked naked and alone to a high hill where I could look out over the place where two great spirits live beneath the Big Water, each claiming this island for his own. It is a place of much power. There I sat for three days and two nights before the Great Kishalamaquon spoke to me. He said to me that one day a woman would come to me from across the water. He said to me that she would be my *oquio*, an untouched maiden chosen to receive the seed of my body. He said to me that I would know her by the fire mark on her brow. He said to me that from this union would be born a *quasis*—a son—who would one day be a leader among our people.''

As Kinnahauk's sonorous voice flowed over her with its hypnotic richness, it was as if the words passed directly into her consciousness. Bridget found herself gazing at the small tattoo high on his broad, smooth chest. The same mark adorned the flap of his *ouke* and the shield that hung beside it. Without thinking, she touched the mark on her brow, and then reached out to touch the one on his chest. They were so much alike . . . yet different.

"As a man and a woman are different," Kinnahauk said softly.

"How did you know what I was thinking?" Startled, she gazed up into his face.

"There is a voice—" He took her hand and placed it over his heart, and she could feel its wild beating, like the pounding of a stormy sea. "It speaks silently. Sometimes it does not say what I wish to hear, and I grow angry. Yet I must heed, for the Voice that Speaks Silently does not speak falsely."

"Is it the voice I hear inside you, hammering against my fingertips?" she whispered, her eyes trapped in the golden depths of his. She could scarce recall the words he had spoken with his lips, knowing only that her own heart echoed the voice of his, and her soul seemed somehow bound up in this man.

"Your own voice has spoken to you, Bridgetabbott. I have seen the truth on your face many times when you look at me. Why do you speak of this man Davidlavender when you know he is not for you?"

All thought of David Lavender slipped away as Kinnahauk leaned closer, so close that she could see the shadow of the beard he had not taken time to scrape from his jaw with the edge of his blade. His breath was sweet upon her face, his eyes gentle yet compelling, kindling a warmth inside her that made her forget the ache of her head and the stiffness of her body.

Vainly she tried to retain a shred of sensibility. "Those things you said to me..." The words—what were the words he had spoken? That she was his woman? That she must bear his children? Her body reacted to the thought with an inner trembling that was frightening in its intensity. "Kinnahauk, how can I believe you? First you go off and leave me here while you try to trade me for corn, and when that fails, you accuse me of—of things..." Instinctively she clamped her thighs together.

His surprise was almost comical. "I did not try to trade you for corn, woman. I left this place to show the stupid white-eyes how to find water. Why do you say things that are not true?"

"How can I know what is true and what is not?" she cried, struggling to sit up. "You did not bother to explain."

"Explain? Kinnahauk is chief," he announced haughtily, as if that were explanation enough.

"A chief who tries to kill his own best friend, who berates me for things that I have not done, nor even thought of doing, and now—"

"It is so." Sighing, Kinnahauk pressed her back onto his soft mat, his hand lingering to caress her shoulder. "And now, my true heart, I confess to you that once more I have acted like a *nanupee yauh-he*—one made crazy from whiskey. Fear and anger rob me of my senses. I say to you that never has this thing happened to me before. Always before, with a woman I have known the right words to say, the right way to reach out for what I would have. You must be more powerful than the greatest *shaman*."

"Are you saying it's *my* fault that you attacked poor Kokom like some wild savage?" The irony of her words escaped her, yet a few months before she would have expected no better of him, having been led to believe that all copper-skinned people were ignorant, bloodthirsty heathens. "Will you at least tell me what you did to Kokom, and why?"

His fingers tightened on her shoulder. "Kokom. Even when I kneel beside you, pleading for that which by rights I could take, you think only of that one."

"Surely someone must, with Gray Otter fair breaking his heart and his best friend trying to cut his throat over some silly misunderstanding."

"I did not hurt him. If you wish to shed tears, shed them for Kinnahauk, who was too blinded with anger to see clearly. Kokom's blade was the only one to draw blood. When your mare bolted I went after you instead of finishing what I had begun."

"You would have killed him?" she asked, shocked. Having known only his gentleness, she could only guess at the depths of his wrath.

"No. The words Gray Otter spoke were true, yet their meaning was false. If it had been otherwise, then I would have vanquished him to live among our people on the mainland." Kinnahauk's eyes moved over her, just as his hands had moved over her earlier. At Gray Otter's sly words, he had ridden out in a blood rage, not taking time to paint his face or his horse. The eagle feathers were still in his hair only because he wore them each time he left this place as a symbol of his office and his brave deeds.

It had been no brave deed to frighten his *oquio* and endanger her life. Her crumpled body had looked so still and small that both men had been terrified that she would never awaken. While Kokom had held on to the two skittish stallions, he had examined her carefully, finding only bruises and the knot on the back of her head. Lifting her, he had placed her carefully into Kokom's arms while he remounted. Kokom had handed her up to him, and Kinnahauk had carried her back to the village, torn between the need for caution and the need for haste.

"I have not shirked my duties to your mother," Bridget said quietly now. "If I spent too much time consoling poor Kokom, it was only because he's so miserable. He has had no luck at all in convincing Gray Otter to move into his lodge."

"This I know."

"I only sought to advise him in ways to capture her interest."

"This I know."

"Kokom is a good man, too good for such a troublemaker, but—"

"Hush, spirit of my heart, and I will show you who is the better man," Kinnahauk murmured deeply. Lowering himself to the mat beside her, he turned her carefully so that she lay facing him. "Your people brought to this land a custom that has spread among our people. It was one of the few good things they gave to us."

"A custom?" It was all she could do to force the words from her trembling lips, for he was staring at her as if he would consume her. In her dreams she had relived again and again the time he had kissed her.

Without replying, Kinnahauk touched her lips with his. They were warm and vital, and as they lingered there, delicate as the brush of a butterfly wing, Bridget felt something sweet and molten begin to flow through her veins. By the time he sank his tongue deep into her mouth, branding her his with every sensitive stroke, she knew only that no matter what happened to her after this, no matter where she journeyed, she would never forget this moment.

The musky male scent of him filled her nostrils. Tentatively at first, Bridget began to kiss him back, meeting the thrust of his tongue with the tip of hers. The guttural sound that emerged from his throat sent chills of excitement racing over her, for she knew that this night he would not leave her alone as he had done the last time she had shared his sleeping mat.

Even now the intense dreams she had dreamed that night haunted her, bringing a flush to her face at the strangest times. And on the day when he had found her crying in the forest, he had touched her in such a way that...

She felt the heat steal over her body, felt her pulses begin to quicken. She had thought she knew all that went on between a man and a woman, but she had known nothing. How could she have known about this sweet, wild melting that made her body stiffen and her limbs tremble?

Kinnahauk's lips moved over her cheek, following the curve of her jaw, to settle in the vulnerable hollow at the base of her throat. When she felt the flicker of his tongue there, she shuddered. Surely these strange feelings that raced through her body like caged lightning were unnatural. He had cast a spell of some sort over her, a spell that made her feel hot and cold, weak and strong—a spell that made her want to tear away her clothing and press herself to him....

"Kinnahauk, what are you doing?" she gasped when she felt his hand on her knee.

"Shh, do not fear, my small one, I will be gentle with you. You are sore and bruised from your fall, yet the voice tells me I must wait no longer to claim you. My body speaks even more clearly," he added with an undercurrent of amusement she found completely captivating.

His hand curved over her knee, and his fingertips strayed to the single dimple behind it. Once more came the sweet lightning that seemed to focus on the center of her body. Bridget moved restlessly. "I feel such strange things, Kinnahauk. Do you think perhaps Soconme ... ?"

His hard, warm palm moved up her thigh, taking her skirt with it. "Soconme cannot help you now, my trembling fawn. Are these things you feel bad?"

"Noo," she breathed as he placed a kiss in the curve of her shoulder.

"Do they frighten you?" he asked, his lips moving on her skin.

"Yess..." The heat from the bed of coals cast its warmth on the bared skin of her hips as he raised her skirt to her waist, yet it was nothing to the warmth of his body against hers.

"Will you not trust yourself in my care, Bridget-abbott?" His voice sounded oddly strained.

Flames flickered among the coals, casting shadows across his face. In the dim light, she could see his eyes, the eyes she had once likened to those of a hawk. He had taken her from the sea and carried her to his home, when by all rights he should have despised her. He had shown her naught but kindness, if sometimes she had mistaken that kindness for something else.

"I trust you, Kinnahauk," she said softly. I love you, she added silently, not daring to surrender the last small piece of her heart.

With a movement beautiful in its simplicity, Kinnahauk rose and removed his vest. Bridget let her gaze play over his powerful body, few of its secrets unknown to her, for even in the coldest weather, the men of Croatoan wore but few garments. Her eyes widened as he released the tie that held his only remaining one, baring that part of him that she had felt stirring against her, yet had never gazed upon.

"Do I frighten you, my small golden *shaman*?"

Lips parted, she shook her head slowly. It could not be. She knew the way of a man with a woman, for had not she seen such couplings at Newgate? Yet never had she seen the male part standing free and unfettered. "It cannot be," she whispered. "I was not made right, for truly, my body cannot accept such a—such a—"

"Such a gift?"

Her eyes pleaded with him. All the dreams, all those strange feelings each time she had seen him—the way she had felt when he touched her or held her in his arms . . . she had thought it would come as naturally as the rain, but that was before she had seen him this way. "Kinnahauk, please—don't ask this thing of me. I will do anything else you ask, only this I cannot do. We are not made for each other, surely you can see this?"

He hesitated only a moment before speaking. "Then I will only hold you while you sleep." He still stood over her, proud and tall, his sleek, coppery body centered by the thatch of dark hair that drew her gaze like a lodestone.

"It is not yet time to sleep, for the sun is still high," she protested weakly.

"You will sleep. When you wake, we will talk more of this matter, but now you must rest."

"You don't have to stay with me," she offered hopefully, her voice pitched higher than usual. She realized she must have landed on her head, for it was beginning to ache, and her wits had scattered like a flock of blackbirds.

"I will stay with you until you sleep, Bridgetabbott. Lift your arms now, for I would remove your shift. If you will not part your thighs for me, at least allow me to hold your body next to mine."

Slowly Bridget lifted her arms over her head, wondering as she did, why she had so little will where this man was concerned. Without her even knowing how it had come about, he held her heart and soul in the palm of his hand. Now he would claim her body, as well. The last time she had known such fear and wonder, she had just signed her name to an agreement to leave behind everything she had known and held dear, beginning a whole new life.

This time the feeling was even stronger.

Kinnahauk tied the flap of his doorway on the inside so that it would not blow open in a sudden gust of wind. He unfolded the red wolf robe and placed it beside the sleeping mat, and then he knelt beside her.

Lifting her gently, he eased the soft shift over her shoulders, drawing it carefully over her head so as not to touch the bruised bump. For a moment he did not move. Then, to Bridget's amazement, he lowered his head and kissed her breast. All the air rushed from her lungs, and her body stiffened. The words he spoke then were in his own tongue. He spoke them softly between kisses. *Waurraupa*. She knew that meant white, and he was kissing her breasts. *Wisto* was the word for the skin of a fawn, *roosomme* meant soft, but when he drew the tip of her breast into his mouth and began to suckle gently, there were no more words.

Bridget's fingers curled into her palm as she fought the urge to touch him as he was touching her. How could a man make a woman feel this way? She had known dry little boy-girl kisses before, and they had left her unmoved. No one had told her that when a man and a woman touched in certain ways, they grew hot and damp and filled with a sweet heaviness unlike anything else in the world!

Kinnahauk took her nerveless hand and placed it on his chest, and she felt the thunder of his heartbeat. Surely this was dangerous! Yet knowing it, she was compelled to court danger, her fingertips moving cautiously at first, and then more boldly.

He was hard and warm, his skin softer than the finest silk, his muscles hard as stone. He moved sinuously so that he was never still, one moment suckling her breast, the next nibbling the soft lobe of her ear, his breath stirring tendrils of hair against her neck. He whispered to her, the words strange, the meaning clear. He intended to do to her that mysterious thing that men did to women—the humping and groaning under bundles of rags she had seen in Newgate—and suddenly it did not seem so impossible after all.

He was touching her the way he had in the forest, and the world seemed to go up in flames. She was burning for him, craving something . . . something. . . .

Breathing heavily, she twisted in his arms, and Kinnahauk grew still. The hand that had been cupping the place between her thighs, the place that was the center of all her longing, ceased its magical movements.

"It is time, my own love," he whispered in her language. At the sound of his husky voice, a fresh course of tremors racked her body.

"Please, Kinnahauk, I don't know what to do, I only know I cannot abide this sweet agony much longer!"

Kinnahauk rose, kneeling beside her. Carefully he lifted her and sat her astride his thighs so that she faced him.

"Put your arms around my neck. Rest your face on my shoulder, my love. We will go only as far as you want to go, and we will do this as slowly or as quickly as you wish. This I promise you."

As she leaned against him, burying her face in the curve of his shoulder, her soft belly pressed against his rigid manhood, he lifted his face and invoked the spirits for patience and control.

He kissed her hair, inhaling the fresh scent of sunshine that always seemed to cling to her, as if the gold of her hair were a gift of *wittapare*. He kissed her eyelids, and as she lifted her face to him, he joined his lips to hers. Her lips parted eagerly for him, but he waited until he felt the restless movement of her hips before he lifted her, cupping her buttocks in the palms of his two hands, and lowered her until the tip of his man part brushed the golden floss to part the petals of her secret place.

She was moist. His nostrils flared as he caught her sweet woman smell. Everything about her was made to please him. She was his! Soon there would be no more waiting. He could feel her throbbing against him, and it took every shred of strength he possessed not to plunge heedlessly. Instead, he lifted his hands to her face, holding her so that he could meet her eyes. "You are the heart of my hearts, Bridgetabbott. If there was a way to do this without hurting you, I would do it, but there is not. The pain will be over quickly, but it is for you to choose."

Bridget chose. With only her instincts to guide her, she allowed herself to settle over his shaft. When the thin veil was torn, his mouth was there to capture her cry.

Kinnahauk waited only for her to grow used to the feeling of him inside her, for she was small and tight, clasping him with a strength that all but drove him beyond recall. His hand slipped down between them, searching until he found what he sought... caressing. At his first touch, she began to move, as if needing only this reminder of why they were joined in such a way. Only then did he rise to his knees. Lowering her back onto the mat, he began to move, feeling himself drawn into her sweet depths as she met each thrust eagerly.

He had hardly dared hope that the magic that sent a man and his woman soaring beyond the skies would happen, but there was no mistaking the flush on her face, the soft whimpers as she clung helplessly to him. He felt the shudders of her release, and his control broke.

When it was over, he held her tightly. He could not withdraw, not when even the echoes of such sweet passion brought a pleasure all their own. It was like nothing he had ever experienced, this joining.

"It is for this I have waited all my life," he whispered with a tender look at the small, sweat-drenched creature in his arms. Gently he brushed the hair from her face and placed a kiss on the fire mark. His. She was his now, and no man could take her from him.

Some time later, Bridget roused to find Kinnahauk bathing her. By all rights, she should be mortified, but had this man not seen all of her there was to see? Had he not known her more intimately than any other creature on God's earth? She smiled and closed her eyes, too weary to think about what had happened to her. Tomorrow would be time enough to think.

Kinnahauk walked out into the water, starlight gleaming on his dripping body. He felt the power of many spirits in the clear cold night. The Spirit of the Cold River and the Spirit of the Warm River were at peace. The spirits of his ancestors whispered approval of his woman. The wisdom of the Great Kishalamaquon was beyond understanding, for had He not known that to lead his people in a world they would share with the white-eyes, Kinnahauk must open his heart to the people he had long despised? They were all creatures of the Great Spirit, for to be less was to have no soul.

He dived under the surface and swam until his lungs were fit to burst. Tomorrow he would begin collecting furs. He

would take the best pelts from his own *ouke*, and the three
gold coins from the safe place where they had rested these
many years, and he would go to the place where many trails
crossed. He would send word that Kinnahauk of Croatoan
would pay gold for the finest pelts. When he had collected
enough, he would go to the place called Albemarle. He
would find this man, Davidlavender, and pay him the bride-
price. In that way, his own honor and that of his woman
would be satisfied.

Chapter Nineteen

Gray Otter had watched the canoes bearing Kinnahauk, Crooked Stick and Calls the Crows slip away in the mist that drifted above the waters. She had been awake when Kinnahauk had passed her *ouke* on his way to see his mother. She had thought to be outside when he passed that way again so that seeing her, he would be reminded that she was more beautiful, more wise and far more passionate than the milk-faced creature he had taken to his mat last night.

In the quiet time that comes before day is born, she had heard him tell Sweet Water that he would use the coins to buy pelts to pay the bride-price for the white-eye woman.

"No good has ever come from the white man's gold coins," Sweet Water had said, for she could not forget that her youngest son had been slain for such a coin. "I would have them gone from our village."

"The trappers I seek are men of honor. They will take our *peage* and the white man's gold and say nothing."

"Go with much care, my son."

"I will be back before moonrise on the fifth day. Be with my woman until I return. She sleeps now."

Gray Otter, who had lain awake all night imagining what was going on in the *ouke* on the ridge, had cut circles in her palm with her fingernails. Slipping through the morning mist, she had stood on the shore and watched them disappear, her heart filled with bitterness. As silent as one of the sentinel cedars that rose from the shallow water, its bones bleached by many suns, she stood there, willing Kinnahauk to turn back.

Take me, take me! I will give you many fine sons who will be great hunters, who will fish the deepest waters, who will walk the fiercest storms. I will give you daughters to care for you in your old age. I will teach our children the ways of our people so that one day they will rise up against this wicked white tide that has flooded our shores, from the Land of Frozen Water to the Land of No Cold Moon.

Even as she watched, the sun began to swallow up the night mist. It was then that she saw the oystering shallop, its sail furled in the morning stillness. Behind it was a wide canoe, its sides low in the water. Englishmen! There were often sails in the distance, but they did not usually venture so close.

Gray Otter would bid them welcome. Three lone men, though they be treacherous white-eyes, would not dare attack a canoe so close to their own village, not when their own sails hung empty of wind. These men could not know how few warriors remained to guard the village.

Moving swiftly, she went directly to Kinnahauk's lodge. She had dared enter only once before, when he had first brought the white-eye woman to their village. Since then there had been only trouble.

The woman they called *Waurraupa Shaman* was still sleeping. On *his* sleeping mat! They had lain together until the sun walked down and the moon had climbed above the highest tree, without food, without summoning Sweet Water or Soconme. He had taken her in on the night of the last storm, but she had returned to Sweet Water's *ouke* with the rising sun. Now he had taken her in again. No man would take a woman into his *ouke* before all his people two times unless he meant to have her for his woman. Kinnahauk had chosen this useless creature to be his first wife.

Gray Otter's face was mottled with ugly color as she stared down at the small, still figure. He had covered her with the red wolf robe that had been a gift from his people on the mainland, who ever hoped to persuade him to live among them. Gray Otter had coveted the thick, red-and-gray pelt from the first time she had seen it.

A glint of metal in the dim light drew her eye, and she gasped softly. There on the robe beside the pale-skin woman was Kinnahauk's copper arm band. She recognized its distinctive pattern of serpents biting their tails, each linked to the next to form an endless circle of endless circles, a symbol of great power. Lying within the arm band was a sprig from the *yawaurra* tree, which symbolized the greatest of all bonds among their people.

By placing such an offering beside the miserable *waurraupa yicau*, Kinnahauk had pledged himself to her in the way of a man who would take only one wife! Pain cut through Gray Otter's heart like a dull blade. Did he not know that the stupid white-eye woman was not worthy of such a great sacrifice? How could such a one even understand its meaning?

Glancing quickly toward the opening to be certain it had closed behind her, Gray Otter bent over and scooped up the arm band and the spray of glossy green leaves, hiding them in the folds of her shawl. Then she stood, angry color fading as her face took on a purposeful look of repose. Was she not the granddaughter of Yatestea Wetkes, the great warrior who had once swam beneath the waters to a Coree war canoe and drowned five braves who had come silently in the last hour of darkness to steal Hatorask women?

Gray Otter's eyes narrowed in speculation. If Kinnahauk had told the woman his reason for leaving, then another way must be found to be rid of her. Yet it was not Kinnahauk's way to explain. Even as a young child he had possessed an arrogance she had admired, acting as he would and explaining to no one his reasoning. If only Kokom were more like him, she thought, allowing herself to be distracted for a single moment. It was good for a man to be strong, but a strong man must have a strong woman by his side, not a pale weakling!

She must move swiftly, before the village began to stir. The oyster gatherers could be planning to leave by first light. Not knowing of the powerful currents near Chacandepeco, they had drifted toward Croatoan in the night. At the first wind they could raise their sail and be off.

"Awake, Bridget." Gray Otter forced a smile to her face. "I bring good news, but we must go quickly."

Bridget stirred. She moaned softly as she attempted to stretch, and then she yawned. Shyly she looked at the place next to her, expecting to see Kinnahauk. There was no sign of him, either on the mat or in the *ouke*.

"Gray Otter?" Her voice sounded rusty. Her very bones felt rusty! Kinnahauk had heated water in the coals and bathed her quite tenderly before she slept, anointing her body with sweet oils and sweeter kisses, but she was still miserably sore, both from her fall and from what had come later. Mayhap he thought she had need of a woman to minister to her, but surely he would not have sent Gray Otter, knowing Bridget did not care for her. "Why are you here? Has Kinnahauk sent you?" She sat up, making an effort to hide her discomfort.

"It is as you say, I have been sent by Kinnahauk to tell you that a boat approaches even now that will take you where you wish to go."

"Oh, but I—"

"You must hurry," Gray Otter said, her face unusually beautiful in its animation. "Kinnahauk had many things to do this day, for he wasted much time *yottoha*—yesterday. He spoke to me of you when he came to my *ouke* before the sun rose. He said that I should say these things for him. He said that you are now free to go to the man who paid your bride-price. He said that he will not ask for corn or bearskins in return as he had planned, such is his regard for you."

"Oh, please—you don't understand, he could not have paid—"

"He said that you could return as his second wife if the man who paid for you no longer wants you, that we will treat you with no little kindness. With such a man as Kinnahauk, I will have many sons. I will have need of a second woman in our *ouke*, for there will be much work." Gray Otter's eyes narrowed as she waited to see the effect of this last offer. If the pale one showed any sign of wanting to linger after such a blow to her pride, then she would think of something else.

Gray Otter had made up her mind many years ago that one day she would be wife to a chief, mother of chiefs, a woman of great wealth and standing. Kinnahauk had much *eage*, the strings of shell beads that represented wealth even to the white man, for there was little gold to be found. He hunted and fished with the other men of the village, though he was chief. Even Sweet Water was content to spend her days scraping skins and drying meat, working until her fingers were as knotted as old Soconme's. When Gray Otter became first wife to the *werowance* of the Hatorask, things would be different. Her corn would be ground for her, her *ouke* cleaned each day. She would scrape no skins, but instead, every man and woman of this village would kneel down before her, laying at her feet their softest pelts. Many years ago she had seen in a dream the pelts of many gray otters piled high around her.

Men were not the only ones who had visions!

Bridget sat huddled in a small knot of misery as she took in the meaning of Gray Otter's words. He was sending her away. After taking her, making her his—*using her!*—he was sending her away as if she were of no more value to him than a broken bowl.

"There is no time to waste, for the wind will soon carry the boat away," Gray Otter said tersely.

Bridget's chin lifted. "I would bid farewell to my friends here."

"There is no time!" Gray Otter repeated, snatching away the thick fur robe and leaving her bare.

Too stunned even for anger, Bridget stiffly reached for the sandy, rumpled shift Kinnahauk had discarded. The ashes in the fire pit had long since grown cold, leaving an acrid dampness in the small enclosure. "Wait outside. I will join you as soon as I am ready," she said with quiet dignity. Pride alone prevented her from crying, from running after Kinnahauk and throwing herself on his mercy.

"Hurry!" Gray Otter ducked through the opening, allowing it to fall shut behind her. It was not done yet, but if her luck held, this woman with her fish-belly skin would be on her way to her own kind. Knowing she had lived among the Hatorask, the oyster gatherers would no longer value her, but would sell her to the highest bidder or use her and discard her, for such was the way of the white man.

Gray Otter closed her mind to the fate of the white-eye woman who had lived among them since the Moon of the White Brant. She did not belong here. Perhaps when she was no longer here to cast her spell over Kinnahauk, he would turn to a woman who was strong enough and bold enough to be wife to a chief. One day he would thank her for freeing him from such a poor creature, knowing it had been for the good of their people.

Descending the hill to the place where the other *oukes* were clustered, Gray Otter spared a single thought for Kokom, who was hunting the great buck whose hoofprints he had seen in the lower woods. Once Kinnahauk took her to his *ouke*, she could no longer meet with Kokom in their secret place. She would miss those meetings, for Kokom was a skilled and tireless lover.

But Kokom was not a chief. He could only become chief if Kinnahauk died before producing a son. Kinnahauk must wait no longer to take a wife. For the sake of his people, he must have many sons. Gray Otter would at last know his virility.

Pausing outside Sweet Water's *ouke*, she stilled her features to composure. "Ho, Sweet Water, I have come from Soconme, who feels the approaching rains. He would not ask you to stay with him, yet I believe it would please him greatly."

"Aiee, my own bones have told me of the coming rain. I will go to him now. We will smoke together, and I will warm the scuppernong wine and speak of the old days, when our bones were not so old."

"One more thing, Bridget asked that I bring her belongings to Kinnahauk's *ouke*."

Sweet Water beamed. "I will take them."

"She would feel awkward to see the mother of her lover this day. It would be better if I take them, for we are of an age."

Shortly afterward, Gray Otter entered Kinnahauk's *ouke* to hurry the white-eye woman on her way. "Sweet Water sends these things." She held out a small bundle rolled in buckskin and tied securely, which contained one faded and worn blue gown, two ragged petticoats, a pair of pantalets that were in shreds and the remains of a stained and worn apron. "She is sorry you must leave us, but she must stay with old Soconme, who suffers greatly before the rains."

"Sits There—"

"Is with Crooked Stick in his *ouke*," she lied. "They would not care to see you now, I think." Glancing outside, she saw no sign of anyone astir. Sweet Water was still inside Soconme's lodge. "Come, we must hurry before the oyster gatherers sail away."

Taking Bridget by the arm, Gray Otter rushed her through the chill dawn air. With a conspiratorial smile, she shoved the smallest canoe off the sandbank. The wind was beginning to whisper in the treetops. Soon the whole village would be moving about. "I will say your farewells, but is of small import. Farewell is not a word in our language. We come when it is timely; we go when it is timely. That is our way."

Cat's-paws ruffled the surface stillness as Gray Otter paddled quietly toward the shallop. Even now the three men stirred into action, unfurling the single sail and hauling up a small anchor. Bridget watched the village where she had come to know so much love disappear in the morning fog that swirled up from the water to embrace the wooded shore. Her heart was a knot of misery, for she had thought Kinnahauk had returned her feelings. But what did she know of such things? Mayhap his people did not know such tender emotions—they had been rare enough among her own kind.

Yet something in her could not accept that truth. Surely the melting looks that passed between Sits There and Crooked Stick signaled something more than an agreement that he would provide meat for her and she would cook and cure his hides and keep his *ouke* clean and warm his sleeping mat. Even between Many Toes and Face of a Horse she had seen many quick touches and secret smiles.

She would miss her friends. Sometimes it seemed that she had only to come to care for someone for them to be taken from her. Stiffening her back, she winced with the pain of yesterday's bruises and then strove for a more cheerful face. "I would thank you for all you have done for me, Gray Otter. Please tell Sweet Water and Sits There and—and—"

"What is this word you say? I do not know *thankyou*. I will tell them that you have gone to this place Albemarle. No more words are needed."

As indeed, Bridget thought with a sigh, they were not.

Lifting her paddle, Gray Otter called softly across the water. "Ho! White-eyes! I have a woman of your kind who would go to the place called Albemarle. Will you take her?"

Her head ached dully as Bridget listened to the old man ramble on. "Aye, they be the saltiest of all the oysters. I've harvested the waters from Chesapeake to Cape Faire. Aye, these be the best." The old man, whose name was Hamish,

O'Neal, nodded to the small flat boat they towed, where bushels of the shellfish were covered with wet canvas. "They'll fetch a muckle o' money for me'n the lads."

Bridget forced a smile in response. The old man had been talking since they had set sail, and Bridget had smiled and nodded, telling herself it was good to be among her own kind once more. The sound of his familiar accent fell like music on her ears, yet she missed the musical cadence of the Hatorask's English, which was uncommonly good except when they grew excited.

The "lads" the old man referred to were his partners, Cormick and Isaac, lately come down from Chesapeake to work with him in the less crowded sounds and rivers of the lower colonies. The two younger men had made several sly references to Hamish's new bride and the cargo of oysters they hauled, leaving Bridget with the impression that the old man had recently taken a wife some years younger than he.

Hamish told her many tales of colonies to the north and the south, of battles fought and skirmishes between trappers, settlers and the heathen redskins. "Aye, not that a man kin blame the poor devils. Still, 'twas too great a land to waste on ignorant savages, that be the God's truth. A man kin only claim what he kin hold on to, be he red or white."

"And we all know what this 'ere old buzzard likes to 'old on to," said Isaac with a sly dig at his friend's ribs.

Hamish roared a threat, and the two younger men snickered. Bridget pretended not to understand. As the day wore on, she began to feel increasingly uncomfortable with Cormick and Isaac, who reminded her of a sort she had known in Newgate.

"Will the journey to Albemarle take long?" she asked after they had been sailing for what seemed an eternity.

"Well now, that depends," the old man drawled, his eye on the sail and his weathered hand on the tiller. "If'n the wind holds to the no'th'ard it be one thing. Then again, if'n she swings around to the south'ard, it be t'other. Where abouts on the Albemarle d'ye say ye wanted to go, child?"

"Ha! Child, ye calls 'er!" chortled Isaac with a leer at the length of leg exposed beneath Bridget's short buckskin shift. "'Pears to me she be some older'n yer new bride, Hamish."

Looking embarrassed, the old man muttered something into his beard, and Bridget tried to stretch the soft skin down over her slender legs. Hamish was old enough to be her father—indeed, her grandfather. The thought brought a small degree of comfort, and she edged along the rough-planked bottom closer toward the stern thwart, as far away as she could get from the two crewmen. "I would like to go to the plantation of David Lavender. Do you know it?"

"Aye, I heard the name. Can't say as I recollect where I heard it, though. Isaac, Cormick—you lads hear tell of a planter called Lavender on the Albemarle?"

The two younger men cast quick glances at each other, looks which for some reason made Bridget even more uneasy. It was Isaac, the swarthy one with the bloodshot eyes, who answered. "I recollect meetin' a man called Lavender last time we stopped in Hoag's fer whiskey. Tall, thin feller—not much gizzard to him."

Cormick grinned, revealing the stumps of several rotted teeth. He was a large man with sandy hair and a fairer complexion, but his expression struck Bridget as dark and sinister. "Aye, no gizzard, them was me own thoughts. You be his woman?"

"I—um—plan to work for him," Bridget said cautiously. She owed these men no explanations. Still, she was a passenger, though she was in no position to pay her passage. The thought occurred to her that she was accumulating such a great debt in this so-called golden land that it would take several lifetimes to repay it.

"Got me a tidy little place on the north bank o' the Albemarle," mused Hamish. "One o' these days when I get too old to work the water, I'll plant me a few acres o' corn, a few acres o' terbaccy, an' set back on me arse end an' raise another crop o' younguns.''

Again, both younger men roared with laughter. They were crude, these three watermen, yet the honest coarseness of the old man did not offend her near so much as the sly looks of the younger two.

The wind held, and the shallow-draft boat moved swiftly over the choppy waters. There was no place to sit save the pile of musty canvas that Hamish told her was the spare sail. From the look of the patched and stained triangle that strained to hold the wind, it might be needed at any moment.

They passed several other boats, some small, some surprisingly large. In the distance she saw several canoes bearing men with coppery skin and black hair, and she bit her lip to hold back the tears.

Other than a few fires along the shore, which Hamish told her were redskins' fishing camps, she saw no sign of a town. Often they were out of sight of any land at all.

Bridget's belly grumbled with hunger. At midday Hamish had offered her a slab of rough cornmeal bread wrapped around a chunk of salt fish, but she had refused, not wanting to take their food when she had no way of repaying them. All three men drank a beer that Hamish said was made of cornstalks, which she also refused. "Where are the cities?" she asked timidly as the sun slipped down under the water in a burst of violent colors.

"Why, London Towne is right around yon point," Cormick taunted, earning a stern look from Hamish.

"Ye'll not have to worry about fancy doin's, lass, fer we be simple, God-fearin', hardworkin' folk along the Albemarle," the old man said with a quick glance at the buckskin shift Sweet Water had sewn for her.

"Oh, aye," put in Cormick, "with simple brick castles and great simple fields of tobacco, and hundreds o' simple sla—"

"They's a few that wears silk, lass, but the rest of us is glad to get buckskin or good honest cotton and linsey-woolsey."

"Aye, in them sawed-off buckskins ye'll make them dandies fair bust their codpieces when we pull up alongside Hoag's docks." Isaac leaned forward, his dark face twisted into an evil grin. "How long'd ye say ye lived with them redskins?"

Hamish scowled. "Mine yer manners, boy. This here little lady weren't taken in no raid, she was rescued by them heathens. If she'd been one o' their whores, they'd a sold her a'ready, or traded what was left of her to another bunch o' savages."

Bridget felt a sickness rising inside her that had nothing to do with either hunger or the constant motion of the boat. Pillowing her head on her arms, she closed her eyes, pretending to fall asleep. Kinnahauk, why did you send me away? she cried silently.

Within moments, pretense became reality, and she slept dreamlessly. Once she roused to feel the cold damp weight of the spare sail settling down over her. "Sleep on, daughter. Ye'll open yer eyes to Albemarle country come morning," Hamish said with gruff kindness. Stirring, she changed position, searching for one that did not press against a sore muscle. Every part of her ached, but no part so much as her heart.

Isaac took a turn at the tiller while Cormick slept, and the old man stood in the bow, his eyes scanning the skies where a few stars glimmered through a light cloud cover. The men's voices drifted back and forth over her head, blending with the constant slap-slap of the water and the creak of the tall mast.

"Aye, it be rich land, lads. Good crops, thick pelts, fish fair jumpin' into a man's boat and good salty oysters fer the taking."

"I'd trade it all fer a drink o' good whiskey to warm me feet," grumbled Cormick sleepily. He tugged at a corner of the canvas that covered Bridget, and she drew her knees up to her chest in an effort to avoid touching any part of him.

"Drink when the journey's done, lad. A man don't drink whiskey on the water, not if'n he wants to keep breathin'. If'n the shoals don't get ye, the redskins will. Pays a man to stay sober less'n he be among friends."

" 'Tis easy enough fer you to say, fer ye'll be sleepin' in yer own bed wi' yer own woman afore first light. Me'n Cormick here, we got a ways to go."

" 'Twas our agreement, lads. I supply the boat, and the pair o' ye do the upriver run."

"What about her?" Isaac nodded to the sleeping woman.

"I conceit this here Lavender fellow will reward ye fer delivering his woman. I'll not ask fer a share, fer I'll not be the one to have to find the devil. Ease off a point, lad, the wind's coming around. I smell rain."

"It ain't rain I smell, it's woman," muttered Cormick, but Bridget had fallen asleep once more under the hypnotic spell of water rushing along a wooden hull and the gentle rocking motion of the boat.

Chapter Twenty

Soft gray mist moved just above the black water, bringing a damp, bone-biting chill to the early-morning air. Bridget winced as new aches were added to the old. The air smelled different here. Less salt. The scent of damp earth, rich mud and resinous pines was laced with a mysterious sweetness.

She eased her numb feet up until she could hug her knees for warmth. The sail had kept the dew from settling on her, but it had scarcely held in the heat. "Are we there?" she whispered, hardly daring break the stillness.

Hamish stood in the bow, a long pole in his hand. Cormick had the helm, while Isaac stood by to fend off the flat of oysters they towed. The sails were slack as they drifted toward the shore.

"Nay, daughter, ye've a ways to go yet. The lads'll get ye to Hoag's Trading Post, and ol' Hoag'll send summon' to fetch yer man."

"But you're not leaving?" Bridget did not dare look at the two younger men for fear they would read the disquiet she felt at the thought of being left in their care. Honest fishermen or not, a more unreassuring pair she had yet to see outside prison.

"Aye, daughter, this here be me own plantation. Me woman'll have grist 'n molasses awaitin', an' coffee on the boil. Sheer off there, boy, afore ye ruin me landin'."

The bow scraped along a weathered plank that appeared out of the mist-ridden bushes along the shore. Bridget caught a whiff of wood smoke as she began to untangle herself from the heavy canvas. Mayhap she could remain here with Hamish and his wife for a spell....

"Three days, lads. I'll meet ye here at the landin'. Don't let that old skinflint Hoag talk ye out'n a fair price, fer he's got custom all the way up the Chowan awaitin' fer these oysters." With that caution the old man leaped nimbly out of the boat and disappeared into the fog.

In strange new territory with two men who made her increasingly uneasy, Bridget felt alone and vulnerable. Even in prison she'd had Meggy and Billy. Aboard the *Mallinson* there had been Tess and Tooly. Even Sudie Upston had been a familiar face, if not a particularly pleasant one.

The longing in her heart had mounted with each passing moment since Croatoan had fallen behind. Kinnahauk! Was she never to see him again? What wicked fate had brought her halfway around the world, cast her into the arms of the only man she could ever truly love and then snatched her away? She'd sooner have been abandoned on the shore than to have reached the gates of heaven only to have them close before her.

Huddled in misery, Bridget was unaware of just when the shallop left the main course of the Albemarle and eased silently up a narrow twisting body of water. Cormick lowered the sails, for no wind could penetrate the dense thicket of cypress trees that edged the banks, their sinuous roots reaching out into the black water like serpents.

"Hoag's Trading Post ain't far. Most like, yer planter'll be comin' in to trade if'n he lives around these parts."

"This is Albemarle?" Bridget asked, her doubts multiplying as she peered through the dense forest that crowded in. She had heard Albemarle called a sound, a river and a settlement, but this was surely none of those.

"In a manner o' speakin'," replied Isaac as the two men exchanged a quick look. "Me 'n' Cormick here, we figgers we be due a mite of consideration fer takin' ye on to Hoag's. Hauling passengers, that be outta our line.''

"Oh, but Mr. Hamish—"

"Don't worry none about the old man. Fer all his gray beard an' his Tessie's squinty eyes, they'll be a-goin' at it by now. Me 'n' Cormick, we thought of a way to liven up the trip some afore we sets ye off at Hoag's place.''

The realization that Tess was Hamish's young wife was forgotten as the two men's meaning became clear, and Bridget looked around her for a weapon. There was naught but the long pole Hamish had used, and that was well out of her reach. "Lay one finger on me and you'll answer to Mr. Lavender.'' The threat sounded weak even to her own ears. Evidently the men thought so, too, for they laughed uproariously, startling the birds into silence.

"Oh, aye, that fine gentleman o' yourn, he'll thank us fer takin' such good care o' his woman—primin' the pump, so t'speak. Shove us over to that clearin' on yonder bank, Cormick—I don't fancy gettin' me arse strung up on bramble vines.''

Easing herself onto her knees, Bridget eyed the bank. The moment they were close enough, she must jump. With a head start, she should be able to lose herself in the forest quickly enough, for the sun had still not risen high enough to penetrate the shadows. She eased one arm along the washboard, ready to launch herself over the side. Isaac was in the stern shoving against cypress roots with a pole, while Cormick stood in the bow with a line.

Suddenly a scream rent the stillness. Cormick staggered, clutching his throat, where an arrow had sprouted. Bridget stared in horror as he toppled slowly into the water, bright blood gushing from his mouth.

"Bastids!'' screeched Isaac. "Savage redskin bastids!'' Stabbing furiously at the water with the shove-pole, he tried to reverse the momentum of the shallop, succeeding only in scraping the side along a sinuous cypress knee and tipping the oyster flat as it dragged over another such obstruction.

Bridget knelt on the bed of canvas, numb with disbelief as she watched three painted savages swarm into the water. A fourth stayed on the bank, his yellow teeth bared in a horrid grimace. He waited only until the other three had pulled the shallop closer before launching himself at Isaac with what appeared to be a stone hatchet in one hand, a rusted knife in the other.

The hatchet crashed down on Isaac's skull, and he slumped forward. Seizing him by the hair, the savage quickly passed his knife around the edges of his scalp and then ripped it violently off, holding it aloft with a fiendish cry of exaltation.

Bridget felt the bile rise in her throat, causing her stomach to heave sickeningly. Only the tenacity that had carried her so far against such great odds enabled her to fling herself over the side and into the black water. Intent only on escaping with her life, she forgot about the other three fiends. The moment she came to the surface, they grabbed her by the hair.

Dragging her up onto the muddy bank, they threw her facedown. One of them knelt beside her and rammed a knee in the small of her back, forcing the air from her lungs. Still holding her hair, he jerked her head back until she could not even cry out. With one finger, he circled her scalp, muttering something in a tongue that was completely foreign to her. Not that she had any doubt as to his meaning. She, too, was going to lose her hair, her life—and more.

The one on her back shifted until he was sitting astride her hips. The other three began plundering the dead bodies, having dragged Cormick's up onto the shore to take his scalp. All were drinking. Between drinks, they threw back their heads and howled like the animals they were. Bridget, numb with horror, felt gooseflesh breaking out. Even without the smell of strong spirits, the stench of the creature on her back was nauseating, yet she dared not try to dislodge him, for he was maddened by drink and blood lust. No one knew better than she just how dangerous such a condition could be.

Think! She must think what to do—how to escape. Once out of their reach, she would be safe, for surely they could not follow her in their condition. Already they were stumbling around, spilling more of the whiskey than they managed to pour down their throats. With each tipple they seemed to grow wilder, giving great cries and whoops as they danced around the dead bodies of their victims. The savage who still rode astride her buttocks began to move, grinding against her so that her hip bones were forced painfully against the hard ground.

And then they began mutilating the two dead men with their knives. Bridget, her cheek pressed against the damp earth, closed her eyes, stifling a moan with her fist. Oh, God, please let them murder me swiftly—*please* don't let them torture me so, she prayed silently.

Yet even then, some spark of determination buried deep inside her refused to give up. When the beast on her back toppled off, attempting to drain the last few drops from his jug, she wasted no time in scrambling as far away as she could get. Diving headlong into a bramble thicket, she began to tunnel under the thorny canes, and was almost completely hidden when one of the savages lunged at her foot and dragged her out.

With a cry of triumph he twisted her ankle so that she had to roll onto her back or see it broken. A fiery pain shot up her leg, reaching all the way to her groin as she lay helpless on her back.

"Con-noowa ware-occa cotshu!"

Bridget had no inkling of his meaning. Was he going to dismember her? "No," she whispered. "Oh, please—no!"

"Cotshu con-noowa," mumbled one of the others, reeling over toward them. "Me take woman."

With sounds that put her in mind of feeding hogs, the other two descended upon them, one falling to his knees beside her head, the other landing on his face nearby. The one beside her head reached for her hands, and before she divined his intent, he wrenched them ruthlessly over her head, leaving her defenseless. With a jubilant cry, the savage who held her foot dropped to his knees and crawled up onto her body. The yellow-and-white diagonal stripes that had been painted on his cheeks writhed sickeningly as his face stretched into a grimace.

He began rotating his body, rolling his hips back and forth as he straddled her. After a few moments he began fumbling with the top of her dress. When it would not tear, he took out his knife and held it poised above her for an endless moment before slashing the lacings and tearing the garment down the front.

At first Bridget could not believe she was still breathing. One stroke of the wicked blade would have ended her life. Then she watched a feral glint enter his bloodshot eyes, and a moment later he grabbed her exposed breast, kneading it with his filthy, bloodstained claws. Oh, God, would that he *had* stabbed her through the heart! Death would be more welcome than what lay ahead.

She knew she must escape, she *must*! If she still lived after they had done their vile deeds, she thought frantically, she would somehow get away, and then . . .

Sudden pain caused her to cry out, and her eyes opened wide. The evil creature had bitten her breast! Horrified, she saw him draw a circle on one pale breast with her own blood, laughing uproariously all the while. With the last vestige of strength she could summon, she kicked out and tugged at her wrists.

It was useless. The beasts only tightened their hold, crushing her bones in their powerful grip until a merciful blackness overcame her. Somewhere in the far reaches of her mind, she could hear someone screaming, screaming . . .

But there was no deliverance. Consciousness returned all too quickly as the three made sport of her hair, her skin, even the nipples on her breasts. They clawed feebly at the torn edges of her dress, but the sturdy doeskin defeated their drunken attempts to tear it from her. At least her thighs had not been parted while she was unconscious. Mayhap they were too drunk to carry out their wicked intent. If only they would fall into a stupor, she might still have a chance to get away. Even as her mind searched frantically for a way to distract them, the tall one with the humped nose, who seemed less drunk than the others, began speaking rapidly, his words a series of unintelligible grunts. He seemed to be ordering the one who sprawled across her to leave, and for a moment her hopes lifted.

But only for a moment. Hump Nose, who had been holding her wrists, indicated that he would take a turn astride her, and Bridget's hopes plummeted. At least the one who rode her now was too drunk to do more than pantomime the act, though he had been able to hurt her badly, even so.

Her feet were released as the four of them argued. With a final vicious twist of her breast, the slavering creature hoisted himself to his feet, wavering as he stood over her. He glared down at her as if she alone were responsible for his condition. Giving in to the agony, Bridget rolled over onto her side, moaning softly. Not until she felt something warm and wet did she open her eyes.

The animal had jerked his tail clout aside and was urinating on her! Like a dog marking his territory. In utter horror at this final degradation, she kicked out wildly, catching him on the leg. He fell and lay there without moving, but Hump Nose loosed a fierce cry. Before she could scramble out of the way, he struck her hard on the side of the head with his forearm, causing sparks to dance before her eyes. Still reeling, she was dragged to her feet, and before she could prevent it, her hands were jerked behind her back and lashed together.

"*Uhnta-hah!*" barked Hump Nose.

Bridget shook her head dazedly, her ears still ringing.

"You come!" he repeated.

"You speak English?" Somehow the fact that such a creature could actually speak her language made his viciousness even more unthinkable. And that, Bridget thought with a glimmer of amusement not untouched with hysteria, was surely ironic in light of all she had suffered from her own kind.

The four men set out in a shambling run, in spite of their drunkenness. A branch whipped into her face, and she fell back with a low cry. Instantly she was surrounded by her captors. All reeked of spirits, as well as their own natural filth, and although they could run through the forest without a single misstep, it seemed they could scarce stand without falling over.

"You come," Hump Nose commanded roughly. For emphasis, he cracked her on the side of the head again, this time with a stick.

"Where are you taking me?" she demanded.

"Where you take me," the savage repeated.

Confused, she tried again. "David Lavender will pay you well for my return."

"Dav'd Lander pay well take me," said one of the others with a look of triumph. "Take me, take me, take me!"

Another savage took up the chorus, and slowly, Bridget realized that not one of the creatures had understood a word she had spoken. They were simply parroting her phrases.

"Oh, God," she wailed.

Tiring of their game, they resumed trotting through the seemingly endless forest, three ahead of her and one behind her. All carried jugs, and she could only hope their supply of drink held out, for had they been more sober, her own fate would have been quite different.

Just as she began to wonder if they were to run all night, they stopped. Bridget crumpled to the ground in a silent heap. She was light-headed from hunger and shock. Her moccasins had been lost somewhere along the way, and her feet were bleeding. One of her ankles was swollen to twice its size, but it had long since grown numb. She knew instinctively that if she could not keep up, she would be dispatched with a stroke of those vicious weapons the heathens wore strapped to their sides.

At least she had not been raped. Yet. There was no new tenderness between her thighs beside that with which she had awakened after Kinnahauk—

"Ah, Kinnahauk," she whispered. "I would sooner have been your second wife than leave you."

The moment she stopped moving, Bridget had felt the cold begin to bite into her flesh. She was light-headed from want of food—surely even animals required sustenance. A fire, a bit of meat, perhaps. Even a handful of acorns would be welcome, with a sup of water to wash them down.

But there was no food, no water. Only more of the spirits. She sat silently, making herself as small as possible, while the four men gabbled in their heathen tongue and tippled from the few remaining stoneware jugs. They seemed to be bragging about something, for now and then one of them would wave one of the still-fresh scalps and slam his fist against his chest, and the others would grunt an approving chorus.

Any moment now I'll wake up, Bridget told herself. Sweet Water will be settling the earthen pot of water and yaupon leaves into the coals for tea, and I must hurry and mix the *appones* and set them to cooking.

She no longer dreamed of Little Wheddborough. Croatoan had become her home, the Hatorask her people. Until they had sent her away.

One by one, three of her captors toppled over, snoring loudly. Hump Nose emptied the last of the jugs and tossed it aside. He wiped his chin with an arm, smearing his paint, all the while staring at her with his dark, red-rimmed eyes. Bridget breathed a prayer of thanks that she had nothing to fear from them this night, for surely even Hump Nose was too drunk to stand. The morrow might bring a new threat, for they were sure to awaken in a foul mood, but she would be gone by then. The moment Hump Nose succumbed, she would slip away. She had no idea where the settlement was, but she would rather trust herself to the wild animals of the forest than to these drunken savages.

Her wrists were still tied. Dared she prevail on Hump Nose to loosen the strips of rawhide? He seemed the most intelligent of the lot. It was worth trying, for she had little to lose. Crawling over to where he reclined, she turned and thrust her bound wrists at him. "Please?" she implored softly. "I cannot sleep this way."

With a grunt, he fumbled at her bonds. She would much prefer he untie her than attempt to use his knife, for in his condition, she might well lose her hands. Unexpectedly she felt his hand on her ankles, and then her feet were jerked tightly together. Losing her balance, she toppled onto her side. "No, please—you don't understand! Oh, please, not that—not my ankles, as well! Leave my wrists, and I'll not bother you again."

Too late she realized her mistake. She had thought he would be too far gone with drink to know what he was about, and now she found herself bound hand and foot. She was still protesting when he passed a rawhide thong around her neck, attaching it to the one on her ankles and tightening it until she was doubled backward like a bow. Sobbing in fresh agony, Bridget pleaded with him for relief, knowing it would do no good. She should have waited and then slipped away while she had the chance. Now even the opportunity was denied her.

Behind her she could hear Hump Nose as he struggled to his feet. In fear of what other fiendish punishment he would devise, she fell silent, scarcely daring to breathe. She need not have worried. Having trussed her up so that she could not move without danger of strangling herself, he staggered into the woods and vomited.

From somewhere in the distance came the hollow cry of

an owl, and Bridget gave a moment's thought to the predator's poor victim as she willed herself to rise above the pain.

What was it Soconme had said—that pain was but another sea for the mind to sail upon? She tried, but there was no escaping the physical agony that beset her. Yet even that was naught compared to the pain of knowing that Kinnahauk had not wanted her.

"Have I truly been so wicked that I must be punished again and again?" she whispered.

Sometime before dawn she drifted into wakefulness, her body numb with cold. Her dreams had grown so fanciful that she could not say which was dream and which reality. Once she was certain she saw Kinnahauk standing tall and silent among the tree trunks. It almost seemed that, breathing deeply, she could smell the scent of wood smoke that clung to his leather garments, the sweet earthy smell of his flesh.

But it was only a dream ... only the whisperings of her aching heart.

Chapter Twenty-One

Bridget had no way of knowing how long she had slept, or what had awakened her. Pain was the only constant reality. She lay still, afraid of arousing her captors. Her hands and feet had grown numb, and she fought against the terror that threatened to numb her mind, as well.

At the sound of a stealthy movement, panic quickened her breath. Over the thunder of her own heart she heard four soft thuds, the last one followed by a gurgle and a muted exclamation. Something brushed past her head, and she shrank instinctively, choking when the thong around her neck tightened. Before she could adjust her position to ease the pressure on her windpipe, she was roughly grabbed and lifted from the ground.

"U-kettawa!" muttered a gruff voice.

"We-waukee?" responded another.

"Neep. E-tau-wa."

"E-tau-wa," repeated several deep voices in the darkness.

"U-kettawa E-tau-wa!"

Bridget felt hands moving over her, hands that were rough, but not brutal. There was a grunt, and suddenly the pressure around her throat was gone, her ankles released. Hardly daring to believe she was being set free, she waited for them to cut the bonds on her wrists, but evidently that was too much to hope for. She tried to straighten up from the bowed position she'd been forced into, but the agony was such that she could not stifle a cry.

The rough male voices suddenly ceased. Intent only on escape, Bridget took a few staggering steps, but her limbs were still numb. She would have fallen had not one of the savages grabbed her. Beyond terror, she could only await more torture.

As hard fingers bit into her arms, she realized that this was all but a game. There was no escape for her. Dear God, could it be that the people of Little Wheddborough had known a truth about her that she had not? Was she indeed a witch after all? What other reason could there be for such fiendish punishment?

By now her eyes were growing accustomed to the gray light that presages dawn. One look was enough to tell her that these were not the same drunken creatures who had captured her. The last shred of hope died. She might have escaped four savages, their senses befuddled by spirits, but what chance had she of escaping so many? These did not even smell of spirits, nor were they painted in the same hideous patterns.

"Kill me now and be done with it," she challenged with a recklessness born of despair.

The man whose fingers bit into her arms stared at her as if puzzled by her words. Biting her lip to keep from crying out, Bridget bore his rude scrutiny until her pitiful store of strength gave out and she swayed on her feet. She would have fallen had he not swung her up into his arms.

"Kill?" He seemed to turn the word over in his mind, examining it as if it were some oddly familiar trinket. "*Neep* kill. *Neep* kill *u-kettawa E-tau-wa*."

Bridget could have wept. She recognized not one of the words they had spoken. These people were not Hatorask. Their tongue was different even from those who had murdered Isaac and Cormick and tormented her. Who were they? What did they intend to do with her?

She sniffed, and then sniffed again. There was a scent about them that was oddly familiar. Musk? She had smelled the same cloying scent on Kokom's hands after he had skinned out a muskrat. Could it be that she had been sold or traded to a band of trappers while she slept?

She began to twist in the arms of her newest captor. Grunting, he shifted position, affording her a look at the place where she had lain suffering through the night.

One look was enough to tell her what had happened. The murdering fiends who had captured her lay sprawled where they had fallen in a drunken stupor, arrows now protruding from their throats and chests. Bridget felt her gorge rise. She moaned, her face turning faintly greenish, and was quickly set on her feet.

Finally, her throat raw from retching, she leaned weakly against a tree, only dimly aware of the low murmur of male voices behind her. Peering longingly into the dark forest, she gauged her chances of slipping away and hiding. She had no illusions about her fate if she were to be caught again, but even a small chance was better than none at all.

She moved carefully away, but before she could take more than a few steps her wrists were caught in an iron grip and jerked upward, causing her to sag to her knees. "Would that I were a man, you wicked heathen," she gasped defiantly. Her wrists were dropped just before the pain became intolerable, and she tried to take heart from the fact that, so far at least, the beasts had not mutilated their victims as her first captors had done. She wondered if that meant they were less uncivilized.

Still on her knees, she studied them in the dim light. As a race, they were broad and squatty, neither handsome nor plain, and with none of the noble bearing of the Hatorask. They numbered six, and all seemed well past first youth. For the moment, at least, they seemed to mean her no harm. "What people are you?" she asked, speaking slowly and clearly.

It was only when she saw the way they were looking at her that she became aware of her ruined dress. Her breasts were exposed, and with her arms still bound tightly behind her, there was nothing she could do to hide herself. The one who wore two feathers in his headband lifted her to her feet and swung her around so that she faced him, her back to the others.

Striving for a look of confidence, she lifted her chin and spoke with scarce a tremor in her voice. "Who are you?" she asked again.

For a moment no one spoke. Then they began grunting and mumbling among themselves. Bridget waited for a moment, and then, addressing the one who seemed to be a leader of sorts, she said, "My name is Bridget. *Brid-get*. I am Eng-lish. I mean you no harm."

The savage's eyes beamed in sudden understanding. Thumping himself on the chest, he said proudly, "Taus-Wicce. *Taus-Wicce*. Poteskeet."

Thus far, so good, Bridget thought with a fresh glimmer of hope. Now if only he could understand her well enough to come to her aid. She struggled to think of a way to explain her needs, but it was near impossible to think clearly when her every bone and sinew cried out for relief and she was dizzy for want of food and water.

She opened her mouth to ask for food in the Hatorask tongue, but before she could speak, dark spots began to dance before her eyes. To her dismay she felt herself begin to topple, but the savage's hands shot out and caught her before she fell. When she cringed away from his touch, he merely grunted and propped her against a tree. "Please, won't you help me?" she whispered.

There followed another terse discussion among the six men, with the one who called himself Taus-Wicce having the last word. Bridget wondered if they were arguing her fate. Somehow she must make them understand that she needed to reach Albemarle.

"Albemarle?" she said hopefully. "David Lavender? If you will but take me to him I'm sure he will pay you well for my safe return."

"Pay?" one of the men repeated. "Pay gold?"

There was another flurry of talk among the men. They broke apart and stared at her in the growing light. One of the closest reached down to touch her hair, which fell in pale tangles over her shoulders, for she had long since lost the bindings that would have held her braids intact. "Ungh! Gold. Pay gold."

In spite of her weakness, Bridget knew she must correct this misunderstanding quickly, for it would not do to give the savages false hopes. She had no notion at all that David Lavender would be willing to pay more than a token for her return, especially as she had no intention of marrying him. In their disappointment, these men could murder David, and her, as well.

It seemed that the savages came in all shades of good and bad, as did the English, and were ever more unpredictable.

"Perhaps trade would be a better term. *Trade*," she enunciated clearly. "That is, Mr. Lavender will trade you something of value—perhaps a knife or some food. Corn?" She knew how dearly all the Hatorask held their corn, never wasting a single one of the colorful grains.

No—not corn. At their lack of response, Bridget recalled hearing that corn grew so well in this rich land that one had only to poke a hole in the dirt and drop in a grain for three to sprout. It was only on Croatoan that it failed to thrive and needed to be taken in trade. What would these men value?

Taus-Wicce turned to her again, his face expressionless. Taking his knife from his belt, he knelt behind her, and just before Bridget's heart stopped beating altogether, she felt the bonds on her wrists give way.

As great as her relief was, the ache, as she tried to move her arms, was near unendurable. Finally she was able to bring them around onto her lap. After several moments she reached up and began fumbling with the torn edges of her dress until she managed to tie it together. With her modesty once more intact, there returned a measure of dignity.

"Thank you," she whispered graciously.

"Pay trade. Hoag. *U-kettawa E-tau-wa* come," the savage grunted, lifting her to her feet. And then as one, the six men broke into a trot, weaving their way through the forest as if it were the broadest street in all London.

Bridget stumbled along after them, grateful that they spoke a few words of English. It had been the words *pay* and *trade* that had turned the tide in her favor. And surely Hoag was the name of the trading post where Isaac and Cormick had been taking her. It seemed that she would finally reach her journey's end after all.

Had it not been for her months of living among the Hatorask, Bridget could never have traveled so far and so fast on feet that were bruised and torn. She had long since grown used to bearing all manner of discomforts, and now pride alone kept her from crying out. When she tripped over a root and fell, her captors waited stoically for her to rise again, neither reviling her nor offering to help. It was as if they looked on her as cargo, something of value to be delivered to the trading establishment.

Bridget had long since learned that the natives of this land never walked, but ran when they journeyed from one place to another. Like the Hatorask, these people—what had they called themselves, Poteskeet?—moved at a swift pace, tempered only by her inability to keep up with them. She had grown surprisingly strong and able during her stay on Croatoan, regaining the strength she had lost in prison, and more, but after the ordeal of the past night, she could only stumble after them and hope they would not lose patience and disappear, leaving her stranded in the midst of the dense, featureless forest.

"Hoag," Taus-Wicce grunted, stopping suddenly. "Trade."

Bridget leaned against the shaggy bark of a huge cedar tree, breathing in the sweet resinous scent. "The trading post? Where?" she panted.

The dark-skinned man pointed, and Bridget strained to see something besides more trees. Was that a rooftop? Indeed, she could make out three small cottages, widely spaced and roughly hewn, yet obviously inhabited by people of her own sort. Relief flooded through her. One of them might even belong to David Lavender. In another few moments, she could be seated at a real table before a warm hearth, drinking real tea and taking her fill of biscuits! Surely under one of those roofs there would be a place where she could rest for a few hours before she must think of beginning to repay her mountainous debts. "Then come, let us hurry so that Mr. Hoag can send for David Lavender."

Taus-Wicce and one other slipped away, and Bridget called after them, "Wait! Surely you don't mean to leave me here?" She took a few steps to follow, but one of the other men took her arm in a firm grasp and held her back. He pointed to the ground before her and said gruffly, "Sit."

Bridget was so astonished that she sat. From that moment on, she was ignored. The four men who remained talked idly among themselves, and after awhile one of them went farther into the woods and came back a moment later adjusting his tail clout.

Nettled by their disregard, Bridget stood, gritting her teeth against the pain of her throbbing ankle, and hobbled off in the opposite direction until she found a bush thick enough to hide her. Afterward she lingered to adjust her dress. There was little she could do about her appearance, for the small bundle that contained her clothing, poor though it was, was still aboard the shallop.

A shudder passed over her as she relived that horrible moment. She was incredibly fortunate to have escaped with her life. The fact that she was ragged and barefoot was naught to cry over now, for surely David would understand when she explained all that had befallen her.

No. Not *all* that had befallen her. She could not bring herself to tell anyone about Kinnahauk and what had passed between them. Even now she had trouble crediting such a thing, yet she had not dreamed it. Nor would she ever forget the single most beautiful experience in her entire life, and the man she had come to love despite all reason.

Weary beyond belief, Bridget was dozing on a soft bed of pine straw, trying to convince herself that she was not freezing to death, when Taus-Wicce and his friend returned. With them was a bear of a man, his sallow face showing blue where he had scraped away his heavy beard, and his oddly pale eyes buried in pouches of sagging flesh.

"Aye, ye be right, heathen. She be English, all right, and a fair piece o' work, at that."

Bridget felt something inside her shrink away from the heavyset man in the dusty dark suit and knee-high moccasins. Could this be David Lavender? Dear God, she would rather have taken her chances in Newgate than tie herself to such a man as this. He fair reeked of evil!

With choppy motions, the man signed something to the savage, who gestured angrily back, shaking his head several times for emphasis.

"Ain't worth all that much, you stinkin' redskin, but I'd jest as leave keep me hair. Salt, two knives and a lookin' glass, an' that's me final price."

Taus-Wicce scowled at the man, then signaled for Bridget to rise and follow. She felt an inexplicable reluctance to trade her savage escort for the company of this rough-looking creature, yet what choice had she?

The man reached out and grabbed her by the chin, angling her face for a better look. Something shifted in his eyes at the sight of the mark on her brow, but he made no comment. Bridget cringed as his gaze moved slowly down her body, lingering on the torn doeskin that barely covered her breasts. If he touched her, she would shrivel up and die!

"We'll clean ye up and see if'n ye're worth what them heathens is askin' fer ye, witch woman. Squaw women ain't worth much in these parts."

Meekly Bridget followed the men past the three houses she had seen, to Hoag's Trading Post. There she learned that her host was not David Lavender, but Boris Hoag. After the Poteskeets had taken their trade goods and gone with scarcely another look in her direction, Bridget cautiously took measure of her surroundings.

The trading post was a rambling assembly of boxlike rooms, each tacked on to the last, with no semblance of order. Inside, casks and barrels, crocks and jugs jostled together amidst iron pots, bolts of dusty cloth, bundles of skins and packets of bright gold tobacco leaves, their stem ends bound together. Lanthorns hung from the overhead timbers, and a crude bar reached across one end, its rough-hewn surface stained and scarred from usage. The stench was overwhelming, partly from so many raw skins and partly from years' accumulation of filth.

"Well, now, witch woman, supposin' ye tell old Hoag how long ye been whorin' fer them savages? Looks like they done treated ye good, tradin' ye off whilst ye was still in one piece. Most white women don't fare so well once them red devils gets aholt of 'em."

Bridget swallowed her wrath and took her time before replying. Even with her body one enormous ache, she had not quite lost her wits. She was suddenly quite sure that the less this man knew about her past, the better off she would be. She was now indebted to him for the sum of a sack of salt and a few trinkets, but that was the least of her worries. Poor David Lavender. She was beginning to dread meeting him after all that had passed.

"I was on my way to join the planter who paid my passage out to the colonies, when the oystermen who were bringing me here were attacked and killed. I, um, was rescued by the men you just met, and they were kind enough to bring me here.''

Hoag's grin revealed a set of tobacco-stained teeth that could have bitten through nails. ''Strikes me there be a mite more to the tale than ye're willin' to own up to, Missy, but it be no skin off old Hoag's nose. What be the name of this planter who bought ye?''

''D-David Lavender. Of Albemarle. Do you know him?'' When there was no response, she thought he had not heard her, but then he began to swear softly.

''Is there some problem?'' she asked timidly.

''Problem?'' Hoag belched and patted his stained belly. He offered her a greasy smile as if to apologize, while his mind turned over rapidly. The little whore! Good thing he had got to her before she'd had a chance to ruin everything! Setting that bitch Sudie up with Lavender as a poor widow in need of protection had been a stroke of genius, and her with the whiskey-maker's brat in her belly. The gibbet bait had sworn to him that the female Lavender had paid passage for had died of the same fever that had taken her own dearly beloved during the crossing, and been buried at sea.

Her ''dearly beloved!'' He had choked on that one. Hoag had known damned well she'd been lying, for he made it his business to know what went on in the territory. She'd lied to him about Fickens, and clearly she'd lied to him about Lavender's woman. The bleeding bitch! Now one word from this redskin's whore, and even a sheep-headed sop like Lavender might lift his noggin out of his grog long enough to start asking questions. It had been a right fair game, with Sudie keeping Lavender drunk and tipping off Hoag's man when it was safe to raid the storehouse or butcher a few head of beef. After each such raid, moccasin tracks were always set near the property, and Sudie spread the alarm about the painted devils who'd been seen hanging around the woods nearby.

Feeling her worried eyes on him, Hoag turned back to Bridget and the present problem. "Lavender, ye say, hmm?" He scraped a thumb across his bristling jaw with audible results as his mind worked feverishly. He had to get to Sudie first, while Lavender was still up the Chowan trying to find out which band of renegades was stealing his cattle. Pity the fool hadn't thought to look into the barrels of pickled beef in Hoag's back room. "I s'pose ye heerd the man took a wife?" He ventured a sly look at the beauty in the ruined doeskin gown to see how she took the news. One way or another, she was going to be a gold mine.

Bridget blinked. Married! Her David Lavender was married? That possibility had never occurred to her—not that it mattered any longer. Had she still been of a mind to wed him herself, she might have been devastated. Now it no longer seemed important. Indeed, with her head buzzing like a swarm of bees, nothing seemed important. "Mayhap Mrs. Lavender would need a maid? I—I'm not afraid of hard work."

"Why weary yerself with hard work? Now, if ye was to stay here, I could find it in me heart to see that ye'd plenty to eat an' a roof over yer 'ead, an' ye'd never have to lift a hand."

Bridget frowned. Muzzy headed or not, she knew she would rather take her chances with the savages who had brought her here than stay on in this stinking hovel. "Mayhap I could have a sup of water and a bite to eat, and we could go to see Mistress Lavender?"

Aye, Hoag thought with a malicious little smile, Sudie would like that just fine, having a tasty little morsel like her underfoot all the time, looking sweet as sugarcane with them little teats jiggling under Lavender's nose. Like as not, she'd end up the same as Fickens did, and he, Hoag, would be out one good whore. He thought that with women scarce as hen's teeth in these parts, he'd be a fool not to make use of what providence had put in his path.

Clearing his throat, he said, "Seems to me they won't want another mouth to feed, what with a babe on the way." The old sow was swole as big as a hogshead and would not take kindly to having a fetchin' little mort like this around, for she was as vain as she was greedy.

Bridget began to grow desperate. She had to get away from this man, no matter what! Oh, why had she let Gray Otter talk her into leaving? Even though Kinnahauk no longer wanted her, she would have stayed with Sweet Water, helping her care for the old ones of the village. Just to see him in passing, just to hear his voice—that would have been enough if that was all she could ever have.

She could scarce breathe in this fetid atmosphere. The man Hoag was as rank as his pigsty. "I saw other houses nearby. Could we not inquire at one of those? I'm quite skilled with herbs, and I can read a bit and cipher."

"Cipher, eh?" Hoag responded absently, for he was busy thinking of how best to make use of his new possession. "Spinnin' and weavin', cookin' and scrubbin', and spreadin' thigh come nightfall, that be what a man needs. Not cipherin' and such. Now if I was to offer ye a position in this here establishment—"

"At any rate, I must see Mr. Lavender first. I owe him for my passage, and I'll not rest easy until I have begun to repay him." Nor will I rest easy until I'm free of you, she added silently, for the man Hoag frightened her in a way she did not quite understand.

The trader seemed to consider for a moment, and then he heaved himself up from the barrel where he'd been sitting, thick thighs sprawled obscenely in the filthy woolen breeches. "Well, old Hoag'll do his best by ye, lassie." He fetched her a gourd of water from a filthy bucket, and she drank greedily. Slipping the knife from his belt, he cut a sliver from one of the hams that hung from the rafters. "I'll ride on out to the Lavender place and tell them ye're here. Ye'll find a pallet in yon corner."

Bridget's eyes widened. "Oh, no—please! I'll go with you!"

Hoag's gaze touched on her face briefly before following the slender outline of her body beneath the filthy doeskin. Seeming to reach some conclusion, he nodded.

Before they had been gone a quarter of an hour, he had thought it through. Seeing the mort would throw a scare into Sudie, all right. She might not have believed him without proof.

Aye, he'd fallen into a heap of luck this time. With a bit of good fortune, he could collect on both ends. Cleaned up, the girl would be a prize. Females of her sort were rare in these parts, and for all she'd been living for God-knows-how-long with the filthy, thieving redskins, she could still pass for an innocent.

For the first time, he was almost glad of the fact that he couldn't use her himself. Were it not for that damned Tuscarora arrow ten years ago that had caught him where it did the most damage, she would have ended up the way all those pretty little squaws had. He would have had to paddle what was left of her out into the creek and sink her with a rock tied around her neck. Ahh, he mused, the good times were gone forever, and him still in his prime. Now all he could do was pay other men to let him watch when the notion took him.

He scratched his crotch absently, and his mind turned to what in recent years had become the driving force behind everything he did. Profit. He would take the little white squaw out to Lavender's and find out how much Sudie was willing to pay to be rid of her.

He turned to the woman who jostled along at his side, looking more dead than alive. He should have given her a dram before they left to keep the blood flowing in her body. "Ye be all alone now that Lavender's got himself a wife?" he asked, adopting an avuncular tone of voice.

"I, um, have friends on Croatoan. And one of the women who crossed with me is married and lives not too far from here," Bridget confessed, thinking it best not to appear *too* alone.

"Croatoan, huh?" So that was where she'd passed the winter. Had she escaped, or had the Haties traded her to the Potes? Not that it mattered. Hoag hated one tribe as much as the other, for all of them cheated him. Even the white trappers, thieving bastards, held out their best pelts, claiming Hoag didn't pay fair prices.

He'd show them fair prices! Wait until he had this little mort stashed away in his back room, her soft white thighs and teats there for the taking by any man that brought in a decent bundle of furs. He'd have them all crawling to his doorstep, just begging for a chance to get at her!

"Funny savages, them Haties," he drawled in a conversational tone. "Keeps to themselves. Seen one or two of 'em up thisaway lookin' to trade tea-bush an' oysters fer corn an' flint, but fer the most part, they stays clear o' us civilized folk."

The rutted trail that wound through the trees turned to run alongside a cleared field, with remnants of last season's corn still standing. Now in the last days of winter, it looked dismal and uninviting. "Lavender place," Hoag said with a nod. "Corn, terbaccy 'n cattle. Not much of a planter, but I reckon if that bunch o' renegade Tuscarora that's been raidin' all up and down the river stealing cows ever moves on, they'll make do. Got a young 'un on the way—ain't nothing like a new young 'un to make an old man's back hairs roach up all proudlike."

"Old?" Somehow Bridget had pictured David Lavender as young, with fine features and clear eyes.

"Some men wears out early. Drinkin' and womanizin' is all right if a man's got the gizzard fer it, but Lavender was wore out when his family shipped him out here to the colonies."

Bridget contrasted that image with one of a tall, vital young man with golden eyes, a man who spoke of honor as if it were as much a part of him as his own shadow. She thought of the simple lodges built of rushes, simply furnished with clean mats of sea grass, moss and spicy herbs as they drew up before the cramped, boxlike structure of unskint logs that sat squarely in the center of a raw clearing. "This is…it?" she asked timidly. No attempt at all had been made to soften the uncompromising lines.

"Aye, this here be the Lavender plantation. I'd be obliged if'n ye'd allow me to speak to Mistress Lavender afore ye joins us, fer her being in the family way and all, she be apt to take a start from seein' a stranger. Beggin' yer pardon," he added in a servile tone as he glanced quickly at the mark on her brow and away again.

His meaning was quite clear. No woman, pregnant or not, would care to be confronted with a woman bearing the mark of a witch. With little choice, Bridget shifted to a more comfortable position on the hard wooden bench. The wagon was crudely constructed, more suited for hauling freight than passengers, but she was grateful not to have to walk, for she was more aware with each passing moment of all the aches and pains in her body. The sliver of salty meat and the water had helped, but her belly still rumbled with hunger, and besides, she was so tired she could have gone to sleep in the cart tracks.

Huddling in the paltry warmth of a setting sun, she watched the broad back of the trader disappear through a low, wide door. All she saw of the woman who had bade him enter was a flash of blue skirt and a pale hand. As shadows stretched longer across the clearing, she shivered. Odd—she had gotten used to the cold on Croatoan until she scarce felt it, but now it seemed to reach into her very bones and leach the marrow from them.

Inside the log house, Sudie paced, one hand to the small of her back, the other tightened into a fist. "Are ye certain she be the same one?"

"She bears the mark ye described, but I doubt she be a witch, or she'd have witched her way out o' the hands o' them heathens afore now."

"'Od's truth, I'd sell me soul fer a decent servant. I'd sell me mother's soul fer a wet nurse, fer the thought of havin' some stinkin' brat swingin' from me paps fair sickens me!"

"She'll not serve ye there, fer I vow she could pass fer a maiden. Aye, she be a fair mort, Sudie," Hoag said slyly. "I vow David'll be thinkin' the same."

Sudie gave him a sharp look. "We be wed fair an' proper."

Knowing the shrewd woman was well aware of her vulnerable position, he weighed his next words carefully. "Aye, but not all knots stay tied, if ye take me meaning?"

The color drained from Sudie's face, leaving her sharp features pasty. She raked a hand over the lank brown hair that was skewered into an untidy knot at the back of her head. "Damn you, Boris Hoag, I told ye it was them redskins that kilt me poor Albert!"

Hoag bared his strong yellow teeth in an evil grin. Knowledge was power, and power was profit in the hands of a man shrewd enough to use it. "Aye, I keeps fergettin'. Still, we'd best both remember what we stand to lose when Lavender finds out his bride's come back from the dead."

"'e's upriver. Won't be back till the morrow."

"Still a-huntin' fer them thievin' bastids that stole his cattle?" he asked with mock solicitude.

Ignoring him, Sudie took another turn around the cramped, cluttered room. "Why the devil didn't the stupid twit drown like she was supposed to?"

"There be ways of gettin' rid of a problem with no one the wiser. Trust yer old friend Boris, fer I'd not serve ye false."

"I'd sooner trust a ditch full of devils. The only one you ever served was Boris Hoag." But Sudie had come too far to turn back now. All her life she had been forced to play the beast with two backs to keep body and soul together. By marrying a weakling now and turning him into a sot, she no longer had to put up with that, at least. A few more years and she'd be set for life. "Get rid of 'er," she said flatly.

"Oh, my, ye'd not ask me to do away wi' an' innocent what never done me a mite o' wrong." Hoag assumed a look of shock.

One look from Sudie's sharp iron-black eyes told him what she thought of his protestations. He shrugged. "If'n I was to take her off yer hands, I'd want some consideration fer me risk. I happens to know yer man gets a nice bit o' gold fer every year he stays away from his lovin' family. Now if'n some o' that gold was to find its way inter safe-keepin', the poor man'd be less likely to be found wi' 'is 'ead bashed in by thievin' redskins." Hoag began to nod with satisfaction. Aye, he was a shrewd one, all right, he thought. From squeezing his way up stinking chimneys with hot coals put to his feet, he'd fought his way in the world single-handed, until now he was owner of the grandest emporium between Virginie and Charles Towne. Balls or not, that made him a man!

"The sot's hid his gold, the snot-nosed miser! Ye'll take a few hands o' terbaccy from the smokehouse or nothing, fer I can't get down on me 'ands and knees and search for it! Once I get shed o' this brat, I'll find that strongbox, an' when I do, I'll buy me way up to Virginie and leave this stinkin' place to the snakes and the redskin savages!" She peered closely at Hoag. "Ye're certain sure she be the same one? Yaller 'air, gray eyes, a mark branded on 'er brow?"

"Look fer yerself," Hoag invited with a shrug. If he had to make do with naught but tobacco for his troubles, he would make sure he got his money's worth from the witch girl, one way or another.

Sudie sidled clumsily up to one of the narrow slots that bracketed the door, constructed to allow a wide view and a good shot. "Aye, it be 'er, awright," she said sullenly. "Pity she didn't end up in the belly of a sea monster."

Chapter Twenty-Two

There was nothing at all in Kinnahauk's expression as he admired the many choice pelts in the cypress dugout to indicate that his heart swelled with pride and anticipation. This would make a fine bride-price. If David Lavender demanded more, he would somehow find a way to pay it, but it would take time, and the waiting would not be easy. Among the Hatorask, a man could offer for the woman of his choice, and once the offer was accepted by her father, she could move into his *ouke*. But honor decreed that no matter how many times they had shared a sleeping mat in the past, once the offer was made, they must live as brother and sister until the full bride-price was paid. This could take many moons.

Kinnahauk had gazed down on the woman of his choice as she lay sleeping on his mat and known that he must move swiftly or risk losing his honor. Leaving the token of declaration, he had taken three men and the largest canoe and headed north at a swift pace, stopping only to send word by runners from the villages along the way. Word had passed quickly that Kinnahauk of Croatoan would give much *peage* for the finest pelts. A meeting place had been named, and partly out of hatred for the white trader, Hoag, many trappers had come forth—Tuscarora, Haynoke and Nottoway—even white-eyes. They brought thick beaver from the high mountain waters to the west, and many soft pelts from the vicious little mink. From a trapper just down from the cold lands to the north had come the finest pelts Kinnahauk had ever seen.

Kinnahauk had dealt fairly with all, trading the valuable black-and-purple *peage*, which was hard and took much time in drilling. He offered gold coin in exchange for the rarest and thickest skins, and both *peage* and one gold coin for the skins of two rare white lynx.

The trading had taken longer than he had planned. Three days had passed before they were ready to leave the Big Bay of the Coritucks. Now they raced to reach Taus-Wicce's village of Pasquinoc near the throat of the Albemarle before the sun walked down.

"My belly rumbles for the feast awaiting us in Pasquinoc," said Calls the Crows.

"Paugh! It is not your belly that guides you to Taus-Wicce's village, but your root. I have seen the way you look upon Little Foot," Crooked Stick taunted.

At the head of the long canoe, Kinnahauk stroked smoothly and silently as the sun slipped down and began to pour its fire onto the water. His gaze followed the low, wooded shore, noting certain trees and stumps that had guided him along this shore many times. He was aware of the quiet voices behind him, but his own thoughts were not on the cook fire of Taus-Wicce's wives, nor on the attentions of the young unmarried maidens of the Poteskeet village. He thought of his *oquio*, of the way her lips parted as she slept, of the sweet scent of her skin and the golden treasure that she had shared with him so sweetly. He thought of her gentle patience with the children of his village and with the old ones who told the same stories many times over. He thought of her quick laughter and her stubborn courage.

She would be his first wife, his only wife.

Kinnahauk's heart bade him journey through the night so that he could return to her more quickly, but years of having to choose between wisdom and the recklessness of

youth demanded otherwise. He would pass this night with
his friends at Pasquinoc and be on his way before first light.
Taus-Wicce would know how to find the man Davidlavender, for little escaped his sharp eyes in the region the white-
eyes called Albemarle.

Hoag had lost little time in telling Bridget that there
would be no work for her in the Lavender household.
"Brought up yer papers, I did, Missy. Lavender's woman
signed 'em over to me fer due consideration, so it be Boris
Hoag that owns ye now."

Bridget was horrified at his words. She might be free of
debt to David Lavender, but she would have sooner owed
a stranger than this man who caused her flesh to crawl with
a look from his colorless eyes.

Word had spread quickly that there was a strange woman
at Hoag's Trading Post. Not only the men, but the women
as well came to gawk at her. At first, Bridget had dared to
hope that she could find someone in need of her skills, but
before three days had passed, it was painfully clear that she
was not welcome in the settlement. At least, not among the
women, who were inclined to glare at the mark on her brow
and whisper among themselves.

The men did not glare. If their eyes seemed to linger on
her more than was necessary to satisfy common curiosity,
it was not at the mark on her brow, but at the swell of her
breasts that showed above the gaping neck of her gown in
spite of all she could do. Even when she took to wearing her
shawl indoors, pulled tightly around her throat, they stared
at her face, her hips and her bare ankles.

Hoag had suggested that she might repay him by acting
as a hostess for some of the men who did business with him,
but at Bridget's flat refusal, he had not forced the issue. In
the end he had agreed to trading food and a pallet in the
corner in exchange for her labors in his establishment. He
had even given her a gown, a shawl and two aprons, all
well-worn and meant for someone half her height and twice

her girth. The shoes he had offered her had been worn beyond use, and she had begged a scrap of spoiled buckskin
and stitched herself a pair of moccasins instead.

Bridget had not dared ask how he had come by such
garments, fearing she would not like the answer. Truly, she
was an ungrateful wretch, for even knowing that he had
saved her from starvation and worse, she could not find it
in her heart to be thankful. The pallet that he had shown
her had been infested with vermin, the food stores that he
expected her to use no better. She had scrubbed her knuck-
les raw those first few days, waiting only until Hoag had
gone to his own room before collapsing onto the mat she
had fashioned from moss and buckskin.

From the beginning, Bridget had been terrified that he
might want to wed her, but he had not insisted on marriage. Nor had he shown any interest in her as a woman,
although she did not much care for the way he watched her,
his beady eyes narrowed as if speculating on what lay beneath her rough garments.

If he appreciated her cooking, he failed to show it, other
than in a series of loud belches. He ignored altogether the
area of cleanliness that was growing larger each day, yet
Bridget continued to scrub, using the bar of lye soap she
had unearthed under a mound of filthy, moth-eaten fleeces.
It would not last long. The crock of tallow she had thought
to use for candles would do as well for soap if she could
find a burned stump for lye water.

Mayhap if she could make enough soap to sell, scenting
it as her mother had done with sweet herbs and spices, she
would be able to buy her freedom sooner. And just yesterday she had unearthed a set of candle molds and thought
that if she made candles as well, mayhap...

Pausing in her labors, Bridget allowed herself a brief
dream of freedom and independence. Beyond that, her
mind refused to venture. If she cried in her sleep, it was only
because her heart had not had time to heal. In years to

come, she would forget all about the man who had taught
her to love.

Oh, aye—when cats swam and fish walked, and the sun
danced round the moon!

To hasten the day when she would be free, Bridget offered to help with the accounts, for she was almost certain
that Hoag could not read. If he could cipher at all, it was
only with the help of knotted strings and notched sticks, but
from the way he glared at her when she ventured her suggestion, one would have thought she had insulted his pride.
If a man like Boris Hoag even knew the meaning of the
word.

So she continued to scrub. On her hands and knees, she
was scouring years of accumulated grease from the floor
around the hearth and trying to avoid being seen by a tart-
tongued woman called Piety Smith, when she heard the
door open and close.

"Why, Mistress Lavender, I've not seen you about for
many a day. Have ye heard the news? If I were in your delicate condition, I'd not set foot in this place for fear my
babe would be marked by Hoag's witch woman."

Bridget's face flushed in anger, but she held her tongue.
In the few days she had been there, she had been pointed
out, whispered about, leered at, jeered at, prayed over and
scorned, and all by the fine, upstanding citizens of the Albemarle settlement. "If I were as wicked and as powerful
as they all seem to think," she muttered under her breath,
sloshing water from her pail as she slid it to another part of
the floor, "I would long since have turned them all to
doormice!"

"Awrr, it's too soon fer me brat to be marked, Piety, fer
I've not been wed but fivemonth come March. Me own
dear mother told me that a babe's still safe in 'is caul till
after sevenmonth."

Sudie was livid. Hoag had promised to rid her of this
threat. Instead, he had brought the wretched mort here
where all could see and gossip about her. If he had delib-

erately set about destroying all their careful work in getting her settled into the household of that whining old crock, Lavender, why he could not have done a better job of it!

"Why, I thought you was closer to lying in than that!" Piety exclaimed.

"Nay. Still, the way me back pains me, I feel the little darlin' may be burstin' out afore 'is time. Impatient like 'is dear old father, is me little lad."

Still hidden behind the counter that separated the kitchen from the public room, Bridget stared unseeingly at the pail of dirty water. Odd how the memory could tease—Mistress Lavender's voice sounded almost familiar.

"G'day to you, Piety," said a third woman just entering the room. "Why Mistress Lavender, I be surprised your man would allow you to set foot out of the house in your condition."

"*Allow* me? Ye've lived so long in these godforsaken colonies yer brains 'as turned to black rot, Johanna Jones. The cock struts and crows, but 'tis the hen that rules the roost."

Bridget grew still, the discomfort of having spent hours on her knees forgotten. Surely her ears were playing her false. 'Twas not possible that Sudie Upston and Mistress Lavender were one and the same—was it? She had to be sure!

"Mayhap," Piety said, "but I'd not trade my cock for any number of hens."

"Wait till your cock takes the food out of your young'uns mouths to trade for skins," jeered Mistress Jones.

"Skins! And me with the best wheel and loom in all Albemarle? Why would Henry be wanting skins?"

"You mean you ain't heard about Hoag's contest?"

There was a spate of whispering, an astonished exclamation, and Bridget, her face burning, heard the one who sounded so much like Sudie give tongue to a string of gutter oaths.

What contest? Bridget knew of no contest.

Crawling forward until she could peer between the table legs, she looked out into the room. One glance was enough to recognize that sallow face with the pointed chin and the narrow black eyes. Sudie was big with child, but other than that she had changed little since they had first met in a cart bound for Newgate. Remnants of beauty could still be found if one looked deeply enough, but on meeting such a mean expression, few would bother.

The women were gone before Bridget could recover her wits. A moment later, the door opened again and three trappers walked inside. Bridget got slowly to her feet and called out to Hoag, who was working in the storeroom. The three men, two white and one redskin, dropped their bundles of furs and boldly stared at her.

"We heared 'bout the contest. Be she the one?" The tall, red-haired man asked Hoag as he joined them.

Bridget thought that her ears must be deceiving her as she listened to their conversation. They spoke about her as if she were not there, discussing such things as whether she was a virgin, how many men she had lain with, if it was true that lying with a witch gave a man certain powers that would enable him to perform beyond his wildest dreams.

As soon as the trappers had gone, Bridget turned on Hoag. "You are not fit to be called a human being! How could you even *think* of doing anything so dreadful?" All color had fled her face, leaving it white as whey.

His small eyes narrowed until they were barely visible in the pouches of yellow fat that surrounded them. "Did ye think to live on Hoag's charity forever, witch woman?"

"Charity! I've fair broken my back trying to turn this pigsty into a decent place! Pigsty, indeed—why, no self-respecting pig would live in such filth! You had no right—"

"Right!" the trader roared. He leaned forward, thrusting out his beard-peppered jaw belligerently. "I'll tell ye about rights! Rights is what you ain't got! Twice I paid fer your rights, witch—oncet from the damned redskins and oncet from Lavender's woman. Hoag ain't never been bested in any deal, and he ain't aboot to start wi' some mealymouthed, scar-faced whore!" By the time he had finished speaking, he was shaking her roughly. Damned woman was more trouble than she was worth, he thought bitterly and pushed her roughly aside.

Asking about his accounts like she suspicioned him of cheating. Looking at him with those great gray eyes of hers like it was his fault she weren't queen of the May! If she could whore for the Potes and the Haties, she could whore for his trappers! This idea he had was going to put an end to the trappers holding out on him. The lazy, lying bastards had got it in their heads that Boris Hoag was in business to make *them* rich! When he wouldn't pay what they demanded, they commenced to whining about a sorry season and held back all but the poorest skins, saving out the rest for some new buyer he heard was fixing to go into business upriver.

The idea of using the witch woman as bait had struck him the first time he'd seen the way they had looked at her. They'd been fair busting their codpieces to get at her, but he'd held back, knowing there was a better way than just to lock her in a room and let them at her for a few shillings a shot.

Hell, she'd have been wore out by now. Yeller hairs didn't hold up as well as a pretty little squaw. He had toyed with the idea of selling her to a planter, but why sell once what you could sell a hundred times over?

Then the idea for the contest had come to him. With trapping season just over, he had put out the word, knowing that the filthy redskins would spread it for him. Just how they managed this feat he had never fathomed, but the thieving bastards knew everything that happened to red and white alike. Just let a settler cut down a tree on the Chesapeake and before nightfall, some Santee down on the Congaree could tell you if it be pine or oak.

Hoag had enjoyed watching the men look from him to the woman and back again with a measure of envy in their eyes. It was clear they thought he had the use of her. Nor had he set them straight the first few days, for none knew of his ruination at the hands of the Tuscarora. He had long since killed the savages who had gelded him, as well as the only white man who had known about it—the planter who had found him bleeding and unconscious.

But gold spoke more loudly than pride, and Hoag was not a man to waste an opportunity when it landed in his lap.

He'd seen no reason to tell the witch woman the details of his contest, but he had let it be known that the trapper who brought in the finest pelts to be sold would have the first use of her. The man who brought in the second best bundle would tumble her next, and so on, each man in turn and all deals final. He had put out the word that she was hardly broken in, deciding against calling her a virgin. Enough that she was small, with a look about her that belied her whoring ways.

Trappers who had not set foot in his establishment in years came to look on his white witch, for the word had spread like wildfire. After one longing look, they hurried away to see if they could buy, beg or steal a bundle of choice northerly pelts or even a few of the buffalo skins that were seldom seen in this neck of the woods.

The day arrived. Hoag had not allowed too much time to pass, knowing that to keep interest high, he must move quickly. One of his many cluttered rooms was quickly cleared and made ready, and under Hoag's watchful eyes, Bridget was set the task of scrubbing it clean.

If Bridget could have escaped, she would have, but he had watched her like a hawk. If she could have got her hands on his knife, she would have gutted the devil and taken her chances in the forest, but she was never given the opportunity. It was as if he read her thoughts.

"Awrr, now, don't be hard on old Boris. I'd only make a livin' fer the both of us, girl. 'Tis better than starvin', ain't it? And it's not like it was something ye've never done before."

She cast him a look filled with hatred, her mind churning as she scrubbed. If she thought he would not catch her and kill her on the spot, she would have flung the scrub water in his face and run, but it would take more than a pail of water to stop such an animal. She must bide her time. Somehow, she was going to get away.

Under the guise of clearing away the heavy bales from the doorway, Hoag continued to watch her. Bridget stood and stared at the room when she was done. When he had first ordered her to clean it, she had refused, knowing what it was intended for. He had struck her on the side of the head, making sure he did not mark her face. For hours afterward, her ears had rung and ached.

Now, tight-lipped, she could barely bring herself to speak. "No matter what you say, I am not going through with it."

"Oh, aye? And what d'ye intend to do about it, climb upon yer broomstick and fly off to yer friends, the Potes?"

"I'd a thousand times rather spend the rest of my life with them than another minute in your presence. Even breathing the air that surrounds you fair sickens me!"

Lashing out before she could duck away, Hoag struck her again, not bothering to avoid her face this time. "Damn yer wicked tongue, woman, ye made me do that!" His regret was not for having hurt her, for pain—either his own or someone else's—meant little to him. But he did not care to have her stand before the trappers tonight with a blue and swollen jaw.

Damn her soul for taunting him so! Then, stealing a sly glance at the knot hole in a dark corner of the room, he allowed his temper to cool. Before another sunrise, he would see her humbled. And count the gold in his pockets every time she spread her thighs! He'd teach her to look down her nose at Boris Hoag!

Chapter Twenty-Three

Bridget watched dully as another trapper, his back bent under a heavy bundle of pelts, came through the door and searched for a clear place to drop his burden. With each one, Hoag's small pale eyes had glittered more feverishly. Had she really believed she could escape her fate? She had no more chance of escaping the cruel trader than she'd had of escaping those who had branded her a witch and thrown her in Newgate to rot.

Hoag's excitement had grown all day, until finally he had made his mistake. Leaving Bridget to get herself prettied up, he had headed for the storeroom to water down another barrel of rum before hauling it into the main room.

Bridget had waited only long enough for him to disappear. Grabbing her shawl, she had slipped out, carefully closed the door after her and darted around to the back, where the horses were kept. From there it was but a short distance to the edge of the woods. Once clear of the settlement, she'd had in mind following the edge of the water until she came to Hamish's Landing. No matter how long it took to get there, she had to try. If she went cautiously and kept her head, she would be all right. The forest may be filled with vicious creatures, both man and beast, but better an unknown fate than the wicked one that awaited her.

At least she would not starve along the way. There were nuts and roots, and freshwater creeks abounded in these parts.

Holding a finger to her lips to caution Hoag's horses to keep silent, she had edged around the corner of the fence, cringing at the soft whuffle and stomp of the slab-sided animals. All she had to do now was dash across the clearing to the woods.

"Goin' som'ers?" Hoag had inquired with that grin that always made her skin crawl. He'd been leaning up against the fence, his massive arms crossed over his grease-stained vest.

"I—my—"

"Ye wouldn't run out on poor old Hoag now, would ye? After all I've done to make ye feel at home? A room of yer own, pretty frocks, gentlemen to entertain ye of an evening? Why I'd call that purely ungrateful now, wouldn't you?"

Her arm had been already purpling with new bruises by the time he had flung her back into her room. From then on, he had not taken his eyes off her for a single moment. To her eternal shame, he had even forced her to scrub herself and dress while he watched.

"If I'm to be bartered so that you can fill your pockets with gold, then I'll stay as I am," she had declared, her skin gray with the grime of her day's work, her hair in tangles, and her misshapen gown wet and stained.

Once more she had been treated to the back of his hand. "I'll scrub ye meself," he had declared, giving her arm a vicious twist before scooping up the filthy rag she had used on the floor.

"Get out," she had choked. He had stood in the doorway, his bloated body blocking any chance of escape. Knowing he meant what he said, she had turned her back and splashed water over her face and neck, expecting at any moment to feel his horrible hands on her body.

"All over."

Knowing that if she didn't, he would, she had complied. As quickly as she could, after scrubbing herself in water from the pail left over from her cleaning, she had tugged her spare gown over her head. "There—I'm done now, you can leave me be."

"Do somethin' to yer hair if'n ye wants to keep it, Missy—it don't even look yeller no more."

Reluctantly she had bent over and dipped her head into the bucket, fumbling for her scrap of lye soap. After rinsing she had wrung the excess water from her hair and tugged it ruthlessly back from her face, tying it with a bit of string. She prayed that the sight of her witch-mark would put the trappers off and they would turn away in disgust. She deliberately left the sash off her gown so that it hung loose on her body, and she anchored her woven shawl closely about her throat, then turned to face her tormentor.

"Mr. Hoag, if you'll just let me go, I promise I'll repay you twice over what you paid Mr. Lavender for me. Somewhere there's *bound* to be someone who needs my skills."

"Aye, an' they be awaitin' fer ye now, woman. Every man in these parts what could skin a cat is here tonight, and more on the way." Grabbing her by the arm, he had begun dragging her through the warren of crowded rooms, the noise from the main room growing louder with each step. Bridget had hung back, nausea bringing a pinched look to her small features as she caught sight of the mass of filthy, leering faces. "No—please, Boris, I'll do anything you say, but not this. Not this..."

Futile hope. He had lifted her bodily up on top of an upturned cask that had been placed in a prominent position, and she had quickly been surrounded by a living wall. "Here she be, lads, just as I promised ye—pure as driven snow, purty as a new-struck guinea."

Scores of trappers, men who had been alone in the wilderness all season without sight of a white woman, as well as dozens of curious planters and even a few tradesmen, had been converging on the trading post all day. as word of the contest had spread from settlement to settlement. Boris Hoag was auctioning off a chance at the white witch to the man who brought in the finest furs by the night of the full moon. In a place where social gatherings were few, it was an exciting event.

Bridget tried to pray, but the noise was too deafening, the stench too sickening. Some small shred of pride that still remained was all that kept her from dissolving into a wailing mass of terror. Rise above it, she commanded herself, and she tried desperately. It did no good. She knew now that she would never be free of the nightmare that had commenced so long ago.

Once she had dared to hope... on Croatoan. Why had she allowed herself to be talked into leaving? Since then she had longed for Kinnahauk until her heart was wrung dry. Now she was glad he was not here, for she would not have him know of her shame.

Hoag strutted back and forth through the crowd, examining pelts, barking orders to his sullen helper to see that each man paid for all he ate and drank. He was obviously taking great pride in his new role as entrepreneur. "'Tis badly stretched, Pearson, and ye call yerself a fur man? Newcomb, them weasels ain't worth sweepin' out the door."

"Weasels! Them critters is mink!"

"Weasels. Look at Kumtewaw and Yellow Feather's bundle if'n ye want to see prime mink."

Thus he continued to spur them on, pitting one against another, red man against white. The trappers, too, did their share of gaming, holding back their best pelts to see what the competition would produce. Bridget looked on dully with a growing sense of doom as one trapper after another went back outside to return with a prize pelt, a special skin they had hoped to save out for a better price from another dealer. Hoag gloated. His prices were disgracefully low, but the trappers were a competitive lot, and he was greatly skilled at exploiting any man's weakness if it would line his own pockets.

"Do she truly be a witch? Ain't that the same as a conjure woman?" asked a young trapper just in from the great swamp after his first season. "Me pa says if a man beds a conjure woman, his pecker turns black and drops off come the next full moon."

There was a murmur of comment, and Bridget felt her face grow hot. She leaned forward and stared directly into the boy's innocent blue eyes. "Aye, your pa told you right," she whispered fiercely. "My mother was a conjure woman, and my grandmother before her! I be a seventh daughter of a seventh daughter, which makes me the most powerful kind of conjure woman! I know spells that not even the devil himself would dare to cast, and I vow that any man who lays a hand on me will—"

She was drowned out by the loud squawk of Hoag's forced laughter. "Aye, me little flower do like to tease, don't she, lads? As if any fool don't know the difference 'twixt a white witch and a conjure woman. Ain't many men lucky enough to come across a genuine white witch, for they's rare in these parts. Take it from old Boris, beddin' a creature like this is what separates the men from the boys, am I right, Newcomb? Pearson? Why, the pleasures they put a man through is downright mystical! The onliest danger be that once a man dips his wick in a white witch, he grows so powerful that women jest won't leave him be. They keeps a-whinin' and a-beggin' fer it all the time!"

There were a few snickers, a few jabbing elbows and a bit of strutting among the white trappers. The few red ones who had joined the rancid-smelling company tended to stand apart, their faces revealing neither pleasure nor displeasure.

Bridget shuddered, willing herself to ignore her surroundings, not to think about what lay ahead of her. Women had suffered and overcome shame and humiliation since the beginning of time. 'Twas but a trick of the mind to rise above the body. Had she not been told as much by Soconme?

Oh, God, even the women were going to witness her shame! Bridget stared in disbelief as Sudie entered with a lank, pinch-faced man in ill-fitting woolens and a soiled shirt. *This* wormish creature was her David Lavender? What fearful tricks the imagination could play, for she had pictured him as sweet and fair as the herb from which he took his name. In truth, he looked little better than Sudie. Even so, how could he stand by and watch what was happening to the woman he had brought over to be his bride?

"David—Sudie, please," Bridget cried out, but her voice was lost under the noise of the drunken revelry. David made his way directly to the bar, and Sudie, her head tossed back and her arms crossed over her bulging belly, smiled in satisfaction as she met Bridget's gaze with no sign of surprise. But of course she had known that Bridget had not drowned. Had she not?

It was all so confusing—and what did it matter now? As the scent of musky, unwashed bodies became suffocating, Bridget fought against nausea. It was barely dark, and the trading post was already bulging with men intent on milking the last drop of excitement from such a rare piece of entertainment. The skins that had been piling up on the floor all day were beginning to smell as the room heated up. Hoag had already broached a third keg of the watered-down spirits he labeled rum, having sold the pure stuff until his patrons were all too drunk to notice.

There were hours yet to go until the contest was declared at an end. Bridget knew that even if she survived those, she could not survive what would come afterward. To a man, the trappers wore knives strapped to their sides. She would steal the knife, she thought feverishly—she would kill if she had to—and this time when she escaped into the forest, she would be armed. In the darkness, she would not be recaptured so easily.

Kinnahauk had not been so filled with fear since he had walked the storm as a youth. They had stopped at Pasquinoc, thinking to feast and rest before going on to find the man, Davidlavender. Instead they had learned of a white woman bearing a fire mark on her brow, who had been rescued by Taus-Wicce and his hunters from a band of drunken Tuscarora renegades and taken where she wished to go—to the trading post of a man called Hoag.

"It is a bad place. I do not like to go there, but the woman spoke of trade. I do not try to understand the ways of the white-eye," said the Poteskeet on learning that the woman was the *waurraupa shaman* he had heard of who had lived with the Hatorask since the Moon of the White Brant.

The two men spoke in a mixture of Poteskeet and sign, for Taus-Wicce had stubbornly resisted learning the language of the white-eyes. "She is my woman," Kinnahauk said, pain in the very timbre of his voice.

"Then I must tell you what is said," the older man said, resting his hand on the shoulder of the young *werowance*. "It is said that she came here to join with the man, Lavender. It is said that Lavender has taken another woman, and that she is the same woman who killed the whiskey maker who lived two days walk from this place. It is said that Hoag holds your woman captive and will give her to the trapper who brings in the finest skins on the night when the moon shows her full face."

"Aiee, there is no time," Kinnahauk said softly, his eyes glittering like cold fire in the grayness that draws forth the night. "I must go now."

"You must not go unprepared. You are few and they are many. You seek a woman who is not of your own kind. This woman is one all men want, for she is good to look on."

"She would make the fairest blossom close its petals in shame."

Taus-Wicce's eyes kindled with sympathy. "It will be dangerous, my friend. These men are filled with lust and spirits. You must walk among them with great care. Four of my best warriors will go with you. Two of them speak the white-eyes's language. They have many friends among the trappers."

Unable to speak his feelings, Kinnahauk nodded. "Let us go quickly."

"My women will prepare food. It is no small distance."

"I cannot wait," Kinnahauk insisted, his soul burning in an agony of fear that he would not be in time. His little one had suffered much, and unless he moved more swiftly than the straightest arrow, she would suffer more. She could not live if that were so.

"Do not be foolish, my young friend. You must learn the patience that comes with age and wisdom, or the fires of youth will consume all you touch. There is a man called Hamish beyond the place where the Yeopim wintered in my father's day. He is a man of honor. Beyond there, you will come to no harm. Blue Feather's drunken men have returned to dust, and no others have come yet to take their place."

"I will kill the man Hoag if he has hurt her in any way."

Taus-Wicce grinned, creasing his lean, weathered cheeks. "He cannot hurt her in *that* way, my friend, for our old enemy Raucaucau robbed him of his seedpods long ago. You must plan carefully and take with you much wealth. I have been saving skins to buy myself another wife, but I can wait. With three wives, two are always fighting with the third. With four, each will have a friend and I will have some peace.''

Bridget narrowed her eyes against the smoke that was so thick in the room it was almost impossible to see to the far side.

A draft of cold air stirred the miasma, and she caught sight of another redskin slipping in, making his way along the wall. Like the others who had entered during the past few minutes, he carried no bundle of furs. Standing against the wall, arms crossed, one hand resting on the haft of his knife, he might well have been a statue for all his lack of expression.

What must they think of the men they called white-eyes, the same ones who called them savages? Bridget acknowledged that she had found far more nobility among those people who dwelt on Croatoan than could be found in a shipload of her own kind, save for a few.

The room was packed, the bundles laid out for judging. Shoulders hunched, she tried to ignore the fever pitch of excitement all about her; tried to pretend that she was back on Croatoan, smelling the clean salt air, hearing the laughter of the children as they played around the lodges; tried to pretend that the constant shuffle of feet against filthy pine floors was the whisper of the surf against the shore. Instead of the lewd comments, she heard the lonely cry of the white brant winging high overhead.

Soconme had once told her that the white brant were the spirits of the departed. Closing her eyes, Bridget could see them, the black tips of their white wings moving in graceful precision as they gazed down on the small island that had once been their home. Would that her spirit could fly with them, leaving behind all pain, all sadness, all loneliness.

Someone pinched her thigh. A whiskey-slurred voice speculated on the fullness of her breasts, and Hoag stepped forward to snatch the shawl from her shoulders. Crossing her arms defensively before her, Bridget sent him a look of sheer hatred.

Hoag laughed and elbowed the man standing next to him. "Did ever ye see such treasures, me lads? There's nary a sweeter set o' melons 'twixt the Northern Colonies and Spanish Florida." Tossing the shawl over a rafter which was hung with traps, hams and bundles of tobacco, he turned to the men. "Come now, don't hold back on old Boris. Let's see the best ye got, fer that's what she'll cost ye, lads. Newcomb be in first place fer all them fine beaver, Yellow Feather stands second fer the size o' that black catamount skin. When yon candle is spent, the contest be finished, so if ye've got anything left to declare ye'd best get on with it, or ye'll not part me little flower's thighs."

There was a flurry of activity as several of the men measured their stacks against those of the other trappers. Those who had held out, hoping not to have to turn over their entire winter's cache to Hoag, made one last hurried trip outside to bring in a few more prize pelts.

Above the clamor, Boris's gravelly voice rang out. "The candle's gutterin', lads. 'Twon't be long afore the winner steps forward to claim his prize. The rest o' ye fine gents can line up and wait yer turn whilst I commence totin' these bundles out to me storehouse an' tallyin' up."

They were crowding in on her. The one called Newcomb sidled closer, and Bridget stared at him in horror. His foul breath sickened her as it rattled in his chest. A string of tobacco-stained spittle dribbled from a corner of his mouth. He grinned at her, revealing the blackened stubs of three teeth. "Woman, ye got a treat in store. Luthor Newcomb'll drive ye plumb wild afore the night's over. I done learnt me a thing or two about diddlin'."

Over the deafening din, Bridget heard Sudie's distinctive cackle. Moaning softly, she closed her eyes. She was going to be sick. Save for the redskins who had slipped in lately, two of them looking almost familiar although they were too far away to be seen clearly, there was not one man in the room who looked as if he had bathed in the past twelvemonth. The one called Newcomb was repulsive beyond belief. In the closed atmosphere, with the stench of hundreds of pelts, of whiskey and tobacco, of overheated, underwashed humanity, the air was as bad as that of Newgate's common room.

A cold draft and a sudden hush made her open her eyes. A current of excitement seemed to run through the crowd, like the tension that filled the air just before a violent storm. Someone new had entered the room, but the wall of trappers that crowded about her blocked her view.

And then the wall seemed to melt away. A tall figure sauntered up to stand before her, and she blinked to clear her vision. Surely she was dreaming. Her mind was seeking the escape that had been denied her body.

"*Kinnahauk?*" she whispered.

There was no response. It was as if she had not spoken. But then, she was dreaming, wasn't she? And dreams did not speak.

Phantom or no, she would have fallen forward into his arms if he had not stepped back at that moment, bending over to lower a great pack of furs to the floor. Only then did he meet her eyes, his own blazing a message she was unable to interpret.

Shock? Surprise? Disgust? Suddenly mortified that he should see her this way, Bridget willed herself to grow smaller until she dwindled away to nothing, like a spent candle. Mayhap he had not recognized her. She had heard one of the women of Albemarle say that all redskins looked alike to her. Wasn't it possible that all English looked alike to the redskins?

His three feathers brushed against a rafter as he turned and confronted the heavyset trader. "I am Kinnahauk of Croatoan," he announced, his demeanor both cool and arrogant. "I claim this woman for my own." Kinnahauk cursed himself for speaking too quickly. He had planned carefully as they had sped across the dark waters, for stealing a white-eye woman from under the noses of such men as these would be more dangerous than walking through a nest of white-mouth snakes during the Song Moon, when they were wild with mating.

"Wait yer turn, ye heathen devil," Hoag replied, kicking the bundle of furs with his toe. "Cut 'er loose. Let's see if ye've got anything in there worth lookin' at. I know you Haties—ain't nothing on two feet or four down there worth more'n a few glass beads."

Bridget saw Kinnahauk's eyes blaze at the insult. Her own skin grew cold to the touch, in spite of the sickening heat from so many bodies thronged together in a closed space. She could not have spoken if her life depended on it.

Kinnahauk signaled with his hand. One of the men along the wall stepped forward. It was Crooked Stick! Bridget could not suppress a gasp, yet he showed no sign of having recognized her. With one sweep of his wicked blade, he cut the strips of rawhide that bound the bundle of furs. Though they had been cured skin side out, all had been turned so that the quality of the pelt was evident.

"Beaver, huh?" Hoag grunted. "Ain't the best I've seen, but it ain't the worst."

"It is the best," said Kinnahauk flatly. He did not look at Bridget at all.

Newcomb edged forward. "What about mine? I got better'n that, redskin!"

Kinnahauk lifted one hand. At the signal, another of the redskins came forward with another bundle of furs. Leaving it bound, he melted into the crowd.

"Open it," Hoag demanded, his pale eyes avid.

"I would examine the woman first. She may be worthless."

"Worthless!" Hoag sputtered. "She be prime flesh, untouched, but ripe fer pluckin'. Ye'll not find her match in all the colonies, I swear it!"

Kinnahauk walked slowly around the cask upon which Bridget was seated. As if recognizing his right to do so, the trappers fell back. Once he touched her, and Bridget felt as if she had been branded all over again. Then he turned away, shrugging. "Paugh! Too skinny," he dismissed, reaching for his bundles of furs.

Bridget's jaw dropped as she stared at his broad back. Quick tears rose to sting her eyes, and she wondered if she had indeed lost her senses. Could he have changed so greatly in such a short time? Could *she*? Had he truly forgotten her so quickly?

As if fearing the loss of his rich profits, Hoag leaped to her defence. "Skinny, aye, but she be strong and spunky for all her lack of meat."

"She is spotted and marked. Not worth the beaver. Not worth the two white lynx. Not worth—"

"White lynx?" Hoag echoed disbelievingly. "*Two* of 'em?"

Ignoring the interruption, Kinnahauk said, "I will get more *peage* for them from the man you call Batts."

"But he ain't even set up yet. Besides, that be a far piece from here."

"A day's journey is nothing. I go." From the men who had sold him their best furs, Kinnahauk had heard of a man who would someday open a trading post near the meeting place of those rivers. In dealing with the white-eye, one must stoop to borrow the white-eye rules, speaking falsely and putting honor aside. He grasped the band of rawhide that held the unopened bundle and signaled for Crooked Stick to pick up the other. Pretending he would leave, he dared not look at his *oquio* for fear of murdering every white-eyed devil in this place and burning it to the ground.

In the sudden hush that fell over the gathering, the sound of thunder could be heard.

"Hold there! Let a man see what he's a-buying, redskin. Open up that second bundle, will ye? Maybe we kin make a deal."

As if it mattered little one way or another, Kinnahauk shrugged off the bundle of beavers and nodded to Crooked Stick, who slit the second bundle open. A gasp arose from those close by as a dozen black mink so glossy they sparkled even in such dim light slid out, followed by the matched pair of albino lynx.

Hoag went down on his knees, his pudgy hand hovering over such treasures as if he dare not touch them. He licked his lips. The trove brought in by this arrogant Hatorask bastard surpassed anything he had seen since he'd escaped the hangman's noose and moved south to the Albemarle some twelve years ago. The mink was as glossy as wet ice, the beaver thicker than any he had seen since the great freeze, and the white lynx... Hell, he'd never even seen one before, let alone a matched pair!

Hoag hated having to deal with the stinking savages, but profit was profit, and the bloody truth was, they could outtrap, outhunt and outfight any white man in the territory. And he was not in business for the pleasure of losing his shirt.

"Tell ye what, redskin—I'll pay ye top money fer this stuff and give ye a whole hour in the back room with the woman. Lusty young feller like you, that ought to give ye time enough to dip yer wick four, five times, at least." He'd flatter the dumb bastard if that was what it took. The high-nosed pup had probably stolen this stuff anyway, what did he have to lose?

Kinnahauk pretended to consider the trader's words. "The woman is marked. She is not worth much."

"There ain't nary a mark on her other than that on her face, and in the dark, that won't matter none. She's prime, lad. A white woman like her would bring a fortune if I was to sell her outright."

Kinnahauk's fingers inched toward the knife at his side. One day soon he would have the pleasure of slicing the liver from this man and feeding it to the bustards. Until then he must play this deadly game with great care. He was well aware of the dangers of a red man's walking among white-eyes and demanding one of their women. The white-eyes were a treacherous lot, even without lust and whiskey heating their blood to boiling. They would as soon put a knife in his back as not. He cast a quick glance about the room, meeting the eyes of the men who waited his signal. Tension burned up the very air until it grew almost impossible to breathe.

Hoag found himself staring into a pair of eyes that put him in mind of a wildcat he had once seen caged by a Mattamuskeet brave.

Only colder. More deadly.

"Kinnahauk does not buy the use of the white man's whore. I will take this much *peage*—" with a concise gesture, he measured the space of a handbreadth "—that is for the beaver. For the woman, I will give you the lynx pelts. I will take her with me. When I am finished with her, I will give her to the women of my village as a slave."

"Thar's no way in hell I'll let you keep 'er!" Hoag roared. "Why should I let a stinking redskin walk outta here with a piece of my property when I can sell it to a hunnert men afore it's wore out?"

Kinnahauk shrugged. Once more he prepared to gather up his pelts while the trader sputtered filthy oaths. Newcomb mumbled a string of drunken curses and tripped over Yellow Feather's beavers. He was promptly dislodged by a well-placed kick.

Kinnahauk ignored it all, yet he was aware of every current that passed through the room. Some of the men present, both red and white, hated Boris Hoag enough to want to see him bested, even if it meant they lost their chance at the prize. How many? Which ones?

He did not dare to look at the woman for fear of triggering an outright war.

A slurred voice cried out an insulting remark about red men and female animals, and an uneasy hush fell over the room. Suddenly the men who had been leaning against the wall a moment before were no longer there. A few sharp gasps were heard. Two bodies slithered to the floor, whether from too much rum or from being suddenly deprived of air, no one could be certain. No one really cared. All eyes were on the two men who stood toe-to-toe in the center of the room.

"There is a man called Nathaniel Batts. I am told he will pay a good price for your furs. If this man Hoag has treated you fairly, you will have no need of another trader." Kinnahauk's voice was lifted so that those who stood nearby had no trouble hearing. A few began muttering softly. "It is said that the man Batts will outfit any trapper who agrees to work for him, and will pay well for his pelts."

Crooked Stick signed to Kumtewah, who signed to another of his brothers. Both men began retying their bundles. Soon a few of the white trappers, those still sober enough to do so, began gathering up their own caches.

"Kumtewah! Blue Nose, hold on there! He's lying to ye! Have I ever lied to ye? What are ye doing?"

No one answered, and Hoag swore. God knows how the heathen devil had done it, but he had every man in the room set to follow him, leaving Hoag with nothing for all his trouble.

"Ye stinkin' bastards, ye ain't even paid fer yer drinks yet! Pearson, get back here! I been buying yer skins fer

eight year now. Ye walk out that door and ye'll not sell another one to Boris Hoag, I promise ye!''

The trappers continued to retie their bundles, ignoring
the screaming man. Hoag was wild. He couldn't believe
what he had just witnessed. Like a flock of stupid sheep,
they were going to follow that redskin devil upriver and sell
to Batts.

Bridget huddled on her cask, hardly aware of what went
on around her. Her hands and her feet were like ice. Her
heart was a stone in her breast. How many times in her life
had she seen her hopes come crashing down around her?
How many times, against all odds, had she learned to hope
again?

Now her last hope was bundling up his furs and preparing to walk out the door. She had not even the will to go on
living now. Kinnahauk had destroyed her as surely as if he
had put his knife through her heart.

Newcomb staggered against her and leered up into her
face, and Bridget gagged. ''White meat ain't oughta be
wasted on no heathen savages, am I right, Pearson? This
here woman's mine!''

And then the fickle tide began to turn as another man
pushed forward to argue with him. ''I got twice the prime
beaver—I say she be mine!''

Suddenly both men were lying on the floor, and Kinnahauk was standing before her. With no sign of gentleness,
he scooped her up and tossed her over his shoulder as if she
were a side of venison.

Hoag battled his way through the mob. ''All right, all
right, you win, you thieving red bastard!'' he screeched.
''Take her and go! I be sick of the sight of the damned
woman, anyway!''

''You pay,'' Kinnahauk said flatly.

''Pay!'' Hoag screamed. ''Ye got the woman! What else
do ye want, ye stinking red devil! Turned 'em against me,
ye did—me own men!''

"Pay," Kinnahauk repeated evenly. The mob fell still, but it was a dangerous stillness, like a snake just before striking.

"Take it then!" Hoag flung a length of peage at him—the pale kind, not the valuable dark. Kinnahauk shrugged and tucked it under his waistband. He owed Taus-Wicce for the white lynx. Then he strode out through the path that had cleared magically before him.

Not until they were outside did Bridget begin to breathe once more. Even then it was difficult, for she was still hanging over Kinnahauk's shoulder. When he started to run, she called out to be released, and to her surprise, he let her go. She slithered down his body, and he held her painfully tight for the time it took her to draw a deep, shuddering breath.

The noise from inside grew louder, and before they were even halfway to the water's edge, the door burst open, and the mob spewed out, crying for the white witch. Grasping her hand, Kinnahauk began to run.

Dear God, it was happening again!

The crowd had not seen them yet, but at any moment they would, for lightning flickered incessantly. Bridget saw the six half-naked warriors put themselves between her and the men that milled about. Crooked Stick dropped to his knees, working at something that was hidden from her.

"Go quickly!" Kinnahauk cried, pushing her forward. "I will join you."

Bridget decided that questions could wait. She ran to the smallest canoe and, kneeling on the stern, pushed it away from the bank.

Not a moment too soon, it seemed. The mob had spotted them. Screaming their rage, they came after them. "Kinnahauk!" cried Bridget. "Hurry—run!"

And then several things seemed to happen at once. A bolt of lightning lit up the sky, turning it a sickly shade of pink. It lingered as if the very heavens themselves had been split asunder. In the impenetrable darkness that followed the blinding light, a series of fireballs streaked across the sky toward the trading post, one after another, until the whole roofline of Hoag's rambling structure was rimmed with flames.

A man screamed something about witchcraft. Another one yelled something about his pelts. Then the sound of voices was lost as a gust of wind caught the fire and sent it roaring.

Blue Violet 571

anader. In the impenetrable darkness that followed the
blinding flash, a screech of rusty strikes, across the sky
toward the leading boat, one shot snapping until the whole
Crushed at Hoag's ramding structure was flanced with
flames.

At one end a ...ing ... ... Another
horse ... ...ing ... ... the sound of
... was ... ...rolled overall breath and sent it ...
... ...flailing.

Chapter Twenty-Four

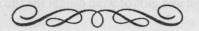

Bridget was trembling uncontrollably by the time the other
canoes appeared silently around her. Kinnahauk stepped
into her shallow craft without making a ripple, and
Crooked Stick reached across the small space to give her a
heavy robe. Her smile of thanks was strained.

Ashore, the blaze started by the fire arrows roared out of
control. Small figures raced about in confusion, silhouetted against the burning building. Horses ran wild, some
pulling carts. Men ran after them, screaming. No one had
time to think of a handful of men and one woman.

"Let us leave this place, for it offends my nostrils," said
Kinnahauk. Crouched in the stern, half kneeling, half
seated, he cut the water in a swift, silent stroke, shooting
the slender craft ahead of the rest. The sky was suddenly lit
by three bolts of lightning, followed quickly by a deafening clap of thunder.

Clasping her knees, Bridget huddled in a ball, half expecting Hoag to spring up before her at any moment.

"I would stay behind and finish what we have begun,"
said Calls the Crows in a tone that fell strangely on Bridget's ears. Tonight she had seen a side of the peaceful
Hatorask people she had never even suspected.

"We will leave this place. It is done. Hoag and the one
called Newcomb are doomed. Their spirits fled long ago to

escape their rotting bodies. To look into their eyes is to see a death from which there is no awakening."

Bridget shuddered, recognizing the truth of Kinnahauk's description and pulled the robe over her.

"No man will sing their death song," said Crooked Stick.

"No man will sing their death song," Kinnahauk agreed solemnly. "The others who came for *Waurraupa Shaman* will take what is not destroyed by fire and go to Batts, or the new trader. Newcomb will not see the Planting Moon. He has the breathing sickness. Hoag will strangle more slowly on his own greed."

"They did not know *Waurraupa Shaman* was your *oquio*?"

"They did not know. Taus-Wicce did not know."

Taus-Wicce. That was the name of the man who had rescued her and delivered her to Hoag. Bridget stared through the darkness from one man to the other. The canoes moved silently, no more than the length of two paddles apart. Then the two belonging to the strangers moved out ahead, and the one bearing Calls the Crows and Crooked Stick fell back to follow behind Kinnahauk.

Bridget's mind teemed with questions, but she knew better than to ask them now. She had no idea where they were going, or who the strangers were. She had no idea where Kinnahauk was taking her. When another flash of lightning split the sky around them, she flinched instinctively. Trees along the shore stood out in stark relief, silhouetted against the sky like outreaching arms. In the momentary brilliance, Kinnahauk's face was etched on her mind so that she carried the vision into the following darkness.

Striding into the trading post, he had looked arrogant and cold. Now he looked grim, almost as if he were in pain, his jaw set, the sensual curve of his lips nowhere in evidence. What could have happened that would change him from the man she had known and come to love into this icy stranger?

She had been told by both Sweet Water and Soconme that even as a youth he had been moulded by the position that would one day be his. While other children played at hunting and warring, Kinnahauk had sat in council with the old men of the village. He had traveled with a teacher to a place where the earth reached up and becomes one with the sky—the land of the Cherokee. While other youths had played with the freedom and joy of a child, Kinnahauk had been learning to be a wise and just leader of his people.

Yet there had been times when Bridget had caught glimpses of the youth Kinnahauk might have been. She had seen him toss back his head and laugh as he raced Tukkao along the shore, seen the pride he could not quite mask when he brought in the biggest buck or caught the largest fish.

She had seen him hold the head of a doe whose heart had burst with terror when she foundered in a bog, gazing down at her while her large dark eyes had glazed in death. His own eyes had been wet with tears, and Bridget had gone away, never letting him know that she had witnessed his moment of vulnerability.

Now thunder rolled across the water as if the very heavens were angry, and she held her breath, Kinnahauk's stern face still vivid in her mind. As they raced the storm, a narrow row of frail canoes on a broad, windswept river, she wanted nothing so much as to throw herself into his arms and hide there, sheltered by his strength and his warmth. But she dared not. They were not safe yet, for the water was growing wilder by the moment.

She could not believe he had truly meant it when he had told Hoag she was to be taken back and used, and then given over to the women. It made little sense, for the women were her friends—all save one. Besides, the Hatorask no longer held slaves, even though Gray Otter would have her believe otherwise.

She was too tired to think this through. Shivering uncontrollably in spite of the robe and the current of warm damp air that swept ahead of the storm, Bridget fought back tears, angry with herself for needing to cry. She had not cried during the worst of her ordeal—why should she cry now that it was over?

In another flash of lightning she saw the gleaming outline of Kinnahauk's sleek, bare torso and found herself staring directly into his eyes. A gust of wind blew her hair over her face, and he leaned forward to brush it away, his fingertips trailing through the wetness on her cheeks. "Do you fear the storm, little one?" he asked, his deep voice soft.

"It's only a squall. Of course I'm not afraid. Salt spray got in my eyes, that's all."

To her amazement, he smiled. All she could see was a flash of white teeth, but it was enough. Suddenly, in spite of the uncertain future, the threatening storm and her empty belly, Bridget felt immeasurably better.

Mist rushed silently across the dark surface of the water, snagging around the trees that crept out from the shore. Intermittent flashes of lightning silhouetted the lofty pines, the angular branches of winter-bare cypress.

"Where will you take me?" Bridget asked.

"We will stop soon. The rains will follow the wind."

With no discernible signal, all four canoes turned into a narrow opening that widened into a small bay surrounded by the tall white cedars. The air was rich with their scent. The strangers slid their craft smoothly up on the low bank and moved off into the darkness without speaking.

Before the first hard drops hammered down, the men had fashioned three small shelters of interlaced branches. Bridget was huddled beneath one, Kinnahauk, Crooked Stick and Calls the Crows under another, and the Poteskeets, whom Kinnahauk had made known to her by name, under the third. The men talked quietly among themselves and Bridget slept, warm under the robe Kinnahauk had spread over her.

The sun was already high when she awoke. The smell of wood smoke and roasting meat set her belly to grumbling, and she yawned widely.

Kinnahauk appeared before her and invited her to eat. Not until she had refreshed herself and devoured the rabbit Calls the Crows had provided did it occur to her that their numbers had dwindled. "Where are the others?" she asked, daintily wiping her fingers on the hem of her gown.

"My friends from Pasquinoc have returned home. Crooked Stick and Calls the Crows are preparing now to leave."

Once more, Bridget's eyes brimmed, and this time it could not be blamed on hunger, for her belly was filled with roast rabbit and dried persimmons ground with corn and nuts, part of the food that had been prepared by Taus-Wicce's wives. "I don't know why I'm acting like such a milksop," she murmured. "I wanted to thank them. I haven't even thanked you for coming for me."

"Did you not know I would follow you?" Kinnahauk's voice had dropped until its soft timbre sent goose bumps racing down her sides.

"Kinnahauk—why? Why did you leave me?" she whispered, suddenly desperate to know.

He lifted his head, allowing the sun to shine down on his closed eyes for a moment. Then he began to speak. "A man can own no thing but his honor, Bridgetabbott, for all else can be taken from him. I am Kinnahauk, *werowance* of all Hatorask. When the first English came among us, they numbered many men and youths, one girl child and a few women. Our grandfathers took them into their *oukes* and into their lives. Many among the white-eye men took our own maidens as wives, but they were not long content to stay where they could not grow crops. Those who would plant crossed the Inland Sea and lived with our brothers on the mainland. A few went in search of white man's gold and now are scattered like the seeds of the forest. Many remained on Croatoan to await their chief from across the 'Big Water.' They learned to hunt and fish. Their children became our own. They accepted our leadership, for their own chiefs did not return for them."

The sound of birds echoed through the dark green shadows of the forest. Sunlight set jeweled raindrops to dancing from every leaf and needle. The spicy scent of juniper filled the air.

"Our people have been divided. Many times the Hatorask who dwell on the mainland have asked me to go and live among them. This I cannot do, yet my strength must be great enough to guide all those who call me *werowance*. I have learned much, Bridgetabbott. But I have learned little about women. This I did not know until lately. I knew only that when a man loses his honor, he has no more strength."

Even without the three feathers of his office, which he had removed when he slept, Kinnahauk had never looked more regal. Surely, thought Bridget, no one could question the honor or the strength of this man.

"A man of honor does not take a woman who belongs to another man, Bridgetabbott. The one called Davidlavender had not claimed you, but he had paid your brideprice. I did what honor demanded."

Honor? Honor was the last thing on Bridget's mind as Kinnahauk took her hands in his and began stroking the pale skin inside her wrist. "I've changed from the frightened girl who washed up on your shores so long ago," she said quietly. "I do believe no one can own another, but that she gives herself of her own free will."

"Yet the old ways have value, Bridgetabbott," Kinnahauk insisted. "You are a woman of great value. All in my village know this. Sweet Water calls you daughter. Soconme would have you learn from him so that when his body releases his spirit you will be medicine chief to our people.''

"And you, Kinnahauk?"

"I value you in ways for which there are no words. If I captured a thousand horses, it would still not be enough to pay." His eyes crinkled unexpectedly at the corners in a way she had come to love. "But then, if there were a thousand horses to capture, and I had the skill to do it, I would still have no canoe large enough to carry them."

"You would not need a thousand horses, Kinnahauk—nor even one," she said, not bothering to hide her heart. "My life was yours the day you fished me out of the water and carried me stinking and blistered to your lodge for all to see."

Kinnahauk drew in a deep breath of resinous air, feeling tall as the tallest tree, stronger than the storm that had passed overhead during the night. It was done. The woman was his. This thing the white-eyes called love—he was not certain how it affected a man. There were many words to describe feelings, yet no word so great that it would begin to describe his feelings when he looked on her. Or thought about her. Or touched her.

Or the feelings he had had when he thought he'd lost her.

"I will say this, and then we will be done with talking. Taus-Wicce has told me all he learned from the man called Hamish who took you from the village. He told me it was Gray Otter who spoke for you, seeking passage in the white-eyes' canoe, and that the men Hamish had left you with were found dead by the hand of the Tuscarora."

He did not tell her all that Taus-Wicce had said before he had learned that Bridget was Kinnahauk's woman—of the cruel way she had been bound, of her torn gown and her bloody breast. His own heart had died a thousand deaths. He had felt like murdering his friend for not taking her to his village and caring for her there, even though he knew that if any Englishman had seen Taus-Wicce with a white woman in torn and bloody garments it would have meant certain death to him and his men, and possibly his whole village.

Even then, the Voice that Speaks Silently had told Kinnahauk that his *oquio* still lived, but for how long? How much could one small woman endure before her senses fled?

He had resigned himself to taking what was left of her back to his *ouke*, where he would care for her for the rest of his days. Perhaps one day he would have taken a wife, for a man needed sons. But no other woman would have had his heart, for the heart could be given but once. He had given it to Bridgetabbott.

Not until Bridget tugged at her hand did Kinnahauk realize he was holding her fingers in a brutal grip. Ducking his head in a most unchieflike manner, he apologized. "I fear it will be many moons before I can sleep without holding you tightly in my arms. I fear I will follow you around like a tame opossum, until you grow weary of seeing my face."

This time it was Bridget who squeezed his hand. Laughing softly, she said, "In a hundred years, mayhap I will grow weary of having you underfoot. Then you'll know the sharp edge of my tongue."

He grinned. "I would not wait a hundred years to know your tongue, woman." Standing, he took her hand and pulled her to her feet.

Bridget placed her hands upon his chest, her fingertips spreading over the sleek, resilient flesh that remained so warm even in the coldest weather. "Kinnahauk, what of Gray Otter? She said—that is, she told me—"

"Gray Otter makes trouble. She twists words until their meaning is false."

"You don't love her? You don't want her for a first wife?"

His eyes narrowed until the gold was barely visible. With a return of his former grimness, he said, "I would not want her had I never met you, Bridgetabbott. There is only one woman I want, one woman who will be my wife, to share my *ouke* and bear my children."

But still she was worried. Tenderly stroking her cheek, Kinnahauk said, "The time has come to send Kokom to live among the Hatorask on the mainland. He will lead them under my guidance. He will be called *Winnee-wau*, which is a proud title."

"And Gray Otter?"

"She will go with him as his wife." He did not say what both Crooked Stick and Calls the Crows had known when they had carried his message to Croatoan—that if Kinnahauk looked on Gray Otter's beautiful, lying face, he would be sorely tempted to take her life with his own hands.

"I am done with talking," he said, taking both her hands in his and gazing at her as if he could still not quite believe she was standing before him.

Bridget allowed her own eyes to roam over his tall, strong body, covered only by a bleached buckskin tail clout and a brief vest that opened widely in the front. He no longer wore his copper arm band.

"Come, Bridgetabbott. I know a place where the sun shines warmly and the earth is soft and fragrant. We will take the robe."

Suddenly she could hardly breathe. Lifting her face to meet his eyes, she met his lips, instead. By the time they drew apart, the warm place was forgotten. Kinnahauk ducked under the shelter and drew her inside with him, holding her almost painfully tight. He whispered words in his own language, words she had never heard—or never heard them spoken in such a way.

She could not get close enough. Her face was pressed against Kinnahauk's chest, the scent of his skin in her nostrils sweeter than the sweetest herbs and spices. His lips moved over her hair, touched the top of one of her ears and lingered on her temple. She could feel his heart pounding under her cheek.

"I thought I would never see you again," she whispered. Tears filled her eyes and overflowed as the magnitude of such a loss overwhelmed her anew. As much as she had suffered before, thinking he had not wanted her, it was nothing compared to being in his arms and knowing how close she had come to losing him forever. "Kinnahauk, I still don't know why you left without telling me."

Kinnahauk lowered her carefully to the robe and came down beside her, gathering her in his arms. His breath was sweet on her face, his hands warm on her body as he gently unlaced the bodice of her ill-fitting dress.

"Did you not know I would return for you? Did you not see the thing I had left—the token of promise?"

"I saw nothing. I only woke to find you gone and Gray Otter—" She breathed deeply, seeking to forgive the unforgivable. Finally she whispered, "I can almost feel it in my heart to be sorry for her, Kinnahauk. Have you ever—?"

"No, my love. I have never," he replied softly, amusement simmering just under the surface of his deep voice. "At least, not with Gray Otter. Any creature who would survive must learn to be wary of traps, no matter how sweet the bait."

Bridget stroked his back, sliding her hands under his vest to reach his shoulders, and then following the shallow valley of his spine down to where it disappeared beneath his tail clout. Her fingertips encountered the haft of his knife, and she withdrew it and laid it aside. 'Twas not his blade, but his spear that he would have need of. She felt bold and hungry, and not at all tired.

Kinnahauk's mouth brushed over hers, soft as the wings of a moth. She trembled. "I do not like this gown," he whispered against her lips, and proceeded to unfasten the bodice without lifting his face. When she felt his hand brush over the sensitive tip of her breast, she gasped at the sensations that radiated to all parts of her body.

Kinnahauk took advantage of her parted lips to seal her mouth with his, easing his tongue between her lips until it encountered hers. The familiar scent of her skin fired his blood. The taste of her inflamed him until he thought he must struggle not to part her thighs and drive himself into the place that was hidden by the soft golden floss. Only the sweet hidden warmth of her woman flesh would ease this intolerable ache.

Gently. He must move gently, for she had suffered much at the hands of men. He must not frighten her. Even the waiting would be good, he told himself, seeking to convince his impatient male part. As the heat of her body rose around him, intoxicating him more swiftly than the strongest spirits, he felt himself surge fiercely.

Bridget arched beneath him, her thighs softening until they were no longer pressed tightly together. He closed his eyes and groaned. "Are you in pain?" she asked.

"It will ease," he said through gritted teeth. "I would not rush you, my own heart, for you have suffered much. Just holding you is enough." Freeing one hand, he reached down and untied the knot at his side, leaving the tail clout in place.

Then, with great care he eased his hand beneath her skirts, wishing he could rid her of the ugly garments quickly. Her skin was as smooth as the down of a newly hatched sea hawk. He stroked her thighs, moving ever higher, drawn toward the heat of her woman flesh.

Daringly Bridget met the thrust of Kinnahauk's tongue with the tip of her own, thrilling to the sensuous textures of the man who lay half covering her. His caresses made her move restlessly, and when his lips left hers and moved down her throat, lingering in the hollow of her shoulder, she thrashed from side to side. Gooseflesh rose, and when he captured one taut nipple in his mouth, she groaned.

Arching her back, she pressed herself against his lips, and Kinnahauk obliged her by taking more of her into his mouth. Skillfully he suckled, taking great care not to hurt her. As his tongue swirled around the sensitive button, his hand moved higher on her thigh, until it brushed the crease of her leg.

"I would see you without this ugly rag you wear, for I have pictured you in my mind many times since last we joined," he muttered thickly. Without waiting, he rose to his knees, forgetting that he had unfastened his own garment in readiness. It slithered to the mat, leaving him naked and boldly aroused.

At his look of consternation, Bridget laughed softly. "And I have pictured you, my love, if not quite so clearly."

"Sehe," he cried softly, laughing in spite of his embarrassment.

Lifting her arms, Bridget slowly drew the gown over her head and tossed it aside. She dealt with the few poor undergarments she possessed and then lay back, lifting her arms.

"Among my people it is said that a seed planted in a storm brings forth a strong harvest," Kinnahauk murmured as he worshiped her with his hands and his eyes.

"But the storm is ended." She stroked his shoulders, then followed the strong lines of his throat, her fingertips brushing his ears. "Yet I still need you," she whispered against his nipple.

"There will be many storms, my heart. And I will need you until the white brant no longer fly over Croatoan."

As he slowly became one with her in a joyous reunion, neither of them knew nor cared about the ring of silent men who stood guard some distance away to keep them safe from harm for this day and this night. It was Taus-Wicce's wedding gift to them. They did not care that no words had been spoken over them, for the words had been spoken in their hearts.

And so they joined, and Kinnahauk cast his seed upon her, and from that union was born a powerful *quasis*, who would lead his people into the future.

*   *   *   *   *

Take 3 of "The Best of the Best™" Novels FREE

Plus get a FREE surprise gift!

Are your lips succulent, impetuous, delicious or racy?

Find out in a very special Valentine's Day promotion—THAT SPECIAL KISS!

Inside four special Harlequin and Silhouette February books are details for THAT SPECIAL KISS! explaining how you can have your lip prints read by a romance expert.

Look for details in the following series books, written by four of Harlequin and Silhouette readers' favorite authors:

Silhouette Intimate Moments #691
Mackenzie's Pleasure by *New York Times* bestselling author Linda Howard

Harlequin Romance #3395
Because of the Baby by Debbie Macomber

Silhouette Desire #979
Megan's Marriage by Annette Broadrick

Harlequin Presents #1793
The One and Only by Carole Mortimer

Fun, romance, four top-selling authors, plus a **FREE** gift! This is a very special Valentine's Day you won't want to miss! Only from Harlequin and Silhouette.

WESTERN *Lovers*

AVAILABLE IN JANUARY

**Another
Western Lovers
ready to rope and tie your heart!**

HEART OF ICE—
Diana Palmer
Denim & Diamonds

The last thing city girl Kati James wanted to do
was spend Christmas with an arrogant, rugged
Wyoming rancher. But once Egan Winthrop got
Kati under the mistletoe, he never intended to let
her go...

HARLEQUIN®   Silhouette®

WL196

Bestselling author

RACHEL LEE

takes her Conard County series to new heights with

A CONARD COUNTY Reckoning

This March, Rachel Lee brings readers a brand-new, longer-length, out-of-series title featuring the characters from her successful Conard County miniseries.

Janet Tate and Abel Pierce have both been betrayed and carry deep, bitter memories. Brought together by great passion, they must learn to trust again.

"Conard County is a wonderful place to visit! Rachel Lee has crafted warm, enchanting stories. These are wonderful books to curl up with and read. I highly recommend them."
—*New York Times* bestselling author
Heather Graham Pozzessere

Available in March, wherever Silhouette books are sold.

You're About to Become a *Privileged Woman*

Reap the rewards of fabulous free gifts and benefits with proofs-of-purchase from Harlequin and Silhouette books

Pages & Privileges™

It's our way of thanking you for buying our books at your favorite retail stores.

PROOF OF PURCHASE
BR-PP96
Offer expires October 31, 1996

Pages & Privileges™

**Harlequin and Silhouette—
the most privileged readers in the world!**

For more information about Harlequin and Silhouette's PAGES & PRIVILEGES program call the Pages & Privileges Benefits Desk: 1-503-794-2499

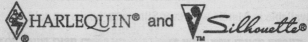

HARLEQUIN® and Silhouette®

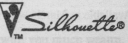

BR-PP96